MURDER LLC

Bryan Cassiday

Bryan Cassiday
Los Angeles
ISBN 9781732976337
Printed in the United States of America
First edition: June 2020

BOOKS BY BRYAN CASSIDAY

Bolt (Scott Brody Thriller 1)
Riptide of Fear
Force of Impact (Ethan Carr Thriller 4)
Wipeout (Ethan Carr Thriller 3)
Dying to Breathe (Ethan Carr Thriller 2)
Countdown to Death (Ethan Carr Thriller 1)
The Bus Stops Here—and Other Zombie Tales
Two Moons Rising
Alien Assault
Comes a Chopper
Zombie Apocalypse: The Chad Halverson Series
Helter Skelter
The Anaconda Complex
The Kill Option
Blood Moon: Thrillers and Tales of Terror
Fete of Death

Chapter 1

Three nuns packing guns under their black habits riding in a silver Range Rover SUV drove up to a small Catholic church in Tula, Tamaulipas, in Mexico on a warm humid night. A knot of ashen clouds drifted lazily in the sky. White wimples covered the nuns' heads, necks, and sides of their faces. Black veils obscured the rest of their faces.

Their butts ached thanks to riding over long stretches of dirt roads and to the Range Rover's janky shocks.

The nun in the driver's seat parked along the curb across the street from the church. The three nuns watched well-dressed parishioners entering the church for evening mass, the men in dark suits and restrained neckties, the women in somber dresses, the children dressed in imitation of their parents.

The nun in the driver's seat took a leather briefcase from the lap of the nun sitting in the middle of the front seat and clambered out of the SUV.

The nun carried the briefcase across the street, kicking out of the way a half-starved stray tan mutt with exposed ribs and a hunched back foraging on the street. The mutt yelped and scurried off.

The nun approached the church entrance. The nun mingled with the parishioners.

"Hello, Sister," said a middle-aged woman, bowing with respect.

The nun nodded at her, as they entered the vestibule.

The nun walked to the corner of the narthex, waited till the narthex was clear of parishioners, and gingerly deposited the briefcase on the floor next to the wall adjoining the church's nave.

A seven-year-old girl in the back of the nave saw the nun angling across the narthex.

"Where are you going, Sister?" she said.

The nun halted briefly and made the sign of the cross.

The nun ducked out of the church and sprinted across the street, a strange sight for a habit-clad nun, and reached the Range Rover. The nun climbed into the driver's seat.

"Shouldn't we leave now?" said the nun sitting in the middle of the passenger seat, as all three nuns watched the church's entrance.

"No," said the driver. "We're supposed to make sure before we leave."

The driver produced a cell phone and punched in a number, which detonated the Czech-manufactured Semtex packed into the briefcase.

A deafening explosion ensued. The church burst into a fireball, hurling fragments of the edifice helter-skelter. Great jagged clumps of burning, smoking masonry showered onto the street, embers swirling in the air as debris from the collapsing church thudded onto the tarmac. Twisted rebar and cement catapulted into the street. The ground shook with the massive fulmination.

The spire bearing a cross toppled from the church roof and slammed into the parking lot's asphalt with an ear-splitting crash like a boulder dropped into a steel Dumpster, kicking up clouds of billowing dust in the moonlight.

Screams from inside the church rent the air.

"OK," said sixteen-year-old Michael Corleone Casa at the wheel of the Range Rover.

"Fucking Zetas," said the nun next to him. "They're on their way to hell."

"That's what they get for attacking Don Gaetano's home," said Michael, the son of Arturo Morales Casa, Don Gaetano's right-hand man, his brown eyes hard.

A sobbing middle-aged woman stumbled out of the church onto the street, her tattered dress on fire, her shoulder-length brunette hair smoking. A mongrel with his black fur on fire bolted down the street in front of her, howling, crazed with fear and pain.

"Help me," said the woman, her arms groping toward the three nuns, as she slogged toward them with a bewildered expression on her charred face. "Have mercy."

The three nuns could smell the stomach-turning stench of her burning flesh.

Michael powered up the driver's-side window and fired the ignition.

The Range Rover peeled away from the flaming, smoking, crumbling church ruins, tires screeching and fishtailing. The woman staggered after it, crying out in pain.

The third nun sitting by the passenger-side door threw up quietly in his lap in the careening vehicle, dislodging the veil from his teenage face with the stream of vomit.

"Don't waste puke on fucking Zetas," said the nun sitting on his left. "Fucking *putas*." He spat into the foot well.

Michael jammed on the brakes. The Range Rover shrieked to a halt.

"What is it?" said the nun beside him.

"I have one more thing to do," said Michael.

He clambered out of the Range Rover, opened the tailgate, whipped out a machete, and jogged toward the blazing church. He slowed when the heat became too intense for him. Grimacing, shielding his face from the heat with his crooked arm, he stared into the flame-engulfed church.

He saw movement.

A thirtysomething man in a smoldering, ragged suit stumbled out of the burning ruins, coughing smoke out of his lungs. He staggered around as if blind.

Michael realized the guy's face was sizzling like bacon grease on a hot griddle.

On account of the intensity of the flames surrounding the guy, Michael couldn't reach him. The overpowering heat forced Michael back.

The guy fell to his knees, but kept crawling through burning debris in the vestibule trying to escape the church, covered with soot as the flames consumed him. Blinded and choking on smoke, still he crawled. He reached a chunk of cement with three bent rebar poking out of it.

At last Michael could reach him. Machete in hand, Michael darted into the lapping flames, snagged the guy's arm, and hauled him out of the conflagration into the street.

Unbelievably, the guy was alive, but Michael knew he wouldn't be much longer.

Standing over him Michael started when he heard a siren's blast.

He gathered his wits. He had to act quickly.

Chapter 2

Brody was standing in the night next to a used rubber splayed on the blacktop in the dim-lit alley behind the Hollywood strip joint waiting for Terri Symonds to finish her lap dance and leave.

The back door of the joint was throbbing as rock music pounded inside. A junkie that was passed out next to a green Dumpster on the blacktop writhed and groaned in his shabby clothes as he awoke from a stupor, his pants hanging halfway down his ass.

Brody tried to open the shuddering metal fire door.

It was locked. All he could do was wait.

He needed to talk to her. She was part of his investigation. And . . . though he didn't want to admit it, he was starting to fall for her—

Thrusting him staggering backward on his heels, the door flew open. Deafening rock blasted into the alley.

The twenty-seven-year-old Terri staggered out, gripping her bloody neck, a crossbow bolt embedded in her torn throat. Her blonde hair awash with blood, her high cheekbones blood-streaked, she collapsed on the blacktop before Brody could reach her.

He scrambled to her prostrate body. Squatting on his haunches beside her he rolled her onto her back and tried to stanch her gaping wound by pressing his hands against it. Blood kept spurting out of her throat through the interstices between his fingers, one of her carotid arteries punctured by the bolt.

She would bleed out in minutes without medical assistance, he knew.

His hands blood-soaked, he punched out 911 on his cell phone, as Terri sprawled moaning beside him.

"Who did this to you?" he said, pocketing his phone.

He lifted her head closer to his face to hear her answer.

Gasping, she coughed up blood that was streaming into her throat. She might drown in her own blood before she bled out, he realized in horror. The ambulance would never get here in time.

He craned to the night sky and screamed in anguish. First, his wife had been murdered. And now Terri.

Covered with sweat, he bolted upright in bed, clutching his sheet, gasping for breath, his eyes staring in shock into his dark apartment. Would the nightmares never end?

Chapter 3

Damian was carrying four hundred thousand dollars in a traveling bag and was sweating bullets as he approached the blackjack tables in Paris Las Vegas.

A trio of half-naked girls were cavorting on a stage in the middle of the eight tables that surrounded them, as Jefferson Airplane's rock classic "White Rabbit" pounded its beat throughout the casino accompanied by Grace Slick's vibrant voice. Spotlights mounted in the ceiling bathed the girls' marmoreal flesh in amaranth pink light.

At the end of the stage was a stationary roulette wheel, its croupier in a low-cut pink satin bustier looking lonely without any bettors at her station.

Erstwhile car mechanic turned cop growing up in El Tapatio, Mexico, Damian had come to the decision he didn't cotton to being on the impecunious side of the law and had switched sides.

Now, at twenty-five years of age, the five-nine Damian was transporting the cash for his current boss of the Jalisco New Generation cartel, Don Gaetano Obrador Ramirez, who had ordered him to launder the drug money in a Vegas casino. Don Gaetano's orders were simple.

Damian was to buy four hundred thousand dollars' worth of casino chips, place a few skimpy bets at a poker table, and cash out. That was all Damian had to do to earn his paycheck. Or he could buy smaller amounts of chips and cash them in at different casinos on the Vegas Strip until he had laundered all of the illicit drug money. Then Don Gaetano would tell him where to deliver the clean money.

If Damian failed to complete his assignment, Don Gaetano had made it clear that he would order Damian's mother and girlfriend both shot in the head, not before having them gang-raped.

His pulse skyrocketing, his adrenaline coursing, Damian wanted to get this over with. He had never in his life held this much money in his hands. It was a heady kick. He felt like an acrophobe standing on the skimpy ledge of a skyscraper a hundred stories up and looking down, fearing he would fall any second—nothing more than his life at stake.

He had no wish to spend the entire week visiting different casinos to wash the cash. He didn't think his heart could endure the turmoil for a week without suffering cardiac arrest. He wanted to launder the cash all at once. Here. At the Paris Casino. With the voluptuous dancers in their pink thongs watching him.

Not that they were watching him. They were too busy doing their numbers on the stage.

Why was he so nervous? he wondered. All he had to do was place a couple of bets, cash out, and wait for Don Gaetano's next orders. What was so scary about that?

Damian told himself to chill out.

But he couldn't relax. This much money in his hands was driving him batshit crazy.

He had grown up in poverty. He had thought he would be a car mechanic for the rest of his life barely making ends meet, working for a cheapskate boss who was screwing him. Then he had tried being a cop and ended up envying the gangbangers in the cartels who had money to burn. Washing out of the police force he had returned to being a mechanic.

And then one day he had repaired a Range Rover for one of Don Gaetano's gangbangers and the guy had recommended him to Don Gaetano as a recruit to the Jalisco New Generation cartel.

Damian couldn't believe it. What were the chances he would ever in his life see almost half a million bucks? Just because he had repaired some guy's SUV, oodles of cash fell in his lap? It was like something out of a movie. A horror movie, it turned out.

The cartel had sent him to a *sicario* training camp for six months in the mountains of southern Mexico, where they had taught him how to kill and dismember victims. He had learned to his dismay that none of the trainees flunked. If you couldn't cut it, they strung you up by the hands to a tree and used you for target practice. You either passed the course and became a *sicario* or lost your life at the end of a rope.

Like the other trainees, he had been required to kill the targets selected for him to pass the course. To show the slightest hesitation in obeying orders meant the trainee's death at the hands of the trainers.

He had learned to murder there.

The only way he could stand killing someone was by pretending he was watching someone else commit the murders that his hands perpetrated. It may have been his hand slitting a guy's throat, he told himself, but it wasn't *him* doing the slitting. He was an innocent spectator watching his own hand slash a guy's throat, watching the blood gush out, watching the guy crumple.

He had slaughtered enough people to pass the course and had become a *sicario*.

As a professional *sicario* he had earned more money than he had ever dreamed of.

But the job had taken its toll on him, turning him into a basket case thanks to fear and paranoia.

Not a day passed without risk. And today in Vegas was no different, namely the threats Don Gaetano had made to his girlfriend Sofia and his mother.

But that was only if Damian didn't complete his mission.

Damian had wondered if he should have said no and refused to accept the job. Somehow Damian doubted it was an offer he could refuse. Don Gaetano wasn't giving him a choice. He was giving Damian an order and would waste Damian along with Damian's mother and Sofia if Damian refused to cooperate.

After all, Don Gaetano's reputation preceded him.
Damian knew the guy was a mass murderer, a guy who could
order a passenger plane shot out of the sky at the drop of a hat
and murder everybody onboard to terrorize the populace
without batting an eye. Or order his men to butcher hundreds
of Zetas, ruthless competing narcos, in broad daylight in the
middle of town, and hurl their corpses into vats of acid, where
they would decompose never to be heard from again.

Don Gaetano never took no for an answer.

Damian had every reason to be terrified. But only if he
failed his mission. If he completed his mission, there was
nothing to fear, he decided, and he would be many thousands
of dollars richer when Don Gaetano paid him.

Still, the notion of this much money in his hands launched
Damian's heartbeat into high gear. In a matter of moments his
frantic heart would shatter his ribs if he didn't settle down.

Grace Slick was screaming in his ears with her mellow
voice telling him to ask Alice as he faced the gambling tables
trying to decide what to do. Before he could gamble he had to
buy chips.

Valise in hand, he wandered around the crowded casino
floor, wending his way between slot machines and fellow
customers until he found the cashier's window.

"I want to buy casino chips," he told the fortyish cashier
with bobbed brunette hair.

"How many?"

"Four hundred thousand dollars."

She stared at him. At least it seemed like she was staring
at him.

"I'll need photo ID," she said.

"Why?"

"For a credit transaction, we always need ID. And, of
course, your credit card."

"This isn't a credit transaction. It's cash."

Now he was convinced she was staring at him. He saw her press a button at the side of her desktop. Maybe she thought he was going to give her a hard time.

"Where's the money?" she said.

Damian lifted his valise, set it on the desktop, and slid it toward her.

Wearing an earbud whose wire coiled down his neck like a Secret Service agent's, an expressionless, square-jawed, clean-cut, six-three guy in a black suit moseyed up to her from inside the cashier's office, looking like he had stepped out of a *GQ* ad.

He searched Damian's face then watched the cashier unzip the valise to reveal the cash—four hundred thousand bucks' worth of neatly bundled hundred-dollar bills secured with red rubber bands. Forty bundles worth ten thousand bucks apiece.

The cashier gazed up at the suit's face seeking instructions.

The suit pawed through the bag's contents, extracted one of the bundles, and riffled it.

"Ten thousand dollars in each bundle," said Damian, watching him.

The suit withdrew one of the bills from the middle of the bundle and held it up to the light to inspect it. He shifted it around examining its authenticity under the glow of the light.

Damian sweated, soaking his shirt under his armpits. He kept his arms down so the sweat didn't show. Could the bills be counterfeit? he wondered. Why would Don Gaetano give him fake money knowing Damian would be busted if it was discovered? Maybe Don Gaetano didn't know the money was fake.

Maybe Damian's next stop would be a jail cell.

Chapter 4

"OK," said the suit, replacing the inspected bill and the bundle of dough into the valise. "We need to count it first."

"Fine," said Damian, his throat dry, barely able to speak, suspecting the suit would find something amiss and blow the whistle on him.

The suit took the valise and disappeared into the back room.

"What's the most expensive chip you have?" Damian asked the cashier, who was picking at her hair, her turquoise fingernails glittering in the overhead light.

"We rarely use them here," she said.

"How much is it?"

"A hundred thousand dollars."

"I'll take three of them and ten ten-grand ones," said Damian, not believing he was really saying the words.

Four hundred thousand bucks' worth of chips! Jesus, he thought.

"When Simon returns, we'll proceed with the transaction," said the cashier, her face blank.

Damian knew the eye in the sky was zooming in on him, scoping him out, trying to ID the new whale in their casino, while Simon was counting the bundles of Ben Franklins. His nerves on end, Damian didn't know if he could stand waiting here much longer. Maybe he should cut and run.

No way, he decided. Not without the money. Otherwise, he'd have to deal with Don Gaetano's wrath.

Why was it taking so long? he wondered. Had Simon called the cops? Were they on their way to bust him? Was the money counterfeit? Get a grip, he told himself.

If he beat it now, the casino security guards would be all over him, the cashier's suspicions of his guilt confirmed. Was she suspicious? he wondered, searching her face, trying to pick up on a tell like a tic or the blinking of an eye. Her expressionless face gave away as much as a cow's chewing its cud. Was this just a routine check everybody making a large transaction was subjected to?

Tempted to check out the eye in the sky, he put the kibosh on the urge, figuring the mere act of looking up at the ceiling would make him appear suspicious. All he could do was stand and wait till Simon returned.

A terrifying thought occurred to Damian. Was Simon tracking serial numbers on the cash? But why would he? The casino didn't care if the money was dirty. As long as it wasn't counterfeit, they'd take it, no questions asked. They could care less where it came from. Hell, this was Vegas. It was built with dirty money by the mobster Bugsy Siegel and his thug cohorts.

Damian listened to Grace Slick belting out lyrics at the top of her lungs, her voice resounding in his head. The music wasn't soothing him. It was jacking him up, adding to his edginess.

He expected the cops to sneak up behind him any minute and slap handcuffs on him. Pulse racing, he whipped his head around.

Nobody stood behind him.

He heard footsteps and turned around to face the cashier.

Simon was returning from the bowels of the office.

"OK," he said, looking at Damian. Simon turned to the cashier. "Four hundred thousand dollars."

The cashier opened her tray of casino chips.

"He wants three of the hundred-K chips," she told Simon.

"We normally give those only to frequent guests of the casino," he told Damian.

"Oh?" said Damian.

"But in your case, the boss said we could make an exception."

Damian felt his heartbeat decelerate. Everything was going according to plan, he decided with relief.

The cashier counted out three of the hundred-K chips.

They were white with a powder blue border and a picture of the Eiffel Tower in the center. Underneath the tower it said $100,000 in powder blue ink. Damian noticed the chip said Baccarat on it.

"It says baccarat. Do I have to play baccarat with it?" he said.

"No," said Simon. "Most high-stakes players play baccarat here. You don't want to play baccarat?"

"No."

"You can't play all the table games with that chip. A lot of them have limits."

Damian remembered the roulette table near the bikini-clad dancers. "What about roulette?"

"No limits."

Damian picked up one of the chips and inspected it. "What's that little dot after the amount $100,000?"

"That's a computer chip. An RFID."

"RFID?"

"A radio-frequency identification tag."

"What's the point?"

"To make sure it's not a fake casino chip."

"What else did you want?" the cashier asked Damian after she had set the short stack of three hundred-K chips in front of him.

"Ten ten-thousand-dollar chips," he said.

She counted out the ten chips in front of him and placed them in a pile beside the three hundred-K's.

He scooped up both piles of chips and deposited them in his trouser pocket.

"Good luck," she said.

He wandered back in the direction of the gaming tables with the bikini-clad girls dancing behind them on a rectangular stage.

All he had to do now was place a couple of small bets and cash out to launder the money. Easy-peasy. He would be out of here in minutes, he decided.

Except—

Chapter 5

After Damian placed ten thousand bucks on red at the roulette wheel and the twenty-four-year-old blonde croupier in her low-cut pink bustier spun the wheel, he won the bet and doubled his money. The easiest ten grand he ever made, he decided, feeling pumped up.

He bet another ten grand on red and became hypnotized by the spinning of the roulette wheel, which seemed to spin forever, as the three-quarter-inch ivorine ball rolled in the opposite direction, bounced around, clicking in and out of slots on the wheel . . . and came to a halt.

He won again.

He had made twenty thousand bucks in a couple of minutes. No sweat.

His eyes blazed with excitement. Adrenaline coursed through his system—not because he was afraid, but because he was turned on. He couldn't lose. Like a basketball player in a zone who knows he can't miss his next shot from beyond the three-point arc, he *knew* he would win the next spin of the wheel.

It wasn't gambling when you knew you were going to win, he decided. It was a lock.

Why not bet it all? a voice inside his head said. After he won he would have over eight hundred thousand bucks. He could keep four hundred thousand for himself and give the rest to the Cobalt Green Tide bagman, who would never know the difference. As long as Damian delivered the freshly laundered four hundred grand to the bagman, Don Gaetano would be satisfied. Damian had no idea what Cobalt Green Tide was. He didn't care, and he didn't care what they would use the money for.

With all that money Damian could retire from the life of a *sicario*, a hit man for the cartel, and start his own business running an auto shop.

Damian was through with being a *sicario* taking orders from Don Gaetano, a ruthless butcher who could retain power only through terror, including terrorizing his own employees. Not only that, Damian lived in constant fear lest enemy *sicarios* whack him any minute with a bullet to the back of the head execution-style.

Few *sicarios* lived past thirty, Damian knew. All the money in the world couldn't make up for a life cut short by a bullet.

The four hundred grand was Damian's way out.

On the other hand, if Damian lost all of the cash entrusted to him on the bet, Don Gaetano would cut off his head with a chainsaw and play soccer with it till it was kicked to a bloody pulp. And do the same to his mother and his girlfriend Sofia. Sofia . . . he didn't even want to think about what they would do to her before they killed her.

But he couldn't lose, decided Damian. The premonition was strong in his mind. He would win the next bet if he put it all on red.

Then he and Sofia could escape the cartel's clutches and live a dream life. Don Gaetano wouldn't send *sicarios* after him because Damian would give the Cobalt Green Tide bagman the laundered four hundred K, minus Damian's winnings at the roulette wheel that Damian would use to start a new life.

Was it an imp of the perverse that was driving him to gamble the entire pile of his chips? Damian wondered. It made no sense to gamble it all, if he thought about it reasonably. Why take the risk? There were no sure things in gambling. That was why they called it *gambling*, he told himself.

Nevertheless, he was certain he would win his next bet on red. Then why not bet it all? Getting out of bed in the morning was risk. Everything in life was risk. The only way you could escape risk was by dying.

"Do you care to place another bet?" said the croupier, after the wheel had come to a halt.

Damian reached inside his trouser pocket and clutched all of the casino chips in it.

Don't do it, said another voice in his head. *Are you crazy? Betting your life on one spin of the wheel?*

Maybe he was crazy, decided Damian. Crazy to ever get involved with the CJNG. Crazy to think he could ever escape them.

"Do you care to place another bet?" repeated the croupier.

Damian squeezed the casino chips in his hand, grinding them together.

Out of the corner of his eye he picked up on Simon, who had appeared at his side like a wraith some six feet away and was standing motionless with his hands clasped in front of him watching with an impassive countenance, feet spread a yard wide, reminding Damian of a Secret Service agent again.

One bet would change his life forever, decided Damian. All it took was the steely nerve to make it.

One bet.

He could feel his palm sweating as he ground the casino chips in his hand.

He placed all of the sweat-smeared chips on red and withdrew his hand.

"Red," he said.

What the fuck did I just do? he thought to himself.

The croupier spun the wheel and rimmed the ball.

Simon watched the proceedings, his expression giving nothing away.

Was he crazy? wondered Damian. To gamble his life on one spin of the wheel? What the hell was he thinking?

He couldn't lose. He couldn't. He was in a zone. He knew the ball would land in the red slot. It was a sure thing. He could see it happening in his mind's eye. There was no way it couldn't happen the way he saw it.

His brow beaded with sweat, Damian felt sweat dripping from his face.

Almost half a million dollars was as good as his, he decided. Christ, was he going to pass out? He felt lightheaded. His knees were turning to jelly. It was all right. He couldn't lose. Red. It was going to be red. *It had to be red.*

The slowing ivorine ball dropped away from the rim and started rattling around on the wheel, trying to find a slot to land in, bouncing out of one and rolling into another, uncertain where to fetch up, driving Damian insane with anticipation.

"Yes," he said, his adrenaline-bright eyes bulging out of his head. "Yes."

A couple more pings of the ball. That was all it would take, he knew. A couple more pings, and the ball would land. It was taking an eternity. Why did the croupier have to spin the wheel so hard? It was like she wanted to prolong his suffering by giving it an extra shove.

She hadn't shoved it half as fast on the previous spin.

The wheel was slowing down, but it wasn't coming to a halt. It was spinning in slow motion. Or did it seem that way because Damian was so jacked up that everything around him looked slow? The casino guests that meandered past him were shambling, their speech incomprehensible because of its slowness.

They schlepped like zombies, mouthing double-talk.

Damian clenched his fists with tension.

Simon was driving him mad with his stoic face watching the ball. Was the guy a robot? wondered Damian. The guy never moved. Did he ever blink? Damian couldn't recall seeing him blink.

"I can't lose," he yelled at Simon, realizing he must look like a maniac with his sweating face and balled fists.

The ball was coming to a halt, Damian could see.

It wouldn't be long now.

Just a few more bounces.

A few more clicks of the ball.

And then he could claim his money.

Yes, he thought.

"Black," said the croupier.

Damian turned white.

The croupier raked in Damian's chips.

Simon walked away, phlegmatic as ever.

Chapter 6

Internet PI Scott Brody was playing Omaha with his poker buddies—Sam Lasko, a thirty-seven-year-old black cop with the West Hollywood Police Department, and Victor Lopez, a thirty-eight-year-old ponytailed ex-marine turned professional bodyguard—in Lasko's Hollywood apartment.

Also present were a couple of friends of Lasko, probably cops, that Brody didn't know.

Open beer cans stood in front of the players.

Victor was clouding the apartment with smoke from a cigar he was puffing.

"If we were living in Santa Monica, you wouldn't be able to smoke that thing in here," said Lasko, sitting beside Victor at the card table in the living room.

"That's why I don't live there," said Victor, tilted his head back, and blew a smoke ring into the air.

"That's Murphy, and that's Pisanelli," said Lasko, nodding at the two men who sat across from Victor.

"I don't care what their names are as long as they got money in the pot."

"We love you, too," said Murphy, a big guy of forty-five with a surly, double-jowled face and small apricot ears, his meaty arms crossed.

He was wearing a sweat-stained madras button-down shirt with a frayed collar.

"My wife broke up with me, and now I gotta live with this clown Murphy," said Pisanelli, a forty-seven-year-old in a black AC/DC T that strained against his potbelly.

Murphy groaned. "Don't tell me we're gonna have to listen to you bitchin' about your wife the whole time we're playing cards."

"Everything's going to hell. Livin' with you's the pits. What did I do to deserve this?"

"Shut up and deal," said Victor.

"You heard the man," said Murphy.

"Did you ever have to share an apartment with another guy?" Pisanelli asked Brody.

"Whatever you do, don't talk to Brody about women," said Lasko. "You'll never hear the end of it. His love life's a train wreck."

"Don't get me started," said Brody.

"Is this a poker game or a lonely hearts club?" said Victor. He rapped his knuckles against the tabletop twice. "Deal."

"I'm doomed," said Pisanelli. "Don't you understand? My wife left me."

"Stop your bellyaching. Shut up and deal. I came here to play cards, not listen to a soap opera."

Brody dredged out his cell phone that was vibrating in his trouser pocket.

"Hello," he said into his iPhone.

"And now *he*'s taking phone calls," said Victor in disgust.

"Deal me out," said Brody, standing up and retreating from the table.

"Did somebody say *deal*? Does anybody here know how to deal Omaha? I'm tired of talking about what's-his-name's wife."

"Do you think I should call my wife and try to make up with her?" said Pisanelli. "Or should I let her cool off and wait for her to call me?"

"You're gonna be in for a long wait, my friend," said Murphy, with a knowing chuckle.

"My life's going to hell in a handbasket."

"I'm outa here, if somebody doesn't start dealing cards in ten seconds," said Victor, glancing at his wristwatch.

"I hate to spoil the party, but I gotta meet a client," said Brody, put away his cell, approached the card table, and scoffed up his chips. "Cash me out."

Victor clutched his forehead. "Are you kidding me? Is this really happening? What happened to our card game?"

"What should I tell my wife to get her to come back to me?" said Pisanelli, his voice plaintive.

"Good luck," said Murphy.

"Crawl to her on your hands and knees and beg forgiveness," said Lasko.

"Why is the only thing we ever talk about at poker is broads?" said Victor, throwing up his hands.

"Crawl on my hands and knees?" said Pisanelli, eying Lasko with a doleful expression.

"And beg forgiveness," deadpanned Lasko.

"I'm doomed."

"Shut up and deal," said Victor.

Brody slipped out the door.

Chapter 7

Brody folded his six-two frame into an emerald green leather-upholstered booth in an Irish pub in Santa Monica and waited for his prospective client who had just phoned him.

He watched a Hispanic woman in her late twenties strut into the room, aware that the male patrons in the pub were checking out her striking looks as she made her way to Brody's booth. A brunette with a full head of hair, electric blue eyes, and a lithe body, she radiated sensuality as she rolled her jeans-clad hips up to Brody and sat across from him, wearing a glossy lime tube blouse.

The pub's patrons lost interest when they watched her take a seat across from Brody.

"You got no taste," a fat guy in a wife beater and jeans sitting at the bar muttered, turned away from her and Brody with his hooded eyes, and took a pull on his beer.

"You're not in her class," his buddy, a crew-cut fortyish guy wearing khaki Bermudas and a loud Tony Soprano button-down, short-sleeved, loose print shirt with sleeves that reached his elbows, told Brody.

Brody ignored him.

Tony Soprano Shirt shook his head in disgust and returned to his drink.

"Are you Scott Brody, the PI?" the woman asked Brody.

"In the flesh," said Brody. "And you're Araceli, the woman I talked to on the phone in need of my services?"

"I need you to find my brother Damian."

"How about a drink?"

"A Tecate."

Brody summoned the waitress and ordered the beer. A glass of Coors stood in front of him.

"Tell me about your brother," said Brody, taking a pull on his beer.

"He went to Las Vegas and disappeared."

"What's his name?"

"Damian Playa."

"Why did he go to Vegas?"

"For a vacation."

"And he never came back?"

"That's right. And I can't contact him. I'm afraid something happened to him."

The waitress brought Araceli's Tecate to the table.

"Describe him," said Brody, after the waitress left.

Araceli fished a photograph out of her scarlet Gucci leather purse and slid it over the tabletop to Brody.

"Here he is," she said.

Brody eyeballed the color photo. A twentysomething rangy guy with a boyish face was sitting on a wooden thwart in a rowboat on a lake, looking relaxed in the bright sunshine, an unidentifiable green tattoo on his upper arm, a fishing rod clasped in his hands as he waited for the next fish to bite. His dreamy eyes gazed into the distance.

"Maybe he just got lost," said Brody.

"I'm convinced something happened to him. He hasn't made any attempt to contact me since he arrived in Vegas."

Chapter 8

"Could you give me some information about him?" said Brody.

"Such as?" said Araceli.

"Has he vanished before?"

"No."

"Could you tell me something about his personality?"

"He's a three-time no-talent loser."

"Hmm," said Brody, taken aback, surprised a guy's sister would describe her brother in such pejorative terms. "I'm getting the impression you don't like him."

"I *do* like him. But he has a way of finding trouble, no matter what he does." She shrugged. "He's a loser. What can I say? It is what it is."

"Your brother the bum."

"He's not a bum. He's a loser. There's a difference. A bum never tries. Damian tries, but fails. He can't find his place in the world."

"Your brother the flop."

"He can't do anything right. Like I said, he's a loser."

"You think he got himself into a scrape in Vegas?"

"I'm sure of it."

"What's his job?"

"He changes jobs faster than I can keep up with. He used to be an auto mechanic and a cop. Now I don't know—"

"A cop, did you say?"

"Used to be."

"Then his going missing might have something to do with that."

Araceli fingered her cold glass of beer. "He's not a cop anymore."

"Maybe he's out of work."

"What can I say? He's a loser."

Brody paused. "Have you tried calling him?"

"Many times. He doesn't answer."

Brody took a pull on his beer.

"My price is four hundred dollars a day plus expenses," he said.

"All right," she said, without arguing.

Brody took the photo of Damian and stuffed it into his trouser pocket.

"Have you filed a missing person's report with the Vegas cops?" he said.

Araceli knocked back her Tecate. "No. I don't want the cops involved."

Brody jacked his eyebrows. "Oh yeah? Why not?"

She leaned toward him, exposing cleavage, lowering her voice. "He might be into something dirty."

"As in illegal?"

"Yeah."

"Why do you say that?"

"He doesn't have a nine-to-five job. He thinks he can get ahead in the world by cutting corners."

"How?"

She rubbed her eyelid with her tapered forefinger. "I can't keep up with him."

Brody sat back in the booth. "I could go to the Vegas cops and check the morgue to see if Damian's there."

"No cops. I don't want the cops involved. That's why I came to you."

"The cops have more manpower than me."

"If Damian's involved in something dirty, like I suspect, I don't want the cops finding out about it. I'm trying to find him, not put him in jail."

"How did he get to Vegas?"

"Search me."

"By car? Plane? Bus? If he took his car, maybe I could have his tag traced."

"He didn't go by car. I know that much."

Brody leaned back in the booth. "I'm going by plane. I don't want to have to make the six-hour trip through the desert to get there by car."

"Whatever."

"What do you want me to do when I find him?"

"Call me." She gave him her cell number.

"I need a nonrefundable five-hundred-dollar down payment from you, and I'm outa here."

Araceli dug her wallet out of her purse, counted out five Ben Franklins, and handed them to Brody.

She stood up, thanked him, and left the pub.

Leering, the male patrons at the bar watched her leave through the green door.

"Whew, she looks even better from the rear," said Tony Soprano Shirt.

"Put your drool back in your mouth," said the bald bartender, wiping a wet glass with a dishcloth. "I don't want OSHA busting my joint for unsanitary conditions on account of your spit."

"When I want your opinion, I'll ask for it, Cue Ball."

Tony Soprano Shirt reached for the bartender's bald head.

The bartender swatted the guy's hand away and retreated down the bar in disgust.

"Is that any way to treat your customers?" said Tony Soprano Shirt.

Chapter 9

Brody drove his Mini back to his small, unkempt apartment in West LA, parked in the garage, entered his room, took a seat in front of his desk, awoke his laptop from Sleep mode, and logged into Elysian Fields, a website that numbered epileptics as members.

He checked in regularly with the website to see how the other members were dealing with their condition, which most people considered a disability. Since epileptics felt stigmatized by society, members of the chat room used code names instead of their real names to keep their identities secret.

Brody used the name Myshkin, the name of the title character in Dostoyevsky's novel *The Idiot* who suffered from epilepsy and was considered a naïve idiot by the people he met.

Myshkin: Anyone here?

Margaux Hemingway: I am, Myshkin.

Teddy Roosevelt: So am I.

Margaux Hemingway: Where's Caligula?

Caligula was dead, Brody knew. Caligula, aka Brad Peltz, had been an FBI plant inside the chat room sent to spy on Elysian Fields' members. Peltz had infiltrated the group, believing it was a subversive organization dedicated to the overthrow of the US government. An unidentified man with a crossbow had fired a bolt through Peltz's heart.

Brody had never told any of the other members about Peltz's death or that Peltz was spying on them. Brody still didn't know if Peltz was working on his own when he had infiltrated the chat room or had been given the assignment by the FBI.

The special agent in charge at the FBI's LA branch Gus Thomason had told Brody the bureau had fired Peltz for emotional instability and a nervous breakdown. They had considered him a paranoid psychotic and ousted him.

Peltz had told Brody Peltz's "termination" from the bureau was in reality his cover story for his clandestine mission of uncovering a cabal within the FBI that was conspiring with the deep state to remove the president of the United States from office using the Twenty-fifth Amendment.

Brody wasn't sure what to believe—the FBI's explanation or Peltz's. The only thing he knew for sure was that Peltz was dead.

Brody didn't know what to tell the other members of the chat room about Peltz, aka Caligula. If he told them Peltz had infiltrated their group to spy on them, they might clam up and resign in fear. But Peltz might have been spying on the group on his own thanks to his psychotic paranoia, without the knowledge of the FBI. If that was the case, why should Brody alarm everyone by telling them Peltz's concocted story about a cabal?

If Peltz was working on his own as a madman when he infiltrated the chat room, the FBI had no interest in spying on the group, and therefore the group had nothing to fear from the FBI.

Why should Brody alarm the group unnecessarily? He decided he should say nothing to them about the FBI till he found out the truth of the matter.

Teddy Roosevelt: Yeah. Where's Caligula? I haven't heard from him in a long time.

Myshkin: Maybe he quit the group.

Margaux Hemingway: Wouldn't he have told us if he did something like that?

Teddy Roosevelt: You would think.

Julius Caesar: I'm new to the group. My name's Julius Caesar.

Teddy Roosevelt: Oh. Nice to have you aboard, Julius.

Margaux Hemingway: Pleased to meet you, Julius.

Myshkin: Welcome.

Julius Caesar: Thanks to all of you.

Until this thing about Peltz was cleared up to his satisfaction, Brody was going to be suspicious of new members. But Brody wouldn't tell Margaux Hemingway or Teddy Roosevelt his suspicions at this time.

Margaux Hemingway: You're welcome. We're always happy to have new members.

Julius Caesar: Are you guys as worried as I am about what people think about you because you're epileptic?

Teddy Roosevelt: Don't let their stupid opinions affect you. Most people are idiots and they shun epileptics out of their own ignorance. Don't pay any attention to them.

Julius Caesar: I don't like being ostracized by so-called normal people, though.

Margaux Hemingway: None of us do. But there's not much we can do about other people's stupidity. You just have to ignore them.

Julius Caesar: I've found the best way to deal with it is not to tell anyone in the first place about my condition.

Myshkin: It's none of their business anyway.

Teddy Roosevelt: Yeah. Fuck them. Who needs them?

Margaux Hemingway: Not everyone has negative feelings about epileptics. Some people are nice and don't look down on us. You guys are too cynical. I've told some of my friends about my condition, and they don't run away from me like I've got the Black Death.

Teddy Roosevelt: I'm not so sure. Oops. Gotta run. My wife's calling me. I'm outa here.

Margaux Hemingway: Let's call it a day.

Brody logged off.

Chapter 10

Damian stood staring at the rotating roulette wheel in the Paris Casino in disbelief. He had backed away from the wheel after his loss, since he had no money left. All he could do was watch the wheel spin and the other players bet.

He wondered if he was still alive. He felt like he wasn't there. Like he had ceased to exist with his loss at roulette.

He desperately wanted to get out of his life of crime, his life as a spear-carrier and a *sicario* for Don Gaetano and the Jalisco New Generation cartel. If he had won just that one bet and doubled his money, he could have walked out of the casino a free man. He could have given the laundered four hundred grand to the bagman and used his winnings at roulette to open his own auto shop.

He had never wanted to be a *sicario*, but the money was too good to pass up. And then there were the girls. Cartel members got all the good-looking girls. The problem was, the life span of a *sicario* was short. It was best to get out of the business as soon as possible—or end up dead from a rival *sicario*'s bullet at an early age.

As a *sicario* he spent his life on the run. He had to keep one step ahead of the cops and rival cartels.

Damian wanted out.

In a trance he watched the roulette wheel spin. One spin of the wheel was all it had taken to decide the outcome of his life.

Now he was on the run again—this time from his boss Don Gaetano. When the *patrón* found out Damian had lost the CJNG's money, he wouldn't hesitate to put out a contract on Damian.

Damian listened to the roulette ivorine ball clicking as it bounced in and out of the spinning wheel's slots, his eyes mesmerized by the omnipotent ball that controlled gamblers' fates.

It didn't matter which number came up now. He had no money at stake. He had gambled and lost. He was a loser. He should have known better. He was always a loser. That was how he had ended up in the drug racket. By losing at everything else in his life, he took the only option remaining to him after he had quit the auto shop and washed out of the police force—joining the drug cartels. It was either that or the hardscrabble life of poverty. His boss at the auto shop would never rehire him if he found out Damian had been working for a cartel. And the cops would toss him in jail if they found out.

Of course, he was going to lose at roulette, he decided. He should have known better than to gamble with the cartel's money. He had lost at everything else he had ever tried. It was preordained he would lose at roulette. What the hell was he thinking? he wondered.

Desperation had driven him to a life of crime. And desperation had driven him to make his last fateful gamble on the spin of a roulette wheel.

It was hopeless, he decided. He was condemned to death. Nobody could escape the long arm of the CJNG. Don Gaetano would have Damian's head—*if* he found out what had happened to the cartel's money.

That was the answer, Damian decided, brightening.

He had to prevent Don Gaetano from finding out. But Damian could prevent it for only so long. Sooner or later Don Gaetano would discover the money was missing. Maybe he already knew, decided Damian.

Damian scoped out the casino suspiciously. Don Gaetano had spies everywhere, Damian knew. Don Gaetano had spies in the Mexican police force and in the government—all bought with heavy bribes. The guy might even have spies in the US. A spy might be watching him even now.

Damian needed help.

He had heard of a Mafia don in Vegas, Armando "Army Brat" Musante, a mortal enemy of CJNG. The US Mafia was always trying to horn in on Don Gaetano's narcotics business. Damian wondered if he could solicit the mobster's help in protecting him from Don Gaetano.

There was one problem with that idea. Musante, who used to work for mobster Tony "The Ant" Spilotro, might wind up whacking Damian if Damian told him he worked for CJNG. There were those that believed Musante had had a hand in Spilotro's violent death. A team of mobsters had beaten Spilotro in his underwear with baseball bats and buried him alive with his brother.

Damian would rather avoid Musante altogether, but Damian was caught between a rock and a hard place. He needed a way to protect himself from Don Gaetano when the guy came after him. Damian couldn't think of anybody else that could protect him.

He couldn't go to the cops. Some of them might be in the pay of Don Gaetano, and they would rat him out in a heartbeat. In any case, Damian was wanted by the Mexican *federales* for murdering two *sicarios* that had worked for the Sinaloa cartel. The Las Vegas cops would be sure to vet him if he went to them for help. And they would find out he was here illegally. Going to them for help was out of the question, Damian decided.

Which left him with Musante.

The girls in their pink bikinis kept dancing behind the ring of blackjack tables and the spinning roulette wheel as the dealers kept dealing, and the rock music kept blaring throughout the casino riddling the walls with sonic blasts, indifferent to Damian's misery.

The way Damian saw it, no matter what he did he was screwed.

But he had to do something.

He wasn't going to sit around and wait for Don Gaetano to send a hit squad of *sicarios* gunning for him.

Chapter 11

The first thing Damian had to do was to keep his mouth shut about what had just happened at the roulette wheel. Nobody must know about the money he had gambled away.

As it stood now, only two people, beside himself, knew of his loss—the roulette croupier and Simon, who had watched the whole thing from a ringside seat.

As long as Don Gaetano hadn't put a tail on Damian, there was no way the guy could know what had happened, decided Damian. Don Gaetano was thousands of miles away in Guadalajara. How could he know?

Why was that woman staring at him? Damian wondered, picking up on a voluptuous thirtysomething brunette with green eyes in a skintight low-cut black Lycra tube top eying him. Was she a hooker looking for a prospective john? After all, this was Sin City.

Maybe she had watched him drop four hundred grand on roulette and figured he must be loaded, he decided.

If she *was* a hooker, she might know how to reach Armando Musante. The Mafia might be pimping for her. In which case, she could serve as Damian's conduit to Musante. It might be worth Damian's while to strike up a conversation with her.

He wandered over to her. Anything to get away from that cursed roulette wheel, which would take pride of place in his nightmares tonight—if he was still alive come nightfall. Was it that bad? he wondered. It was if Don Gaetano had sent spies to follow him and they had seen him lose the cash.

He had to find a way out of this mess, Damian decided. The four hundred grand had been a ticket to freedom. Now that he had lost it, it was a ticket to hell.

"Can I buy you a drink?" he asked the brunette, approaching her.

He could speak English. Maybe that was why Don Gaetano had chosen him to launder the cash. Damian's mother Esmeralda was bilingual and had taught him English, along with Spanish. His father Pedro had taught him nothing. Pedro was a drunkard. He had disappeared when Damian was five years old, and his mother never mentioned his name in their house again. Damian had no idea if the guy was alive or dead.

It was OK with Damian, since the rummy used to beat him when he tied one on. After multiple beatings at his drunken father's hands, Damian had developed the good sense to avoid Pedro after the guy had been hitting the tequila.

Later on in life, long after Pedro had vanished from the family, Damian had decided Pedro saw himself as a failure and was taking it out on his son by beating him.

"Why not?" said the brunette.

"My name's Damian," he said.

"I'm Melody."

He wondered if she was a hooker. Wearing a low-cut blouse didn't make her a hooker. He couldn't very well ask her if she was one. If she wasn't one, she would be offended if he asked. What he really wanted to know was whether she could put him in touch with Armando Musante.

"Did you know the Mafia hangs out here?" he said.

"Oh really? How exciting."

He couldn't tell anything from her answer.

"Let's find a bar," he said.

They wended their way through the idling mélange of customers and beeping, flashing slot machines that crowded the casino till they located a bar.

Entering the bar Damian turned around to see if anyone was following him.

"Are you waiting for someone?" said Melody, watching him.

40

"No—uh, no. I—uh—thought I heard someone say my name. Let's sit here."

"Why not?"

Damian looked behind him one more time to make sure nobody was following him. If they were, they weren't tipping their hands.

Chapter 12

Damian and Melody sat on a banquette with garnet leather upholstery with brass studs running along the perimeter of the seat back.

"Have you been watching me?" said Damian

"Whatever gave you that idea?" said Melody.

He wasn't sure how to take her response. Was she being sarcastic, meaning *of course*? Or was she being indignant? He couldn't tell anything from her tone or visage. For all he knew, she could be the one that was Don Gaetano's spy. He doubted it, though. She was a gringo.

They both ordered margaritas from the tall thirtyish waiter who had a walleye and spoke with an English accent. The waiter disappeared behind the bar.

"What do you do for entertainment in these parts?" said Damian.

"The same as everybody else. Drink and gamble. There's nothing else to do here."

She withdrew a pack of cigarettes from her purse, shook out a smoke, and lit up.

"Did you know the Mafia hangs out in Vegas?" he said.

"Yeah," she said, exhaling a cone of tobacco smoke. "You already told me."

"Oh, right."

"Can you think of any other entertainment they have here?" she said, quirking an eyebrow.

"Maybe a Mafia mobster would know."

She giggled.

"Do you know any?" he said.

"Me?" She unleashed a throaty laugh. "I'm just a lifeguard. What would I know about mobsters?"

Damian shrugged. "You never know."

"What about you? What do you do?"

"I'm—uh—I'm into delivery."

"Like FedEx?"

"Yeah," he said, not wishing to elaborate.

"Vegas is for losers. Losers from all over the world gather here, thinking they can make a fast buck," she said, scanning the casino from their table.

Damian cut to the chase. "Do you know Armando Musante?"

"He sounds like a magician or something. Musante the Great," she said with amusement. "Or the Great Musante."

"I guess that means no."

"I don't know anyone. I'm a lifeguard—uh, I *was* a lifeguard. I hurt my back while diving," she said, rubbing her back and wincing. She leaned toward him and said, "I'll let you in on a secret. My husband's trying to kill me."

He had thought *he* was the one with problems. "Why?"

"I asked him for a divorce. When he heard that, he came after me with a knife. I ran out of the house. I'm still running. I'm convinced he'll kill me if he finds me."

Damian clutched his head. "I just lost four hundred—"

He caught himself before he told her how much money he had lost. The fewer who knew about it, the longer he would stay alive, he figured.

"You lost four hundred dollars on roulette?" she said.

"Uh, yeah."

"I saw you over there, looking like you were gonna pass out."

"Easy come, easy go," he said, his face blank.

"Everybody's a loser in Vegas, one way or the other," she said, and sipped her drink. "And we're all running from something."

She got that right, decided Damian. Did she know more about him than she was letting on? Did she know the cartel was after him? How could she?

"Did you report your husband to the cops?" he said.

"Oh, no. It wouldn't do any good. It would just make him madder."

"How mad can he get? You said he already wants to kill you."

"I've had it with him. I'm gone. I'll be OK, as long as he doesn't find me," she said, biting her lower lip.

"Maybe Musante could help you."

"Who's this guy Musante you're talking about?"

"He's a Mafia don."

"What do I want with a mobster?"

"The mob offers protection. Maybe he would protect you from your husband—for a price."

"You want me to hire him to kill my husband?" she said, searching his face.

"He wouldn't have to kill him. Just dissuade him from attacking you."

"He's a good persuader?"

"Baseball bats, tow chains, and blowtorches help him out."

She started. "*That* kind of persuasion. I'm not looking for that."

She either wasn't taking his hints, or she had no idea how to get in touch with Musante, decided Damian, in which case she was useless to him.

"What *are* you looking for?" he said.

She paused a beat. "Could he get me painkillers for my back?"

"Don't you have a doctor?"

"The stuff he gives me isn't strong enough. I need something stronger."

Heroin, Damian was thinking. He could get her skag or fentanyl from Don Gaetano easy enough—if he ever saw Don Gaetano again. Bad idea. If he *did* see Don Gaetano again, the guy would blow him away for losing the four hundred grand.

"What's wrong with your back?" said Damian.

"I got a herniated disc. My doctor used to get me OxyContin. But he stopped prescribing it for me after they found out it was addictive. Doctors refuse to prescribe it anymore."

He gave her a look. "You really don't know Musante, do you?"

Damian felt his burner vibrate in his trouser pocket. He knew who was calling. His pulse quickened. He withdrew the cell phone and checked the caller ID. Private, it said.

"I have to take this call," he said, excusing himself from the table.

Chapter 13

Cell phone to his ear, Damian left the restaurant and found a deserted spot among the dollar slots in the casino where he wouldn't be overheard.

"It's me," said Don Gaetano.

"Hello, *patrón*," Damian managed to say, despite his gnashing teeth.

"Is it done?"

"Uh—um—no. Not yet."

"What's taking so long?"

"I'm—uh—doing it a little at a time."

"OK. When it's done, I'll tell you the name of the guy I want you to deliver it to."

"All of it?"

"Is that a problem?"

"No. Not at all, *patrón*."

Don Gaetano terminated the call.

Damian had to get rid of this burner. That was the deal. Use it once and discard it. He knew he should stamp on it first to destroy it, but doing so would draw too much attention here in the middle of the casino with so many onlookers.

Idling toward a wastebasket he dug out his handkerchief from his back pocket and wiped his prints off the cell phone when he saw that nobody was watching him. Concealing the cell in his handkerchief he dropped the cell into the wastebasket, returned his handkerchief to his rear pocket, and headed back to Melody at the bar.

He wondered which guy Don Gaetano wanted him to give the money to. Don Gaetano hadn't told him yet. The guy was a bagman for Cobalt Green Tide, was all Damian knew.

Don Gaetano's latest instructions might benefit him, decided Damian. Maybe he could bluff his way out of the mess he was in. Since he didn't have to deliver the cash to

Don Gaetano, how would the boss know what Damian had really done with it? No, that wouldn't work. The bagman who was supposed to get the money would report Damian if the cash wasn't delivered to him as Don Gaetano had ordered.

Damian returned to the banquette and scooched in beside Melody.

"Something important?" she said.

"No," he said, trying to shrug it off.

"You look pale."

"I—I'm just hungry. I get pale when I haven't had anything to eat. I haven't eaten all day. I didn't even have breakfast."

Chapter 14

When Brody walked out of the pub in Santa Monica, two guys in dark blazers, neckties, and sunglasses accosted him on the sidewalk. They stood on either side of him, sandwiching him. One of them grabbed Brody's arm.

"Hey," said Brody, trying to break away from them.

"Come with us," said the taller of the two, whose breath stank of cigarette smoke and garlic.

"Why should I?" said Brody, not cooperating.

The thickset one drove his meaty fist into Brody's solar plexus. Gasping, Brody doubled over. The guy had nice shoes, Brody could see.

They shoved Brody into the backseat of a black Range Rover and sat on either side of him.

"What the hell?" said Brody, doubled over, grimacing.

"You know what they say about sleeping dogs?" said Tobacco Breath, who had the trace of a harelip.

"I have no idea what you're talking about."

"He's saying, mind your own business," said Meaty Fist with a raspy voice.

"What's it to you what I do?"

"We work for the FBI," said Tobacco Breath. "That's all you need to know."

Brody sat up straight. "Where are your badges?"

"We don't have them with us."

"Why not?"

"We're working undercover. Do you think undercover agents carry badges? Think again."

"I'm not telling you how to do your job. Why do you think you can tell me how to do mine?"

"Because we work for the Federal Bureau of Investigation."

"I got a job to do, I do it. That's what I'm paid to do. I'm a private investigator."

Tobacco Breath grabbed Brody's hair and rammed Brody's head into the back of the front seat.

"Stick to your job of peeping through windows and snapping photos of cheating husbands in skeevy dives," said Tobacco Breath. "Don't stick your nose in our business."

Brody blacked out as his head slammed into the seat back. He thought he might suffer an epileptic seizure as a result of the blow and pass out. A blow to the head could trigger an epileptic episode.

He regained consciousness seconds later.

"Is that a threat?" he said.

"Think of it as sound medical advice," said Tobacco Breath. "If you stop turning over rocks, you'll live longer."

"Sounds like a threat to me. Threats are illegal in the state of California."

"Think of us as doctors," said Meaty Fist. "You're sick, and we're giving you medical advice."

"You're *not* doctors, and I'm *not* sick."

Meaty Fist stepped out of the Range Rover.

Tobacco Breath shoved Brody across the backseat toward the open door, rearranged himself on the backseat, and, with a quick thrust of his legs, used his heels to propel Brody out of the SUV. Brody tumbled out of the vehicle and crumpled on the sidewalk in front of Meaty Fist's nice shoes. Not pricy John Lobbs, decided Brody. Not a special agent in charge. Just a special agent who worked in the field.

"Next time we won't be so gentle," said Tobacco Breath.

"There isn't gonna be a next time," said Meaty Fist. "Is there, Brody?"

On his back on the sidewalk Brody propped himself up on his elbow and glared up at him.

"He's gonna follow his doctors' orders and save himself from a life-threatening disease," said Meaty Fist.

"Since when does the FBI have a license to rough people up?" said Brody.

"Ask your senator."

"At least, tell me what this is all about."

Meaty Fist sidestepped Brody's body, shut the Range Rover's back door, climbed into the driver's seat, yanked the door shut after him, revved the SUV, and peeled away from the curb, leaving Brody disheveled on his back on the sidewalk.

Watching the Range Rover drive away, Brody wondered if they were really feds. Feebs didn't go around beating up innocent people the last he'd heard.

The last feeb he had dealt with was Peltz. And Peltz had ended up dead at the hands of a hit man. That was another story.

His body aching, Brody got to his feet, none the wiser.

How had they got onto him, and for what reason? Brody wondered. He would have to keep a lower profile. He didn't want to have to keep looking over his shoulder for feds.

An important part of his job as a PI was asking questions. If he stopped asking questions and "turning over rocks," as the feds had put it, how could he do his job? They were putting him out of business with their warning.

He didn't want to tussle with the government, but he had a job to do. His job right now was to locate Damian Playa for Damian's sister Araceli.

Brody would have to give Tobacco Breath and Meaty Fist the slip.

Chapter 15

"Did you ever want to disappear?" Damian asked Melody in the bar at Paris Las Vegas.

"What do you mean?" she said, nursing her drink. "Like a ghost?"

"Like vanish so nobody knows where you are."

"You mean, vanish off the face of the earth without a trace?"

"Not really. I don't think anyone would want to cease to exist as though they'd never lived. That would be scary."

"I don't want my husband to know where I am. I'd like to disappear from him—if that's what you mean."

"I'm not expressing myself correctly," said Damian, frowning in thought. "I mean, *disappear*—as in become somebody else and leave your old life behind."

"I don't think I'd want to do that. Becoming another person would be too frightening. It would be like dying."

"Or like being reborn."

"It's impossible anyway. You can't become a different person. You are what you are."

"Sometimes my life feels like it's suffocating me. Like I'm locked into a death spiral because of choices I've made."

"I know what you mean. I married the wrong guy. I should've known better. I didn't figure in my wildest dreams he would try to kill me."

"You understand, then."

"But you can't change the choices you already made. So why even think about it? It's pointless. It's just a parlor game."

Damian felt the other burner phone in his trouser pocket vibrate. He withdrew the burner from his pocket and checked the screen.

"I gotta take this," he said, and slid out of the banquette, the seat of his pants squeaking against the leather upholstery.

"You get a lot of calls," said Melody.

Damian nodded and retreated to a deserted spot in the casino next to a roulette slot machine—unfortunately. He would be much happier if he never saw another roulette wheel.

It was Don Gaetano again.

Damian wished the guy would stop calling him. How could he get anything done if Don Gaetano kept pestering him?

"Have you finished?" said Don Gaetano.

"No, *patrón*," said Damian.

"You don't understand your job?"

"I do, *patrón*."

"I guess you don't want to see your girlfriend Sofia again."

"*Patrón*—"

Don Gactano hung up.

What was he doing to her? wondered Damian in anguish. Had the bastard kidnaped her?

Damian remembered his orders. He had to ditch the burner after making or taking one of Don Gaetano's calls. Idling toward a trash basket he wiped his fingerprints off the burner with his handkerchief. He disposed of the burner when nobody was looking.

Before he did anything else he had to return to his room to retrieve another burner in case Don Gaetano attempted to contact him again. Damian had no more burners in his trouser pockets. The guy might call any minute. There was no telling what the son of a bitch would do to Sofia if Damian didn't answer a call. Damian didn't want to find out the hard way. He had to get another one of his burners.

He hurried back to the bar.

"I have to return to my room," he told Melody. "I'll be right back."

Don Gaetano was letting him know who was boss, harassing him, decided Damian. Cutting across the casino floor, he hustled to the elevator that led to his room, entered the elevator, and rode up to his floor.

He used the key card to enter his room and retrieved two more burners from his suitcase that lay on the portable nylon and aluminum luggage rack near the bureau under the wall-mounted flat-panel HDTV.

Breathing a sigh of relief he deposited the two burners in his trouser pockets.

He left his room, took the elevator to the main floor, angled past the slots, and returned to the bar to meet Melody at the banquette.

The banquette was empty.

The waiter spotted him, rushed over to him, and demanded payment of the bill.

"Did the lady at my table tell you where she was going?" said Damian, digging out his wallet and paying his bill.

"She left when I wasn't looking," said the waiter.

Damian scanned the casino floor. No sign of her.

Maybe it was for the best, he decided. She had said she didn't know Musante, which meant she wouldn't be able to lead Damian to him. Damian didn't know what her game was. Maybe it was like she said. She was on the run from her murderous husband.

Chapter 16

At Don Gaetano's hacienda in Guadalajara, Michael
Corleone Casa strode across the cement and terrazzo pool
deck to Don Gaetano Obrador Ramirez, aka "El Padre," who
was lounging on his back on a chaise longue idly watching
two bikini-clad women floating on inflatable rubber rafts in
the pool, a margarita in a frosty glass in his hand.

Minus his nun's habit, Michael was carrying a cooler in
one hand. Unlike most of the cartel members, Michael had no
tattoos. He was tall, but not quite as tall as his father, with a
hatchet face.

The six-foot-tall Arturo Morales Casa, Michael's father,
an intimidating scar slicing his cheek, was sitting beside Don
Gaetano studying his cell phone in one hand, gripping a
tequila in the other.

"*Patrón*, I took care of the Zetas as you ordered," said
Michael.

With a half-inch-long beard the fifty-two-year-old Don
Gaetano squinted his black eyes in the bright sunlight at
Michael and sat up. "You blew up the church they worship
at?"

The black eyes that looked like they never slept, decided
Michael. Even when they were half closed they saw
everything.

"It is done, *patrón*," said Michael.

Arturo looked up from his cell phone and smiled at his
son, stretching the scar on his cheek. "Good boy."

"I'm not a boy anymore, Papa."

Arturo nodded. "No, you're right. You have proved
you're a man."

"They were at mass?" said Don Gaetano.

"*Sí, patrón*," said Michael.

"Good job."

"They had to pay for attacking us at your mother's wake."

"When they hit us, we hit back twice as hard."

Don Gaetano's son Juan drove across the pool's deck toward him on a metallic crimson tricycle, smiling as he peddled furiously.

"Fuck Zetas," said Arturo, and spat on the deck. "Nobody messes with *Jalisco Nueva Generación.*"

Don Gaetano smiled at his son, as Juan parked in front of him.

"You're getting faster and faster every day, my son," he said, patting Juan's head.

"I want to be a race-car driver," said Juan.

"I thought you wanted to be the captain of a ship."

"That was before. Now I want to race cars."

Don Gaetano chuckled. "You have a long way to go before you have to make up your mind."

Juan smiled. "I can be anything I want."

"Exactly. And you have plenty of time to decide." Don Gaetano turned to Michael. "Not that I doubt you, Michael, but do you have the proof?"

"My son doesn't lie," said Arturo.

"I don't doubt that. But this is his first assignment for me. I treat all my employees equally—even the son of my best friend and trusted lieutenant. Everyone needs to show me proof."

"My son's word is good as gold. I stand by him."

"If you didn't, I would fire you. Blood is thicker than water and binds us together. Still . . . there's the matter of proof."

"Not a problem, Papa," said Michael, stepping toward Don Gaetano and depositing the cooler beside him. "Here it is."

Don Gaetano rearranged himself on his chaise longue and studied the cooler. "Open it."

"*Sí, patrón.*"

Eyes wide with curiosity, Juan dismounted his tricycle and walked over to the cooler.

"What about the kid?" said Michael.

"He has to get used to seeing how we deal with our enemies," said Don Gaetano, his face impassive. "I don't want him to grow up to be *un cobarde*." Coward.

Michael lifted the cooler's lid.

The charred face of a human head stared back at him, most of the flesh consumed by fire. It was the head of the dying parishioner Michael had decapitated with his machete at the church.

"Excellent," said Don Gaetano.

Juan goggled at the dead white eyes that gazed out of the cooler.

"Death to Zetas," said Arturo, and spat again. *"Pendejos."*

Don Gaetano looked disgusted and waved his hand in front of his face. "The stink. Cover it."

Michael replaced the cooler's lid.

Chapter 17

Brody was getting ready to leave his apartment and drive to LAX to catch his flight to Vegas when he heard a knock on his apartment door.

A middle-aged clean-cut guy in a navy blue business suit and a maroon tie was standing in the hall. He removed a badge from his suit's breast pocket and displayed it to Brody.

"Special Agent in Charge Gus Thomason."

The fed's name sounded familiar, decided Brody, but he couldn't place it.

"What can I do for you?" said Brody, not looking forward to talking to another fed.

"Mind if we have a talk?" said Thomason.

"Your buddies beat you to it."

"What?" said Thomason, puzzled.

"I was on my way out," said Brody with a trace of a smile, glancing at his packed suitcase sitting on the carpet.

Thomason took in Brody's words with dark eyes that didn't smile. "This is important."

Thomason didn't budge.

There was no way Brody was going to get through the doorway with Thomason planted there.

"Come on in," said Brody, stepping back into his living room.

"Thanks."

Thomason entered the room and closed the door behind him.

"Are you Scott Brody?" he said.

"Yeah."

"You're the one I talked to on the phone about Brad Peltz."

Now Brody recalled Thomason's name. "You're the head of the FBI's Westwood branch?"

"Correct. And Peltz was murdered."

"I know. I saw it go down. Do you want something to drink?" said Brody, glancing into his kitchenette.

"This shouldn't take long."

"Good. I don't want to miss my flight."

"I'm not gonna beat around the bush. What exactly did Peltz tell you when he contacted you?"

The thing was, Brody couldn't tell Thomason anything that Peltz had told him about the cabal within the FBI that was plotting with the deep state and Vice President Dealey to remove President Ransom from office using the Twenty-fifth Amendment. Brody had signed an NDA for Peltz. According to Peltz, to violate the NDA would get Brody sued and thrown in prison for the rest of his life for violating the Espionage Act.

But did the NDA continue to be enforceable even after Peltz's death? wondered Brody. He decided it must, because the NDA he signed was with the FBI and not with Peltz personally. At least that was what Peltz had told him. Peltz was dead, but the FBI still existed. Brody didn't want to end up tossed in the joint.

The question that had nagged at Peltz was, who in the FBI was involved in the conspiracy? Peltz hadn't given any names to Brody. Peltz hadn't trusted anybody, not even fellow agents in the bureau.

Brody thought about it. If the conspiracy was real, then Thomason might be a coconspirator in the cabal. Which meant Brody could end up dead like Peltz if he revealed what Peltz had told him after Brody had signed the NDA.

"He didn't tell me anything," said Brody.

"He told you nothing," said Thomason, sarcasm dripping from his lips.

"Right."

"Then why did he contact you? Your story doesn't wash. Do you see what I'm getting at?"

"He wanted me to help him with a case he was working on, but he wouldn't go into detail about it."

Thomason shook his head. "How could you help him with a case if he didn't tell you what it was about?"

"That's what I told him. I didn't get it either."

"You're not leveling with me."

Brody said nothing.

Chapter 18

"You could go to jail for withholding evidence from the FBI," said Thomason nonchalantly, touching his eyelid with his forefinger's knuckle.

"I'm not withholding evidence."

"You're a fool if you think you can fight the bureau. We have the means . . ."

It sounded like Thomason was about to threaten him before he trailed off, decided Brody.

"I'm not fighting the FBI," said Brody. "I'm a private investigator doing my job for my clients."

"You were working for Peltz, an ex-FBI agent."

"He told me I had to. And he never told me the FBI had fired him. I thought he was an agent on active duty."

"What did he tell you about the case he was supposedly working on for the bureau?"

"We're going around in circles. I already told you, he told me nothing," Brody lied.

"Lying to an FBI agent is perjury. You could do a lot of time for perjury."

Brody was aware of the law. No matter what he said or did, he could go to the slam. He was either committing perjury or violating the Espionage Act. Zugzwang, they called it in chess.

He decided not to trust Thomason. He knew nothing about the guy. If Peltz hadn't been a paranoid nut case as Thomason had called him, he might have been right when he claimed that Thomason was part of the cabal. In which case Brody would be cutting his own throat by telling Thomason the truth about what Peltz had told him.

"Peltz didn't confide in me," said Brody. "I wish I could help you, but he was tight-lipped. I got the impression he thought he was smarter than me and didn't have to tell me anything."

Thomason shrugged. "That sounds like him. You know how these paranoid schizophrenics are. They think everybody else is an idiot. They're the only enlightened ones."

Brody couldn't tell if Thomason believed him. Was the guy pretending to? Was he changing tactics by pretending he did, trying to get Brody to relax and divulge the truth in an offhand moment?

Brody said nothing.

"These psychos are something else, aren't they?" said Thomason, acting like Brody's friend.

"Yeah."

"Some of them are slippery as hell. At times they can sound believable."

"Yeah."

"There's a lot of suspicion about the FBI these days. Certain groups think we've become politicized. We never used to deal with that back in the day. The bureau was respected as an objective enforcer of the law."

"Times change."

"If you can recall anything Peltz told you, notify me immediately. He might've stumbled onto something the bureau needs to know about. He *was* paranoid, but he had his lucid moments—and he *was* a good investigator before his attacks of psychosis."

Brody couldn't make up his mind to trust Thomason. The guy could be on the up and up, decided Brody, and not part of the cabal. If that was the case, Brody should tell him about the conspiracy so Thomason could foil it.

Brody didn't want to take the chance of believing Thomason. Too much was riding on it. In any case, Peltz's belief in a conspiracy could have been a delusion, which meant it didn't matter to anyone. So why bother to bring it up? decided Brody.

"If that'll be all, I really have to catch my flight," said Brody.

Hiking his eyebrows Thomason scratched the back of his neck. He fished his wallet out of his trouser pocket, extracted his business card, and handed the card to Brody.

"Call me when you remember something," said Thomason, and retreated toward the door. He balked and wheeled around. "You're not planning on leaving the country, are you?"

"No."

"Don't. I'll yank your passport if I have to."

"No need."

"Where are you headed?"

Brody didn't think it was any of Thomason's business. He believed information shared between him and his clients was privileged.

"Out of state," said Brody.

"I can find out easy enough. All I have to do is check with the airlines."

Brody knew Thomason was right on that score. The FBI could do whatever it wanted. Brody didn't want to sound like he was hiding anything.

"Vegas," he said.

"That wasn't so hard, was it?" said Thomason, and opened the door. "One more thing," he said, turning to face Brody.

"Yeah?"

"Did you ever hear of Cobalt Green Tide?"

Brody shook his head no. "What is it? Some rock group?"

Thomason left the room without saying a word.

Brody didn't like the idea that the feds were tailing him. He didn't even know which feds they were. Were they the real deal? Or were they the cabal inside the bureau that was attempting to oust the president from office, according to

Peltz? Did the cabal even exist outside of Peltz's paranoid delusions?

First things first. He had to track down Damian Playa for Damian's sister Araceli.

Chapter 19

"Where are the three amigos you captured?" Don Gaetano asked Arturo, as they strolled along the deck of his Guadalajara hacienda's pool past an inflatable white unicorn that floated across the water borne by a gentle breeze that rippled the water's surface.

They angled across the lawn under the hot afternoon sun, their guayaberas clinging to their sweaty chests, the air thick with the odor of fresh-mown grass.

Sporting jeans, a brown leather vest, and python cowboy boots, Don Gaetano swatted at a swarm of midges gathered in a cloud around his head and scratched his beard. He inhaled a batch of the midges, coughed, and spat.

"I hate breathing those things," he said.

"I know. They get in my eyes," said Arturo, blinking uncomfortably.

"Where are they?"

"The Zetas?" said Arturo.

Don Gaetano nodded yes.

"In the south quadrant," said Arturo.

"Did they talk?"

Don Gaetano coughed, hawked, and spat again, clearing his mouth of the insects.

"*Sí, patrón,*" said Arturo. "They said the Zetas put out a contract on you."

Walking with Arturo, Don Gaetano shrugged in the afternoon heat. "Tell me something I don't know. I always expect someone's trying to kill me. It's how I stay alive. Business as usual. Is that all they told you?"

"*Sí, patrón.*" Arturo paused. "Can I talk to you about something, *patrón.*"

"Of course, Arturo. You are my right-hand man. We have no secrets from each other," said Don Gaetano, brushing beads of sweat from his brow with the back of his hand, relieved he had passed the swarm of midges.

"Have you noticed anything about my son Michael?"

"Noticed what?"

"He seems—I don't know how to say it. He seems— uh—withdrawn."

"How do you mean?"

"I feel like I'm not reaching him sometimes when I talk to him. It's like he's not there, like he's thinking about something else and not paying attention to me."

"Thinking about his dick, huh, my friend?"

"I think it's something else. I don't know."

Don Gaetano patted Arturo on the back. "He's young. He's growing up. That's what he's doing. You remember what it was like being a teenager, huh?" Don Gaetano grinned. "Horny like a bull all the time, huh? Huh?"

"Maybe you're right."

"Of course, I am." Don Gaetano changed the subject, his face grim. "Where are the Zetas? I don't see them."

"Behind the stand of mahogany trees."

They approached the mahoganies, walked under them, and entered a clearing where they spotted three crucifixes, each with a half-naked man nailed to it. Groaning, the blood-streaked men writhed in extremis.

"Did you whip them?" said Don Gaetano.

"I had to get them to talk."

"Did they have anything more to tell us?"

"*Nada.*" Nothing.

Don Gaetano addressed the Zetas. "Do you want to be turned into fertilizer?"

The three Zetas moaned.

"Have mercy," said one of them.

Don Gaetano turned to Arturo. "Where is it?"

"In the shed," said Arturo, nodding at a small wooden hutch under a nearby mahogany whose long boughs arched above it as if in protection. "Want me to get it?"

"Wait. I'm having second thoughts about Damian. I don't think we can trust him. What do you think of him?"

"What do you mean?"

"He hasn't reported back to me from Vegas. When I called him he said he hadn't completed the job. It shouldn't take this long to launder money at a casino."

"You think he's planning to split with the money?"

"We can't rule it out. I have someone tailing him, but we need to send backup to Vegas to get my money and take care of him. A team of *sicarios*."

Arturo nodded yes.

"Do you want me to get it now?" he said, staring at the shack.

"Call the men first."

Arturo dug his cell out of his trouser pocket and punched out a phone number on the keypad. "Tell the men to report to the south quadrant."

Chapter 20

Dressed in jeans, T's, and leather cowboy boots or jogging shoes for the most part, a score of CJNG men, who had been eating lunch, some of them wiping food from their mouths, gathered near the copse of mahoganies, AK-47s strapped over their shoulders.

"A mission, *patrón*?" a wiry twentysomething gangbanger named Roberto asked Don Gaetano, clutching his AK-47's stock, an intent expression on his face.

Roberto always had a half-grin or -sneer plastered on his face, decided Don Gaetano. He was never sure which. All he *was* sure of was that Roberto was a sociopathic serial killer.

Don Gaetano didn't answer. He turned to Arturo. "OK. Get it."

Arturo retreated to the hutch, opened the door, entered the hutch, and exited carrying a flamethrower. He took the flamethrower to Don Gaetano and handed it to him.

Don Gaetano turned to his men. "This is what happens to anyone that opposes me."

He aimed the flamethrower at one of the crucifixes and pulled the trigger. Propane gas burst through the gun assembly and, ignited by piezo-ignition at the end of the barrel, cast a blue flame with a golden tip spewing from the barrel, which incinerated the Zeta nailed to the crucifix.

The Zeta howled in agony, his flesh consumed by flames.

The other two Zetas watched in horror. Don Gaetano ignited them one after the other. The two Zetas emitted ear-piercing screams.

"Let's toast some marshmallows," said Roberto, eyes gleaming.

The air fast became thick with the stench of burning human flesh.

Some of the cartel members looked sick. Others watched the spectacle stone-faced—except for one, who guffawed.

"Getting roasted alive is too good for them," said Roberto with his trademark grin/sneer. "*Maricones*."

"I need six of you to do a job in Vegas," said Don Gaetano.

"I volunteer," said Roberto, brandishing his AK over his head.

Don Gaetano nodded. "Do you all know Damian Playa?"

"I knew he was no good. He used to be a cop before he joined us. You can never trust a cop."

"A lot of CJNG used to be cops before they realized where the real money is. Then they got smart and joined us."

"I still say you can't trust anyone that used to be a cop," said Roberto under his breath.

"Do you think you can handle him?" Arturo asked Roberto.

"Piece of cake. Let me do it alone. I don't need help taking out a cop *pendejo*."

"Take men with you," said Don Gaetano.

"I don't need any help."

Don Gaetano locked his gaze on Roberto's face. "Take at least three *sicarios* with you. I want this taken care of."

"*Sí, patrón.*"

"As soon as you get back my four hundred grand from him, call me."

"*Sí, patrón.*"

"I need a margarita," said Don Gaetano.

His satphone wailed *The Good, the Bad and the Ugly* soundtrack in his trouser pocket. He handed the flamethrower to Arturo, retreated from the others, and took the call.

"It's me," said his wife Carmen. "The neighbors are complaining about the smell of burning flesh coming from our hacienda."

"They must be mistaken, *querida*."

"And the mayor called. He wants a donation."

"Of course, he does. A politician who doesn't want money isn't a politician."

"Will you get back to him?"

"Of course."

"*Te amo.*" I love you.

"*Te amo, querida.*"

He terminated the call. *And I love Valentina*, he thought. *With her black jackboots, black leather thong bikini, ice blue eyes, and riding crop. All I want is love. If the Zetas loved me, I wouldn't have to burn them at the stake. All I've ever wanted is love.*

"An important call, *patrón*?" said Arturo, approaching Don Gaetano, flamethrower in hand.

"My wife."

"Ah."

Don Gaetano eyed the three smoldering crucifixes and the crumpled charred bodies that hung from them, the reek oppressive in the hot humid air.

"When those things have burned to the ground, bury the mess and plant grass on top," he said, gesticulating, and departed.

Chapter 21

Before Brody left his apartment for his flight to Vegas, he got onto his laptop and logged onto the Elysian Fields website as Myshkin.

Myshkin: Anybody there.

Margaux Hemingway: I'm here.

Julius Caesar: So am I.

Teddy Roosevelt: All present and accounted for.

Myshkin: Anybody having problems with their epilepsy?

Margaux Hemingway: Nothing untoward. How about you?

Myshkin: Do you think this is a subversive organization?

Margaux Hemingway: Are you joking? How could we be subversive? Is epilepsy considered subversive now?

Myshkin: Somebody once told me this kind of chat club is subversive.

Teddy Roosevelt: He must've been pulling your leg.

Julius Caesar: Do you discuss politics here?

Margaux Hemingway: No. We discuss problems we have with other people's reactions to our condition, and we also discuss our condition.

Julius Caesar: Are you sure that's all you discuss?

Teddy Roosevelt: Oh. So belonging to an online chat club makes you subversive. Give me a break. That's crazy.

Julius Caesar: It depends on what you talk about in this secret club. I'm playing devil's advocate here.

Margaux Hemingway: We don't talk politics.

Teddy Roosevelt: Politics bore me. All politicians do is lie. It's BS.

Julius Caesar: Then you're a nihilist?

Teddy Roosevelt: Because I think politicians are congenital liars?

Julius Caesar: A nihilist would say something like that.

Teddy Roosevelt: I'm not a nihilist, and I didn't come to this chat room to discuss politics. I'll go to QAnon or 4chan to do that.

Julius Caesar: You're a member of QAnon?

Margaux Hemingway: What's Q whatever?

Teddy Roosevelt: I never said I was a member of QAnon.

Julius Caesar: You said you go to QAnon to discuss politics and nihilism.

Teddy Roosevelt: That's *not* what I said. You're twisting my words.

Julius Caesar: You don't believe a clandestine ring of wealthy pedophiles controls our government and the media?

Teddy Roosevelt: No, I don't. And what if I did? That's got nothing to do with our chat room.

Margaux Hemingway: What are you two talking about? That's crazy stuff. A clandestine ring of pedos controls the government and the media?

Teddy Roosevelt: He's talking about QAnon conspiracy theories.

Margaux Hemingway: I guess I live a sheltered life. The only Q I've heard of is *GQ*.

Teddy Roosevelt: Julius Caesar brought it up. Not me.

Julius Caesar: Not true. You brought it up.

Teddy Roosevelt: I said we *weren't* QAnon or 4chan. I never said we *were*. I said I'd go to QAnon and 4chan to talk politics, not here.

Julius Caesar: When you talk politics, you go to QAnon and 4chan.

Teddy Roosevelt: No, I don't. You're twisting my words again.

Julius Caesar: But you *have* heard of them. A lot of people haven't.

Teddy Roosevelt: I plead guilty to reading a lot.

Julius Caesar: You're upset with the way things are, though. That's why you do so much reading.

Teddy Roosevelt: I read because I like to read.

Julius Caesar: And you believe a ring of rich pedophiles controls the country.

Teddy Roosevelt: I don't believe the convicted sex offender Jeffrey Epstein committed suicide in a New York jail, if that's what you mean.

Julius Caesar: The ring of pedophiles closed ranks? They hired an assassin?

Margaux Hemingway: What does any of this have to do with epilepsy? We're straying off the subject. We come here because sometimes we think we're pariahs because of our condition. My dog is barking. I think he needs to take a pee.

Julius Caesar: I know how you feel. Our condition puts a wall between us and others.

Teddy Roosevelt: I need to take a pee.

Myshkin: Then you know what it's like, Julius.

Julius Caesar: Of course. That's why I joined.

Margaux Hemingway: We always welcome new members.

Julius Caesar: You're trying to increase the size of the group?

Margaux Hemingway: We're not a closed group.

Julius Caesar: You want to spread the word? WWG1WGA.

Margaux Hemingway: WWG—what? Is that some kind of code? We don't speak in codes here.

Julius Caesar: Where We Go One We Go All. It's a slogan of QAnon.

Margaux Hemingway: Never heard of any of it. My dog—

Julius Caesar: And yet you all ~~have~~ secret identities.

Teddy Roosevelt: You think Elysian Fields is a front for QAnon? That's nuts.

Myshkin: We come here to discuss the problems epileptics face in society. Sometimes we feel like outcasts.

Julius Caesar: You're antisocial?

Myshkin: Society in general is misinformed about epilepsy.

Julius Caesar: And you want to change society because of that?

Teddy Roosevelt: I'm not here to change anything. I'm here to discuss, not change.

Julius Caesar: Me too. I'm one of you.

Margaux Hemingway: I'm here to learn of other epileptics' experiences and share my own.

Julius Caesar: Because you're upset with the way things are?

Margaux Hemingway: Who's upset? My dog's upset. I have to go. He's going crazy. Good-bye, everyone.

Myshkin: I should be at the airport.

Julius Caesar: Where are you headed?

Myshkin: Vegas.

Julius Caesar: Good time for a vacation.

Teddy Roosevelt: It's always a good time for a vacation.

Julius Caesar: I got things to do and places to go. Bye.

Brody logged out of Elysian Fields, shut down his computer, grabbed his suitcase, and headed for the door.

As he locked his apartment's door behind him, he felt his cell phone vibrate in his trouser pocket.

It was Araceli.

"My mother just called me," she said. "She says she fears Damian is in grave danger."

"I'm on my way to Vegas," said Brody. "Do you have any idea where he's staying?"

"All I know is, he likes to gamble."

"He must be somewhere on the strip, then."

"As soon as you find him, let me know."

"Will do."

Chapter 22

Don Gaetano sat in the spacious living room of his Guadalajara hacienda, luxuriating in the cozy ambience of the room's stucco walls under a glittering chandelier and rich mahogany exposed beams in the cathedral ceiling. Satphone in hand, he was sitting on a brown leather sofa reading a list of numbers that he had placed on the acrylic-topped coffee table.

Reading one of the phone numbers he punched it into his satphone.

Carmen entered the room, wearing a scarlet dress, running the pearls on her necklace through her fingers.

"Is everything OK?" she said, noting his concerned expression.

"Just checking up on one of my men."

Nobody answered the call.

He punched out the next phone number on his list.

"He doesn't answer?" she said.

"He has about a dozen burner phones. I don't know which one he's carrying so I have to call each number till he picks up."

"It would be easier if he had only one phone."

"It would be easier to trace, too. He throws out every burner after he uses it once to avoid being traced."

"Sometimes I think you're paranoid, dear."

"Because I have a lot of enemies?"

"There you see. You *are* paranoid."

"If I wasn't paranoid, I'd be dead."

She laughed. "You say such funny things."

"The truth can be amusing."

"Do you like my dress," she said, smiling and pirouetting.

"*Sí, querida,*" he said, staring at his satphone, listening to it ring.

Coming to halt she frowned. "You're not even looking at it."

He looked up at her. "It's beautiful."

"It makes me feel free," she said, pirouetting again.

"Free?"

"Because it's so light and loose. I barely know it's there."

"It goes with your raven hair."

No answer on the satphone. He punched out the next number.

"There must be an easier way of doing that," she said.

"The secure way is the most difficult way and the best way."

He listened to the phone ring.

Arturo strode into the room.

"*Patrón?*" he said deferentially.

"*Qué pasó*, Arturo?" said Don Gaetano.

"I have heard from our bribed informants in the government. They have checked all the flight manifests of jets flying from the United States into Guadalajara. There's no sign of Damian Playa."

"Then he hasn't snuck back into the country. I wanted to make sure. I thought he might try to see his mother and sister on the sly."

"The informants found three suspicious names on the manifests that might be CIA or DEA agents."

"All right. Check them out and get back to me."

Arturo nodded and walked out.

Don Gaetano punched out the next number on his satphone and listened to it ring.

Chapter 23

Damian had just passed by a faux marble statue of the Roman god Neptune wielding a trident in a fountain and was window-shopping in the airy hall of the first story of the three-story Caesar's Palace Forum Shops when he felt his burner vibrate in his trouser pocket.

His heartbeat accelerated.

He ducked into a hallway leading to the restrooms so he would be alone when he took the call.

"Did you do the laundry?" said Don Gaetano.

Damian's throat tensed. He didn't know what to say. He couldn't stall any longer. Don Gaetano would become suspicious.

"Your mother and sister would like to know," said Don Gaetano when Damian didn't answer.

"It took longer than I thought," Damian managed to say, his voice husky and barely audible.

"What was that? I couldn't hear."

"Yeah, I did it," said Damian.

"*Bueno*. Now I want you to give the laundry to Ned Bates."

Damian registered surprise. "Who is Ned Bates?"

"I'm sending Roberto to help you, since you're having so much trouble."

"I don't need help—"

Don Gaetano terminated the call.

Burner in hand, Damian stood frozen, stunned.

Roberto was a stone killer, Damian knew. The psychopathic *sicario* had racked up more than a hundred hits of Don Gaetano's enemies and he was only in his twenties. Roberto was the last guy Damian wanted to see as help. If Roberto was the "help," it meant Don Gaetano had sent him to whack Damian.

And who was this bagman Ned Bates? wondered Damian. How was Damian supposed to recognize the guy? Damian had never met him.

Damian would have to avoid Ned Bates. Damian had no money to give him. As soon as Ned Bates found out the money had vanished, he would contact Don Gaetano, and that would be the end of Damian. But how could Damian avoid Ned Bates when he had no idea what Ned Bates looked like?

Realizing he was clutching the burner in his hand, he knew he had to trash it. He disappeared into the restroom, dropped the burner under the sinks, stomped on it with his heel, picked it up, wiped it off with a paper towel, and flicked it into a wastebasket half full of crumpled paper towels. He washed his hands, wiped them off with paper towels, and pitched them over the burner, covering it, just as a fat guy grunted, opened one of the stalls, and walked to the sinks, hawking.

Ned Bates? wondered Damian. Hell, he was going to be seeing Ned Bates in his dreams.

Damian strode out of the restroom, not knowing what to do.

He couldn't think straight. Lightheaded, he wandered into the capacious hallway. Not only were his mother and sister in Don Gaetano's sights, so was he. And then there was Roberto.

Roberto was a killing machine. Nothing interested him other than killing.

If Don Gaetano had given Roberto the contract to waste Damian, Damian was as good as dead. *If* Don Gaetano had put out a contract on Damian. Don Gaetano had not said he had. He had said he was sending Roberto to "help" Damian.

But Damian couldn't trust Don Gaetano. Why send Roberto of all people to help him? Damian wondered.

Both Roberto and Ned Bates were to be avoided, decided Damian. If Ned Bates found out Damian had lost the four hundred grand, he would tell Don Gaetano. The problem was Ned Bates would be difficult to avoid, since Damian had no idea what the guy looked like.

Chapter 24

Damian maundered down the hall in a daze, passing the window-shoppers who were checking out the upscale stores like Gucci, Rolex, TAG Heuer, John Varvatos, and Emenegildo Zegna, none of them with a care in the world other than possessing luxurious merchandise.

He hated the window-shoppers. Why was he enduring this nightmare while they were wallowing in the luxury that surrounded them? he wondered.

He kept walking. He couldn't blame them. They had nothing to do with inducing his wretchedness. It was his own fault for gambling away Don Gaetano's four hundred grand. Now he hated himself. Why couldn't he do anything right?

Lost in his thoughts, he all but bumped into a big red-bearded guy built like a Hell's Angel wearing jeans and a black motorcycle jacket with zippered slash pockets, holding his arms up at his sides, his fists clenched downward, like he was lifting a barbell to his waist. The porcine-faced guy glared at him.

Damian hurried away. Shooting a guy in the middle of the ritzy hallway wasn't an option. Too many witnesses. A fistfight was out of the question. He wasn't about to get into a mano a mano with a guy built like a linebacker for the Steelers, decided Damian. The guy had more than a hundred-pound advantage over him.

He told himself to pay attention to what he was doing. He had to be aware of his surroundings because Ned Bates might approach any minute. Anybody could be Ned Bates. Even the Hell's Angel.

The good news was Don Gaetano didn't know where Damian was staying. Damian had told Don Gaetano before he had left Guadalajara that he would stay at the Mirage. Damian had changed his mind when he had landed in Vegas at McCarran Airport and had checked in at the Paris.

With any luck Ned Bates was looking for him at the Mirage, decided Damian as he reached a splashing fountain with white statues of rearing horses and Roman gods enthroned in it. Tourists aiming their cell-phone cameras surrounded the fountain snapping pictures of relatives posing near the plashing water.

He wouldn't be visiting the Mirage any time soon.

He *would* be visiting the Mafia capo Musante, as soon as he found out where Musante hung out. Musante was the only guy that could protect him from the long arm of Don Gaetano.

Damian pulled out his handkerchief and mopped sweat from his brow.

The air was cool thanks to the AC, but he was burning up inside with the fever of apprehension.

Damian felt a tap on the back of his shoulder and cringed. He whipped his head around, tensing his body and preparing to attack. Was it Roberto? Ned Bates? The Hell's Angel?

"Excuse me," said a jolly-faced middle-aged guy in a Day-Glo green aloha shirt. "You dropped your comb." He held up a black plastic pocket comb.

Damian accepted the comb with relief. "Thanks."

"Don't mention it."

Damian decided he must have dropped the comb when he pulled out his handkerchief.

The guy walked away.

Was the guy a Good Samaritan or was he a spy? Damian wondered, contemplating the comb in his hand, strumming his thumb along the plastic tines.

His nerves were stretched to the breaking point. Maybe the best thing for him to do was to hole up in his hotel room and figure out how to get in touch with Musante. Damian couldn't take the chance of having Roberto or Ned Bates seeing him—if either of them was even in town.

Damian figured at least Ned Bates was.

Damian left Caesar's Palace.

On his return to the Paris, he encountered the suit Simon who had watched him lose four hundred grand at roulette.

"The boss wants to see you," said Simon.

Damian gnashed his teeth. What could the casino boss want with him? he wondered. It couldn't be anything good. His life was on a downward trajectory. Why should it turn upward out of the blue?

"Can't this wait?" he said, preparing to break away from the suit.

"The boss doesn't wait for anyone," said Simon, latching onto Damian's elbow and ushering him to the bank of elevators that led to the hotel rooms.

Chapter 25

When Brody's forty-five minute flight from LA touched down at McCarran International, it was 111 degrees in Vegas. His travel bag in one hand, a plastic bottle of water in the other, he stood in the heat outside the terminals and waited for a shuttle to the Vegas Strip.

The heat squeezed him like a vise. He wondered if his brains would start boiling out of his ears if he stood out here much longer. He put down his bag, unscrewed the cap on his water bottle, and gulped water, his face sweaty.

The shuttle arrived.

He gave the driver his bag and climbed the metal steps into the shuttle. The driver packed Brody's bag in the rear of the shuttle.

The shuttle had air-conditioning, but it must have been set on low, since Brody continued to sweat. He drank frequently from his plastic bottle of water. The shuttle drove through Vegas's heavy traffic at a snail's pace.

Brody spotted an ambulance parked near the curb in front of the Flamingo. Two paramedics in dark blue uniforms were tending to a red-faced bald guy suffering from heat prostration lying supine on the sidewalk. An EMT rolled a gurney toward them.

The Venetian was the shuttle's third stop.

Meanwhile, the shuttle dropped off tourists at other hotels, driving over a plethora of speed bumps located at the hotels' entrances. Brody was already feeling queasy from the heat. The shuttle's juddering over the speed bumps made him feel worse.

He got off at the Venetian on wobbly legs. The driver retreated to the back of the shuttle and retrieved Brody's bag. Brody tipped him a buck and made his way to the Venetian's entrance, which consisted of a dozen plate-glass doors.

The coolness of the air-conditioning in the Venetian's lobby revived him.

He wondered how he was going to find Damian. Brody didn't see any quick way of doing it. He would have to pound leather and ask around. Damian might have left Vegas by the time Brody got a lead to the guy's whereabouts.

After Brody checked into his room, he milled around the slot machines and showed the cocktail waitresses the photo of Damian that Araceli had given him to see if any of them recognized him.

No hits.

Brody sighed. This was going to take a while.

There were thirty casinos on the Las Vegas Strip. There were forty-five casinos in the entire city of Las Vegas. And there were thousands of tourists cramming the strip's sidewalks, despite the intense heat.

How many more thousands were walking around inside the casinos? he wondered.

He decided his best bet was to file a missing person's report first with the Las Vegas Metropolitan Police Department. They must have CCTV cameras posted on the streets that might have filmed Damian Playa.

He took a cab driven by a short, bow-legged, reedy Vietnamese hack to the Convention Center Area Command station on 750 Sierra Vista Drive. The sign on the two-story grey building said Joseph Lombardo, Sheriff.

"Don't stay out in the sun too long," said the hack with a grin, and drove away.

Sweating, a half-full plastic water bottle in his hand, Brody entered the foreboding building, a stark contrast to the palatial casinos on the strip. At least it was air-conditioned, he decided.

He remembered Araceli had told him not to contact the Vegas cops, but he needed a clue to Damian's whereabouts. The cops had CCTVs on the strip that could provide valuable intel. There was no way she could find out he had visited the cops unless he told her.

He approached the watch commander, a bulky fortyish guy with a dark shaving-brush mustache, a pencil wedged above his ear, sitting in a butternut uniform behind the front desk reading a report in his hands with dark eyes.

"Hello. Do you have CCTV cameras on the strip?" said Brody, and took a swig from his water bottle.

"Who wants to know?" said the watch commander, looking up from his report.

"The name's Scott Brody."

"And?"

"And?"

"And why do you want to know?"

"I want to file a missing person's report. Maybe the guy I'm looking for appeared on one of your videotapes and you could ID him with your facial recognition software."

"Maybe we could do that."

"Good. Because I'm worried about this guy. He could be a victim of foul play."

Chapter 26

"Do you have a photo of him?" said the watch commander.

Brody withdrew Damian's photo from his wallet and handed it to the watch commander. "His name's Damian Playa."

"You'll need to fill out missing person's forms," said the watch commander, glancing at the photo of Damian fishing.

"No problem."

"He likes to fish, huh?"

"I guess."

"Maybe he's at Lake Mead. They got some nice striped bass."

"Do they have hotels there?"

"Sure do."

Brody thought about it. It was a possibility he should keep in mind. After all, Damian was fishing in the photo. But—

"His sister says he likes to gamble," said Brody.

"How long's he been missing?"

"Five days. Could you run his face through your facial recognition software and see if you get any hits? I'd like to know where he was last seen. You *do* have CCTV cameras set up on the strip, don't you?"

"That's police business," said the watch commander, getting uppity.

"I want to get some idea where I should start looking for him."

"Where was he staying?"

"I dunno."

"Why don't you know where he was staying?"

"He didn't tell me."

"Then how do you know he was even here?"

"His sister told me he's here. She got a postcard from Vegas from him."

"Why do you think he's the victim of foul play?"

"His sister hasn't heard from him in five days, and she has no way to contact him. He's not answering his cell phone."

"We need something more than that to make this top priority."

"What more do you need?"

"Was he on the lam from creditors or from alimony payments? Something along those lines."

"Not that I know of."

"There could be a number of reasons he's not answering his cell phone, other than foul play. Maybe he lost it."

"Now that I think of it, he owes child-support payments to his ex."

Brody was making this up on the fly. The more specific he made his lie, the more likely the watch commander was to believe it.

"That might be important," said the watch commander.

"Exactly."

"Why was he in Vegas?"

"For a vacation, he said."

The watch commander mulled it over. "His ex could've sicced a skip tracer on him to get him to pony up his alimony, I suppose."

Brody nodded. "Damian's life could be in danger."

The watch commander made a strange noise in his throat. Brody figured it for a sigh.

"I'll make a copy of the photo and see if any of our CCTV cameras spotted him," said the watch commander, plucking Damian's photo from the desktop and retreating out of sight into another room.

Chapter 27

The watch commander returned after a few minutes, planted his bulk on his chair like a bag of cement, looking like he was planning on remaining sedentary for the remainder of the afternoon, and handed the photo back to Brody.

"Well?" said Brody.

"It's gonna take a while. Meanwhile, you can fill out these forms."

He handed Brody half a dozen forms that he fished out of his desk drawer and produced a clipboard and pen for him.

Brody accepted the forms, not looking forward to filling them out. Paperwork was paperwork.

"Have a seat over there," said the watch commander, pointing to a series of uncomfortable-looking orange plastic chairs lined against the wall.

Brody took a seat on a lopsided chair, took a pull on his water bottle, and commenced filling out the forms.

He handed the filled-out forms on the clipboard to the watch commander, who accepted and skimmed them.

"It says here you're a private investigator," said the watch commander, looking up at Brody.

"Yeah."

"How much do you get?"

"Not enough."

"My buddy's a PI. He used to be a cop. He says he has trouble getting clients."

"It's not easy."

"I told him he needs to advertise."

"How long till you get a hit on the facial ID?" said Brody.

"Depends."

"It's an emergency. Damian could be in danger."

"Still depends."

"I don't get it."

"We have a lot of emergencies here. You're not the only one."

"I need to get some idea where to start looking for him."

"We got your cell number. If you don't want to wait, we can give you a call when we get something."

Brody took a pull on his water bottle, thinking it over.

His cell phone in his trouser pocket vibrated. He took the call.

"Have you found anything?" said Araceli.

"Not yet."

"I'm worried. The longer he goes missing, the greater the chances he's in danger."

"Vegas is swarming with tourists. He could be anywhere. It's easy to disappear here."

The watch commander answered his ringing phone and said, "Vegas Metro."

She terminated the call.

Brody put away his cell, puzzled why she had ended the call so abruptly. Had she overheard the watch commander on the phone? he wondered, his pulse ratcheting up. Was she going to can him because he contacted the cops?

He didn't think she was. She would have canned him on the spot if she was. She wouldn't have hung up without saying anything.

If Damian had a sheet with the cops, it could open a can of worms Brody would rather keep closed. To the best of his recollection, Araceli hadn't told him Damian had a criminal record. She had said he might be involved in something dirty. She hadn't said anything about an arrest warrant with Damian's name on it.

The watch commander jerked Brody out of his thoughts. "Good news."

"What?" said Brody, putting away his cell and turning to face him.

"We had a sighting at Caesar's Palace," said the watch commander, gripping the desk phone's handset.

"Thank you, Officer."

Brody couldn't tell from the watch commander's expression whether the cops had discovered Damian had a record when running Damian's photo through the facial recognition software.

Brody was of two minds to ask him. The intel would be good to know, but the mere act of asking the watch commander would arouse the cop's suspicions of Damian to the point where the cops might hang a tail on Brody to see if Brody would lead them to Damian so they could bust Damian. Brody decided to keep his mouth shut.

Off to Caesar's Palace, he decided.

Chapter 28

Damian and Simon stepped into the elevator with two tourists who were speaking German.

The tourists got off at the thirtieth floor.

The elevator kept rising. Damian wondered when it was going to stop. It didn't stop till they reached the penthouse.

The stone-faced Simon inserted a key into a red plastic button above the control panel to open the elevator doors electronically and ushered Damian out onto the corridor's marble floor.

Palms sweaty, Damian wondered what this was all about. Why did the casino boss want to see him? It had to be because of the four hundred grand he had bet on roulette. Had the boss somehow found out it was drug money Damian had bet? Why else would the guy want to see him?

Damian thought about making a run for it. He could easily break out of Simon's grasp.

Walking down the hall, listening to his footsteps echo, Damian was convinced nothing good could come of this meeting. He knew the cops were waiting for him in the casino boss's penthouse. In his mind's eye he could see them standing in there, handcuffs in their hands, waiting to clap him in irons.

Damian had to make up his mind before it was too late.

Jacked up with the adrenaline of fear coursing through him, he broke free from Simon's clutches and pelted to the elevator, whose doors remained open. He sprang into the elevator and punched the Lobby button.

Damian noticed Simon wasn't running after him. He couldn't hear Simon's footsteps racing down the corridor's marble floor to the elevator.

He noticed something else.

The elevator doors weren't closing.

He slammed the Lobby button with his open palm, urging the doors to close.

Still, the doors didn't close.

Frantic, he pressed the button with his thumb and didn't let up on it. His thumb turned red and throbbed in pain.

Simon walked into view in the doorway.

He didn't look happy. Damian doubted the guy ever looked happy. On the other hand, Simon didn't look angry either. He looked like he was weary of dealing with a misbehaving brat.

"I locked the elevator in place when we got out," he said. "You're not going anywhere without the key."

Odd, decided Damian. Even though the elevator wasn't moving, he felt like it was hurtling to the bottom of the shaft where it would crash.

"Come out," said Simon. "The boss doesn't like to be kept waiting."

Damian walked into the hall. He glanced at the other two elevators.

"Don't waste your time thinking about it," said Simon. "None of the elevators can reach the penthouse unless someone unlocks the penthouse floor on their control panels. Only me and a couple other guys have keys."

Damian considered overpowering Simon and stealing the elevator key. A big guy, Simon looked like he knew how to handle himself. Damian nixed the idea.

Hangdog, Damian trudged with Simon to the boss's penthouse suite. Simon knocked on the door.

"Give me a second," said the voice from inside. A minute or so later he said. "Come in."

Simon opened the door. He gestured for Damian to enter before him.

Gulping, his face breaking into a sweat despite the AC, Damian set foot into the suite waiting in dread for the cops to slap cuffs on him.

Chapter 29

Above him Damian saw a life-size naked pink blow-up woman hanging from the suite's cathedral ceiling. A row of stuffed animals on a shelf on the wall included several stuffed green frogs. Damian noticed two massage tables in the expansive suite.

"I'm a connoisseur of fine art," said a fortyish man reclining on a ruby crushed velvet sofa. "Warhol made that sculpture," he said, nodding at the blow-up doll.

Though only five seven in stature, he had a large tonsured head supported by his thick neck. The crown of his head gleamed under the overhead light as if waxed. He was wearing a white terrycloth bathrobe with the initials *AM* stitched with gold thread on the breast pocket. He projected arrogance, thrusting his chest out as if daring someone to attack him even as he sat.

Two slender teenage girls, a blonde and a brunette, in bikinis were sitting in large comfortable chairs looking on, the blonde with her long legs crossed.

They looked awfully young, decided Damian. Maybe they were AM's daughters. And yet . . .

AM glanced down at his bathrobe. "I was getting a massage when Simon knocked."

He glanced at the massage table to his left.

An uncomfortable silence hung in the air.

Damian didn't know what to say. He had no idea why he was here. Where were the cops? He was relieved they weren't here, but their absence left him with nothing but questions and misgivings.

"Hello," said Damian.

"You're not what I was expecting," said AM. "What's your name?"

"Damian. What were you expecting?"

"I was expecting a whale."

"Whale?"

"Simon told me about the bet you made on roulette. Only a whale would put down a bet like that. I expected you to be older. Then again, look at all these techie kids like Elon Musk who run around in torn jeans and dirty sneakers with billions of dollars in their bank accounts. Times are changing."

AM reached for a box of cigars on a glass-topped square coffee table at the edge of his sofa.

Damian nodded. "Silicon Valley's taking over."

"How about a cigar?" said AM, opening the cigar box.

"Sure," said Damian, and approached AM.

"These beauties are from Havana."

"Why did you want to see me?" said Damian, feeling more relaxed, welcoming the offer of a cigar.

"I like meeting whales."

"Do you work here at the casino?" said Damian, selecting a Montecristo #2 that nestled next to a Bolivar Belicoso and a Cohiba Behike. He sniffed it with pleasure.

Chuckling, AM selected the Cohiba Behike. "I own the place. I'm Armando Musante."

Damian did a double take.

The Mafia capo, decided Damian. Just the guy he wanted to see. *Thank you, Simon, for the introduction.*

Armando clipped the cap off his Cohiba Behike with a cigar cutter, tossed the cutter to Damian, inserted the cigar in his mouth, ignited the tip of his cigar with a lighter, commenced puffing, and blew a smoke ring out of his mouth. He sat back on the sofa, draping his arm over the sofa back.

Damian clipped the cap off his cigar and lit up.

"I need to talk to you," he said.

"Whales are always welcome here," said Armando with a smile. "Do you want a massage?" he said, nodding at the two girls watching them.

"Not right now."

"Then what do you want? Do you want to make another bet on the roulette wheel, hey, my friend?"

Hell no, thought Damian.

"I need your protection," he said.

"I own casinos," said Armando, puzzled. "Do I look like I sell insurance policies?"

Damian had to confide in someone. He couldn't go to five-o. Musante was the only one who could help him. Damian didn't want to sound like he was begging for help. He took a puff on his cigar, enjoying its bittersweet aroma. The cigar relaxed him.

"A hit team of *sicarios* is here to kill me," he said, his face grave.

"*Sicarios*?"

"Hit men."

"You need to tell the cops," said Musante, glimpsing Simon, who was standing nearby, his hands clasped in front of his waist.

"No cops," said Damian.

"Why not? That's their job. To protect and serve."

Damian debated how much he should tell Musante. Damian got the impression the guy wasn't going to help him unless Damian leveled with him. On the other hand, giving Musante too much info posed risks—especially if Musante wasn't with the mob. Was the guy really just an honest casino owner? That wasn't what Damian had heard on the street. They even knew of the guy in Guadalajara.

Damian blew cigar smoke out his mouth and took a deep breath.

"I work for a cartel," he said.

Musante pricked up his ears. "What kind of cartel?"

"Is there any other kind?"

"A Colombian drug cartel?"

Damian shook his head no. "Mexican. The Colombians are old hat. Pablo Escobar is dead. The Mexican cartels are calling the shots now."

"The Sinaloans?"

"Jalisco New Generation."

"What kind of drugs are we talking about?"

"Everything. You name it. We got yayo, smack (both Mexican mud and China white), crack, crystal meth, moon rock, bennies, special K, monkey juice, murder 8—"

"What don't you have?" said Musante, listening with interest.

"If we don't have it, we can get it. Anything you want."

"So why does a team of *sicarios* want to hit you?"

"They're working for the Zetas. The Zetas hate CJNG."

"I want to help you because . . . ?"

"We'll give you a direct drug pipeline over the border," Damian lied.

Musante massaged his chin in thought. "I don't know if I want to get involved in a turf war between cartels."

"All I want from you is protection from the *sicario* hit team sent here to whack me."

"And in return you can cut a deal for me with the Jalisco boys?"

"What kind of deal?"

"One where we can start moving drugs into the States as partners."

Damian wasn't empowered to cut any deals for CJNG, but Musante had no way of knowing that.

"Absolutely," said Damian.

Musante puffed on his cigar, blowing a smoke ring that floated languorously across the room past the dangling pink blow-up doll.

"I think we can work something out," he said. "We could use more yayo. The stuff sells like hotcakes. Silicon Valley, Wall Street, DC—they eat it up. I have connections and distribution networks in place everywhere in the country. All I need is product—your product."

Chapter 30

Brody needed a gun. He had left his at his LA apartment. He couldn't get his gun past TSA security at the airport, and he had a feeling things would get nasty.

He was no stranger to Vegas. He knew where he could get a gun.

He took a taxi to the gun shop he used. The shops were everywhere, since Nevada was an open-carry state. Guns were even allowed in casinos. The only caveat was no concealed weapons without a permit.

As soon as Brody stepped out of the air-conditioned taxi onto the sidewalk, a wave of heat hit him. Its impact stopped him dead in his tracks for a moment.

Recovering, he entered the coolness of the gun shop. A sign behind the counter said Make My Day, a line from a Dirty Harry movie.

"Long time no see," said Maggie, the thirtysomething owner standing behind the counter in jeans and a short-sleeved white blouse, a couple of tattoos of roses on her tan arms.

A Glock 17 hung in a Velcro holster on her hip.

"Hi, Maggie. I need a gun," said Brody, approaching the counter.

"How come the only time I ever see you is when you want a gun?"

"I'm usually in LA."

"That's no excuse. Why don't you drop in and say hello to me sometime just to chat?"

"I'd like to, but I'm here on business."

He couldn't very well tell her any woman he got involved with died by violence. A charming serial killer had strangled his wife, and a psycho assassin had thrust a crossbow bolt through the carotid artery of an actress he was starting to fall for.

"You should make time," said Maggie, flirting.

My wife was strangled to death. How about a date with me? It didn't sound like a winning pickup line. *We could bet on how long you live after our date.*

"I guess you're right," he said.

"You know I am. Now what do you want?"

"I need a SIG Sauer P365."

She clomped across the floor in her suede tan leather cowboy boots to the end of the glass counter, fetched the SIG, and handed it to him.

"You plan on carrying inside a casino?" she said.

"Why not? It's legal," said Brody, inspecting the pistol.

"It's legal, but most of them ask you to leave if they see you with a gun."

"Then I won't let them see it. Concealed carry's OK in casinos."

"Not unless you have a Nevada concealed carry permit."

"I have a California one."

"The cops might hassle you. Some of my customers say the cops hassle them if they don't have the Nevada permit, particularly for handguns. Rifles not so much."

"How do you conceal a rifle?"

"In your pants, of course."

He gave her a look.

"I'm not gonna conceal this," he said. He inserted the SIG in his waistband, the butt clearly visible.

"The cops are funny about the definition of the word *conceal.*"

"I heard you gotta be a resident of Nevada to get the permit."

"Just saying. Credit or cash?"

"Credit."

"I'll need ammo, too," he said, dredging his wallet from his trouser pocket and withdrawing his credit card.

"No problem. Take whatever you want," she said, accepting his credit card.

Brody selected a cardboard box of fifty 115-grain full metal jacket nine mils. Maggie handed him his credit card and a plain white plastic bag for his purchases. He deposited the gun and the ammo in the bag. Bag in hand, he headed for the door.

"If you drove here instead of flying all the time, you wouldn't have to keep buying guns," she said.

"But I wouldn't get to see you, either," he said, turning to look at her.

She gave him a flirtatious smile.

He smiled back and opened the door.

"Don't stay a stranger," she said.

You're better off if I do. You'll live longer.

He left the store. He didn't look back.

Chapter 31

Brody returned to his room at the Venetian and logged onto the Elysian Fields website. Something was eating at him.

Myshkin: Anybody there?

Margaux Hemingway: What's up?

Myshkin: Do you ever feel like you should be doing something else with your life? Like you're not the right fit for your job?

Margaux Hemingway: You mean, because you're an epileptic?

Myshkin: I'm not sure if it's that or it's because I meet all the creeps in the world in my job. It's bumming me out.

Julius Caesar: It sounds like you're not happy.

Myshkin: Is your job supposed to make you happy?

Teddy Roosevelt: I don't know if *happy* is the right word for it. A feeling that you're doing something that people appreciate is what my job gives me.

Margaux Hemingway: That's a good way of putting it.

Teddy Roosevelt: I'm a paramedic, and I feel like the people I help on the job appreciate me. This gives me a sense of satisfaction.

Myshkin: I don't think I'm getting that satisfaction. I mostly deal with creeps in my job.

Julius Caesar: Maybe you're a malcontent. Do you feel like you want to change the way things are?

Myshkin: Not really.

Margaux Hemingway: Maybe you need therapy.

Julius Caesar: You sound like you want to change the status quo, Myshkin. Are you mad at society for stigmatizing you for being an epileptic?

Myshkin: It's my job that's bumming me out.

Margaux Hemingway: It could be time to get another.

Myshkin: The problem is, I don't have any interest in another.

Julius Caesar: Do you blame society for your dissatisfaction?

Myshkin: I'm not blaming anyone. I'm trying to deal with my job.

Margaux Hemingway: You sound like a workaholic. You need to relax. Take time off to enjoy your life with your wife.

Myshkin: I'm not married.

Margaux Hemingway: A bachelor workaholic. You're asking for trouble. Your heart attack is right around the corner.

Teddy Roosevelt: You're just having a bad day, Myshkin. That's all. Happens to everyone. I don't think this has to do with epilepsy.

Margaux Hemingway: Why not get a pet? I have a Belgian Malinois. He's a beautiful dog and my best pal.

Myshkin: I'm not really a dog person. I do a lot of traveling. The dog would end up in a kennel most of the time.

Julius Caesar: It sounds like you got a problem. Are you political?

Myshkin: It doesn't have anything to do with politics.

Margaux Hemingway: My dog is barking. He needs me. Gotta go. He's very demanding. Sometimes I feel like *he* owns *me*.

Chapter 32

Don Gaetano was reclining in a chaise longue sipping a tequila and watching Valentina float in a mauve bikini on an inflatable white unicorn in his Guadalajara hacienda's shimmering pool.

In her twenties Valentina was a striking brunette with transparent blue irises. Gazing into them was like looking into the swimming pool's water—drowning in it, decided Don Gaetano.

Arturo was sitting beside him in a lawn chair, nursing a mojito. Like Don Gaetano he was wearing jeans, a guayabera, and huaraches in the sultry afternoon heat.

Out of the corner of his eye Don Gaetano spotted an aging fifty-year-old bald hipster by the name of Brockton Root angling toward him across the cement and terrazzo pool deck. A professional grade camera hanging from a leather strap around his neck, Root wore khaki Bermudas and a white silk shirt with its top buttons undone, exposing a forest of grey chest hair and a chichi silver necklace nestled in it like a cobra.

"*Hola*, Don Gaetano," he said.

"*Qué pasa*, Root?" said Don Gaetano.

"I want to do a fashion spread with the lovely Valentina," said Root, glancing at her floating on the unicorn.

"That's up to her," said Don Gaetano, smiling at Valentina, his beautiful and erotic mistress, who favored wearing black jackboots and a black leather bikini while she whipped him in bed.

She was one of the few who understood him, understood his need to be loved by everyone. His whole life was about acquiring more love. He saw it as a commodity that could be bought if people were unwilling to give it to him of their own volition. If he couldn't buy it from them, their only other choice was . . . not pleasant.

"Root, you know Vegas, don't you?" he said.

"Of course. I do a lot of shoots there. Magazine editors like the palatial casinos and the glitzy neon-lit strip."

"I need you to go to Vegas with Roberto to keep an eye on him."

"What for?" said Root, not keen on the idea.

"Take along some models and do a shoot there as well."

Root's face brightened almost as much as his bald head. "Valentina?"

"She stays here. This is too dangerous for her."

"Sounds good," said Root, disappointment in his voice. He paused. "What's with Roberto?"

"Sometimes he goes off half-cocked. I don't want him shooting up Vegas."

"I'm a photographer, not an enforcer. How am I supposed to stop him?"

"Report to me if anything happens. He's supposed to get my money back. Make sure he gets it."

"Why me?"

"I trust you more than him. He's a hothead psycho killer. And he might get greedy."

"And me?"

Don Gaetano smiled at him with his black eyes that saw all. "You know which side your bread's buttered on. These young guys . . . you never know with them. They get stupid ideas in their heads. They want to advance their careers in one fell swoop. They have no patience. They want the Ferrari without putting in the long years of work to buy it."

"All right."

"You've done work for me before. You don't lose your cool. And"—he paused for effect—"you know how it goes if you don't do your job," said Don Gaetano, his visage turning hard.

Root clapped admiring eyes on Valentina floating in the pool without a care in the world, absorbing the sun's rays. "Could I get Valentina to pose for me now?"

"I want to see her in the house first."

"No rush."

"You're the only gringo I trust, you know, Root."

"My father's a gringo. My mother's Mexican."

"You appreciate beautiful women like I do. We have the most voluptuous women in the world in Mexico."

"I do indeed," said Root, and smiled at Valentina.

Don Gaetano started in his chaise longue when he heard an explosion, spilling some of his tequila as he sat bolt upright.

Chapter 33

Half a second later, a portion of his hacienda's backyard blew up some thirty feet from the pool, hurling loam and sod into the air.

"What the hell?" said Don Gaetano. "Arturo."

Arturo didn't need to be told what to do. He sprang from his chair knocking his mojito over. He belted across the pool deck toward the source of the discharges, somewhere out of sight beyond the driveway.

Another burst rent the air.

The yard exploded again, closer to the pool, hurling clods of dirt and turf fifteen feet into the air. The earth shook.

Valentina screamed in terror, scrambled off the unicorn, swam to the edge of the pool, hauled herself out of the water, and fled toward the house.

Arturo disappeared from view. A car's ignition sounded, followed by screeching tires in the driveway.

"It's a frigging mortar," said Don Gaetano, as he heard another discharge.

The ground erupted again, flinging dirt and grass, this time ten feet closer to the pool than the previous projectile.

"What's happening?" said Root, preparing to cut and run.

"Zetas. Must be. *Putas* don't believe in the sanctity of the home."

Don Gaetano spat onto the deck.

He heard a gunshot in the distance near the source of the mortar fire. He got to his feet, tequila in hand.

A fire engine red Jeep Wrangler Rubicon came tearing down the hacienda's driveway from the direction of the mortar toward the pool. Watching, Don Gaetano took a pull on his tequila.

The mortar fire had stopped for the time being.

The Rubicon screeched to a halt on the asphalt.

Arturo and a twentysomething CJNG cholo clambered out of the Rubicon with a teenager in baggy jeans and an olive drab wife beater, his arms green with tattoos. They frogmarched him to the pool, where Don Gaetano awaited them. Don Gaetano could see the teen's face was bloody from blows to the head.

"We caught this fucking Zeta firing a mortar at the hacienda," said Arturo.

"They got no respect," said Don Gaetano.

Arturo and the cholo came to a halt, holding the Zeta's arms pinned behind his back.

"What do we do with him?" said Arturo, taking control of the Zeta.

"Does he have a gun?"

"Not now."

"Was he alone?"

"We shot the other one. They had Goat Horns, along with the mortar."

Nodding, Don Gaetano understood cartel slang for AK-47s.

"You desecrated my yard," Don Gaetano told the Zeta, pointing at the three gaping holes in his lawn. "You got no respect."

The teen was shivering with fear, sweat beading his grimacing, blood-streaked face as he struggled to break free.

"What should we do with him, *patrón*?" said Arturo.

"Let him go."

Surprised, Arturo released the Zeta.

"I believe in giving him a sporting chance, even though he gave us none when he blew up my yard. That's what makes us different from the Zeta *putas*." Don Gaetano faced the Zeta. "What is your name?"

"Pablo."

"Do you believe in God, Pablo?"

Petrified with fear, Pablo didn't speak.

"I don't," said Don Gaetano. "Do you wish to pray?"

Pablo remained tongue-tied.

"A waste of breath, I'm afraid. But you can try praying, if it'll make you feel better."

Speechless, Pablo shivered.

"Are you praying to God to strike me dead?" said Don Gaetano.

Clutching his heart and gasping, he rolled his eyes, staggering forward.

Pablo watched, stunned.

Straightening, Don Gaetano laughed. "I had you going. Didn't I?" He turned serious. "Make a run for it, Pablo."

Terrified, Pablo stood glued to the spot, uncertain, shifting his eyes everywhere, seeking an exit.

"If you stand there, you will die," said Don Gaetano, lifting his Belgian FN Five-seveN pistol with a gold-plated stock from the small white metal grillwork patio table that stood next to his chaise longue.

He always had a gun with him—if not on his person, within reach.

Pablo made a run for it.

Without missing a beat Don Gaetano shot him in the back of the head.

At such close range Pablo's head cracked and exploded into pink mist under the impact of the aluminum-core hollow-point 5.7 x 28 mm round.

Appalled, Brockton Root flinched as blood splattered him.

"Use the chain saw on him and FedEx the pieces back to his mother, one piece at a time, one day at a time," Don Gaetano told Arturo.

"*Sí, patrón*," said Arturo, striding over to the crumpled corpse to drag it to the shed where Don Gaetano kept the chain saw.

"And fill in those craters in my yard."

Chapter 34

Roberto came charging up the driveway to the hacienda's backyard, wrestling on a polo shirt as he ran, clad in jeans.

"*Qué pasó?*" he said, breathing heavily when he reached Don Gaetano.

"Zetas attacked us," said Don Gaetano, watching him finish putting on his polo.

"I was pulling three girls when I heard the blasts."

"Save your energy for Damian in Vegas."

Roberto surveyed the cratered ground. "Looks like a war zone. Lucky they didn't hit the house."

"I'm sending Root here with you to Vegas."

"I don't need any help to take care of Damian."

"Root needs to go there for a fashion shoot."

Roberto eyed Root. "Who is he?"

"He's a fashion photographer."

"I never heard of him."

"You're missing the point. He's going with you to Vegas."

"He's gonna get in the way."

"It'll be good cover for you. You can pretend you're part of his photography crew so they won't hassle you in Customs."

"All right, *patrón*," said Roberto, not happy with the idea.

Don Gaetano's satphone vibrated in his trouser pocket. He answered the call. It was Damian.

"I hope you're calling me to tell me you contacted Ned Bates," said Don Gaetano.

"I haven't been able to find Ned Bates," said Damian. "That's why I'm calling. Where am I supposed to find this Ned Bates?"

"Ned Bates will find you. Don't worry about it."

Don Gaetano terminated the call.

Life was all about trust, he decided. Trust and love. And, last but not least, money and power.

Was Damian trying to pull a fast one on him? Don Gaetano couldn't tell. He hoped he was overreacting by sending Roberto after Damian. When doubt replaces trust, send a *sicario*, was Don Gaetano's motto.

"Can I trust you, Roberto?" said Don Gaetano.

"With your life," said Roberto.

Like life, building an empire was about trust, decided Don Gaetano. Trust was the mortar that held the bricks of the empire together. Without trust, the empire collapsed. He couldn't expand the empire without trusting people. And yet it was all but impossible for him to trust anybody.

"I will reward you well if you accomplish your mission," said Don Gaetano.

"No problem, *patrón*," said Roberto. "I will take care of Damian."

Don Gaetano watched Arturo dragging Pablo's corpse across the backyard to the toolshed.

Wearing a yellow dress Carmen, her brunette hair braided in a ponytail, emerged from the house with Valentina in a bikini, their footsteps tentative, apprehensive after the mortar attack.

"What were those explosions?" Carmen asked Don Gaetano.

"Zetas blew up our yard," said Don Gaetano, fuming about the Zetas' disrespect.

"I thought I was gonna be killed," said Valentina, holding her chest.

"I would never let that happen."

"The neighbors called and complained about the fireworks coming from our yard," said Carmen.

"Don't they have anything better to do than to call us and complain all the time?" said Don Gaetano. "I ought to go over there and knock some sense—"

"It's not important."

"I'm glad it's over," said Valentina.

"Is Valentina going with us to the photo shoot in Vegas?" said Root.

"Valentina is staying here," said Don Gaetano. "Don't keep asking me that."

"I thought maybe you changed your mind."

"What's this about Vegas?" said Valentina, her interest piqued.

"You can go to Vegas another time." Don Gaetano turned to Root. "Take other models with you."

"Models are going with us to Vegas?" said Roberto.

"Part of the photo shoot."

"This is sounding better and better," said Roberto with a toothy grin.

"Don't lose sight of your mission."

"*Sí, patrón.*"

Juan burst out of the house riding his crimson tricycle, head bent down over the handlebars to reduce drag and increase speed. He drove up to Don Gaetano.

"Where are the fireworks?" said Juan, eyes glittering with anticipation. "I wanna watch the fireworks."

Don Gaetano watched Arturo drag Pablo's corpse into the toolshed then looked at Juan, smiling.

"You want an ice cream cone, Juan? Ice cream's better than fireworks," said Don Gaetano.

"Yes, Papa," said Juan, his face beaming.

Nodding, Don Gaetano patted Juan on the head. "Let's go inside and get an ice cream cone."

Juan dismounted his tricycle. He and Don Gaetano walked to the house.

"What kind of ice cream do you want?" said Don Gaetano, rubbing Juan's hair.

"Pistachio."

"I'll take maple walnut."

The racketing grind of Arturo starting up the chain saw in the toolshed ripped across the yard.

Chapter 35

His loaded SIG P365 hidden in his waistband tucked behind his back underneath a loose leather vest he was wearing, Brody wandered through Caesar's Palace questioning the cocktail waitresses that offered drinks to the gamblers at the slot machines. They were dressed in short white dresses resembling togas and tended to be in their twenties, yet some were older.

Brody showed them the photo of Damian and asked them if they had seen him. So far, none of them had.

Brody decided Damian must have been here at some point in time, since the police CCTV had recorded him outside the casino. Of course, if Damian had entered the casino, it could have been during the shifts of different waitresses from the current staff, in which case his queries would yield no results. There was also the possibility Damian hadn't played the slots, so he wouldn't have accepted drinks from the waitresses.

If Damian wasn't playing the slots, what was the guy doing here? wondered Brody. There wasn't a whole lot to do in Vegas other than gamble. They didn't even have movie theaters on the strip. All they had were casinos, restaurants, shops, musicals, and comedy shows.

His sister had told him Damian liked to gamble. That didn't necessarily mean he liked to play the slots. Maybe he played table games like poker, blackjack, baccarat, and roulette. The waitresses should have seen him, though, since they worked the gambling tables as well as the slots.

Maybe one of the waitresses had seen Damian, but hadn't recognized him from the photograph Araceli had given Brody.

Brody started approaching the card dealers. One of them could have seen Damian. A lot of them weren't even dealing. Their tables were empty, and they were staring ahead like statues. Answering his questions gave them something to do, though they'd rather be dealing him cards.

He walked up to a slender thirtyish Chinese woman with short brunette hair who was wearing a gold lamé vest and waiting for a customer at her blackjack table. He showed her Damian's photo.

"Have you ever seen this guy?" he said.

She shook her head no.

He sauntered through the casino to the race and sports book, where scores of flat-panel HDTV screens bolted to the high wall featured different sports events. Several college football games were playing.

Brody loved to watch football. It reminded him of life. The opposing players were doing everything they could to cut you off at the knees so you couldn't achieve your objective. Somehow you had to carry the ball and score a touchdown, despite the opposing players trying to tackle you.

He scoped out the gamblers sitting watching the TV screens. He didn't see Damian.

He buttonholed a twentysomething cocktail waitress with long blonde hair carrying a tray full of cold drinks past him. He showed her the photo.

"Did you ever see this guy?" he said.

"Why?"

"I'm trying to find him. I'm a friend of his."

"I might've seen him, but I wouldn't swear to it. I dunno. His face isn't very distinctive. It could've been someone else." She let out a sigh. "I see so many people every day, faces become a blur. Like they're going by on a merry-go-round on speed."

"When do you think you saw him?"

She thought about it. "Ah . . . yesterday." She grimaced. "This tray's getting heavy. Gotta run."

She scuttled away, tray in hand.

Not a firm ID, he decided, watching her leave. Even if she had seen Damian, it didn't mean he had a room here. Throngs of tourists roamed in and out of the palatial casinos day in, day out.

He wasn't making any headway.

He could do with a cold beer. He continued walking through the casino. Maybe he would stop off at Cleopatra's Barge for a drink.

His cell phone vibrated in his trouser pocket.

Araceli. "Have you found him yet?"

"No. But he's in Vegas, or he *was* here. I saw a photo taken of him walking on the sidewalk."

"How did he look?"

"He looked fine."

"That's a relief. I thought something had happened to him. But I'm still worried. I'm convinced he's in trouble. You gotta find him ASAP."

"Have you heard from him at all?"

"Nothing."

"Is there any way you could trace his cell?"

"The calls aren't even going through to voicemail. It makes no sense. That's why I thought something had happened to him."

"Maybe he lost his phone, or the battery's dead."

"He's running out of time."

"All I can do is keep searching for him."

She terminated the call.

Pocketing his cell phone Brody wondered what Damian was into. To inspire such dread in Araceli it had to be something illegal.

Chapter 36

Across the street from Caesar's Palace Damian was angling across the bustling casino floor in the Paris, a three-hundred-pound brawny guy with black hair strutting beside him. Musante's gift to him for protection, decided Damian.

The thirtysomething bodyguard named Dominick was wearing black jeans, a black T, a black blazer, and a holstered Glock 19 on his broad hip. Damian figured the guy wasn't planning on going outside in the oppressive heat in such a getup.

Roberto would be in for a surprise if he came gunning for Damian, decided Damian. On the other hand, Roberto was a psycho stone killer who probably wouldn't bat an eye when he spotted Musante's goon Dominick. And Roberto would have a team of *sicarios* with him, guys whose only skillset was committing murder.

Maybe Damian's best play was to blow town here and now and never look back. He knew Roberto, though. The homicidal maniac would never stop searching for him no matter how long it took to find him. Damian knew what was driving Roberto wasn't merely Don Gaetano's orders, it was Roberto's animus for Damian. Roberto hated Damian for being an ex-cop.

The problem was, Damian didn't know what to do. Did he really think he could escape the wrath of Don Gaetano once Don Gaetano found out he had lost CJNG's cash? Damian's only hope lay in convincing Don Gaetano he still had the cash.

What was he supposed to do when his bluff was found out? Damian wondered. He would have to disappear off the face of the earth. Not easy. CJNG had long tentacles. Its reach covered the world, and Don Gaetano didn't flinch at committing murder. CJNG had assassinated hundreds of its enemies with the belief that the only good enemy was a dead enemy.

It was no secret the other cartels had given CJNG the wry nickname "Murder LLC."

How long could Musante and his mobsters protect him once Don Gaetano discovered the truth about CJNG's four hundred grand? wondered Damian. And Musante wouldn't protect him forever. The deal Damian had cut with Musante was access to the cartel's drug pipeline in exchange for protection. Musante had no idea Damian was powerless to deliver drugs without the support of CJNG.

Damian broke into a cold sweat just thinking about the fix he was in.

"What's the matter?" asked Dominick, picking up on Damian's discomfiture. "Did you see a hit man?"

"Uh—no. It's the heat," answered Damian, plucking at his collar.

Wandering around in the casino gaming area was exposing him to the danger of having a *sicario* spot him—if the hit team had already arrived in Vegas.

"Maybe I should go back to my room," he said.

"If somebody's bothering you, I can take care of him," said Dominick, scoping out the gaming floor, where an endless stream of tourists milled.

"It's OK."

Damian headed to the bank of elevators that led to the guest rooms, Dominick in tow.

Standing in front of the elevators, Damian decided he needed to concoct a plan to extricate himself from his dilemma. He racked his brains trying to come up with a solution . . .

An idea struck him.

He wondered if he could pull it off.

It might work. It just might work.

He couldn't bear any more of this standing around waiting to be whacked.

His burner in his trouser pocket vibrated, startling him. Don Gaetano.

Damian didn't want to take the call. But he didn't see any way out. If he didn't answer it, Don Gaetano would be convinced Damian was cheating him.

"I'm glad you answered," said Don Gaetano.

"Why wouldn't I?"

"Have you met Ned Bates yet?"

"No. No sign of him. Maybe he got lost in the shuffle."

"Make sure you're out and around so Ned Bates can see you. Better yet, tell me which casino you're staying at."

Damian's heart skipped a beat. *No way.* He lost his voice. His throat withered into a tight knot.

"Are you there?" demanded Don Gaetano.

"Bally's," Damian squeaked.

"What?"

"Bally's."

"*Bueno.* You like the showgirls, huh? I'll pass on the intel to Ned Bates."

"But I'm not always there—"

Damian gazed at his burner. He realized he was talking to dead air.

"You don't look so good," said Dominick.

"The heat," Damian muttered, white-faced, as one of the elevator doors opened.

"If you can't take the heat, you're not gonna last long in Vegas."

The way I'm going I'm not.

Chapter 37

Serving cocktails to the slot players at the Paris, Melody wondered why she had no luck with men, culminating with her marriage to her current husband Dan, a trucking company owner who wanted to kill her because they didn't have any kids and because he thought she was flirting with everyone.

The night he had tried to kill her he had come home late from work fit to be tied and had flipped out when their dinner was cold. He had been a victim of road rage he told her. Some guy in an SUV had cut him off. Dan had honked at the guy in anger. Then the guy had slammed on his brakes trying to get Dan to rear-end him.

Dan had accused her of deliberately serving him a cold dinner. He had taken a swing at her. Smelling his breath she realized he had been drinking. He swore he was going to kill her.

She knew it wasn't the cold dinner that was the actual cause of his violence. It was their lack of kids and his misguided obsession that she was flirting with everyone. The cold dinner was merely a trigger that had brought everything to a head.

She had fled for her life.

The guy had problems, she could see that now. But that didn't give him the right to take out his issues on her. She wasn't going to stand for it. And she believed him when he had said he would kill her. It wasn't the first time he had vented his anger on her with violence, but it would be the last, she decided.

She refused to live on a daily basis in fear for her life. She wondered if he could track her to Vegas. She had taken an Uber from their house to a bus station then a couple of more buses to get here from New Mexico.

She didn't see how he could have followed her, though he claimed he had powerful friends in Black Cube, an Israeli international security agency, who could find anyone they wanted.

Boasting of his supposed powerful connections was one of his ways of terrorizing her into staying with him. That and punching her in the face, so she had to wear dark glasses when she went out in public to prevent anyone from seeing the bruises.

Not anymore, she decided.

She was always getting mixed up with the wrong men. Her natural good looks attracted them like honeybees to flowers. Well, she wasn't going to let herself go to pot out of fear of men pursuing her. Nature's blessings could turn into curses sometimes. What was she supposed to do? Have breast-reduction surgery so men wouldn't look twice at her? That was crazy if women had to live in terror of men, she decided. They couldn't all be like Dan.

She had a sister in LA. Maybe Melody could go live with her while she looked for work in California. She couldn't make a decent living in Vegas working as a cocktail waitress. The job was temporary till she figured out her next move. For now, it kept her alive and out of the hands of her homicidal husband.

She had a good mind to sic the cops on him. But then she would have to see him again when she testified against him. Right now she never wanted to set eyes on the rat bastard's face again. And what if the cops and the courts sided with him? Then where would she be?

She would never go back to that creep. He would have to find himself another slave. She had wasted too much of her life already trying to please a jerk.

But what if he found her? she wondered with apprehension.

She all but spilled a glass of ginger ale she was carrying on her tray to a henna-haired middle-aged woman playing a slot machine.

Was the guy going to haunt her dreams for the rest of her life? Melody wondered.

Melody served the ginger ale to the woman, who reached into her black leather pocketbook and gave her a crumpled dollar.

Melody thanked her with a smile and picked up on a guy sitting at another slot signaling to her to come over. The slot machines pinged around her as she approached him. He looked like he was in good shape. Now that she was single— except she wasn't single. Legally she was still married to Dan. She hadn't had time to file the divorce papers with the court. Not only that, Dan had threatened to kill her if she did.

The way she figured it he was going to kill her no matter what she did. She would file the papers as soon as she felt safe from Dan. Whenever that happened. *If* ever that happened?

Chapter 38

"Something to drink?" she asked the guy that had beckoned her.

It was time for her to stop thinking about Dan, she decided. The guy was destroying her life even when he wasn't present by taking up permanent lodging in her mind like a bogeyman spying on her every move.

"Have you ever seen this guy?" said the player at the flashing slot, handing her a photo of a fisherman in a rowboat.

She *had* seen him, but she wasn't sure she wanted to admit it. It was Damian, the guy who was talking about wanting to disappear and the Mafia. Was this guy holding the photo working with the Mafia? Could he be hunting Damian?

"Why do you want to know?" she said.

"His sister's looking for him. She thinks he might be in trouble."

"Oh."

"Does that mean you saw him?" said Brody.

"I was just wondering."

"I really need to find him. If the wrong people find him before I do, it's gonna get ugly for him."

"I see a lot of people during my shift. You wouldn't believe how many people go in and out of this casino."

"What are you trying to say?"

"I'm saying, faces tend to fade quickly from my mind, leaving no trace."

"Does that mean you haven't seen him?"

She didn't know this guy from Adam. She wondered if she should tell him about Damian. Then she saw that he was sitting awkwardly in his seat, his back at a weird angle. On closer inspection, she picked up on a bulge in his back that was pressing against his vest, which had ridden up his back.

He had a gun wedged in his rear waistband, she realized with a start.

She knew Nevada was an open-carry state, but this was the first time she had seen anyone in the casino, other than security guards, carrying a gun.

"No, I haven't seen him," she said, now more than ever reluctant to confide in him.

Why was he packing a gun? she wondered, becoming anxious.

Brody stood up. "His name's Damian. If you see him, let him know I need to meet him. I want to help him."

He gave her his business card.

"You're a PI," she said, reading it. Which would explain the gun. *Or pretending to be a PI*, she thought.

"And I can help him."

"Is he in trouble with the Mafia?"

"Why do you say that?"

She laughed. "I guess I watch too many Martin Scorcese movies. You know, *The Godfather* and *Casino*."

"Coppola directed *The Godfather*, not Scorcese."

She shrugged. "I guess I'm not a cineaste."

"Damian's sister thinks he's in danger."

"If I see him, do you want me to tell him you're looking for him?"

"Call me before you talk to him."

"OK."

"What's your name, so I know who's calling?"

She didn't know if she should tell him her name. She still wasn't sure about this guy.

"Melody," he said, reading her name tag on her dress.

"Scott Brody," she said, reading his business card.

"At your service."

She didn't have much room for a business card in her cocktail waitress outfit. She decided to tuck it inside her bra. Which he noticed. Of course.

She hadn't decided what she was going to do. She needed to mull it over before making a decision. This guy looking for Damian seemed on the level. And a good-looking guy, too. Maybe he really was trying to help Damian. And who the hell was Damian, anyway? she wondered. She had met him for the first time a short while ago.

The more she thought about it the more she realized she didn't know much of anything about Damian. She had told him more about herself than he had told her about himself.

Empty tray in hand, she strode away to another customer.

Chapter 39

Crossing the casino floor to question another waitress, Brody wasn't sure Melody was telling him the truth about her not seeing Damian.

When Melody had first set eyes on Damian's photo, Brody had thought there was a glimmer of recognition in her eyes.

He could have been mistaken.

The question was, if she *had* recognized him why hadn't she told him? Why would she pretend she hadn't seen Damian? He couldn't figure any reason she would lie about it—unless she was trying to protect the guy from being found. But why would she want to protect him? Had Damian alerted her to the fact somebody with bad intentions was looking for him? But why should she help Damian? Did they know each other?

Brody had told her he was trying to help Damian. Why hadn't she believed him? Brody wondered.

Then again, he wasn't convinced she was lying. Maybe she really *had* never seen Damian.

So far, she was one of the few people he had talked to who might have seen Damian. Brody hoped she would call him and admit she had seen the guy.

Brody approached a thin Japanese waitress with brunette hair halfway down her back like a tarred plank of wood who was sashaying by him with her empty tray.

"Would you like a drink?" she said with a smile.

Brody showed her the photo of Damian. "Have you ever seen this guy? He's a friend of mine. He's supposed to meet me here, and I can't find him."

She squinted at the photo. "No, I don't think so."

Brody noticed a burly suit built like a professional wrestler with brown eyes staring at him from across the room.

Brody had seen the guy before. Might be a rent-a-cop working for the casino, Brody decided. Maybe he was drawing too much attention to himself by seeking out every waitress he could find and asking her about Damian.

Brody turned away from the guy, not wanting to challenge him. Brody decided he better stop asking about Damian for a while. Brody ducked into a nearby pizzeria in a food court to order a pizza.

Maybe the rent-a-cop thought Brody was macking on the waitresses, decided Brody, ordering a cheese pizza wedge and an ice-cold Coke and taking a seat at a white metal table in the food court. He realized he was hungry.

Out of the corner of his eye he caught sight of the wrestler making his way toward the food court.

Brody hoped the guy wanted to order a pizza. But he doubted it.

Brody continued munching his pizza wedge, paying no attention to the guy's approach, playing it cool. He licked mozzarella off his fingertips and smacked his lips.

The wrestler towered in front of him. "The boss wants to see you."

"Whose boss?"

"My boss."

"Your boss isn't my boss."

Scowling, the wrestler advanced toward him.

Brody looked up at the guy's broad face. "I'm eating lunch."

"He doesn't like waiting."

"I'm not finished yet," said Brody, and took a bite out of his pizza wedge.

"I don't want to have to ask you again."

"You ought to try this pizza. It's not bad. Don't you get a lunch break?"

"Don't *you* understand English?"

"What's this about?"

"Let's go," said the wrestler, motioning to him.

"Tell him to come over here and we'll share a pizza. Where is he?" said Brody, casting around the casino, as he chewed his pizza.

"He's in his penthouse. Come on," said the wrestler, reaching toward him.

Brody figured the guy might try to strong-arm him and in the attempt find out Brody was carrying. Brody didn't want the guy to find out. It wouldn't help his cause, he decided. It would no doubt get him thrown out of the joint.

"I'm not in a good mood when I can't finish my lunch," he said.

"Tough titty. Time to haul ass."

Brody put down his pizza wedge and stood up. "You spoiled my appetite. Where?"

"To the elevators."

Brody headed to the elevators, the wrestler in tow.

"You should be happy," said the wrestler. "It's not everybody who gets an invitation to see the boss."

"I told you, I don't like having my lunch interrupted."

"You can always eat lunch. Meeting the boss—that's like a once-in-a-lifetime event. You should feel honored."

They reached the bank of elevators to the guest suites.

They took the next elevator to the penthouse. The wrestler inserted a key into the red button that said Penthouse beside it.

Whoever wanted to see him was a big deal, decided Brody. The penthouse was on a private floor.

With muscle like the wrestler working for Mr. Big, Brody was in no mood to meet him. Brody considered decking the wrestler, but his curiosity got the better of him. He wanted to meet Mr. Big and find out what was going on.

Maybe not a good idea, Brody decided. After all, the proverbial cat had learned about curiosity the hard way.

The elevator halted on the penthouse floor.

126

Chapter 40

The wrestler knocked on the penthouse door at the end of the hall. Two short, one long.

Brody heard two locks disengage in the door.

They entered the penthouse.

Flanked by two young bikini-clad teens who were sitting in recliners, a fireplug with a tonsure wearing grey sweatpants and a white T stood in the capacious room staring at him with intense eyes.

The guy looked familiar, decided Brody. The spitting image of the Mafia capo Armando Musante. The main capo in Vegas from what Brody'd heard. What would the Mafia want with him?

"Welcome to my humble abode," said Musante.

"I didn't have a choice," said Brody, surveying the well-appointed room.

The first thing that caught his eye, after the people inside it, was the human-size pink blow-up doll hanging from the cathedral ceiling.

"I got good taste, huh?" said Musante, picking up on the direction of Brody's gaze.

"A family reunion?" said Brody, casting a glance at the girls flanking Musante.

"Not exactly. You know, the movie actor Rick Kane lives in the suite at the other end of the hall. He likes 'em young. A lot of guys I know do," said Musante with a smirk. "You wouldn't believe how many clients I got in DC. Senators and representatives. They all like my girls."

Brody was losing his patience. "Did you bring me up here to admire your blow-up doll? How many do you have in your bedroom?"

Musante ignored the remark. "It's come to my attention you're asking a lot of questions in my casino."

Musante strutted to the picture window that overlooked the strip, the blue sky filling most of the view, a skyline of posh casinos in the foreground, walnut desert and knuckles of mountains in the background, a glinting silver jet threading the sky above.

"What of it?" said Brody.

"It bothers me."

"I'm looking for a friend of mine, is all," said Brody.

"This is my eagle's aerie in the sky." Musante gestured to the teeming gaming metropolis below. "All this is mine."

"The world is yours."

"What?" said Musante, turning to face Brody.

"The sign at the end of *Scarface*."

"That Al Pacino movie?"

"It's also in the original *Scarface* with Paul Muni."

Musante gazed out the window again. "It's a beautiful view, and when somebody makes waves in my city, I don't appreciate it."

"I'm not making waves. I told you, I'm looking for my friend."

For the first time, Brody noticed a white cockatoo preening in a cage near the window, fanning its feathers.

"Maybe you've seen him," said Brody.

He reached for his wallet to retrieve Damian's photo.

"Don't budge," said Musante.

The wrestler moved closer to Brody to make sure Brody followed instructions.

"I just wanted to show you a picture of my friend," said Brody. "His name's Damian."

The wrestler bolted in front of Brody and jabbed him in the solar plexus with all his bulk behind the blow. As brawny as he was, the guy moved surprisingly fast. The sucker punch caught Brody flatfooted. Gasping, Brody doubled over and stumbled backward.

"No more questions," said Musante. "Leave my town alone. Get the message?"

Brody was having trouble breathing.

"And don't go to the cops," said Musante. "You'll be wasting your time. I own the cops in this town." Musante rubbed his thumb and forefinger together.

Wincing in pain, Brody managed to straighten up, taking his time in the effort.

"Yeah?" he said. "What about the Nevada Gaming Commission?"

Musante scoffed. "Five members. I own three. Majority rules. There's nobody ever been born that money can't buy."

"What about the Nevada Gaming Control Board?"

"They take their marching orders from the commission. No worries about the control board as long as the commission's in my pocket."

"What about me?"

Musante laughed. "You? Why do I want to buy you? Don't flatter yourself. You're worthless. If you don't toe the line, I'll tell Dominick to whack you. End of story."

Brody glanced at the wrestler. "He's Dominick?"

"He's part Apache," said Musante. "That's why he moves so fast and so quiet. The rest of him, the good part, is Sicilian."

Brody's immediate impulse was to retaliate and slug Dominick. Then Brody saw three other goons move into view. He stifled the impulse. He wasn't here to start a war with the Mafia. He was here to help Damian.

"I don't want my boys seeing you asking any more questions around here," said Musante.

Brody saw no percentage in arguing with the mob capo. What Brody couldn't understand was why Musante gave a damn about Brody's asking questions about Damian. Was Damian a member of the Mafia? That would explain it.

"I got only one question left," said Brody.

"Spit it out and beat it," said Musante.

"Do you use a stepladder to screw your girlfriend?" said Brody, eying the blow-up doll dangling from the ceiling.

Dominick delivered another blow to Brody's solar plexus. Doubling over again, Brody felt the urge to throw up. Somehow he restrained it.

"Get him outa my sight," said Musante.

Dominick frog-marched Brody out of the suite, the other goons backing him up.

Brody lucked out they didn't see his piece, concealed by his vest. The SIG P365 was a small piece and didn't stick out much. If they had seen it, they might have whacked him. If nothing else, they would have swiped it.

Dominick shoved Brody into the elevator as it opened, followed him inside, and produced an H&K VPN as the door closed.

Brody got the message.

The elevator descended, humming.

He wondered how Musante had found out he was questioning the cocktail waitresses about Damian. Had one of them reported him to Musante? Why would they? Brody couldn't figure it. Unless Musante was somehow expecting him to show up at the casino looking for Damian and had put out the word to the waitresses to be on the lookout. Why would Musante do that?

Brody was glad he had bought the SIG. He might yet need it.

The elevator opened at the lobby. Dominick concealed his H&K inside his jacket with a surreptitious move of his hand.

"Leave," he said, shoving Brody out and following him.

Dominick escorted Brody to the casino exit.

Chapter 41

Damian stood in his Paris casino suite gazing down at the pedestrian-clogged sidewalks of the strip through his floor-to-ceiling window, the AC on full blast. Truth to tell, it was a bit chilly in here.

He realized he was standing directly over the AC vents that were spewing cool air up at him from the floor. He took a step backward to get out of the draft.

His biggest worry at the moment was this character Ned Bates. As soon as Ned Bates met him, Ned Bates would demand the four hundred grand. Damian couldn't stay in his room all day hiding from Ned Bates, though.

Locked up in here day after day would drive Damian up the wall. He was already getting cabin fever. For sure he couldn't lock himself in this room for the rest of his life without ever going out.

He had to figure a way out of this mess. Which brought him back to the idea he had had earlier. He thought the idea had potential. It would get Roberto's hit team of *sicarios* off his back.

All he had to do was fake his death, decided Damian. It had to be convincing enough that Don Gaetano would buy it and drop his search for Damian.

The only way Don Gaetano would go for it hook, line, and sinker was if he saw Damian's corpse with his own two eyes. Don Gaetano might believe a photo of the corpse, but not necessarily. Everyone knew photos could be doctored. Even videos these days could be AI deepfakes. With AI you could put a celebrity's face on a porn queen in a porno, and nobody could tell it was phony. Did Don Gaetano have high-tech savvy? Damian believed the guy did or had an employee that did.

Bryan Cassiday

Damian knew firsthand that nobody was more suspicious than Don Gaetano. The guy was suspicious to the point of full-blown paranoia. Everybody in the cartel used burner phones or encrypted apps to communicate. Sometimes Don Gaetano used carrier pigeons to communicate with his crew. Damian had heard stories that Don Gaetano even bugged his own cartel members' phone calls, suspicious of moles in his organization.

With so much money at stake, Damian didn't see how he could make his faked death believable to Don Gaetano, who would believe it only if he saw Damian's corpse in person.

Damian eighty-sixed the idea and paced away from the window, deep in thought.

He had another idea.

This guy Ned Bates was the main problem Damian could see. Besides, of course, Roberto and his hit team of *sicarios* preparing to descend on Vegas—if they weren't here already, decided Damian.

So far, Damian had been going out of his way to avoid Ned Bates by staying in his room. What if he took the opposite approach and sought out Ned Bates, luring him into a trap so he could waste Ned Bates? With Ned Bates dead, nobody could report Damian's loss of the four hundred g's to Don Gaetano.

Ned Bates's death would buy Damian time—if nothing else. Damian could use the time to figure a way to deal with the *sicarios* coming for him.

There was a problem, though, with Damian's plan. If Don Gaetano found out Ned Bates was murdered, he would suspect Damian was the perp and seek revenge on Damian.

It would behoove Damian to make Ned Bates's death look like an accident or make the corpse disappear so nobody could find it. Then again, Don Gaetano would be suspicious of Ned Bates's "accidental" death. Damian decided Ned

132

Bates had to vanish off the grid. Don Gaetano would have no idea what happened to him.

Who was this guy Ned Bates, anyway? wondered Damian. Why would Don Gaetano entrust four hundred grand of laundered money to Ned Bates? And what was Cobalt Green Tide besides being the organization Ned Bates worked for as a bagman?

Damian shrugged. Maybe it was better not to know. The less you knew, the less you could spill to the cops. A favorite maxim of Don Gaetano's, Damian recalled. Which was why Don Gaetano kept the CJNG cartel compartmentalized. He kept the cartel members in the dark about what other members were doing.

Damian retreated to the spacious bathroom and combed his hair. He admired the bathroom's marble floor and counter around the sink. Not a bad place to hole up, all in all—if he didn't have to worry about running out of money and running into cartel hit men.

It was time to lure Ned Bates into a trap.

Damian wished he knew what the guy looked like, but in the name of compartmentalization Don Gaetano had refused to tell him.

Which left Damian with only one way to find Ned Bates. He would have to make his presence known to Ned Bates so Ned Bates could find *him*. He would have to go downstairs to the lounge and make himself visible to the casino's endless stream of tourists.

Ned Bates had plenty of motive to find him. Four hundred grand did wonders for motivation.

If only Damian still had the cash.

Chapter 42

Sporting an unbuttoned glossy peach guayabera shirt, three gold necklaces, and loose jeans, Don Gaetano lazed in a chaise longue beside his hacienda's swimming pool in Guadalajara's sultry afternoon heat, a frosty glass of tequila in his hand, watching the bikini-clad Valentina drifting in the water on an inflatable unicorn, her hand trailing in the cool turquoise water like a moccasin.

Idly, he wondered if his wife Carmen suspected his affair with Valentina. He decided Carmen was too vain about her looks to suspect Gaetano's affections might wander.

Out of the corner of his eye he picked up on a figure in jeans, snakeskin cowboy boots, and a grey polo clomping across the pool deck toward him.

"*Qué pasó?*" said Don Gaetano.

"I'm still concerned about my son Michael Corleone, *patrón*," said Arturo. "I think he needs a shrink."

"What did he do now?"

"It's like I told you before. I can't reach him. He's like in a shell."

"I'm telling you he's horny. All he needs is a girlfriend."

"I wish I could believe you," Arturo said with concern.

Don Gaetano sat up and sipped his tequila. "Any word yet from Roberto?"

"No."

"He should be in Vegas by now."

"Maybe he *is* there, but hasn't reported in."

Don Gaetano shook his head. "I don't like it. This was a simple deal for Damian. Launder the money and deliver it to a bagman. It's going south, and I don't know why. Where the hell is Ned Bates?"

"Michael isn't paying attention to me," said Arturo, preoccupied.

"You worry too much. Think about what's important."

"He *is* important."

Don Gaetano leveled a penetrating gaze at Arturo's eyes. "What is the most important thing, Arturo?"

"The cartel, *patrón*. Always the cartel. CJNG, forever."

Don Gaetano nodded with approval. "Maybe we should send Michael to help Roberto. That would give him something to do."

"He's too young to go around killing people all the time. He needs to mature first. I'm concerned the bombing of the Zeta church had a bad effect on him. Maybe he got PTSD from it."

"He has to learn how to become a member of the cartel."

"I dunno. Maybe he's too young."

"You're never too young to joint the cartel. Some of our *sicarios* are ten years old. You know that."

"What if he's got PTSD? That could screw up his head for life. A psychiatrist could help him with that."

Don Gaetano put down his tequila on the small white metal patio table.

"Sit down, my friend," he said.

Arturo sat on a lawn chair.

"I have to be honest with you, Arturo. It wouldn't look good if one of our boys went to a shrink. Think of what the other members would say. They would look down their noses at Michael as a coward who didn't have the cojones for the job. His reputation in the cartel would be ruined forever. I can assure you, Michael will be furious with you if you suggest he see a shrink."

"I'm thinking of his well-being, *patrón*. He's my only son, my flesh and blood."

"Perhaps you're being too protective of him for that reason. You're letting your emotions color your judgment."

"Does that mean you won't allow him to go to a psychiatrist?"

"He would never forgive you if you sent him to a shrink. Believe me."

"PTSD could damage him forever."

"You don't even know if he has PTSD. You worry too much. He's a good boy. You yourself have told me he's a tough kid who never backs down."

"That was before he blew up the church and all the people inside it."

"He's not tough anymore?" said Don Gaetano, his voice accusatory.

"He's tough as nails." Arturo hung fire. "But maybe he's too tough. It's not natural."

Don Gaetano grinned. "Nobody's too tough for CJNG. The tougher the better."

Arturo clucked. "My wife has expressed concern about Michael, too."

"Xochitl? How is she?"

Arturo nodded. "Fine."

"Women don't know what it's like being a teenage boy with all those hormones driving you nuts. Let him work it out by himself. In the end we're all left to our own devices. He has to gut it out on his own, like the rest of us did when we were young. It's all about cojones."

"*Sí, patrón.*"

"Look at Hitler."

"Hitler?"

"He had only one ball. Can you imagine what the world would be like now if he'd had a pair? We'd all be singing *Deutschland Uber Alles* and saluting the Third Reich's swastika flag."

Don Gaetano's satphone vibrated in his trouser pocket.

Chapter 43

"Hello," said Don Gaetano into the transmitter.

"This is me," said Damian. "Where's Ned Bates?"

"You haven't met Ned Bates yet?"

"No."

"It shouldn't be taking this long."

"That's why I called. What should I do, *patrón*?"

"Keep waiting."

Don Gaetano terminated the call.

"What's wrong, *patrón*?" said Arturo.

"Everything."

"We should've laundered the money through the banks, like we usually do."

"I don't trust bankers. They steal from their clients all the time. I know they've stolen from me."

"How about our lawyers? They know how to launder money through shell companies and offshore bank accounts."

"They also know how to line their pockets with my money without my knowledge, and they know how to charge over a thousand dollars an hour for their services."

"What should we do?"

"I never should have trusted Damian. This is a simple job. Make a couple of small bets at the casino, cash in your chips, and bingo, the money's washed. Give the cash to Ned Bates. Easy-peasy. It's the simplest way to launder money— and no bankers or shysters can scam you in the process. What the hell happened?"

"The hothead Roberto will take care of Damian. There's bad blood between those two in the first place."

"That's why I chose Roberto to go to Vegas."

Don Gaetano heard a disturbance emanating from the driveway that led to his hacienda's backyard. He picked up on the young CJNG cartel member Jaime toting an AK-47 and prodding its muzzle into the back of a twentysomething short, scrawny guy in an olive drab tank top with tattoos on his throat and arms, his forearms cratered with track marks.

The junkie had a green tattoo of a sinister joker with a red face on his upper arm and a yellow and green tattoo of Santa Muerte (Saint of Death) worshiped by cartels on his throat. Between his eyes was the tattoo of a skull, the mark of a *sicario* who had racked up a high body count.

On his wrist was the letter *Z*, identifying him as a Zeta. Either that or the junkie had tried to slash his wrists without success, decided Don Gaetano.

"I found this Zeta spying on us," said Jaime wielding the AK.

"When will they ever learn?" said Don Gaetano.

"We want to make a deal with you," blurted the Zeta.

"I don't make deals with spies."

A troupe of four mariachis gripping their brass horns paraded onto the patio from the driveway. Two of the mariachis were thin, the other two paunchy. Clad in black *charro* outfits with tight black bolero jackets with brass buttons and tight black pants with decorations down the sides of the legs, the mariachis halted on the patio deck, raised their horns to their lips, and started to play.

Interrupted by their music, Don Gaetano glowered at them.

"Not now," Arturo yelled at the mariachis above the music.

Disappointed, the leader of the mariachis signaled to his band to stop playing.

"We always play at this time," he said. "The *patrón* says it relaxes him."

"It does," said Arturo, "but the *patrón* is busy now. He needs to take care of business. Come back later."

"*No problema.*"

The mariachi leader signaled to his group, and they left.

"Where were we?" Don Gaetano asked the terrified Zeta.

"We want to make a deal with you. We want a ceasefire for a month. I have the power to negotiate with you."

"I don't negotiate with spies. Listen to me. What do you know about the food chain?"

The Zeta shook his head at a loss, not understanding the question.

"I will tell you," said Don Gaetano. "Do you know who the king of the sea is?"

The Zeta pulled a face. "The great white shark?"

"That's what a lot of people think because they saw *Jaws*. It's actually the killer whale, aka the orca. The great white has only two natural predators." Glancing at the toolshed Don Gaetano gestured with his hand to Arturo.

Arturo understood. He crossed the pool deck with Jaime at his side to the shed in the backyard.

"The two enemies are man, of course," Don Gaetano told the Zeta, "and the orca. Sharks live to be about seventy years old. An orca can live to be a hundred. The great white is terrified of orcas. If it knows an orca is in its proximity, it flees for its life. Do you want to know what the orca does to a great white when it attacks?"

The Zeta's anxious face didn't express interest.

"I'm going to tell you anyway. The orca tears the pectoral fin off the great white and squeezes the shark's liver like toothpaste out of the shark's body and into the orca's mouth. The orca consumes the nutritious liver and swims away, leaving the mortally wounded shark to float away and die. The orca knows exactly what it wants from the shark, takes it, and leaves." Don Gaetano paused. "What do you think?"

The Zeta said nothing.

"Do you think the orca believes that eating the great white's liver makes him stronger than the great white? How does the orca know that it wants to eat the great white's liver and nothing more? The information must be in its DNA. Don't you think that's amazing? The orca is programed to eat the great white's liver, and its genes tell it the best way to kill the shark in order to get to the liver is by tearing off the shark's pectoral fin and squeezing the liver out through the hole."

"My boss wants a ceasefire. That's why I'm here."

"Or do you think the orca *learns* how to kill the great white?"

"What?" said the Zeta, confused.

"Does the orca inherit the knowledge through its DNA or does it learn from experience how to kill the great white?"

The Zeta looked helpless. "My boss—"

"Nature is a battlefield."

Arturo and Jaime returned to the pool. Jaime carried the chain saw with him.

"Cut out his liver," Don Gaetano told Jaime.

Jaime looked puzzled.

"Where is it?" he said, eying the Zeta.

"Never mind. Cut him in half at the waist. We'll find the liver later. I'll let you have the pleasure of eating it."

Screwing up his young unlined face Jaime yanked the chain saw's string to start the machine.

The thundering clatter of the two-stroke grated on Don Gaetano's nerves.

He heard the mariachi band start to practice in the driveway, as the chain saw's blade sliced through the Zeta's waist.

The Zeta's scream sounded like a yelping dog.

Chapter 44

Brody was sitting at a table in a sequestered area of the BLT Restaurant in the Mirage eating a burger and fries and contemplating his options when a suit sat across from him.

One of Musante's muscle heads come to harass him, decided Brody. But Musante hadn't told Brody to stay away from the Mirage, only the Paris. It was possible Musante controlled both casinos. He could control several casinos, for all Brody knew, maybe even all of them.

"Expecting company?" said the clean-cut suit, a black leather attaché case in his hand.

He had fanatic's eyes. Brown and intense. Eyes that wouldn't tolerate resistance.

"No," said Brody, holding his hamburger near his mouth. "Do you mind? I don't like to be interrupted when I eat."

"This won't take long. Special Agent Coscarelli. I work for the FBI."

Brody didn't know what this was about. He knew he didn't like talking to feds.

"Could I see a badge?" said Brody.

Coscarelli produced his FBI badge and displayed it to Brody.

"Do I need a lawyer?" said Brody.

"Have you done something illegal?"

"No."

Coscarelli adjusted his powder blue microfiber tie. "Then let's talk. Is your name Scott Brody?"

"Yeah."

"Do you know a person by the name of Ned Bates?"

"No."

"What about Damian Playa?"

Brody didn't want to reveal anything about the case he was working on. On the other hand, he didn't want to commit perjury by lying to a fed.

"Maybe," said Brody, uncertain how to proceed.

"Do you or don't you?"

"I never met the man." Which was true, decided Brody.

"What about Cobalt Green Tide?"

The name sounded familiar, decided Brody. Hadn't somebody else asked him about it?

"What is it?" said Brody. "I don't know anything about it."

"We've had our eyes on you and think you're involved."

"Involved in what?"

"The conspiracy."

Brody put down his hamburger. "I don't know anything about any conspiracy."

"Do you know what the Twenty-fifth Amendment is?"

Twenty-fifth Amendment, decided Brody. Did this have anything to do with the murdered FBI agent Peltz? The same Peltz that had duped him into signing an NDA to prevent him from talking about a conspiracy within the FBI Peltz claimed to have uncovered? A conspiracy among certain FBI agents and others in the deep state who were determined to remove President Ransom from office.

"The president's cabinet can remove him from office if they think he's unable to function as president," said Brody.

"Close. There has to be a majority of the principal officers of the executive department that consider the president unable to act as president. Then they can remove the president and replace him with the vice president. However, that's not the end of it. The president can disagree with their decision and demand his office back after the vice president has assumed the role of president. Then the House and the Senate have to vote with a two-thirds majority in each to remove the original president, or the president resumes his position."

Brody picked up his hamburger. "Complicated."

"Are you willing to help us?"

"'Help *us*,' meaning who?" said Brody, confused.

"The FBI."

"How can I possibly help?"

Coscarelli leaned closer to Brody. "What do you know about Cobalt Green Tide?"

"Nothing. You already asked me that."

"We have reason to believe Ned Bates is involved with Cobalt Green Tide."

"Why do I care?"

Coscarelli laid his attaché case on the tabletop, opened the case, and withdrew several papers stapled together.

"Are you willing to sign an NDA?" he said. He sniffed the air. "I smell fish."

Brody looked at the hamburger in his hands. "I'm eating a real hamburger made of beef. Not fish."

Coscarelli sniffed the air again. "Then why do I smell fish?"

"This is a burger joint."

"How do you know that isn't a vegan burger?"

"I didn't order a vegan burger."

"Maybe it's a fish burger."

"It's not."

"How do you know?"

"Because it tastes like beef."

"It could be some weird vegan stuff they invented in a test tube that's supposed to taste like beef."

"Then why would it smell like fish?"

Coscarelli sighed. "You don't know what you're eating these days."

Brody put down his half-eaten hamburger. "I'm losing my appetite."

"Where were we?" said Coscarelli, sniffing the air.

"You were getting ready to leave."

"Not yet," said Coscarelli. He glanced at the document in his hands. "Oh, yeah. Are you willing to sign an NDA?"

"With you?"

"With the FBI."

"Why?"

"I can't tell you anything about the conspiracy unless you sign the NDA."

Peltz had inveigled Brody into signing an NDA, and Brody's life had taken a drastic downward spiral afterward.

"I'm not sure I want to know about this conspiracy you're talking about," said Brody, getting up to leave, glancing askance at the half-eaten hamburger on his tray.

Chapter 45

"I can tell you this much," said Coscarelli.

Brody resumed his seat, listening.

"Then you decide whether to sign the NDA," said Coscarelli. "We have reason to believe Cobalt Green Tide is a shell company, an LLC, set up in Delaware. Nobody knows who runs the company because the state of Delaware doesn't require the owners of the company to sign their names on the articles of organization."

"I don't understand what this has to do with me."

"Are you part of the conspiracy?"

"Of course not."

"Then why are you looking for Damian Playa?"

"Who said I am?" said Brody, becoming edgy.

"I've been asking cocktail waitresses about him, and several of them said somebody else asked them the same question. One of them named you."

"It has nothing to do with any conspiracy. I'm working on a case that involves Damian Playa."

"And Damian Playa just happens to be part of the conspiracy?" said Coscarelli, frowning and leaning back in his seat. "That's a huge, unbelievable coincidence."

Brody didn't want to tell Coscarelli any more than he had to, but he didn't want to be charged with being a coconspirator in league with Damian, either, which was what Coscarelli was threatening the feds might do—if Brody was reading Coscarelli right.

"I have no idea what Damian's doing here," said Brody. "His sister hired me to find him. She believes his life's in danger."

Coscarelli pulled a face. "Possible. But it sounds too pat. You know what I mean?"

"I'm telling you the truth."

"Do you want to help us bust the cabal that's trying to stage a coup?"

"I do. But why me?"

"Because you can get us close to Damian Playa. We got questions for him. A boatload of them."

"How can I get you close to him? I've never even met him."

"You're not a member of the bureau. Some of these cartel guys can smell FBI agents a mile away. He won't suspect you."

"Are you saying Damian's a narco?"

Araceli hadn't told him anything about Damian's cartel connections, decided Brody.

"We suspect he's a *sicario* for the Jalisco New Generation Cartel," said Coscarelli.

Brody shook his head in disbelief. "This is crazy."

"Believe me, I wish I was making it up."

"If he doesn't suspect me of being a cop, why doesn't he reveal himself to me? He must know I've been asking around for him."

"No more questions until you sign the NDA. I've already told you too much. Are you with us or not?"

If he wasn't with them, they'd figure he was against them, decided Brody. He knew how feds' minds worked. He better play ball.

"I'm with you," he said, grudgingly.

He hated signing NDAs. No good could come from signing them, as he saw it. They skewed in favor of the issuers.

"Good." Coscarelli held up the document he had taken out of his attaché case. "You need to sign—"

Coscarelli's head pitched forward and landed on the tabletop with a thud.

Brody flinched in bewilderment. *What?*

It didn't take Brody long to figure out what had happened.

Coscarelli had a small-caliber bullet hole in the back of his head, where a tuft of his hair was matted with blood. Not much blood, because the guy had died within seconds of getting shot. Brody guessed a .22. The favorite piece of mob hit men. A low velocity hollow-point bullet that didn't exit through the skull, but bounced around inside the brain wreaking maximum damage on the tissue. A .22 fitted with a suppressor, since Brody hadn't heard the shot. Another earmark of a professional assassin.

The mob, Brody decided. Did Musante have anything to do with the hit on Coscarelli? Was the Mafia tied up in this conspiracy Coscarelli was talking about? All Brody knew was that Musante was helping Damian. Brody didn't know why.

Brody had no time to think about it. He had to beat it.

Sitting in front of an FBI agent with a bullet buried in the back of his skull wasn't a good idea if you valued your freedom—and your life.

He scoped out the surroundings trying to pick up on someone with a gun or someone fleeing the scene. The hit man must have left, he decided, noticing no suspicious characters.

As if he hadn't a care in the world Brody left the restaurant, not wanting to draw attention to himself nor the corpse sitting at his dining table.

He walked out of the casino into the hot sun baking the sidewalk and felt sick from the crushing heat, wondering if he would be the next target on the hit man's list.

He came to a halt for a moment, fearing lest he pass out. He felt dizzy, disoriented. He needed to collect himself. Was it the heat, or was he having a seizure?

He waited for the episode to pass, as cars whooshed and honked down the jammed boulevard.

He had been sitting in front of a murdered FBI agent. Maybe it was just now sinking in. Was that why he felt lightheaded? he wondered. He was lucky the assassin hadn't blown him away as well. What if the assassin was stalking him even now?

Brody whipped his head around, trying to catch sight of someone following him. He couldn't tell. Nobody seemed the least bit interested in him. In this case, it was a good thing. Of course, if it was a professional tailing him, the guy wouldn't be easy to spot.

Brody returned to his room, glancing behind him fitfully to make sure he hadn't picked up a tail.

Chapter 46

Naked save for a towel wrapped around his waist, Don
Gaetano was lying on his stomach on his bed stripped of
pillows in his hacienda bedroom waiting for the delectable
Valentina to arrive and treat him with one of her massages.

His mouth watering, he heard his bedroom doorknob click
open. He cast a furtive glance in the direction of the door,
which was opening by degrees. He turned his gaze toward the
full-length mirror that hung from the wall abutting the
headboard, his arms crossed underneath his chin.

Valentina slipped into the room, dressed in a black leather
Gestapo trench coat that reached her ankles, spit-shined black
leather jackboots, and an Allgemeine SS officer's black hat
with the emblems of an eagle above a skull and bones on its
brow.

He heard her boots' hard heels clacking against the
parquet floor as she approached him. He could see her in the
mirror.

She opened her trench coat to reveal she was wearing
only a black leather thong. She pulled something out of the
trench coat's deep pocket. She let the trench coat slip off her
shoulders, down her sensuous body, and onto the floor. In her
hand was a black riding crop.

She tossed the towel from his waist and flung it to the
floor. She raised the riding crop over her head and slashed
Don Gaetano's naked buttocks.

Don Gaetano clenched his teeth with delight.

Valentina was getting ready to bring the riding crop down
again when Don Gaetano heard his satphone bawl *The Good,
the Bad and the Ugly* on the bureau.

He cursed and launched himself from his bed to retrieve
the satphone.

"This better be important," he said into the transmitter.

The caller ID said Private, like most of the calls he received. The callers didn't want to expose their identities.

"This is Ned Bates."

"Did you get the laundry from Damian?"

"My flight out of Reagan National in DC was delayed. I just got in to Vegas. It's too damn hot. Where do I meet him?"

"You know what he looks like because I e-mailed you his picture."

"There are hundreds of thousands of people here. I need to know where he's staying."

"He says he's staying at Bally's."

"Did he check in using his real name?"

"I doubt it."

"I'll head over there."

"As soon as you get the laundry, call me."

Don Gaetano terminated the call.

Things were finally coming together, he decided, putting down the satphone.

"Is that all you can think about it?" said Valentina, flicking her riding crop against her palm, staring at him with her fiery blue eyes, her prominent breasts jiggling.

He glanced down below his stomach, realized what she was talking about, lunged toward her, and threw her on the bed.

Chapter 47

In his room at the Venetian Brody got out his laptop, sat at the desk near the window overlooking Las Vegas Boulevard, and logged onto the Elysian Fields chat room as Myshkin.

Myshkin: Anybody there?

Margaux Hemingway: Hello, Myshkin.

Teddy Roosevelt: We were beginning to think you were dead because of your long absence.

Not funny, decided Brody, considering his recent experience at the BLT.

Myshkin: I have a question. Did any of you ever experience a seizure on account of the heat?

Teddy Roosevelt: I don't know. I don't think so.

Margaux Hemingway: Did the heat cause you to have a seizure, Myshkin?

Myshkin: I'm not sure. It may have been something else.

Margaux Hemingway: Who knows what causes epileptic seizures? Even the doctors aren't sure. I've had seizures in stressful situations. A hot day could be considered stressful. Did it ever happen to you before when it was hot?

Myshkin: No.

Julius Caesar: What did I miss?

Teddy Roosevelt: Myshkin is back from the dead.

Maybe at another time Brody would have considered Teddy's humor funny, but not after his hairbreadth escape from an assassination.

Margaux Hemingway: Did you ever have a seizure on account of hot weather, Julius?

Julius Caesar: No. I don't believe I ever did.

Margaux Hemingway: What brings yours on?

Julius Caesar: It's hard to pinpoint an exact cause. Sometimes I can get one out of nowhere. Did you pass out from the heat?

Margaux Hemingway: It was Myshkin.

Myshkin: I didn't pass out. I felt the onset of a seizure.

Julius Caesar: You must be under stress.

Myshkin: Yeah.

Julius Caesar: It probably wasn't the heat alone.

Brody felt his cell phone vibrate in his trouser pocket.

Myshkin: Gotta run.

Brody logged out of the chat room and took the call designated Private.

"Let's meet," said the woman's voice.

"Who is this?"

"Don't you recognize my voice?"

"Melody?"

"That's better."

"What's this about?"

"I may have information you want."

About Damian, Brody hoped.

"Where do you want to meet?" he said.

"In fifteen minutes at Ruth's Chris steak house in Harrah's."

She terminated the call.

Chapter 48

Damian was wandering around the Paris's gambling floor waiting impatiently for Ned Bates to find him. It wasn't happening. Where was the guy? he wondered. He couldn't whack the guy if he never met him.

Damian commenced walking around in the center of the casino the better to be spotted by Ned Bates. What more could he do to draw the guy's attention? He was in midstride when it dawned on him that he had told Don Gaetano he was at Bally's, since at that time Damian hadn't wanted to run into Ned Bates.

Ned Bates had to be at Bally's, decided Damian. Ned Bates would never find him here at the Paris. Don Gaetano would know that Damian had sent Ned Bates on a wild-good chase because Damian had lied to Don Gaetano about being at Bally's. If Don Gaetano didn't already believe Damian had ripped him off, he would when Ned Bates called him and told him Damian wasn't at Bally's.

Damian hurried out of the Paris to Bally's, a sheathed Gerber Prodigy knife wedged inside the waistband of his jeans. He had slit several throats with the Gerber. It was a fine tool. He couldn't remember how many people he had killed. Was it two? Or was it four? Or six? And how many more at the training camp? It was funny how memory played tricks on you.

He didn't see any way around killing Ned Bates. If Ned Bates reported back to Don Gaetano, he would tell Don Gaetano Damian had no money. Don Gaetano would put out a contract on Damian—if he hadn't done so already.

On the other hand, if Ned Bates never reported to Don Gaetano, Don Gaetano might believe it was Ned Bates rather than Damian who had ripped off the four hundred grand. It was worth a try, anyway, decided Damian. He didn't see any other viable options. He had to throw suspicion off himself and onto someone else.

The problem was, Ned Bates had the upper hand, decided Damian. Ned Bates knew what Damian looked like, but Damian didn't know what Ned Bates looked like. If Don Gaetano had empowered Ned Bates to kill Damian in case something went wrong with the exchange of cash, Damian was risking his life by meeting Ned Bates.

Damian knew nothing about Ned Bates. That was the way Don Gaetano wanted it, Damian was sure.

Ned Bates was a bagman for Cobalt Green Tide, was all Damian knew about him.

Cobalt Green Tide was going to be royally pissed after Damian took out Ned Bates. Damian would be able to add another member to his list of enemies that wanted him dead, a list that was growing by the second and decreasing his chances of dying from natural causes.

Sick of the raft of killings he had perpetrated as a *sicario*, Damian couldn't see any way out of his predicament without yet another killing—wasting Ned Bates. Ned Bates would be Damian's last kill. Then Damian would retire from the dog-eat-dog assassination racket.

After losing Don Gaetano's four hundred grand, Damian had no options remaining other than retirement and vanishing into thin air.

Chapter 49

Brody met Melody for a late lunch at Ruth's Chris in Harrah's.

They sat at a table next to a window that overlooked the sidewalk bustling with assorted characters strolling it—street people with the bare minimum of clothes on, including teenage girls impersonating Vegas showgirls clad in thong bikinis and crowns of white plumage sprouting from their heads eager to have their pictures taken with male tourists for a price. And then there were the guys in nothing but thongs, cowboy hats, and cowboy boots soliciting photo sessions with the female tourists.

And, of course, it wouldn't be Vegas without the occasional Elvis impersonator wearing a sequined white outfit strolling the sidewalk.

Brody and Melody ordered beers and filet mignons, Brody's medium rare, Melody's well done.

Melody wasn't wearing her cocktail outfit, but the low-cut blouse she was favoring was even more revealing, Brody couldn't help but notice, despite his resolve not to get mixed up with another woman any time soon thanks to his recent experiences with women he had been attracted to—namely, his wife Jennifer and a Hollywood actress/stripper named Terri Symonds he had met after a charming serial killer had strangled Jennifer.

A psycho killer had promptly severed Terri's carotid artery, and Brody had helplessly watched her bleed to death in his arms in a condom-strewn alley behind a strip joint as he waited for the ambulance to arrive.

He didn't have a promising track record with women and wasn't in any mood to try his hand at it again.

Melody nudged his foot under the table with her toe.

The waitress delivered their beers and left with a brittle gait.

Brody took a pull on his beer.

"What did you want to talk to me about?" he said.

She leaned over the tabletop toward him, squeezing her breasts together.

"I think I saw that guy you're looking for," she said.

"Damian Playa?"

She nodded yes. "The fisherman in the rowboat."

"Where'd you see him?"

"At the Paris."

"Are you sure it was him?"

"I remember him because I talked to him."

"About what?"

"He looked upset about something. I wondered what was bugging him."

"What did he say?"

"He said he lost a couple hundred bucks on the roulette wheel."

"Why didn't you tell me this when I first met you?"

"He told me he was in trouble, that somebody had it in for him."

"And you thought that somebody was me?"

She nodded yes and sipped her beer.

"I'm trying to help him, like I told you before," he said. "His sister sent me to find him."

She shrugged. "How was I supposed to know you weren't lying?"

Brody could see her point.

"It was odd, though," she said, recalling Damian.

"What?"

"He wanted to know if I knew any Mafia guys in Vegas."

Brody thought about it. "Were the Mafia guys the ones that had it in for him?"

"I dunno."

The waitress brought their filet mignons. Brody would charge them as business expenses when he billed Araceli.

"Don't touch your plates," said the waitress. "They're hot."

Brody heard the filet mignon sizzling on his plate, making his mouth water.

"I love filet mignon," said Melody, ogling her cut.

Brody glanced at her cut then told himself to think about something else.

"Do you know if he's staying at the Paris?" he said.

"No. He could be staying anywhere."

She was right, of course, he knew.

"Did he happen to tell you where he was going?" he said.

"No."

"This is the first time you ever met Damian?"

"Yep."

"And you've been working at the Paris how long?"

"A couple of days. I just started waitressing. I used to be a lifeguard."

"What changed?"

"I injured my back, and . . . ," she trailed off.

"Not to be nosy, but what else changed?"

"My husband."

"I don't understand."

Melody debated whether she should tell him.

"He decided he wanted to kill me," she said.

Brody took a pull on his beer.

"I fled from my home in New Mexico and got a job here," she went on.

"There many beaches in New Mexico?"

"I was a lifeguard at a hotel swimming pool, not at a beach, and I worked at the Y in the winter. Do you always ask this many questions?"

"It's my job. I'm a PI."

"You make me feel like I'm lying."

"I didn't mean to. It sounds like you have a serious problem with your husband."

"I do."

"What is it?"

Frowning, she rubbed her forehead. "I don't really want to talk about it. I want to relax and enjoy my meal."

"Maybe after we eat?"

"Maybe."

She eased out a little smile.

"Right," he said. "Let's tuck in."

Chapter 50

Five minutes later Melody said, "Maybe *you* could help me."

Brody stopped cutting his meat. Warning bells went off inside his head. He didn't like working for women he was attracted to. He knew it would end badly for them. They would come to a violent end—like his wife and Terri Symonds.

"I don't see how," he muttered.

"Don't private detectives provide help for their clients?"

"I'm already working for someone," he said, ducking her question.

"Can't you handle two cases at once? You look like a capable guy."

"I'm also expensive," he said, playing with his filet mignon distractedly.

"You think I'm trailer trash or something," she said, getting angry.

"No, no, no," he said, trying to calm her down.

"Then what's the problem?"

"I want to take your case."

He wanted her to settle down. He had no idea she was going to fly off the handle.

"So?" she said.

"I want to help you."

"Good. Just because I got a bonehead asshole for a husband doesn't make me trailer trash."

"I never thought that."

"I know how people think. We lived in a house, by the way. Not in a trailer park."

She had an explosive temper, he could see.

"Let's enjoy our suppers right now," he said.

Bryan Cassiday

She nodded and returned to eating her steak, her face expressionless.

He could tell she was thinking about her husband. Should he tell her he didn't want to take her case because he was afraid she'd end up like his wife? It might put a chill in the atmosphere. But there already was one.

"I don't want you to end up like my wife," he said.

"What?" she said, looking up from her steak. "You're married?"

He cleared his throat. "A charming serial killer strangled my wife."

She didn't know how to take his words. He saw surprise and puzzlement on her face. Maybe he shouldn't have told her.

"I'm sorry," she said.

"I don't like talking about it."

"I understand. But why do you think I'll end up like your wife?"

"Any woman I get involved with dies by violence."

"No. That's crazy to think like that."

"She wasn't the only one."

"And you think your getting involved with them caused their murders?"

"I'm sure of it."

"You must believe in curses, then."

"No."

"What other explanation could there be?"

"It is what it is."

"Is this your way of saying you don't like me?" she said, irritated.

"Just the opposite, actually."

She shook her head in confusion. "I don't understand you."

"I'm trying to explain if I help you, you'll get murdered."

160

She became upset. "If you *don't* help me, I'll get murdered—by my husband."

"It has to be strictly as a business relationship if you want me to help you."

"What do you think I wanted? That's my real reason for coming here. To get you to help protect me from Dan."

"Dan's your husband?"

"Right. I don't care about this Damian what's his face. I hardly know him. I forgot about him as soon as I met him. That's why I didn't tell you about him the first time you met me."

"The problem is, I'm on another assignment."

Melody thought about it. "What if we make our deal as an on-call job? You don't have to do anything for me unless I call you and ask for your help to protect me from Dan."

That might work, decided Brody. He didn't want her husband to harm her. If he fought off his attraction to her and kept this as a business relationship, maybe he could help her.

"Are you still in love with your husband?" he said.

"No way. I just want to get away from him and never see him again."

Brody stabbed his filet mignon with his fork and lifted the succulent morsel into his mouth. He finished chewing and swallowed.

"I'm not cheap," he said.

"You're gonna be working on call, only when I need you. Hopefully, I won't need you at all."

"What if I'm needed for my current case and can't get away to help you?"

Melody knocked back her beer. "We'll cross that bridge when we get to it."

Brody had misgivings about taking on her assignment, but he thought if he could keep their relationship on a business level, rather than on a personal one, Melody should end up surviving. Whenever he let his feelings become involved, he ran into problems on the job.

Did it mean he was superstitious if he was convinced she would be murdered if he became involved with her? All he knew for sure was his prior experiences had ended up with dire consequences. There were two corpses in his life to prove it.

"I think you're afraid," she said.

"Of what?"

"Of getting involved again."

"Wouldn't you be with the results I've had?"

"The results I've experienced haven't been too uplifting. I wouldn't have married Dan if I knew he'd turn into Attila the Hun. I had no idea."

"Then you understand."

"I'm not gonna live the rest of my life in fear because of one guy that wants me dead. They can't all be monsters."

Brody didn't want to talk about it. He had to concentrate on his job.

He glanced out the restaurant window down at the sidewalk, where sweaty teenagers cavorted, grinning despite the intense heat.

"Do you ever feel like you're missing out on something?" he said.

"There may be hope for you yet," she said.

He guzzled his beer. Maybe if he was drunk he wouldn't think about his train wreck of a private life, he decided.

"Death follows me around," he said.

He wasn't going to elaborate and tell her he had just witnessed an FBI agent's murder. Melody didn't look like she was listening. He wondered if he had bitten off more than he could chew by taking on her assignment as well as Araceli's.

Chapter 51

Ned Bates idled through Bally's gaming room.

The casino was one of the older ones on the strip, along with the Flamingo, that were still in operation. It was showing signs of age. It might soon follow the course of another aging casino, namely the Riviera, which the owners had imploded at the other end of the strip.

A valise in hand, Ned Bates wound through the slot machines and scoped out the milling crowd of gamblers for any sign of Damian. Ned Bates wanted to get the laundered cash and split. Ned Bates would carry it in a valise.

Ned Bates spotted Damian sitting at a taco joint in a food court.

# # #

Damian was sitting at a plastic table munching a hard taco, alternating between feeling bored, anxious, and helpless. He didn't know how he could lure Ned Bates other than by keeping a high profile at Bally's. On the other hand, he didn't want to make a scene and draw everybody's attention, especially if he was going to end up whacking Ned Bates.

Ned Bates had to go, decided Damian. Ned Bates was the only one that could verify to Don Gaetano that Damian didn't have the four hundred grand.

The worst thing about all this waiting was Damian had no idea what Ned Bates looked like. Hence the helplessness Damian felt.

A slender, thirtyish blonde with her hair piled on top of her head, wearing a navy blue pantsuit, walked up to him.

"We got a problem," she said.

Taco in hand, Damian looked at her in bemusement. "You're the one with the problem, lady. You can keep it to yourself."

He didn't want to be rude to her. She was pretty good-looking. Another time, another place . . . who knew? But he was here to meet Ned Bates.

"I don't mean to alarm you," she said.

"You *are* alarming me. Do I look like someone who wants your problem?"

"It's *our* problem."

"Look, lady, you don't understand. There's some mistake."

"No mistake. My problem is your problem."

It reminded Damian of the courteous Mexican saying *mi casa es su casa*, except *mi problema es su problema* was not only discourteous it was flat-out threatening.

"I don't know what your problem is, and I don't *want* to know," he said. "Good-bye."

Damian returned to munching on his taco drenched in jalapeño sauce.

"What's your game?" she said with annoyance.

"*My* game? You're the one that came over here and started harassing me."

"It's no good pretending you're not Damian Playa."

Damian started at the mention of his name, halting his dripping taco on its way to his mouth. Who *was* this woman? he wondered. He had never seen her before. He couldn't get his head around it. Why was she looking for him, and how in the world did she know his name? He hadn't told anyone his name in Vegas. He hadn't even checked into his hotel with his real name. Wait a minute. He had told that cocktail waitress he had met at the roulette wheel his name. Was this woman a friend of hers?

Uninvited, the blonde sat on a seat across from him.

"Don't make a spectacle," she said.

"Who the hell are you?"

"Ned Bates, and lower your voice. Attention is the last thing we want."

Damian couldn't believe his eyes. *Ned Bates* wasn't a woman's name.

"You don't look like any Ned Bates," he said.

She must be an imposter, he decided. But it was obvious she was a woman. She wasn't exactly hiding her breasts, which weren't small. How could she hope to con him by pretending to be a man? And, more importantly, why was she pretending to be Ned Bates? *How did she even know about Ned Bates?*

"N-E-D Bates to be precise," she said.

"What's the difference?"

"The name's Natalie Eames-Dixon Bates."

This was the bagman he was expecting? decided Damian in befuddlement. She could still be an imposter, since Damian had no idea what Ned Bates looked like. Damian wasn't convinced she was the real McCoy.

"And, like I said before, we have a problem," she said, sitting with her arms in her lap.

"All right, I'll play along. What's the problem?"

She kept her voice low. "I found a fed asking about you."

"A fed? That can't be."

Ned Bates was full of surprises, Damian decided. He didn't want to hear anymore. But he had to know what she was talking about.

"The feds have no idea I'm in Vegas," he said, keeping his voice low as well.

"They're not supposed to. Their knowing you're here is a problem."

"What can we do?"

"I took care of it. I took care of him, I mean. He was talking to another guy I overheard asking questions about you."

A *sicario*? was Damian's first thought. A fed was talking to a *sicario*? Roberto or one of his hit team? Were they in Vegas already?

"Who did you take care of? The fed or the other guy?" said Damian.

"The fed."

"A fed?" said Damian, incredulous.

"Which begs the questions," Ned Bates went on, "how many more people know you're in town? This was supposed to be a private meeting between me and you."

"I don't know who any of these people you're talking about are." He paused a beat. "What do you mean, you 'took care' of the fed?" he said, wanting to be sure he understood Ned Bates.

"I took him out," Ned Bates said without hesitation. "It had to be done."

"How did you do it?"

"A .22 hollow point."

"What about the other guy?"

"He didn't look like a cop. I had to beat it. I let him live."

"But he knows the feds are looking for me," said Damian, scratching his cheek.

"The fed didn't get a chance to tell him everything the FBI knows about you before he died. I made sure of that."

Chapter 52

Damian couldn't understand how the feds had got onto him. How had they found out he was in town?

"What do we do?" he said.

"You give me the laundry. We blow Vegas chop-chop," said Ned Bates, and chopped her open palm with the side of her other hand.

That was what he was afraid she would say—the part about giving her the laundry. He had to take her out. But she was packing heat. Taking her out wouldn't be as easy as he had originally thought.

He scoped Ned Bates out. She could be packing in her valise. Unless she had ditched the rod after the kill shot. There was no way to tell. Best to assume Ned Bates was armed, he decided.

Damian picked up on Dominick, Musante's muscle, strolling toward him with a roll to his gait like a sailor through the food court.

Damian had almost forgot he had Dominick to protect him. The guy had followed him here without Damian's knowledge.

Could he have Dominick whack Ned Bates? Damian wondered. All he had to do was tell Dominick that Ned Bates was going to blow him away. As Damian's bodyguard Dominick would have to deal with Ned Bates. But would Dominick whack her out or just bust her up and warn her to stay away? The latter solution did Damian no good. Busted up, Ned Bates could still call Don Gaetano and tell him Damian hadn't turned over the cash. Don Gaetano would have Damian whacked for ripping him off.

Damian couldn't allow Ned Bates to make that call. The only sure way to stop her from blabbing about him was to clip her.

Ned Bates slid her valise onto the tabletop. "Put the laundry in my valise."

Damian's pulse ratcheted up. He had to stall for time.

"Here?" he said. "We can't do it here."

"Why not?"

"Somebody'll see me do it. We could get jacked."

"Do it under the table so nobody can see."

"I—I—uh—can't do that."

"Why not?" said Ned Bates, narrowing her eyes with suspicion.

"I—I—uh—don't have it with me."

"You left it in your room?" she said in disbelief.

He had to think of a credible explanation, he decided, palms sweaty.

"I wanted to check you out first to make sure you're on the up and up," he said.

"How do you know somebody won't rip it off in your room?"

"I—I—put it in the safe."

Dominick lingered off to the side fifteen feet away from Damian. Pretending he wasn't watching Damian, he took a seat at a table.

Ned Bates dug her cell phone out of her pantsuit pocket.

"What are you doing?" said Damian, widening his eyes.

"I better call this in to Don Gaetano. He's already pissed this is taking so long."

"Nooo," said Damian, waving his hands in front of him like he was washing a window. "Don't bother him. He hates being bothered by bad news."

Ned Bates started punching numbers on her cell with her long slender fingers like a havestman's legs spinning silk. "He's having a cow this is taking so long. I'll tell him I found you—"

"Stop. You'll look bad if you say you haven't got the laundry. He'll chew your head off. Maybe even put you on a hit list. I know how he works."

"I don't take orders from him. I work for the company."

"You think that'll prevent him from whacking you? Think again."

Ned Bates halted punching numbers and gazed at Damian. "The longer it takes me to get the laundry, the madder he'll get."

"That's why you shouldn't talk to him until you have the laundry in your hands."

Ned Bates made a moue and put away her cell.

Damian glanced at Dominick, who looked relaxed sitting by himself at another table. The guy must've figured a woman couldn't be a *sicario* and therefore wasn't a threat, decided Damian. Damian knew better. There were plenty of women working as *sicarios*. Some of the most successful killers in the business were women, good-looking women at that. Their targets expected sex. Instead, they got a bullet between the eyes.

Damian didn't motion to Dominick because he didn't want Ned Bates to know Dominick was working for him as a bodyguard.

"I have one question," said Damian. "Who are you working for?"

"Cobalt Green Tide LLC," said Ned Bates.

"What kind of outfit is that?"

"You don't need to know." Ned Bates stood up. "Let's get the laundry."

Damian couldn't figure out why Don Gaetano was paying Cobalt Green Tide four hundred grand.

"What service does this Cobalt Green Tide provide?" said Damian, remaining seated.

"The more you know about it, the shorter your life expectancy."

"Something to do with insurance?" said Damian, puzzled.

"You could put it that way. Now let's get going," said Ned Bates, valise in hand.

Getting to his feet Damian felt the knife wedged in his waistband press against his belly. It might be best if he took care of Ned Bates himself, without involving Dominick.

If Dominick took Ned Bates out, he would tell his boss Musante, and Musante would want to know who Ned Bates was. Damian didn't want to go into it with Musante. Musante was the type of guy that wanted to know everything about any financial transaction and how he could score a percentage.

Damian and Ned Bates cut across the gaming floor's worn carpet, through a glass-enclosed tunnel, out the entrance, and into the stifling heat on the sidewalk.

Where was he going to waste her? he wondered.

Chapter 53

Brody was asking a cocktail waitress at the Cosmopolitan under a diamond chandelier fashioned of obvious paste if she had ever seen Damian when a bald fiftysomething guy with two slender good-looking girls a couple inches taller than baldy buttonholed him.

The guy looked like an aging swinger with his silk shirt half unbuttoned revealing his grizzled hairy chest with a fancy camera hanging from his neck, a pair of fashion models in sheer loose dresses at his side, decided Brody.

"I hear you're looking for Damian Playa," said Brockton Root.

"Have you seen him?" said Brody, turning away from the cocktail waitress wearing a copper taffeta outfit, who returned to serving her customers at the slots.

"I'm looking for him, too," said Root.

Brody didn't like the sound of that. The last person who had said something similar had ended up with a bullet in the back of his head.

"You can take a break now, girls," Root said with a wide smile to his companions. "We'll meet up later."

The two beauties wandered away eying the slots, chattering to each other, flicking at their hair as guys checked them out.

"We're on a photo shoot," said Root, touching the camera hanging from his neck. "Very beautiful, aren't they?" he said, watching the two models wander away.

Brody nodded yes.

"We share the same interests, it seems," said Root.

"I don't know what you mean," said Brody, wary of Root's hail-fellow-well-met routine.

"Damian Playa."

Brody looked blank. He didn't know this guy from Adam.

Lowering his voice Root moved closer to Brody. "My name's Brockton Root. I'm working for the CIA. We have reason to believe Damian Playa is involved in a conspiracy to overthrow President Ransom."

Brody didn't know whether Root was on the level.

Root ushered him to a less crowded area on the gaming floor near the high-roller slots.

"The CIA doesn't work on domestic soil," said Brody.

"This is part of an operation with its origins in Mexico."

"Why are you telling me?"

"Damian Playa's life is in danger."

Brody was beginning to suspect as much after Coscarelli had been shot dead in front of him.

"Why?" said Brody.

"A cartel is after him. They believe he stole their money."

"I don't know anything about that."

"What do you know about Cobalt Green Tide?"

Coscarelli had mentioned that name, decided Brody. He didn't know if he should tell Root about it.

"Nothing," said Brody.

"We believe the money Damian stole was earmarked for Cobalt Green Tide, but we don't know why. They're a shell company. We don't know who's operating it."

Brody didn't know if he could believe Root. Was the guy really CIA?

"I thought you were a fashion photographer," said Brody.

"It's my cover story. We know you're a private investigator. Have you found out anything about Damian's whereabouts?"

"No."

Brody didn't tell Root about Melody's meeting with Damian.

"We're trying to find out who operates Cobalt Green Tide," said Root. "It's a Delaware LLC so they don't have to publicize the names of their operators. We have no way to find out that information. We have suspicions, but no proof."

"I never heard of this company."

"Do you know if Damian stole the money?"

"I can't help you."

Root reached into his trouser pocket, fished out his wallet, and produced his business card with a phone number on it.

"Call me at this number when you find Damian," he said. "Since you're a private investigator, you may be able to find him before us. The bottom line is, we have to find him before the cartel does. They already put out a contract on him."

"I don't get it. How does Damian fit into this conspiracy you're talking about?"

"He's a bagman for the cartel."

"The Sinaloa cartel?"

"CJNG. The Jalisco New Generation cartel."

"Then why do they want to whack him?"

"They think he ripped them off. They sent a hit team of *sicarios* here to waste him." Root hung fire, letting his words sink in. "If you find Damian before I do, send him to me. The CIA can protect him."

"Does he know the hit team is coming for him?"

"All I know for sure is, he hasn't delivered the money to the Cobalt Green Tide bagman. That's why the cartel is so angry. They think he took the money for himself and split."

"Maybe he *did* split with the money."

Root shrugged. "Anything's possible. The thing is, the agency doesn't want Damian dead. The cartel *does*. We want him alive. We don't care if he ripped off the cartel. We want intel on Cobalt Green Tide. We can protect him. Tell him that."

Root turned to leave.

"I haven't found him yet," said Brody.

Root turned back to face him. "If we don't find him before the cartel does, he's dead meat."

Chapter 54

"Have you ever been to Madame Tussaud's?" said Damian as he walked with Ned Bates down the strip.

"The wax museum? Isn't that in London?"

"There's one here. Right over there. Let's go see it."

"They got everything here. The Eiffel Tower, the Brooklyn Bridge, a pyramid. And Madame Tussaud's. We don't have time." Ned Bates held up her valise. "I need the delivery."

"It won't take long. Ten minutes max."

"I can't stand this heat," she said, wiping sweat off her brow.

"The wax museum will cool us off. Ten minutes won't make any difference to our mission."

"Anything to get out of this heat for a few minutes. I'm feeling ill."

They took the travelator to the entrance to Madame Tussaud's, purchased their tickets, and entered the darkened museum.

Damian glanced behind him to see if Dominick was following them. Dominick saw them enter the wax museum, but didn't look concerned about it. Dominick didn't follow them inside. In case Dominick changed his mind, Damian would have to act quickly.

Wax statues of actors stood in the cool, dark museum. Damian was amazed at how realistic they looked. He expected them to move and start talking any minute. He found himself reacting to them as if they were human, as though they were returning his gaze.

At first, he didn't want to stare at them because people didn't like being stared at. He thought the statues would object. Then he remembered they were indeed statues. He could stare at them to his heart's content.

He had no time for admiring the statues.

He cast around for the darkest area of the museum, out of view of guests. He picked up on a shadowy nook near the statue of Rick Kane.

"Let's go over here," said Damian.

"I'm starting to feel better," said Ned Bates, accompanying him.

He spun her around, held her from behind, whipped out his knife, and jammed it to the hilt through the back of her neck between vertebrae beneath her skull, severing her spinal cord. She collapsed in his arms like a ventriloquist's puppet. He withdrew his knife. He sat her corpse in the dark corner a few feet away from Rick Kane's statue. Her vacant eyes stared out of her head.

Ned Bates looked like the other wax figures in the museum with their glassy eyes, decided Damian, concealing his bloody knife and stealing away from her in the shadows.

He had to get out of the museum before Ned Bates's corpse was discovered.

He didn't run. Running wasn't necessary. Worse, it was conspicuous. He walked briskly, glancing at the statues, feigning interest, as he found the exit. Just another customer, not a murderer leaving the scene of the crime.

Dominick picked up on him leaving the museum and waited for Ned Bates to appear at the exit. When Ned Bates didn't show, Dominick followed Damian.

Dominick had no idea Damian had whacked Ned Bates, and Damian intended to keep it that way.

On the hot crowded sidewalk Damian knew Don Gaetano would be suspicious when Ned Bates didn't call him, but he would be suspicious of Ned Bates as well as of Damian. Ned Bates could be the one ripping him off, for all Don Gaetano knew, casting less suspicion on Damian. Maybe Don Gaetano would revoke the contract on him.

Damian wasn't off the hook by any stretch of the imagination, he knew. A hit team was after him, and he figured they had orders to kill on sight. The other alternative was worse. That they had orders to torture him to find out where the money was before they killed him.

Roberto didn't mess around. He had racked up more kills than any other CJNG *sicario*. And Damian knew Roberto hated his guts because Damian used to be a cop.

Damian had one advantage. He had the protection of Armando Musante, which Don Gaetano knew nothing about.

Damian sidestepped a drunken bum sleeping on the sidewalk. Even though Damian was a loser, he felt like a hotshot with his very own bodyguard accompanying him.

Then again, Damian knew one bodyguard wouldn't stop an entire hit team of *sicarios* once they located him. He tried to lose himself in the throng of pedestrians, hoping to avoid detection by Roberto's team. With the beefy Dominick behind him, the hit men would have to think twice before going in for the kill.

Damian decided he couldn't stay in Vegas forever. But he had no idea where to go. Would anyplace be safe with *sicarios* out to whack him who would stop at nothing to complete their mission?

The only sure way to get Don Gaetano off his back was to give him his four hundred grand, Damian knew. Where was he going to get four hundred grand? Money was the impossible dream to him. He never had any.

Chapter 55

Wearing a grey sweatshirt with cut-off sleeves and grey sweatpants, Armando Musante was standing under the pink plastic blow-up doll hanging from his ceiling in his penthouse, talking into a burner.

A skinny teenage redhead all of fifteen named Toni was standing next to one of his massage tables in a bikini, her body oiled, watching him, prepared to give him a massage whenever he wanted.

"I'm glad I got ahold of you, Don Gaetano," said Musante.

"I'm always glad to talk business," said Don Gaetano at the other end of the transmission.

"It has come to my attention you're looking for a guy named Damian."

"Why would that be your concern?"

"With all due respect, I have found out this guy Damian might be in my territory and therefore would be under my protection."

A pause.

"Damian works for me and is accountable only to me no matter whose territory he's in," said Don Gaetano.

"He works for you?"

"Yeah."

"He says he can cut me in on your yayo and murder 8 network."

Don Gaetano laughed. "He's a bottom-feeding flunky. A *pendejo*. He has no power to cut deals for me."

"He says he can set me up nice."

"He can't tie his shoes without my permission."

"Why did he tell me he can cut deals for you?"

"He's trying to go into business for himself. The cockroach. I need to talk to him. He doesn't understand his position."

"He says you're forcing him to go into business for himself."

"How does he figure that?"

"Because you're trying to take him out."

Don Gaetano chuckled. "Why would I do that to one of my own?"

"Could there be a misunderstanding?"

"I need to talk to Damian. Can you put me in touch with him?"

"He's not here."

"But you can find him."

Restless, Musante roamed around under his blow-up doll. "I want to cut a deal with you."

"Why do I have to cut a deal to talk to my own employee?"

"I'm not gonna beat around the bush. I need yayo and murder 8. You can make that happen."

"Ah, and why do I want that to happen?"

"I'll give you Damian in return for a piece of your action. I can connect you to an army of buyers who have wads of dough to throw around."

Silence.

Musante figured Don Gaetano was mulling over the proposal. What was there to mull over? wondered Musante. It was a win-win proposition. Everyone was a winner. Musante won a cut of Don Gaetano's drug action, and Don Gaetano won thousands of new customers. Not only that, Don Gaetano would get his hands on Damian.

Whether Don Gaetano wanted Damian in order to whack him or hang him from a church spire was of no interest to Musante. Don Gaetano could do whatever he wanted with Damian.

Musante was a businessman, pure and simple. When he talked to Don Gaetano he smelled money. Damian was a bargaining chip, his life otherwise valueless to Musante.

"Let me get this straight," said Don Gaetano. "Are you saying you're protecting Damian?"

"I'm saying I'll give him to you for a piece of your action."

"Your thirty pieces of silver?"

"A lot more than that."

"You won't give him to me otherwise?"

"Why should I?"

"Because he works for me."

"He's afraid you're gonna take him out."

"Tell him his worries are baseless."

Musante was becoming impatient. "What's not to like about my offer? Everybody wins."

"I feel like you're twisting my arm."

"No such thing. We're conducting a perfect business transaction. Everything is perfect."

"I don't believe I'm getting anything out of this deal I couldn't get by myself."

"You're getting Damian."

"I already got him. He works for me, not you."

Musante became annoyed. He fought to bridle his temper. An outburst would torpedo his offer.

"This is a great deal," he said.

"I need to think it over," said Don Gaetano, and terminated the call.

Put out, Musante flung his burner onto the sofa.

"Throw that into the incinerator," he said, gesturing to the burner.

Toni rushed over to the burner.

"Not now," said Musante. "I'm tense," he said, rocking his head back and forth and stretching. He rubbed his back. "I need a massage."

Tossing off his sweatshirt he strode to the massage table.

He lay on his stomach. "Start with my feet then work on my back. And remove my pants."

Don Gaetano was a hard nut to crack, decided Musante. These cartel bastards all were. In the end the guy would see it Musante's way. Musante was sure of it. Until that time he would continue to thwart Don Gaetano and protect Damian. Musante wanted to make Don Gaetano's life as difficult as possible until Don Gaetano cut him in on his drug trade.

Now it was time to relax, he decided, as he felt Toni's gentle touch massaging his feet.

Chapter 56

Melody jerked awake, terrified at the realization she was a victim in life. She didn't want to be a victim. She wanted to be a helper. It was one reason she had become a lifeguard.

She didn't feel like a helper anymore. She felt like a victim, turned into one by her murderous husband. She wanted to scream.

She had no idea where she was. She looked around.

She was sitting in a twilit restaurant in a corner booth, a glass of Sancerre wine in front of her.

She must have fallen asleep while she was drinking her wine. She hadn't slept for two days out of fear her homicidal husband would find her.

Out of the corner of her eye she thought she glimpsed him striding through the restaurant near the bar. She tensed with fear. He disappeared from view. If it was him, he hadn't seen her thanks to the dim track lighting of the restaurant.

Could it really have been him? she wondered. How could he have found her? Maybe she was only half awake in a dream state. She could have dreamed Dan in the restaurant. But she didn't think so.

She was scared. Her sleeplessness was destroying her life, turning her into a nervous wreck. She needed to be able to relax and sleep a solid eight hours.

She wondered if she would ever be able to sleep again.

She rooted through her purse and dug out her cell phone. She called Brody.

"I need your help," she said.

"What happened?" said Brody.

"I think Dan found me."

"You saw him?"

"I'm pretty sure it was him. It's dark in here."

"Did he see you?"

"I don't know. I fell asleep in the restaurant. When I awoke, I saw him."

"If he had seen you, wouldn't he have confronted you?"

"I guess. Unless he didn't want to cause a commotion in the restaurant."

"Have you seen Damian?"

"No. I need your help."

"Is Dan still in the restaurant with you?"

"I don't see him. But the lighting here is bad. He could be here at another booth."

"Tell me where you are."

She told him. "How fast can you get here?"

"Ten minutes. Sit tight."

Chapter 57

Brody made his way down the busy sidewalk, his face gleaming with sweat, narrowly avoiding a white-clad Elvis impersonator riding in an electric wheelchair speeding down the cement with indifference to pedestrians.

"Fake," somebody cried after him after dodging the wheelchair and falling on the sidewalk.

A vagrant rolling his life's belongings in a suitcase laughed. "He needs some jailhouse rock."

Brody felt an arm grab him from behind and force him into an alley.

A wiry twentysomething guy in an olive drab wife beater shoved him.

Stumbling, Brody prepared to defend himself.

"I hear you're asking questions about Damian," said Roberto, a green and yellow tattoo of Santa Muerte on his neck.

"What's it to you?" said Brody, regaining his balance.

Roberto bent over and whipped out a piece from an ankle holster. He trained the muzzle on Brody.

"Stay out of this," said Roberto with dead eyes.

Brody thought about reaching for his SIG snugged in his rear waistband. He figured the gangbanger could waste him before he got his hand on the grip.

His face sweated even more than it had been. Heat-and-fear sweat. He had no idea who the gangbanger was. The guy must have had something to do with Damian.

Brody moved his hand.

Roberto's sweat-gleamy face took in the movement. Roberto thrust his piece's muzzle toward Brody.

"Don't move," said Roberto.

"I need to talk to Damian."

"He's mine. Stop asking questions and get out of town."

"I'm not ready to leave yet."

"You don't like living?"

It was true Damian was mixed up with gangbangers, decided Brody.

"I have news for Damian," he said.

"I have news for you. Get out of town or die."

"I have a job to do."

"This is your final warning. Next time, I'll shoot you dead before you know what hit you."

"Do you want to go to the slam that bad?"

Roberto scowled. "You think this is a comedy routine? I just said you'd be dead."

With Roberto's gun trained on him Brody felt his heart jackhammering. The guy could pull the trigger any second, Brody knew. Showing fear wasn't the way to handle him.

Maybe the gangbanger would change his mind and squeeze the trigger now, decided Brody. The notion did nothing to alleviate his apprehension. Brody could still make a play for his SIG P365. But the laws of physics must be obeyed. He couldn't bend them to his will. There was no way he could reach his pistol and bring it to bear on the gangbanger before the gangbanger let loose a shot at him.

True, Brody would have the advantage of surprise if he made the first move. But the advantage would last no more than a nanosecond—the time it took for the gangbanger to perceive Brody's hand moving.

Brody didn't move.

The gangbanger looked like a hothead who could flip out on a dime, decided Brody. The guy could be wired on crank or yayo. His sweat-slick face was sneering and grimacing at the same time, body taut.

It wasn't the time to taunt him, decided Brody.

A black Cadillac turned into the alley from the strip and drove past him and Roberto. A chauffeur pushing forty in black livery, complete with a black cap, tooled down the alley, glancing at Brody.

Roberto concealed his pistol and darted out of sight back into the mob of pedestrians that crammed the sidewalk.

The Caddy drove to the rear of the casino.

Brody wiped sweat from his forehead.

Another player who wanted a piece of Damian, decided Brody.

Brody bolted to the sidewalk casting around for Roberto, eying the sweat-shiny faces around him. No sign of him. The guy could have cut back out of sight into a casino, decided Brody.

He wondered why the gangbanger hadn't shot him. Because of the throng of pedestrians spilling over the sidewalk no doubt. Murder in plain sight was never a good idea. A professional assassin like the gangbanger would know this. The tattoo of Santa Muerte indicated the guy was a *sicario*.

Araceli was right to be worried about her brother, decided Brody. Somehow Damian was involved with *sicarios*, the FBI, and the CIA. *Sicarios* worked for drug cartels, making a cartel another player. The CJNG, if you could believe Root.

Brody didn't know how he was going to get to Damian before all of these other players.

He felt his cell phone vibrate in his trouser pocket.

He took the call.

"Where are you?" said Melody, her voice panic-stricken. "I don't want Dan to find me here."

"I got delayed. Give me a couple minutes."

He put away his cell phone.

He made for the Mon Ami Gabi Restaurant at the Paris, but not before scanning the crowd one last time for sign of the gangbanger that had bushwhacked him. Brody didn't catch sight of him. Just as well, Brody decided. His job was to find Damian, not to hunt down *sicarios*.

Chapter 58

Brody walked into the Mon Ami Gabi.

He didn't see Melody right off. Coming in off the blinding strip he needed to let his eyes adjust to the dim-set restaurant lamps before he could make out anything. He blinked his eyes, waiting for his pupils to adjust.

The AC-cooled air felt chilly on his moist face.

His vision adapted to its new environment.

He scoped out the booths, walking toward them.

He saw her huddled in a dark corner of a booth meant for a romantic assignation with its candle-lit table.

She started when she saw him approach, mistaking him for her husband Dan, he supposed.

She sighed with relief when she recognized him.

"I thought you were Dan," she said.

He sat across from her. "Is he still here?"

"I haven't seen him since the first time."

"Are you sure it was him?"

She rubbed her eyes. "I'm not positive. I was half awake when I saw him."

"Why?"

"What?"

"Why were you half awake?"

"I haven't slept in two days. I can't sleep till I know he can't get me."

"Where are you staying?"

"Some dive at the edge of town. I don't feel safe there. The locks on the doors are a joke. They're not even dead bolts."

She sipped her glass of iced tea.

He wouldn't call her beautiful in the classic sense of the word. Her nose wasn't quite straight. But there was a sensuousness about her, especially in the full lips and the supple figure—

He told himself to concentrate on his job.

She picked up on his interest in her.

"Maybe you could stay with me tonight," she said. "It would make me feel better."

"I'm working for my first client."

A waitress breezed by their table.

"Could I get you something to drink?" she asked him.

"A bottle of cold Perrier."

She disappeared.

"It's too hot outside," he said.

"You're telling me," said Melody.

"We need to make sure this is a business relationship."

"Why are you so concerned about that?"

"It's important for your health."

She looked bemused.

"I don't want to alarm you, but I better tell you the truth," he said.

"Yeah."

"My father was a drunkard and a serial killer," said Brody. "He killed five women before the cops caught up to him."

Nonplussed, she stared at him.

Chapter 59

The waitress gave Brody a glass and poured Perrier from a green bottle into it.

"Thank you. That'll be all for now," he said.

She retreated to another customer.

"Really?" said Melody, still reeling from Brody's revelation.

Brody nodded yes.

"It's not your fault your father was a murderer," said Melody.

"No. But it might have something to do with my relationships with women."

"Are you saying *you* killed your wife and that Hollywood actress you were seeing?"

"It wasn't me. Psycho killers did them," he said, taking a pull on his Perrier.

"Then it wasn't your fault."

"Then why does it keep happening?"

"Are you saying it's some kind of curse on you?"

Brody didn't know what he was saying. He was trying to look at it objectively.

"I don't believe in curses," he said.

"Sins of the father . . .?"

"I don't go around murdering women. But the women I get involved with *are* murdered."

"You're not lucky with women, is all." Melody paused in thought. "And I'm not lucky with men, it seems."

"I don't believe it's just luck. I can see it happening once and figure it's bad luck, but not twice."

"Maybe you're suffering from PTSD. What you've gone through had to be traumatic."

Brody swigged his Perrier. "I'm all right. I can do my job, so I'm all right. If I couldn't function and do my job, I'd agree with you."

"But it's obvious something's eating you."

"My wife and a girl I was starting to like a lot both died at the hands of murderers. What are the chances?"

"It was a fluke. These things happen."

"Nobody's luck is that bad." Brody chewed it over. "It's more like it's my fate that my relationships with women end badly."

"If you really believe that, they *will* end badly. You're psyching yourself out."

Brody felt like he was being psychoanalyzed. He didn't like the feeling.

"I'm just telling you what I'm bringing to the table," he said.

"It's anecdotal. It's not based on fact."

"My experiences in life are facts to me."

"I'm getting a headache thinking about this. We're both damaged goods. Maybe that's why we get along with each other."

"Maybe," said Brody, but he wasn't convinced.

He believed there was a black cloud hanging over him. He didn't know why it was there. How could you know the why of anything?

He looked around the restaurant. "Do you see your husband here?"

"No."

He faced her. "You could've imagined seeing him. You said you were half awake. It could've been a bad dream."

"It seemed real."

"Do you want to inspect the restaurant to make sure he's not here? *I* can't do it because I don't know what he looks like."

She picked up her pocketbook and rummaged through it till she dug out her wallet, which contained a photo of Dan. She showed Brody the photo of a middle-aged guy with a rugged face.

It reminded Brody of the guy that used to do Marlboro commercials on TV, the guy in a cowboy hat and a fleece-lined jacket who sat on his horse smoking, his face dried out by the sun and rough like sandpaper.

"Have you seen him here?" she said, accepting the photo back from him.

"I'll take a look around," he said, got up, and ambled around the restaurant, pretending to look for the men's room.

He wandered onto the patio that overlooked the sidewalk. The cool air-conditioned air dissipated in the open patio area, and he could feel the heat from outside, despite the spritzers on the border of the patio that continuously sprayed cold water vapor onto the edge of the patio and onto the sidewalk.

The heat muddled his mind. The restaurant's AC was much more effective than the spritzers at cooling the temperature.

He saw smiling diners around him enjoying their meals and their company. He didn't see Dan.

He returned to the cool interior of the restaurant, scoped out the banquettes, the bar, and the booths, and took his seat across from Melody.

She eyed him expectantly.

"He's not here," he said.

She sighed with relief. "He must not have seen me and left."

She took a pull on her wine.

He knocked back his Perrier.

"I better get back to my job, since you're OK here," he said, fixing to leave.

Concern on her face, she reached across the tabletop and grabbed his hand. "Do you have to leave so soon?"

"He's not here. You don't need my protection."

"Maybe he'll come back."

"We're not sure he was here in the first place."

"He was."

Brody stared into the distance and started rubbing his hands together like a fly.

"What's wrong?" said Melody.

Brody snapped out of it. "Nothing. I have epilepsy."

A mild seizure, he decided. Why did he tell her? he wondered, instantly regretting it. He had an unwritten rule never to tell his clients his condition lest they fire him. Why had he let his guard down? It showed he was getting too close to her. He needed to back off.

"Maybe you *are* cursed," she said.

"I don't believe in that superstitious nonsense."

"It must be hereditary. Did your father have it?"

"I have no idea what he had. He never told me anything about himself. If you see Dan again, call me."

He left, not looking back. *Strictly business*, he told himself. *Keep it that way.* Or she would end up murdered.

Chapter 60

Clad in white boxer shorts, Don Gaetano was lying on his stomach on his bed in his hacienda peering into the mirror on his bedroom wall waiting for Valentina to open the door. He saw the mirror's reflection of the glistening doorknob turn and the door nudge open.

Valentina slipped into the room, wearing her black Allgemeine SS hat and a black leather Gestapo trench coat that reached the ankles of her glossy black jackboots.

The heels of her jackboots clacked across the parquet floor. She came to a halt in the middle of the floor and shucked off her trench coat, which slid in a puddle around her jackboots, to reveal her nakedness.

Valentina stooped to retrieve her riding crop from her trench coat's pocket, her breasts swaying, and straightened up, snapping the crop on her open palm.

She walked slowly toward him.

Don Gaetano couldn't wait for her to reach him. He ached for her touch. She understood that all he ever wanted out of life was love—

The satphone on his nightstand wailed.

Cursing, he sat up, leapt out of bed, and latched onto the satphone.

"Talk," he said.

Disappointed, Valentina stopped striking her palm with the riding crop.

"It's me," said Roberto at the other end of the encrypted transmission.

"Did you find Damian?"

"Not yet."

"Then why are you calling me?" said Don Gaetano, scowling.

"I found out Root is working for the CIA."

Don Gaetano paused. "No, he isn't."

"I overheard him talking to someone asking questions about Damian. Root said he worked for the CIA."

"Listen to me. He doesn't work for the CIA. Take care of Damian and call me back."

"But, *patrón*, I'm sure I heard him say—"

Don Gaetano terminated the call.

He flung on jeans and a guayabera shirt and left the bedroom.

Valentina pouted with dismay.

Shutting the door behind him so Carmen wouldn't see Valentina, Don Gaetano stormed out of the bedroom, across the capacious living room, and out onto the patio, where he caught sight of Arturo.

"Arturo," he said.

"*Sí, patrón*," said Arturo, who was sitting on a lawn chair drinking a tequila.

He bolted out of his seat and approached Don Gaetano, all ears.

"Roberto says he knows Root works for the CIA," said Don Gaetano.

"How did he find out?"

"It doesn't matter."

"Did you tell him the truth?"

"No. It's not his place to know. You and me are the only ones that know the truth. That Root is our mole in the CIA. They think he works for them, but in reality he's our eyes and ears in their agency. That's how we always know when CIA spooks fly into Guadalajara. Root tells us."

"The CIA stupidly thinks Root works for them."

"We know better, but don't tell Roberto if he asks you about it. I don't want anyone else to know about Root. It could blow his cover, and one of our guys might end up shooting him. We can't let that happen."

"No, *patrón*."

"We need Root's intel. He can ID CIA spies on flight manifests into Guadalajara. With our connections we have access to all flight manifests into the city."

"We're always one step ahead of those *pendejos*," said Arturo with a grin.

Don Gaetano picked up on two figures approaching from the driveway to the pool deck.

It was Michael, and he was holding a Goat Horn on a twentysomething pudgy short guy in a white T, baggy jeans, and sneakers.

Chapter 61

"*Patrón,*" said Michael, "this guy says he wants to join us, but I know he's a Zeta. I swear I've seen him with Zetas."

"That's a lie," said Pudge, his face sweaty. "I'm no Zeta. I hate Zetas."

"You're calling Michael a liar?" said Don Gaetano.

"No, no. I mean, he's mistaken. He saw somebody else, not me, with the Zetas, *patrón.*"

Teeth clenched, Michael jabbed his AK's muzzle into Pudge's belly. "You're calling me a liar?"

"Ow." Pudge doubled over in pain.

"Do you know who you're calling a liar?" Don Gaetano asked Pudge.

"I'm no Zeta. Fuck Zetas."

"This is Michael Corleone, son of my right-hand man Arturo."

"He's mistaken, is all. I'm no Zeta."

"The Zetas have tried to infiltrate my cartel before. They've never succeeded."

"I hate Zetas."

"Get an oil drum and the chain saw from the toolshed," Don Gaetano told Arturo.

"The chain saw, too?" said Arturo, puzzled.

"You heard me."

Arturo made for the toolshed across the backyard, whistled, and signaled to two of his armed men who were guarding the driveway to accompany him.

"Nobody calls Michael Corleone Casa a liar," Don Gaetano told Pudge.

Arturo's two men wheeled a fifty-five gallon oil drum out of the shed on a dolly. They rolled the dolly across the lawn toward the pool. Arturo carried a chain saw.

Don Gaetano raised his hand and gestured for them to stop. "Leave it there."

Arturo had his men spin the oil drum off the dolly and deposit it on the lawn.

"Take the Zeta to the drum," Don Gaetano told Michael.

"I'm no Zeta," said Pudge.

"Get going," Michael told Pudge, goading him with the AK's barrel.

"You're making a mistake," said Pudge, shoved by Michael to the oil drum.

"You're the one that made the mistake of coming here," said Michael.

He prodded Pudge across the lawn to the drum.

"Put him in the drum," said Don Gaetano, watching from the pool deck.

Arturo's two men struggled to lift Pudge into the drum.

"No," said Pudge, squirming frantically.

"Don't fight them or I'll shoot you," said Michael.

The two CJNG gangbangers tried to stuff Pudge feet first into the top of the oil-filled drum. Oil splashed out of the drum as they packed him inside.

"He won't fit," said Michael with a smirk. "His belly's too big."

"Cut it off," said Don Gaetano.

Arturo cranked the chain saw, as his two men held Pudge in the oil drum.

"No," screamed Pudge.

Arturo raised the churning chain saw above his head and nodded to his men.

They stepped away from the oil drum.

Arturo brought the chain saw's blade down on Pudge's belly, slicing through it so Pudge would fit into the drum.

Blood jetted out of Pudge's stomach.

Pudge screamed in horror.

"He's making too much noise," Don Gaetano said under his breath.

Pudge slid farther down into the drum as the chain saw completed its swath through his belly. His bloody entrails unraveled out and slid down the side of the drum.

"Step away from the drum," Don Gaetano told Arturo.

The chain saw in his hands, Arturo stepped away from the oil drum, where Pudge bled out.

Don Gaetano's father Javier rode his electric wheelchair out of the hacienda to Don Gaetano. Confined to a wheelchair thanks to his Alzheimer's, Javier looked at his son, wondering what was going on, his mouth gaping.

"It's nothing, Papa," said Don Gaetano.

Javier glanced at Pudge's bleeding body and tried to talk to Don Gaetano. Gobbledygook issued from Javier's mouth.

"Use the dragon," Don Gaetano told Michael.

Michael gathered the flamethrower from the corner of the patio and trained it on Pudge.

Arturo watched Michael with concern.

Michael paid no attention to him. He pulled the flamethrower's trigger.

Sizzling blue and yellow flame spat from the nozzle, arced thirty feet across the yard, and engulfed Pudge and the oil-filled drum.

Pudge let out a bloodcurdling scream.

Carmen called out from the living room, "The neighbors are complaining about screams."

"We have the worst neighbors," Don Gaetano told Michael, shaking his head in disgust. "Why can't we have decent neighbors?"

"Want me to shut them up?" said Michael, lowering the flamethrower.

"No. We can't go around killing our neighbors, can we? Then we'd have anarchy."

"Bitches should be whacked."

"I'll be the judge of that. Your father's coming."

"I think my father is . . . ," said Michael, trailing off.

"Is what?" said Don Gaetano.

"I've been meaning to tell you, he's showing signs of weakness," said Michael, keeping his voice low.

"Arturo? Ha! Not Arturo. He's the toughest hombre I ever met. There's nobody I'd rather have on my side than your father," said Don Gaetano, smiling.

Michael didn't look convinced as he watched Arturo approach.

"You did a good job blowing the Zeta spy's cover and using the dragon on him, Michael," said Don Gaetano, watching Pudge's charred upright skeleton smoldering in the oil drum, a rictus in its skull blowing fitful puffs of smoke.

Michael nodded and put away the flamethrower.

Javier gazed in horror at Pudge's corpse wedged inside the oil drum.

"Can we talk in private, *patrón*?" said Arturo.

"Of course," said Don Gaetano, draping his arm around Arturo's neck. "Let's go inside." To Michael he said, "You can go now."

Javier muttered incoherently.

"Papa, don't stay near the pool unless someone else is present," said Don Gaetano.

Javier kept staring at the smoking oil drum.

"He loses control of his wheelchair sometimes," Don Gaetano told Arturo. "It's his Alzheimer's. It's eating away at him, killing him a little bit at a time."

Arturo nodded, face glum. "Death by a thousand cuts."

"I don't want him left here by himself because he might drown in the pool."

"I can watch your father," said Michael.

"Thank you, Michael."

Don Gaetano and Arturo disappeared into the hacienda.

Michael grabbed Javier's wheelchair from behind, turned off its power switch, and rolled Javier toward the swimming pool.

"Want to go for a dip?" said Michael.

Clutching the armrests of his wheelchair with clenched fingers, Javier gaped in fear as he neared the water.

Michael pushed the wheelchair to the edge of the water, which rippled in the sunlight.

"Are you ready?" he said.

A scream of terror caught in Javier's throat as he held onto his wheelchair for dear life, his fingernails digging into the leather armrests, his knuckles white.

Michael lifted the wheelchair from behind and tilted Javier toward the pool. He had thought Javier would weigh more.

"How many laps can you do around the pool?" said Michael.

Javier made a gargling sound in his throat, his eyes huge, as his face neared the pool water. He held onto the armrests tighter in fear of falling into the water.

"What?" said Michael. "I couldn't make that out."

Javier's wheelchair wobbled precariously at the pool's edge. Javier refused to release his grasp on the armrests.

"Let go of the armrests," said Michael.

Javier didn't budge his fingers.

Michael heard the pool water lapping as a humid breeze swept over it.

"How long can you hold your breath?" he said, towering over Javier from behind.

"Javier, where are you?" called Carmen from the hacienda.

Michael lowered the back of Javier's wheelchair and rolled him away from the pool's edge.

"He's over here," he told Carmen.

Chapter 62

As Don Gaetano and Arturo entered the living room, a four-foot-long green iguana scampered past them heading out the door. The iguana had a round mark in its neck that looked like one of Frankenstein's neck bolts. Its baggy dewlap hung halfway to the floor.

"Where's the fire, Mojo?" said Don Gaetano, watching the iguana shoot out the door.

The iguana kept going, ignoring him as it made for the pool deck and the hot sun.

"Do iguanas make good pets?" said Arturo.

"You have to pamper them or they die young."

Carmen entered the living room, wearing a scarlet dress, her raven hair tumbling onto her shoulders, her heels clacking on the hardwood floor like castanets.

"I just got off the phone with the mayor," she said. "He wants more money."

"Of course the mayor wants more money," said Don Gaetano. "Was ever a politician born without his hand out 24/7?"

"He said he'll be visiting us for a donation to his campaign for reelection."

"And I'll give it to him. Or I'd have to put out a contract on him."

"*Plata o plomo, eh, patrón?*" said Arturo with a sly grin. Silver or lead.

"It's how we do business. He lets us know in advance whenever the cops are gonna make a move against us. He's our stoolie-mayor."

"He knows which side his bread's buttered on."

"What do we do about the neighbors?" said Carmen. "They keep complaining to me."

Don Gaetano shrugged uncertainly. "Maybe you shouldn't even talk to them anymore."

"If only they'd stop complaining about us."

"They need to get a life."

"That woman griped a few minutes ago that she could smell burning oil coming from our yard."

"Is that all they do all day? Sit in their hacienda and spy on us?"

"I'm getting tired of them."

"That's why we have trees surrounding our property—to keep out prying eyes."

"Still they complain," said Carmen, stalking out of the living room.

"What did you want to talk about, Arturo?" said Don Gaetano.

"I think you're being too hard on Michael."

"I don't know what you mean."

"You're making him grow up too fast, giving him assignments meant for adults. He's just a kid."

"He has to grow up fast if he wants to join CJNG."

"But it's messing up his personality. It makes him withdrawn."

"He doesn't seem withdrawn to me."

"He won't talk to me."

"That's between you two."

Arturo paced to the sofa, deep in thought. He turned around and faced Don Gaetano.

"He's too young to be handling this kind of pressure, *patrón*," said Arturo.

"What pressure?"

"Blowing up a church full of parishioners. Using a flamethrower on a Zeta. He's too young for that."

"No, he's not. He's doing just fine." Don Gaetano approached Arturo and patted him on the back. "I can understand your trying to shelter him from the jungle of the real world because he's your flesh and blood, but he doesn't need it, Arturo. You're being overprotective. You're mothering him."

"I don't want him to take on more than he can handle. It could get him killed." He bowed his head. "I don't think I could stand it if he died while I was alive. I would blame myself for the rest of my life."

"You're overreacting. Michael can take care of himself. You'll see."

Chapter 63

Brody returned to his room at the Venetian and awoke his laptop from Sleep mode. He logged into the Elysian Fields chat room as Myshkin.

Myshkin: Anybody here?

Margaux Hemingway: Hello, Myshkin. How are you?

Myshkin: Do you think our condition is a curse?

Teddy Roosevelt: Like something a witch puts on you? Not at all. I don't believe in curses.

Myshkin: Some people think it's a curse.

Teddy Roosevelt: It just shows they don't know anything about it.

Margaux Hemingway: You hang around with the wrong people, Myshkin.

Julius Caesar: What kind of people are you hanging around, Myshkin?

Myshkin: I meet a lot of people in my job.

Teddy Roosevelt: I've met a lot of jerks when it comes to our condition. That's why I don't tell anyone I have it.

Julius Caesar: Are you afraid to say what you believe?

Teddy Roosevelt: What's that got to do with anything? Epilepsy is a condition, not a belief.

Julius Caesar: We're talking about epilepsy?

Teddy Roosevelt: What did you think we were talking about? Why do you think you're in this group? People need to be educated about it.

Julius Caesar: Are you blaming the government?

Teddy Roosevelt: I'm just saying. That's why we're here in this chat room.

Myshkin: I don't believe in curses, but other people do.

Julius Caesar: We can make changes if we want.

Myshkin: What kind of changes?

Julius Caesar: Isn't that why we're here?

Margaux Hemingway: We're here to talk about our condition. Oh. My dog needs to go out. I have to go. Bye.

Brody felt his cell phone vibrate in his trouser pocket.

Myshkin: Yeah. Till next time.

Brody logged off. He answered his cell.

"This is Araceli. Have you found Damian yet?"

"No," said Brody. "The guy's leading a double life, though."

"What do you mean?"

"He's got *sicarios* after him."

"*Sicarios*?"

"They're hit men that work for cartels."

"I knew he was in trouble. You gotta find him before they do."

"Why would they be after him?"

"I have no idea. I know he's a loser, but I didn't know he was involved with any cartels."

"I found out he's still in Vegas. I'll keep looking for him."

"Is he OK?"

"I haven't made contact with him yet."

"Let me know as soon as you find him."

"Will do."

He terminated the call.

Chapter 64

Roberto wanted to find Damian before anyone else did, especially before Brockton Root. Roberto wished Root hadn't come with him to Vegas and didn't understand why Don Gaetano had sent Root with him.

As soon as Roberto and Root had arrived in Vegas, they had gone their separate ways, which was fine with Roberto. Without Root as an anchor on his activities, Roberto could go about his business and whack out Damian without interference.

Roberto never had any intention to allow Damian to live. Roberto knew Don Gaetano wanted his money back more than anything and hadn't ordered Damian's death. Not yet, anyway. Don Gaetano wasn't sure if Damian had ripped him off or something had happened to the guy.

Roberto, on the other hand, wanted Damian dead from the get-go. The guy was an ex-cop. Don Gaetano should never have hired Damian in the first place. No cop could ever be trusted.

Roberto was walking over a pedestrian bridge spanning Las Vegas Boulevard on his way to Bally's, where Don Gaetano had told him Damian had said he was staying. The bridge had cement parapets topped by sheets of Plexiglas to keep pedestrians from jumping into the traffic and committing suicide.

Sweating from the heat Roberto saw a homeless bum sitting on the cement walkway selling bottled water for a dollar to tourists.

"Want a cold water?" the vagrant asked Roberto, holding up a sweaty plastic bottle of Dasani water.

Roberto fished out a twenty-dollar bill and Damian's photo from his wallet and showed them to the bum.

"Have you seen this guy around here?" said Roberto.

The bearded bum gazed at the photo with his bleached-out blue eyes, a strand of drool depending from the corner of his mouth.

Roberto felt a wave of pity for the bum. What a life. Sitting all day in the boiling sun, his face sunburnt and peeling, his lips chapped, hawking water. What had happened in his life to turn him into a vagrant?

The bum made to grab the photo so he could see it better.

Roberto pulled it away from him. "Have you seen him here?"

"I wanted a better look, is all, to make sure."

"You saw him?" said Roberto, waving the twenty in front of the bum.

"Yeah, I saw him."

"When?" said Roberto, eyes intent.

The bum scratched his long scraggly unwashed sun-bleached hair. "Not long ago."

"How long?"

Shielding his eyes, squinting, the bum gazed into the sky, trying to locate the sun.

"I don't have a watch," he said. "I can't be sure. From the direction of the sun, I'd say an hour or two."

"Was he going in the same direction as me?"

"Yeah."

"Are you making this shit up?"

"No. Why would I?"

"To get this twenty," said Roberto, flapping the bill in the bum's face.

"I saw him, I tell you," said the bum, holding out his empty hand for the twenty, squinting up at Roberto.

Roberto gave him the twenty and looked around the bridge.

Seeing nobody on it he reached down, withdrew his piece from his ankle holster, shot the bum in the temple, and retrieved his twenty from the bum's now dangling hand.

The bum slumped against the bridge's cement parapet like he was sleeping off a drunk.

The feeling of pity had left Roberto.

Chapter 65

Brody was surprised to see Brockton Root walking beside him down the strip.

Maybe he shouldn't have been, decided Brody. The guy could have been following him, thinking Brody could lead him to Damian.

Root's face gleamed with a film of sweat on it, like Brody's. Two shiny faces glittering under the sun. Root's bald head was especially bright with sweat and red with sunburn, decided Brody. Root's ritzy camera hung from a leather strap around his neck.

"They murdered Ned Bates," said Root under his breath.

Brody stopped in his tracks. "What?"

"They took out Ned Bates in Madame Tussaud's Wax Museum."

"Who did and who's this Ned Bates?"

"She was a bagman for Cobalt Green Tide."

They were strolling down the sidewalk in front of the Planet Hollywood Casino among a gaggle of gibbering Chinese tourists taking selfies, some of them using selfie sticks. Brody jerked his head back to avoid getting poked in the eye by one of the sticks.

"What's Cobalt Green Tide?" he said.

"They're a shell company," said Root. "They shuttle money behind the scenes so there's no record of it exchanging hands. So-called dark money."

"Who's running it?"

"That's the sixty-four-thousand-dollar question," said Root, jabbing his forefinger at Brody's chest.

"And who killed Ned Bates?"

"The cops don't have any suspects."

"Do you?"

"The cartel had something to do with it, since Ned Bates was supposed to get money from CJNG's bagman Damian."

"Why would the cartel kill Ned Bates?"

"Maybe somebody in the cartel got greedy and jacked the money from Ned Bates after Damian handed it off to him."

"Who?"

"Anybody who knew Ned Bates had four hundred grand on her—if she *did* have it on her. Maybe Damian hadn't given her the dough yet."

"You're saying the cops didn't find the money on Ned Bates?"

"Exactly."

"What's this got to do with me?"

"It has to do with Damian, and you're trying to find him to help him. Meaning your life's in danger."

"I don't see how you can help me."

"I believe you know more than you're telling me about this. Otherwise, why would you be talking to the FBI?"

"You mean Coscarelli."

"Yeah."

Brody didn't know how much he could tell Root about Coscarelli, since Coscarelli had wanted him to sign an NDA. Brody hadn't signed it, but he *had* signed the one deceased Special Agent Peltz had given him. Since Peltz was dead, did that mean the NDA wasn't valid? Brody didn't know the law on NDAs, especially ones you signed for the feds—or ex-feds, which had been the case with Peltz. Peltz had told him he would be guilty of violating the Espionage Act if he violated the NDA.

But Root was CIA, decided Brody. Didn't that mean Brody could talk freely about what Peltz had told him about the cabal plotting inside the FBI to remove President Ransom from office using the Twenty-fifth Amendment and replacing him with Vice President Dealey?

How was he violating the Espionage Act if he confided in a CIA agent? wondered Brody. Did the cabal number CIA as well as FBI agents in its ranks?

"How do I know you're really CIA?" said Brody.

"You have to trust me. I'm working undercover so I can't go around carrying a CIA badge. You understand that?"

"I guess."

Root *did* seem to know a lot about what was going on concerning Damian, decided Brody.

Brody didn't know what to do. He could use help against the cartel's *sicarios*, but he didn't know how much help the CIA could actually supply—if any.

It would be nice to have someone on his side, decided Brody.

The Chinese tourists continued grinning and snapping selfies of each other as they paraded down the boulevard.

"If Cobalt Green Tide's bagman was killed, aren't they gonna be angry?" said Brody.

"A lot of people are gonna be angry. The thing is, we don't know who's running Cobalt Green Tide. We've been unable to ID anybody in the LLC."

"How do you know Ned Bates was working for them?"

"I got the skinny straight from the horse's mouth, the leader of CJNG."

"Why doesn't he tell you who's behind Cobalt Green Tide?"

"If I ask too many questions, he might decide I'm really working for the CIA."

"Don't ask me. I have no idea who's in this shell company."

"Whatever they're doing is illegal. They're accepting four hundred grand of narco money to fund what we don't know. What we do know is, Ned Bates came to Vegas from Reagan Airport in DC. We therefore suspect Cobalt Green

Tide is based in DC and could be aiming to destabilize our government. How we don't know."

"You think this narco money could be earmarked for funding a coup?"

"Why do you say that?" said Root, leaning closer to Brody and screwing up his eye.

"Just asking."

Brody wondered if Cobalt Green Tide had anything to do with Peltz's contention that conspirators were plotting within the FBI to overthrow President Ransom. He wasn't sure he should tell Root.

"Where are your girlfriends?" said Brody.

"It's too hot for them. They're like delicate flowers. They wilt under the hot sun."

Brody and Root were walking past an ice cream parlor when Brody heard a gunshot and glass cracking behind him. He whipped his head around and saw a bullet hole in the parlor's window. He whipped his head back in the opposite direction. He didn't spot anyone with a gun.

"Let's beat it," said Root.

They bolted down the sidewalk, dodging pedestrians, and ducked into Harrah's.

Chapter 66

Once inside Harrah's air-conditioned gaming room, Brody checked to see if anybody was following them.

He didn't see anyone.

Standing beside Brody, Root checked as well.

"Was that slug meant for you or me?" said Root.

"Me," said Brody. "I had a run-in with a *sicario* earlier."

"For a hit man, he's not a very good shot."

"He could've missed intentionally as a warning."

"You need to tell me what you know. Maybe the agency can help."

"Let's get a drink," said Brody, his throat parched from the heat.

They bellied up to a bar, commandeered stools, and ordered beers. Brody also ordered a glass of water.

Brody decided he better come clean, in spite of the NDA he had signed for Peltz. If Root didn't know about the NDA, how would he ever find out about it? decided Brody. At rest in a coffin, Peltz couldn't tell him or anyone else. If nobody knew Brody had signed the NDA, nobody could report him for violating it. The question was, had Peltz shared the NDA with anyone else? Since the FBI had given Peltz the boot, Brody figured the answer was no. Unless Peltz had a friend he had confided in . . . like a fellow fed . . .

Wearing an earring a hatchet-faced gaunt bartender with a Russian accent and an open collar served their beers and Brody's water.

Brody twisted around on his stool and scoped out the casino gaming room in search of the shooter. The coast was clear. He faced forward.

"An FBI agent told me a cabal within the FBI is plotting to remove President Ransom from office using the Twenty-fifth Amendment," he said. "Vice President Dealey and the cabal are working in cahoots."

"Who told you this?" said Root.

"I don't know if I should tell you his name."

"Did he give you any proof?"

"No. The FBI said they fired him because he had a nervous breakdown."

"He uncovered this conspiracy on his own?"

"I guess. I don't know if we can believe anything he said. He was going nuts toward the end."

"Toward the end?"

"He was killed."

"Why do you say he was going nuts?"

"He accused me of being a traitor and tried to shoot me. He was seeing traitors under the bed. He was diagnosed as a paranoid schizophrenic, according to the FBI, but what if . . ."

"What if what?"

"What if what he said was true? What if he uncovered the truth and it helped drive him completely mad?"

"What else did he tell you?" asked Root in earnest, and took a pull on his beer.

"He said—and again he never showed me any proof—that the cartels hated President Ransom because he was opposed to open borders, but they liked Vice President Dealey because he favored open borders."

"So they could smuggle their narcotics into our country easier."

"Right."

"That makes sense. Ransom is a hardliner on the border. He went to Harvard, but he grew up on a ranch in Texas, and his son OD'd on fentanyl. He sees drugs as America's public enemy number one, and a lot of those drugs are flowing into his home state. He's gonna do everything he can to seal the border. Dealey, on the other hand, doesn't have the same motivation. He grew up in Connecticut and went to Yale. Sealing the border isn't on his list of priorities."

Root took out a pen and started writing on a paper napkin on the counter.

"Go on," he said.

"So what if a Mexican drug cartel is trying to fund the conspirators? How would they go about it? It's illegal for them to contribute to a US election, so what would they do?"

"Create a slush fund in a shell company in order to finance the conspiracy. Is that what you're saying?"

"Isn't it possible?"

"Being possible doesn't make it true." Root slid the napkin across the counter in front of Brody. Brody saw the dots Root had drawn. Brody watched Root draw lines to connect the dots. "We need something to connect the dots. All you've got is speculation."

"This Cobalt Green Tide LLC could be coordinating the slush fund. And you said CJNG sent laundered money to their bagman Ned Bates."

"We have no proof who's running Cobalt Green Tide LLC. If Ned Bates was still alive, we could've questioned her about the LLC, but with her dead, we have no leads. Also, how exactly did they plan to use the money to help the conspirators?"

"This is above my pay grade. I'm just a PI trying to track down my client's brother."

Chapter 67

Feeling his brain overheating, Brody knocked back his glass of water.

"There's a germ of truth in your idea of a cabal," said Root.

"It wasn't my idea. It was the ex-fed's."

"I think we should pursue it. Right now nobody would believe a word you're saying. They might accuse you of being a traitor and lock you up."

"Exactly what the ex-fed did—except he tried to kill me instead of locking me up," said Brody, and took a pull on his beer. "That's why I believe we need to take what he said about this cabal with a grain of salt. He was losing his mind."

"Don't tell anyone about this. Let's keep it between you and me."

"No problem. I just want to find Damian and blow town."

"A lot of people are gonna try to stop you from doing that."

"I'm finding that out. That bullet outside was meant for me."

"You're right."

Taken aback, Brody had hoped Root would disagree. "Even if there really is a conspiracy, what could we do to stop it?"

"*You* couldn't do anything. Of course, the conspirators would still want you dead because you know too much."

Brody gave him a look. "Is this your way of trying to get me to help you?"

Root ignored him and pursued his line of thought. "However, the CIA could stop this cabal."

"Wouldn't that be the FBI's purview since it's domestic?"

"Ordinarily. But if the bureau is corrupt and riddled with cabal members like you say, CIA has a counterintelligence department that could step in."

Brody rubbed his eyes in concern. "I hope Peltz was wrong about this plot."

"Peltz?"

Oops, thought Brody. A slip of the tongue. He hadn't intended to divulge Peltz's name, but the cat was out of the bag.

"That was the name of the FBI agent who told me about the conspiracy," he said.

"Ah." Root leaned back on his stool. "It doesn't really matter what his name is. When they fired him for mental issues, they shot down his credibility. Nobody would believe a psychotic."

"If you ask me, he went too far down the rabbit hole and lost his marbles. I'm having trouble believing his conspiracy theory."

Brody recalled what Nietzsche had said: *If you gaze long enough into the abyss, the abyss will gaze back into you.*

"Peltz's theory would explain DC's involvement with Cobalt Green Tide and Cobalt Green Tide's involvement with CJNG," said Root.

"But, like you said, there's no proof."

"We need to find out how the cartel's money was gonna be used to support the cabal's conspiracy." Root went back to his napkin and drew a connection between two more dots.

"I need to find Damian."

"You're in this whether you like it or not."

"I had a feeling you'd say that." Brody paused in thought. "The Mafia's involved, too."

"Mafia?"

"Armando Musante is providing protection for Damian. It may be one reason we're having so much trouble locating Damian. He doesn't want to be found, and he has protection."

"I don't see why the Mafia would want to help Damian. What's in it for them?"

Brody shrugged. "Is the Mafia connected to Cobalt Green Tide?"

"Your guess is as good as mine. And why does Damian want protection? Protection from who? From Don Gaetano? Does he know Don Gaetano sent a hit team after him?"

Brody tilted his head. "He must think someone's out to get him."

Root rubbed his chin in thought. "He must be worried about Don Gaetano." He frowned. "But why would he be? Don Gaetano is the one that hired him in the first place."

"You don't go to the Mafia for help unless you're desperate."

"Damian must know Don Gaetano sent Roberto here."

"Who's Roberto?"

"He's a hit man with hundreds of scalps under his belt."

"Wonderful."

Brody's situation was becoming more untenable with each passing moment. He felt surrounded by hit men and conspirators.

"Take care," said Root, paid for his beer, and left.

Brody made as if to stop him, but, thinking about it, he realized he had nothing to say to Root. After all, Brody was on his own, the way he always was. Root was just another player caught in the squeeze with his own agenda.

How was he supposed to find Damian if the guy didn't want to be found? Brody wondered. He had to find a way.

Chapter 68

Don Gaetano was sitting on a chaise longue on his pool deck in navy blue swimming trunks eating a papaya when he got the call on his encrypted satphone. He put the papaya down on a plate on the small coffee table beside him, wiped his hands off on a paper napkin on the tabletop, and took the call.

"It's me, *patrón*," said Root.

"Did you find Damian?"

"No."

Crestfallen, Don Gaetano slumped in his seat. "Then what is it?"

"I thought you should know. Somebody took out Ned Bates."

Don Gaetano straightened in his chair. "Are you sure?"

"I saw the cops at the scene of the crime and saw them wheel out Ned Bates's stiff."

"Fuck. And what about the four hundred g's?"

"They didn't find the money on the stiff."

An AK-47 strapped to his back, Arturo trotted up to Don Gaetano and nodded at him.

"What is it?" said Don Gaetano, covering his satphone's transmitter.

"Pedro and Raoul are missing."

Don Gaetano waved him off. "I'm busy." He uncovered the satphone and spoke into the transmitter. "Where the hell's the money?"

"Maybe the killer took it. Or maybe Damian didn't make the exchange yet."

"Why would somebody take out Ned Bates? It makes no sense unless the killer jacked the money."

"How would the killer know Ned Bates had that much dough?"

"Maybe Damian knows something about this. You have to find him ASAP."

"Another thing. The CIA knows about Cobalt Green Tide."

"What?" said Don Gaetano in surprise. "How did they find out?"

"I don't know their source."

"What do they know about it?"

"That it exists."

"They don't know what it's up to?"

Root paused a couple beats. "No."

"That's something in our favor. Good work. Keep me posted."

"What's Cobalt—?"

Don Gaetano terminated the call.

Who clipped Ned Bates? Don Gaetano wondered. Had CIA assassins done it? If they had, it would mean they knew the purpose of Cobalt Green Tide. Root had said otherwise, and Root was the cartel's mole in the CIA. His intel was the true gen. If CIA hit men didn't whack Ned Bates, who did? Did somebody know what Cobalt Green Tide was up to and want it stopped?

Don Gaetano heard buzzing overhead. Whirring rotors. He spotted something flying slowly in the cloud-mottled azure sky.

He saw three more of the flying objects, measuring three feet in diameter.

UFOs? he wondered. No. He knew what they were.

Arturo followed the direction of Don Gaetano's gaze. "*Qué pasa, patrón?*"

"Drones," said Don Gaetano, putting away his satphone.

One of the drones dropped something from the sky.

"Bomb," yelled Arturo, and ran for cover.

Don Gaetano squinted at the object falling from the drone. The object landed with a thud on the lawn. It was a human foot. The next drone dropped a hand. Additional drones appeared in the sky, dropping human organs. A human head landed in the pool with a splash.

"Fucking Zetas," said Don Gaetano.

He rushed into his hacienda, retrieved a Mossberg Scorpion 12-gauge pump-action shotgun from a gun rack near the fireplace on one of the stucco walls in the living room, returned to the pool deck, and commenced shooting the drones out of the sky like skeet.

Arturo shouldered his AK, drew a bead on one of the drones, and let loose a burst. The barrage of bullets shattered two drones, which wavered and veered off course then plummeted to the ground as their severed spinning propellers catapulted into the sky.

There were at least twenty of the drones overhead now, all of them dropping body parts on the lawn and patio.

One of the remaining drones dropped another head into the swimming pool.

Don Gaetano recognized the head as it bobbed in the water, the expression on its face frozen in terror.

"We found Raoul," said Don Gaetano, stone-faced.

"*Putas*," said Arturo.

"Scumbags," roared Don Gaetano, and shouldering his Mossberg blasted the offending drone out of the sky.

A dog commenced barking next door.

Carmen ran out of the living room onto the patio. "The neighbors are complaining about gunshots."

Lowering his shotgun Don Gaetano slewed around to face her.

"Tell them it's my car backfiring," he said. "It needs a tune-up."

"Why don't *you* tell them? I'm sick of their complaints."

"I'm busy. We're being invaded," he said, pointing at the drones clustered in the sky.

"What the hell?" said Carmen, picking up on the drones. "Blow every last one of those motherfuckers out of the sky."

"My pleasure."

Carmen's face turned ashen as she saw a human head plummet into the backyard.

"They're dropping body parts," she muttered.

"The Zetas wasted some of my men and are letting me know it."

"You can't let them get away with this, *querido*."

Carmen turned to go.

The neighbor's dog continued barking.

"And tell them to put a muzzle on their dog," he said. "It's making too much noise."

Don Gaetano swung his Mossberg upward and blew apart another drone, which shattered and strewed the ground with pieces of plastic and metal.

Juan ran out of the hacienda and cut across the patio into the backyard. Wide-eyed, he gaped at the drones flying overhead.

"Toy planes," he yelled, pointing at the drones.

Don Gaetano stopped shooting. He didn't want his son hurt by flying debris from crashing drones.

Juan spotted one of the drones that had crashed to the ground, approached it, crouched on his haunches, inspected it, and withdrew a severed hand from the wreckage.

"Don't play with dead things," said Don Gaetano. "Come back here."

Juan tossed the hand away in disgust.

One of the drones hovering overhead dropped a blood-streaked human thigh that landed six feet from Juan.

Juan leapt to his feet and scampered back to Don Gaetano.

Don Gaetano swung up his Mossberg, took aim at the drone, and blew it to smithereens.

Chapter 69

Sitting at the bar in Harrah's, Brody ordered another beer. He felt bummed out, knowing he had a legion of enemies hell-bent on wasting him.

It reminded him of when he was a kid. Whenever he had an epileptic attack, the other kids would either scream and run away from him or stand watching him, laughing their heads off, pointing and jeering at him.

He could hear the other kids' voices now:

"What's wrong? You a spaz?" said ten-year-old Johnny, the neighborhood bully, a cop's kid, and guffawed.

"What's that stuff on your lips? Foam," said Brody's nine-year-old neighbor Mikey, tracing a finger along his lips as he watched Brody suffer a seizure. "You got rabies like a dog?"

"Man," said Johnny, "that's disgusting. Let's beat it."

Brody had to get used to the jeers willy-nilly. He was the odd kid on the block.

Sometimes he wondered how he had ever survived childhood. Everyone putting him down. His father a drunken serial killer who couldn't care less about him.

Brody was a survivor, though.

And then there were the fistfights.

Whenever the kids on the playground picked fights with him, he always got up when they knocked him down no matter how many times they hit him.

"Stay down, spaz, so I don't have to keep knocking you down," said the big-for-his-age Johnny, who kept punching Brody in the face and flattening him one day on the blacktop playground.

His nose bleeding, eyes black and blue, Brody kept getting back up after Johnny beat him to the ground.

"Want me to kill you, spaz?" said Johnny in frustration, blowing out his cheeks, standing a head taller than Brody. "Stay down and I won't hit you anymore. Are you a retard as well as a spaz?"

The other kids had formed a circle around them and were egging on Brody, who was slipping in and out of consciousness, holding on by a thread, determined to stay on his feet and not pass out, his fists raised in front of his chest in defiance. He felt the warm blood that leaked from his nose stream down his lips. He was going to keep getting up no matter how many times Johnny knocked him down.

"Want me to help you commit suicide, is that it?" said Johnny, struggling to figure Brody out. "Suicide by cop's kid?"

Brody kept his ground, his lips torn and bleeding, his face pulpy from Johnny's blows, his fists balled in front of him, waiting for the next onslaught.

Exasperated, Johnny picked up Brody's metal Peanuts lunchbox, smashed it on the ground, and stamped on it, flattening it.

"There," he said.

"Can't you take it?" said Brody, not sounding convincing—even to himself, as he brandished his fists in front of his mutilated face.

Johnny snagged Brody's wrist and shook it. "Look how skinny he is," he told his buddies.

They laughed.

Johnny threw Brody's wrist down and shoved him backward.

Brody stumbled backward a few steps but kept his balance. Thinking he might pass out any second, he shambled forward and brandished his fists again.

Shaking his head in disgust, Johnny turned around to face his gang. "He's dead on his feet, but he's too stupid to know it. I could blow him over with my breath. Let's get out of here."

His gang split their sides. They jeered at Brody.

"Who's next?" said Brody, having trouble speaking thanks to his sore jaw.

They guffawed at him.

"You look like shit," said Johnny. "I beat the crap out of you. Look at yourself in the mirror. That's what a loser looks like."

Johnny beckoned to his gang and strutted away.

Laughing at Brody they followed Johnny.

"Stupid spaz," said Johnny. "You don't even know how to fight. You're too stupid to know you lost. It's over."

Departing, Johnny gave a dismissive wave at Brody, his amused gang in tow. His knees rubber, Brody stood, holding his ground, not knowing when to quit. No matter how tough the fight, he never quit.

When he returned home, his mother chewed him out for getting into a fight and cleaned him up. His father was sleeping off a drunk.

Now in Harrah's, Brody took a pull on his beer, chasing the humiliating memory of his playground beatdown out of his mind. He wasn't going to quit this case.

He didn't drink the rest of his beer. He didn't need it. His miserable childhood was behind him. Only the memories remained seared in his mind. He had to face the here and now.

He had to find Damian, no matter how many players wanted to stop him dead before he did.

Chapter 70

Brody was returning to his room at the Venetian, cutting through the gaming room to the bank of elevators that led to his floor when Special Agent in Charge Gus Thomason accosted him.

"Well, well. What are the chances I'd bump into you here, Brody?" said Thomason, clad in a navy blue suit and sporting a yellow silk moiré necktie.

"Accidentally on purpose?" said Brody, surprised to see Thomason in Vegas.

"We need to talk."

"That's what I figured," said Brody, not looking forward to their conversation. "How did you find me?"

"We're the FBI. We can find anybody we want."

Brody wondered if they could find Damian Playa for him. He wasn't going to ask. He didn't want the feds searching for Damian. They might end up busting Damian for working for a cartel.

"What's this about?" said Brody, making a beeline for the elevators, passing brightly lit beeping slots played by gamblers staring like zombies with bloodshot eyes at their machines.

"Let's go somewhere private."

Brody hoped the guy wasn't here to bust him. Bust him for what? Brody wondered. He hadn't done anything illegal. Why was he worried? You never knew with the feds. They played by a different set of rules than the rest of us because they had more power. In many ways the bureau was omnipotent. And, like the man said, power corrupts, and absolute power corrupts absolutely.

Brody and Thomason detoured into a deserted corner of the gaming room.

"What do you know about Ned Bates?" said Thomason.

"Never heard of her," Brody lied.

"You said 'her.'"

Brody said nothing. Not good, he decided, realizing his faux pas.

"How did you know Ned Bates was a she if you never heard of her?" said Thomason.

"*Was?*"

"You didn't answer my question."

Brody groped for a reasonable explanation. "Uh—uh— the way you said her name. Had to be a she."

Thomason snickered. "I'm not buying it." He paused. "She was murdered, by the way."

"What's this have to do with me?"

"That's what I'd like to know. You say you never heard of her, and yet you know Ned Bates is a she. Everybody knows *Ned Bates* is a man's name."

"Not necessarily. There are a lot of names used by both males and females, especially these days. There are even people that claim they have no gender. They call themselves 'they' instead of 'he' or 'she.' You need to keep up with the times."

"I never heard of any woman called Ned Bates. I'm losing patience. How do you know her?"

Brody decided he better level with him. "Oh, now that you mention it. I did overhear cops saying that name. And I saw them drag away her body on the strip not long ago."

"That's better. So why did you pretend you didn't know her?"

"The name meant nothing to me when you first said it. I guess in my subconscious mind I recognized the name and knew Ned Bates was a she because I had seen her corpse."

"You expect me to believe this cock-and-bull story?"

"It happens to be true," said Brody, his palms sweaty.

"What do you know about Ned Bates, other than she's dead?"

"Nothing."

"Do you know why she was in town?"

"No."

"Do you know who she was working for?"

"No."

Narrowing his eyes Thomason searched Brody's face. "I'm asking you for the last time. What do you know about Ned Bates?"

"Nothing."

As long as Brody didn't know if there really was a cabal of conspirators within the FBI, he was going to keep his mouth shut about what he knew about them since he had no idea who belonged to the cabal and which feds he could trust. Spilling what he knew to the wrong fed could spell his death.

"Did you have anything to do with Ned Bates's death?" said Thomason.

"Of course not. That's ridiculous."

Thomason wasn't laughing. "Why? As soon as you come to Vegas, Ned Bates ends up dead."

"Thousands of tourists come here every day."

"They don't end up dead."

Why were the feds interested in Ned Bates's homicide? wondered Brody. You would think the local Vegas cops would be investigating it. Maybe the cops thought the killer was from out of state, in which case they would contact the feds. It wasn't his business. He had a job to do.

"Do you know who took out Ned Bates?" said Thomason.

"No."

"I got a good mind to haul you in for questioning and sweat you at headquarters."

Brody had to find Damian. The clock was ticking on the guy's survival. The longer it took Brody to find him, the less chance Brody would have of finding him alive. Brody had no time to spare dicking around with the feds.

"You'd be wasting your time," said Brody, his heartbeat accelerating, cold sweat like steel pellets rolling out of his armpits.

"As long as I'm on the clock, I'm not wasting my time."

"It's just about money with you."

Thomason did a slow burn. "There's a lot more at stake here than money. How about the security of your country? Start talking."

Brody said nothing.

Thomason stared at him.

Brody kept his lips sealed.

Thomason walked away. "I'll be seeing you."

Brody started when he saw Damian ambling through the gaming room with muscle.

Chapter 71

Don Gaetano was sitting in his spacious living room under a chandelier in a lime guayabera shirt and blue jeans watching his five-nine fifty-three-year-old lawyer Antonio Quintana enter from the patio in a bespoke dark business suit and vest. Greying hair at his temples, broad-shouldered, barrel-chested, he radiated an air of clubby refinement, someone who had attended the best schools and was socially at ease with the rich and powerful.

"*Mi abogado favorito*," said Don Gaetano, getting up to greet Quintana with a smile and a pat on the back. My favorite lawyer. "*Mi casa es su casa*."

"Don Gaetano," said Quintana, smiling back at him.

"Have a seat, Antonio."

Quintana sat on a sofa. "Why do you want to see me?"

"I want to know what the politicians are doing," said Don Gaetano, continuing to stand. "Are they planning to move against me?"

Quintana was about to speak when Mojo the iguana scampered across the living room floor and out the open door to the pool.

"He won't hurt you," said Don Gaetano with amusement.

Quintana straightened his jacket's lapels. "They are worried about the onslaughts of violence among the cartels."

"That goes without saying. The question is, are they gonna do something about it?"

"Of course, they will send out the police to arrest some cartel members. The usual to placate the populace and give the newspapers something to publish."

"They don't plan to escalate their war on us?"

"What do you mean?" said Quintana, plucking at an imaginary piece of lint on his jacket.

"I mean, are they gonna start taking down leaders?" said Don Gaetano, fixing a baleful stare on Quintana.

Relaxing, Quintana leaned back on the sofa. "Not to worry."

"I never worry. I take precautions, is all. I'm always ready to do battle. I need to know what my enemies are planning against me and when they plan to do it."

"They won't make a move on you, Don Gaetano. They know how that works."

"Meaning?"

"They know if they cut off the heads of the cartels, the number of homicides will escalate as the lower echelons jockey for power. Keeping the cartel bosses in power actually helps hold down the homicide rate. They learned that the hard way."

"Like when they took down El Chapo," said Don Gaetano with a nod and a knowing smile.

"Exactly. His territory exploded into some of the worst violence we've ever seen in this country after they put him away."

"Then what is the problem?"

"The governor isn't in any hurry to try to take you down. But he has to do something or the populace will rise up in outrage and throw him out of office. The upshot is, expect some of your cartel operatives to be busted."

"The price of doing business."

Don Gaetano retrieved an ornate cigar box from the mahogany coffee table and offered Quintana a cigar.

"No, thanks. My wife tells me they cause cancer."

"But you don't inhale."

"Cancer of the mouth," said Quintana, massaging his mouth.

"You worry too much," said Don Gaetano, and selected a Cuban Montecristo Petit No. 2 from the cigar box.

He scoffed up a guillotine from the coffee table, cut the head off his cigar with a quick decisive snip, inserted the cigar into his mouth, and lit it with a wood match that he drew from a box of matches on the tabletop.

"Never use cardboard matches to light a cigar," he said. "They destroy the flavor of the tobacco."

He puffed contentedly.

"Speaking of worrying," said Quintana. "What about your problem with Damian? Is that resolved?"

"No," said Don Gaetano, his face somber.

"I told you, you should have let *me* launder the money for you. I could've laundered it through shell companies and offshore bank accounts in the British Virgin Islands, over to Cyprus, over to Latvia, over to Panama . . . Nobody would ever be able to trace it to you. Instead you used Damian to launder it in a Vegas casino."

"No middlemen. I don't trust bankers. How do I know they're not skimming my money?"

"Well, who can you trust?"

"With all due respect, I don't trust lawyers either. Not to put too fine a point on it, a law degree is nothing less than a license to steal."

Don Gaetano blew a smoke ring which floated lazily across the room.

Quintana grinned with shark's teeth. "Like Shakespeare said, 'The first thing we do is kill all the lawyers.'"

"Have you heard my favorite lawyer joke? What's the difference between a dead snake in the road and a dead lawyer in the road?" said Don Gaetano, returning the grin.

"I don't know."

"The dead snake has skid marks in front of it."

Quintana couldn't help but chuckle.

He turned serious. "Next time, hire *me* to launder your money. You pay me to do a job, I do it. Your money gets laundered, and everybody's happy. This bottom-feeding clown Damian can't even figure out how to launder money at a casino, the easiest way there is. This isn't the guy you send to do a man's job."

"Hindsight is always twenty-twenty." Don Gaetano paused. "That's not the worst of it."

"What do you mean?" said Quintana, head cocked.

Chapter 72

"The CIA knows about Cobalt Green Tide," said Don Gaetano.

Quintana sat up straight on the sofa. "They know who's running it?"

"No. They couldn't have found that out."

"Exactly. Because it's a shell company set up in Delaware. Which is why I set it up there. LLC owners have perfect anonymity in Delaware. The corporate shield is secure, even from the CIA."

"There's another thing."

"What?"

"The money to be laundered has vanished," said Don Gaetano, furrowing his brow.

"How could it?"

"The bagman for Cobalt Green Tide was whacked. The money wasn't on her."

"Damian must still have it. He didn't make the exchange."

"Then why didn't he tell me?"

"What's his explanation?"

"I can't contact him," said Don Gaetano, taking an angry swipe at the air.

"Because he jacked it and doesn't want to talk to you. He could be anywhere by now."

"He could be dead for all I know."

"If only you had allowed me to launder it, none of this would've happened—"

"Next time, consigliere," said Don Gaetano, holding up his hand to halt Quintana. "That money has got to go to Cobalt Green Tide. They need it to implement our plan in Washington. It needs to grease the palms of one of The Fifteen. Where the fuck is it?"

"Do you have any blow?" said Quintana, looking around the room.

"Is the pope Catholic? The vial on the coffee table," said Don Gaetano, nodding at the vial.

"Mind if I do a bump?"

"Feel free."

Quintana latched onto the glass vial, poured blow onto the back of his wrist, and snorted it.

"Ah," he said with pleasure, tilting his head back.

Carmen glided into the living room in a scarlet dress with a plunging neckline, a wide smile on her full lips that glowed with crimson lipstick.

At the sight of her, Quintana stood up, approached her, leaned forward, and kissed the back of her hand.

"Always a pleasure to see you, Carmen," he said.

"The pleasure's mine, dear Antonio," she said with a flirtatious smile playing on her lips.

Feeling a twinge of jealousy Don Gaetano stepped over to Carmen in his python cowboy boots and kissed her smack on the lips, holding his Montecristo away from her, knowing she didn't appreciate the aroma.

"Could I offer you something to drink?" she asked Quintana.

"He was just leaving," chimed in Don Gaetano.

Quintana looked surprised. Nevertheless, he took the cue.

"Another time, I hope," he said, smiling at her. He turned to Don Gaetano. "Good day, Don Gaetano."

Quintana strode out of the room.

"If I didn't know better, I'd say you two were seeing each other," Don Gaetano told Carmen.

"I ask legal advice from him from time to time, not that it's your business."

"Your business is my business."

"And what about Valentina?" she said, confronting him.

"What about her? I like her."

"You like her a tad too much."

"It's none of your business."

"Your business is my business," she said, parroting him.

"Let's not quarrel. I have more important issues to tend to."

"Maybe I can help."

"I doubt it. I can't contact Damian. He jacked my money. Or someone wasted him and swiped it."

"You need to take your mind off this."

She seized his arm and twisted it behind his back.

"What are you doing?" he said.

"I know you like to play. I've seen you with Valentina."

"What are you talking about?"

"Don't you want to fuck me like a bull now?" she husked.

"I don't under—"

She dropped his arm in anger. "You're no fun."

She stalked out of the living room, six-inch Lucite high heels clacking on the hardwood floor.

Maybe she *had* seen him with Valentina in the bedroom, he decided with concern. *Damn.* Carmen was a savvy businesswoman. She was a vital part of the brain trust in charge of CJNG. He needed to keep her happy. He needed to be more discreet about his sessions with Valentina.

There was no way he could part with Valentina. He remembered with a tingling sensation between his legs the time he snorted yayo off one of her naked breasts . . . He could never part with her.

On the other hand, the last thing he wanted was a divorce from Carmen.

Chapter 73

Don Gaetano heard rapping on his door. "Who is it?"

"It's me. Arturo."

Don Gaetano strode to the door and let Arturo in. Wearing jeans and a grey polo, Arturo looked preoccupied.

"*Qué pasó?*" said Don Gaetano.

"We have a problem with the police chief."

"Why?"

"He's giving preferential treatment to the *Toros Rojos* cartel."

"You need to change his mind."

"I know this police chief. His name's Roderigo Zendeja. A fucker. He has it in for us."

"You're practiced in the not-so-friendly art of persuasion. Change his mind. Or demote him."

Arturo clucked. "I'm gonna have to demote him, *patrón*."

Don Gaetano nodded yes. "Send Michael to take care of it."

"Michael is doing too much. I can take care of it, *patrón*."

"Michael can handle it. I need you here."

Arturo balked at the suggestion. "Michael is too young to take on so many assignments."

"You and I both know we all need to grow up fast in this business or die."

"He just blew up a church and burned a Zeta alive."

"And he's doing a fine job. He deserves another assignment for his good work."

"But, *patrón*—"

"No more ifs, ands, and buts. Give him his orders."

"*Sí, patrón*," said Arturo, standing to attention.

"Excellent. We got another problem. Damian's turning into a clusterfuck."

Arturo cocked his head. "Didn't Roberto take care of him?"

"The problem is, bagman Ned Bates got whacked," said Don Gaetano, not answering him. "Ned Bates didn't have our money on her. So where's my four hundred grand?"

"Damian must have it."

"Why hasn't he called me and told me about Ned Bates?"

"He must have the cash. Where else could it be?"

"That money is earmarked for Cobalt Green Tide. Once they have it they'll be able to replace President Ransom with our man Dealey. He'll open the border for our deliveries."

"We ship most of our product by sea. Do we really need an open border with the gringos?"

"We do. And I'll tell you why. It gives us more options. The more options we have, the less chance there is that the DEA, the DHS, ICE, the Border Patrol, and the ATF will intercept our shipments. They can't be everywhere at once. If they're patrolling the sea, we can smuggle by land, and vice versa. If the sea and land are covered, we smuggle by air. It's all about options."

"Our tunnels are our best bet."

"Our tunnels are always in play, my friend."

"What about Damian?"

"He's dead."

"You said you don't know what he's doing. How do you know he's dead?"

"I'm talking about his future—or lack of it, in his case. He's dead whether he's got my money or not. The only thing I want to know from him now is, where's my money? Then Roberto or one of his hit team will waste him. Damian's assignment was a piece of cake. How the hell could the *pendejo* have blown it? This is what I get for trusting him."

"How do you want me to handle the police chief?"

Don Gaetano puffed on his cigar, mulling it over. "Tell Michael to get him to confess on videotape that he showed favoritism to the *Toros Rojos* cartel after they bribed him. Viewers of the video won't feel sorry for a corrupt cop after he turns up dead by execution. They'll know he's a criminal and deserved it."

"What if he doesn't want to confess?"

"Torture him and chop off his hands with an ax while he watches. He'll confess."

"Then what?"

"Deliver the videotaped confession to the local rag."

"And?"

"I thought that would be obvious. Chop off his head with the ax and toss his corpse and the rest of him on the roadside."

"*Está bien*," said Arturo, nodding. "Out with the old boss, in with the new boss."

"Make sure you find out who they're hiring to take his place and get to him with *una mordida*." A bribe.

"*Sí, patrón.*"

"We need the chief in our back pocket."

Don Gaetano spotted Mojo the iguana scampering through the open door into the living room swishing its tail. The iguana's nails clicked on the hardwood floor.

"What if he can't be bought?" said Arturo.

"Whack him out and buy the next appointee for chief. *Plata o plomo.*"

"Now you're talking. These *pendejos*, they don't know who they're messing with."

"They'll know when we're done with them. We'll take out every last one of them in the police department if they don't come to heel. We'll blast their choppers out of the skies with RPG-7s. Hell, we'll blow up their whole damn station like the Zeta church if we have to."

Chapter 74

When Brody set eyes on Damian, he wondered if the muscle with Damian was protecting Damian or holding him hostage. Damian appeared comfortable with the muscle at his side, so the muscle must have been acting as Damian's bodyguard, decided Brody.

Getting a better look at the muscle, Brody recognized Dominick. Brody owed the guy a couple of punches.

Brody started to approach the pair when he saw a guy withdrawing a piece and commencing to take aim at him. Brody didn't recognize the guy. Another hit man? Brody wondered.

Brody bolted to the stairs on his right and rocketed up them two at a time.

The hit man didn't loose a shot thanks to the people on the staircase impeding his aim. Instead the hit man pelted after him, concealing his gun inside his Windbreaker.

Brody tore onto the landing and made for the massive concourse of the Grand Canal Shoppes, intersected by a meandering turquoise canal complete with black-painted gondolas plying its waters helmed by crooning gondoliers wearing boaters and red and white striped jerseys. A fake azure sky arched across the cathedral ceiling as in a diorama.

Sightseeing tourists jammed the concourse. He darted among them, hoping to lose the hit man.

He glanced behind him and picked up on the gunslinger giving chase.

Brody dashed into another throng at a jog in the canal.

He glanced over his shoulder. The guy was gaining ground, shoving people out of his way and knocking others to the ground. A tall crew-cut tourist shook his fist angrily and yelled at the guy.

Brody scanned the canal. He saw a gondola inching along the canal under the gentle prodding of the gondolier who wielded a long black pole.

Brody sprang onto the cement parapet and dove into the canal six feet in front of the gondola's bow. He swam to the other side of the twenty-foot-wide canal. The gondola glided over his wake, as the gondolier watched him with surprise. Dripping wet, Brody scaled the other side of the canal.

His pursuer leapt onto the opposite parapet, drew a bead on Brody, and fired.

Brody scrabbled up the side of the parapet and pulled himself over it as the bullet slammed into the cement two inches from Brody's arm and ricocheted into the throng.

Panicked guests fled amok at the crack of the gunshot.

"He's got a gun!" a suit yelled, fleeing.

The shooter fired again at Brody.

Brody tumbled over the parapet and into the crowd, which was dispersing helter-skelter.

The shooter's bullet took out a middle-aged grey-haired woman rolling a baby carriage. She crumpled to the ground, sending the abandoned baby carriage rolling out of control.

The shooter aimed at Brody.

Taking cover behind the parapet, Brody whipped out his SIG P365, shook the water off the barrel, braced his gun arm on the parapet, and trained the muzzle on the shooter. The shooter stood on the opposing parapet and fired at Brody. Brody ducked.

Brody lined up his shot again, hoping the gun would fire even when wet. He squeezed off two shots. The shooter's head exploded into pink mist. He nosedived into the canal, dyeing the water with crimson streaks.

The cops would be here any minute, Brody knew. He could wait for them and explain away the shooting death as self-defense. But he didn't want to waste the time. He needed to get to Damian, who he hoped was still downstairs. He concealed his weapon.

The problem was his wetness. It would draw suspicion.

Gun drawn, a hotel security guard dressed like an Italian carabiniere dashed toward the commotion and inspected Brody, who was walking past him.

"I heard a gunshot and jumped into the canal," Brody said, sheepishly.

"Who fired the gunshot?" said the carabiniere.

"I dunno."

Face determined, the carabiniere plowed his way through the panicked mob to try to find the shooter, who was floating in the canal facedown.

Brody fought his way through the terrified mob and descended the steps to the gaming floor where he had set eyes on Damian and Dominick. Brody scoped out the place seeking them.

In his sodden clothes he felt chilly in the coolness of the air conditioning. He shrugged it off. He could change clothes later. Right now he had to find Damian.

Brody had to work fast. The cops might order the casino locked down after the shooting. Certainly they would close the Grand Canal Shoppes so they could inspect the crime scene.

Had Damian heard the gunshots and fled? wondered Brody.

Chapter 75

Brody became alert. He saw someone that could be Damian strolling near a bank of slots thirty-odd feet away. The guy was turned sideways to him so Brody couldn't discern his whole face.

Then Brody saw Dominick get up from his seat at a slot and approach Damian.

Brody could see Damian's face. He strode toward Damian, his mien not too determined lest he panic Damian. After all, Damian had no idea who Brody was.

Brody disguised his interest in Damian, scanning the rest of the gaming room as if trying to select an interesting slot to play as he neared Damian.

"Aren't you Damian?" said Brody.

"Who wants to know?" said Damian, taken aback. "I never saw you before in my life."

Dominick stepped within a couple inches of Brody challenging him.

"Can I have some breathing room?" said Brody, feeling crowded.

"Do you know this guy?" Dominick asked Damian.

"No," answered Damian.

"He's bad news. Want me to escort him outa here?"

Brody held his ground, despite Dominick's invasion of his space.

"Your sister sent me," Brody told Damian.

"Wait a second," Damian told Dominick, motioning for him to back off.

Dominick backed away a step. He didn't look happy.

"What about my sister?" Damian asked Brody.

"She thought something might've happened to you," answered Brody. "She sent me to find you."

"You found me. So?" said Damian, holding his palms open at his waist.

"I'm here to help you."

"Help me what?"

"You're in danger."

"Even if I am, how can you help me? Maybe I don't want your help."

His worst-case scenario for this assignment—a missing person that didn't want to be found, decided Brody.

"I can get you out of Vegas," said Brody.

"Want me to eighty-six this joker?" Dominick asked Damian.

"Can we talk in private, Damian?" said Brody.

Brody thought Damian might be afraid of speaking his mind on account of Dominick's presence.

Damian thought about it.

"I don't trust this guy," Dominick told him. "He's been asking around for you."

"He says he's trying to help me," said Damian.

"And you believe him? Look at him. Why's he all wet? Maybe he's on drugs or something."

"It's so hot outside I jumped into the swimming pool," said Brody. "Have you been outside? It's a furnace out there."

"Man, you're stupid."

"Let him have his say," said Damian. "You can go play the slots while we talk."

Brody and Damian wandered over to a cocktail lounge. Hanging back, Dominick watched them with eyes narrowed in suspicion.

Chapter 76

Brody and Damian claimed stools at the bar. Brody ordered a beer. Damian ordered a guava margarita.

"Who the hell are you?" said Damian.

"The name's Brody."

The thirtysomething waiter brought their drinks. He scratched his eye. He had pinkeye, Brody noticed. Probably from rubbing his eye too often with dirty hands. The guy retreated, scratching his itchy eyelid.

"Is the muscle holding you hostage?" said Brody.

Damian glanced in the direction of Dominick, who was staring with dark eyes at him and Brody.

"He's my bodyguard, if it's any of your business," said Damian.

"Why do you need a bodyguard?"

"I have my reasons."

"Because your life's in danger, and you know it."

Damian sipped his ice-cold guava margarita. "He's helping me."

"How long do you think that's gonna last?"

"Meaning?"

"He's Mafia."

"Maybe."

"He's got mobster written all over his face. How long do you think it'll be before he turns against you?"

"He's not gonna turn against me."

"How can you be sure? What do you know about his boss?"

"You ask too many questions."

Brody took a pull on his beer. "What did you promise Musante in return for protection?"

"Who's Musante?"

"Come off it. It's no secret he's the Mafia capo in these parts. He takes his marching orders from the Gambino family in New York."

"I don't know anything about that."

"What did you promise him in exchange for a bodyguard?"

"I don't have to tell you anything."

"I'm trying to help you. Don't you know who your friends are?"

"No, I don't. I'm new in town."

"And your life's in danger if you're palling around with the mob."

Face morose, Damian stared into his margarita. "My life's in danger *without* them."

"I heard you got *sicarios* gunning for you."

"You got big ears. You know what I'm saying?" said Damian, glowering at Brody.

"Listen to me. How long do you think you can trust Musante to protect you?"

Damian chewed it over. "It's not like I have much choice."

"I can help you before he turns on you like the rattlesnake he is."

"You?" Damian snickered. "You're one guy. How can you give me more protection than the Mafia?" He shook his head in despair and stared into his drink again as if he could glimpse the gathering clouds of a dark future.

"What did you offer him?"

"Are you a cop?" said Damian.

"I'm a PI."

"And my sister hired you?"

"Yeah."

Damian thought about it. "OK. I promised Musante a piece of the cartel's drug trade if he gave me protection."

"Can you deliver on that promise?"

Damian bridled. "You're too nosy."

"You're working for a cartel?"

"You're asking way too many questions," said Damian, preparing to leave.

"Sit down. I'm trying to help. Did you antagonize a cartel somehow? Is that why cartel *sicarios* are after you?"

Damian swigged his guava margarita.

"When Musante realizes you can't provide him a pipeline to drugs, he's gonna turn you over to the cartel and cut a deal with them," said Brody.

"How do you know that?"

"Do you think he's protecting you because he likes you?"

Damian took umbrage at Brody's sarcasm and paid him back in the same coin. "Why should I throw in with a peephole PI like you? Please."

"I'm the only chance you got."

"Then I'm dead," said Damian, tapping his margarita's glass with his forefinger, knocking loose some of the salt grains on the glass's rim.

"You work for a cartel?"

Damian said nothing, kept tapping his glass.

"What did you do to piss them off?" said Brody.

"I got greedy and did something stupid."

"You stole their money?"

"Look. I'm trying to get out of this business. I want to open my own auto shop. I'm tired of looking over my shoulder all the time, running from another enemy with a gun."

"You need to get out of Vegas."

"I need to disappear."

"I can help you."

"How do I know you won't turn me over to the cops?"

Brody leaned back on his stool. "I'm not here to bust you. I'm working for your sister."

"How is my sister? Is she OK?" said Damian with concern.

"She's fine."

"I heard otherwise," said Damian, preoccupied.

"You heard wrong. She wants to see you ASAP."

"If I go with you, where will we go?"

"Somewhere safe till this blows over. We'll go to ground till the *sicarios* lose interest in you."

"I'm safer here."

He polished off his guava margarita and stood up.

Brody dug out his wallet from his trouser pocket and handed Damian one of his business cards.

"Call my cell if you change your mind," said Brody. "And I think you will, 'cause Musante's gonna hang you out to dry. The question is, will you tumble to it before it's too late?"

Damian snagged the card, crammed it into his trouser pocket, searched Brody's face one last time, and left.

Dominick strode over to Damian. Dominick glared at Brody and looked like he was going to confront him. Damian changed Dominick's mind.

Brody watched them depart, unsure of his next move. He couldn't force Damian to go with him. Then again, why not? He could hold Damian at gunpoint and blow Vegas with him in custody. But Damian would fight him every inch of the way, making Brody's job of rescuing him twice as difficult. Not only would Brody be fighting Damian, he would be fighting the *sicario* hit team out to waste Damian. Brody didn't consider it a viable option.

He saw half a dozen Vegas cops enter the casino, all business, bent on investigating the shooting at the Grand Canal Shoppes.

He paid for the drinks and returned to his room.

Chapter 77

Brody took a shower and changed into dry clothes in his room.

Gazing out his window at the thronging strip below Brody called Araceli on his cell phone.

"I found your brother," he said.

"How is he? Is he OK?" she said, her voice urgent.

"He's fine—for now."

"What do you mean?"

Brody watched a myriad of cars drive down Las Vegas Boulevard hundreds of feet below. He wondered if and when the cops would lock down his hotel. If any of the tourists that had been visiting the Grand Canal Shoppes ID'd him to the cops and the cops found him, he would tell them the truth. The shooter had fired at him first. Brody had returned fire in self-defense.

"A team of hit men are after him," said Brody.

"Then get him out of there."

"There's one problem, and it's a big one."

"What problem?"

"He doesn't want to go with me."

"Did you tell him you're working for me?"

"I did."

"I don't understand."

"He thinks he's safer here in Vegas. He doesn't think I can protect him."

"Why would he be safer there if hit men are after him?"

"He's got an arrangement with the local mob here. They're giving him protection while he's staying in town."

"Mob?"

"As in *The Godfather*."

"Why does he feel safe with them?"

"I told him it's not gonna work out for him. They'll turn on him any second."

"What did he say?"

"He doesn't believe me."

"You need to get him out of there. That's your job."

Brody paced around the room, his cell to his ear. "I'm hoping he'll change his mind. My only other option would be kidnaping him."

She paused. "All right."

Brody stopped pacing. "All right?"

"Kidnap him. You're saving his life. He'll thank you later."

"I didn't sign on to take him by force."

"You refuse?"

"No, no. I have to think about this. It makes my job more difficult."

"I'll pay you a bonus of a thousand dollars."

Brody mulled it over. "A hit man tried to take me out today."

"Hello? What are you saying? You're breaking up. Hello? I can't hear you."

Her voice sounded fainter. Maybe her cell was losing its charge, Brody decided.

"I'll call you back later," he said, raising his voice, hoping she could hear him, and terminated the call, uncertain what she had heard.

He thought of another problem. Where was he going to take Damian once they left Vegas? They would need to find a bolt-hole, a place where they could defend themselves if attacked by a hit team.

If he took Damian straight back to Araceli in LA, the hit team might follow them and blow all of them away at one fell swoop, eliminating all witnesses. It would be best to take Damian to a hideout where they could lie low till things died down, decided Brody.

He wondered if he should call Root and Thomason and tell them he had touched base with Damian. On the other hand, did he really want the CIA and the FBI involved with Damian? Brody didn't know which outfit he could trust. Could he trust either one of them?

Root might have valuable intel on CJNG's plans since he had infiltrated them, posing as a fashion photographer. He might know how Brody and Damian could avoid the cartel's hit team, decided Brody.

He retrieved his damp wallet from the desktop, where he had left it to dry out, and found Root's business card. The card was still damp, but the ink hadn't run. He could read Root's phone number.

He called Root on his cell phone and arranged a meet.

Chapter 78

Brody took the elevator to the lobby, which was crawling with cops by this time. They had locked down the second floor, where the Grand Canal of Shoppes was located, but the lobby floor remained open, allowing tourists to continue entering and leaving the casino.

Brody cut across the lobby floor making no attempt to hide from the cops, looking interested in their presence like the other tourists, but not too interested. The cops didn't pick up on him.

Maybe nobody had ID'd him as the guy that had blown away the shooter, decided Brody. The panicked crowd around the canal had been so busy fleeing for their lives they hadn't noticed who had shot the assailant.

That might not be the end of it, decided Brody. There had to be CCTVs located in some of the shops that skirted the canal, and they could have recorded his blowing away the shooter.

Brody couldn't worry about it now. He had to meet Root.

In any case, if any of the CCTVs had recorded the shooting, the videotape would bear out Brody's claim that he had shot the shooter in self-defense.

As long as the cops didn't stop him on his way out of the casino . . .

Brody made it to the casino's front doors without incident and, relieved, strode out onto the sidewalk. Even though the sun was going down, it remained over a hundred degrees outside.

The heat pounded down on him like a sledgehammer.

He crossed the traffic-jammed street to Caesar's Palace, trudging through the heat with a mob of pedestrians. Like slogging through a stream of lava.

Brody met Root at Cleopatra's Barge, a nightclub in the shape of the ancient Egyptian vessel with a golden figurehead of Cleopatra's torso jutting from the prow. Oars stuck out of the ship's hull into the water around the barge. Dim track lighting illuminated the nightclub's interior.

Brody spotted Root sitting at a booth with two of his fashion models. Root told them to leave at Brody's approach. Looking bored, they wandered to the bar, their Jimmy Choo spiked heels clacking on the floor.

"How do you like my fashion models?" said Root, watching them depart with a smile.

"A pair of lookers," said Brody, eying them, but not in the mood for women at the moment.

"Not only are they beautiful, they're smart. Teresa, the taller one, is a former Miss Guadalajara. She's fluent in four languages. Yolanda, the one with the boobs, can play the piano and the drums. She's a member of a rock band. They're pretty good, I hear."

"We need to talk."

"What's all that cop activity across the street?"

Brody sat across from him. "A *sicario* tried to take me out."

"They wanted you to leave town, and you didn't."

"I'm not done here yet."

"As far as they're concerned you are."

"Are you siding with them now?" said Brody, annoyed.

"I'm trying to find Damian," said Root, nursing a mojito. "Whoever finds him first I'm siding with. I need to know what he knows about Cobalt Green Tide."

"I'm getting the feeling you're gonna switch sides at the drop of a hat."

"I'm a realist. At the CIA we deal with realpolitik."

Brody was having second thoughts about confiding in Root about meeting Damian. Brody's only other option was the fed Thomason. And Thomason might bust Damian to get him to talk. Brody couldn't figure Thomason. Was the guy a stand-up fed without political motives or part of the deep state conspiracy and a member of the cabal to remove POTUS?

Full of misgivings, Brody decided to side with Root.

"I met Damian," said Brody.

He signaled to the waitress, a twentysomething brunette with a very pale complexion and a red tint to her hair that cascaded to her shoulders. He ordered a Coors.

"Where?" said Root, after the waitress departed.

"Not far from here."

Root leaned across the tabletop. "Did you tell him I want to talk to him?"

"There's a problem."

"Does that mean no?"

"It means, he doesn't want to leave town."

"Did you tell him there's a hit team gunning for him?"

"I did."

"The guy's a bigger moron than I thought."

"He thinks he's got a better deal with Musante protecting him."

"Musante? The Mafia capo?"

Brody nodded yes.

Root leaned back, shaking his head. "That's not gonna last. He'll turn Damian in for two bits."

Root stretched and feigned a yawn, pretending he was tired as the waitress brought Brody's beer and left.

Root leaned over the tabletop, getting in Brody's face. "I can't emphasize this enough. I need to know everything Damian knows about Cobalt Green Tide and the conspiracy against POTUS."

This was the response Brody was angling for.

"Can you provide him with asylum?" he said.

"*Political* asylum? What kind of asylum?"

"A bolt-hole. Somewhere me and him can go to ground till this flap blows over."

Root sipped his mojito, his mien reflective.

"He doesn't want political asylum?" he said.

"I didn't ask him. Can you grant it? Can you get him into the witness protection program?"

"The US Marshals Service runs the witness protection program. The CIA doesn't, and the attorney general decides who gets into it. Not the CIA."

"Does that mean no?"

"I didn't say that." Root paused. "The CIA can create new identities for high-value assets."

"Damian might go for that."

"I can't make any promises till I find out what he knows. He might not know anything about the conspiracy—in which case he's useless to us."

"What about a safe house where we can hide from the *sicarios*?"

Root thought about it, running his forefinger along the lip of his mojito glass. "I can handle that. A friend of mine has a cabin at Big Bear Mountain in California. It's off the beaten path. Nobody would find him there."

"That could work."

"You just said he wouldn't leave town with you."

"If I tell him about the cabin, maybe he'll change his mind."

Root dipped his forefinger into his mojito. "The safe house is stocked with HK MP5s and spare magazines—just in case."

"You CIA spooks go all out. If nobody knows we're there, we shouldn't need them."

Root deliberately licked the mojito off his forefinger's tip. Brody stood up to leave.

"I suggest you act quickly," said Root. "Musante contacted Don Gaetano. Musante wants to cut a deal."

Brody wasn't surprised. He knew the Mafia would turn on Damian. There was no percentage in protecting him.

Damian had promised them a drug deal that he couldn't deliver on.

Brody strode out of Cleopatra's Barge.

Chapter 79

Twenty-five minutes after Brody left, Roberto entered Cleopatra's Barge, picked up on Root, and made a beeline for Root's booth.

"How long have you been here?" demanded Roberto.

"A while," said Root, unruffled.

Roberto plunked himself down across from Root. "We got a problem. We need your help finding Damian."

"I thought I saw him here."

Roberto scoped out the nightclub. "I don't see him. Where are your girls?"

"At the bar," said Root, gesturing in his models' direction.

They had their legs crossed on the bar stools, exposing a good foot of thigh.

Roberto leered at them.

"Do you fuck 'em?" he said.

"Does a bear shit in the woods?"

Roberto screwed up his face. "Does that mean you fuck 'em?"

"I don't blame you for being jealous."

"What do they see in you?" said Roberto, the blood rushing to his face. "A rock's better looking than you and has more personality."

Root said nothing.

"I wanna fuck their brains out," said Roberto. "Two of 'em at once. After we nail Damian, I pull 'em both."

Root waited for Roberto to cool off.

"That's up to them," said Root.

"No. It's up to me."

"What's the problem you were talking about?" said Root.

Roberto couldn't stop thinking about the girls. "They're dying for it. Those are two prime pieces of tail. Why are they sitting over there?"

"I couldn't keep my hands off 'em."

"Now you're talking," said Roberto, leering. "I wanna squeeze their—"

"The problem?"

"What? Oh. That PI dick whacked out one of my best men across the street. I warned that rat bastard to blow town. I told him he'd pay if he didn't beat it. Now I'm gonna whack his ass, cut his head off, and mail it to his mother. Stinking *puta*."

"I saw a bunch of cops over there," said Root, nodding.

"That *puta* makes me so mad," said Roberto, flecks of saliva flying out of his mouth. "He killed Julio."

"You on blow?" said Root, drawing back from the airborne spit.

"What's it to you? The *patrón* is fuming. He wants his money. I just got off the phone with him."

"What if Damian doesn't have the dough?"

"He has to have it. Where else could it be? Ned Bates didn't have it."

"How are we supposed to get the money to Cobalt Green Tide without Ned Bates?"

"The *patrón* didn't tell me. First, we need to glom onto that dough. You need to help me find Damian."

"I told you, I thought I saw him here."

"Well, he's not here. So why are you hanging around drinking?"

"I was making calls, asking around. I know people in Vegas. I've done shoots here."

Roberto got to his feet. He leaned his fists on the tabletop.

"The boss told me the guy that finds Damian first gets a ten grand bonus," he said.

"A lot of money."

"And I'm the one that's gonna score it. You can sit here all day on your ass getting drunk if you want."

Roberto slewed around and headed toward the exit. He waved at Teresa and Yolanda at the bar and smiled.

"Hello," he said. *"Hasta la vista."*

They looked at him with confusion.

Idiots, he thought. They would change their minds when he had time to mack on them.

He turned away from them and stalked out of the nightclub, grinding his teeth. Business before pleasure. First he had to whack out Damian.

Chapter 80

Root sipped his mojito. His cell phone vibrated in his trouser pocket. He answered.

"Is this Brockton Root?"

Root didn't recognize the voice. "Who wants to know?"

"This is the FBI. We need to talk."

Root couldn't understand why the feds would want to talk to him. Were they going to try to bust him for working for CJNG? he wondered. He had to figure out how to play this.

"I'm listening," he said.

"Not on the phone. Where are you?"

Root could lie about his whereabouts, but he wanted to find out what was what. The thing was, he doubted the feebs knew he was a CIA agent that had infiltrated the Jalisco New Generation cartel. Then why would they want to talk to him? He had to find out.

"I'm at Cleopatra's Barge," he said.

"Great. I'll be there in five minutes."

The fed hung up.

How could the guy get here so quickly? wondered Root. An idea dawned on him. The cops across the street investigating the cartel hit man's murder. The fed must be over with them now. But how did the guy know Root was in Vegas?

Root had to find out how much the feds knew about him and how they had found it out.

Teresa and Yolanda were in no rush to leave the bar. They liked it here on the barge.

He couldn't blame them. The nightclub had a laid-back vibe that relaxed him.

He sipped his mojito and waited.

It didn't take long.

A five-nine suit entered the club. Navy blue threads. Standard government blah. The monotony broken up by a turquoise-and-black-striped rep silk tie.

Fed, decided Root. Trying to show off his taste with his tie, though he had none.

The guy spotted Root and angled across the floor to Root's booth.

"I'm glad I caught up with you, Root," he said, and sat at the booth, face stony.

"You have me at a disadvantage."

"Shenk. Special Agent Max Shenk."

Max Shenk withdrew his badge from his jacket's inside breast pocket and displayed it to Root.

Root nodded. "Should I call my lawyer?"

Max Shenk returned his badge to his pocket. "I hope not. Those sharks charge over a grand an hour in DC. The nerve."

Root couldn't tell where Max Shenk was coming from. Max Shenk's round face displayed little. The face of one of the pod people in *Invasion of the Body Snatchers*. Pushing forty. Intent eyes. Blue. Inchoate furrows in his forehead with a clear complexion. Had all his hair. Went straight from college to law school to the bureau. Never a cop. White collar all the way.

"Then why do you want to talk to me?" said Root.

"I want to make sure you understand who you're talking to."

"Max Shenk."

"That's right. I went to Phillips Exeter and graduated from Princeton."

"A good college, I hear. F. Scott Fitzgerald went there."

"I got my JD from Yale Law School."

"Lucky you." Root wondered if any of it was true, and if it was, why was he supposed to care?

"There was a murder committed recently on the strip that interests us. We think you may know about it."

"That one across the street?"

"The one in Madame Tussaud's."

"I'm not a cop. Why would I know about it?"

"Let's not beat around the bush, Root. You're CIA."

Root sipped his mojito. "Why would you say that?"

Max Shenk signaled to the waitress. "I'll have a gin and tonic."

The waitress retreated.

Max Shenk kept his own counsel till the waitress served his drink and decamped.

Chapter 81

"Ned Bates was murdered," said Max Shenk.

Root looked blank. "If you say so."

"Ned Bates was a bagman for Cobalt Green Tide LLC."

"Never heard of them."

"I think you have. In fact, that's why you're in Vegas."

"I'm here on a photo shoot. If you know my name, you must know I'm a professional fashion photographer."

Max Shenk snickered. "You're CIA. Ask me how I know."

"Do I have to?"

"I work for Cobalt Green Tide."

Taken aback, Root paused. "Cobalt Green Tide is an FBI shell company?"

"Don't act surprised, Mr. CIA agent. If you spooks can do it, so can we feds. The CIA ran shell companies during the Vietnam War when they were dealing drugs and again during the Iran Contra scandal in Nicaragua, again dealing drugs. And I'm sure they're running them even as we speak."

"Where's this leading?"

Max Shenk took a pull on his gin and tonic. "Which fraternity were you in?"

"I wasn't in one."

"What? Are you a communist?"

"Because I wasn't a frat boy?" said Root, amused.

"What are you drinking?"

Root glanced at his drink. "A mojito."

He didn't understand the segue.

"Cobalt Green Tide has members of the CIA in it as well as bureau members," said Max Shenk.

"That's nice," said Root, not knowing whether to believe it. "*I'm* not in it."

"You weren't invited."

"Because I didn't belong to a frat house?"

"Let's cut the small talk." Max Shenk leaned toward Root. "We know you infiltrated CJNG and you're here because of a delivery to our bagman Ned Bates."

"Why would you think that?"

"I told you. We have some of your CIA buddies in Cobalt Green Tide. We're deep state. We know things. And we want that money meant for our bagman."

Root was getting the picture. Except—

"What's the money for?" he said.

"It's for Cobalt Green Tide, is all you need to know. It's our money. Where is it?"

"Why do you think *I* know?"

Root didn't know who this Max Shenk really was. The guy might have been trying to sound him out, to get him to admit he was CIA. Whoever Max Shenk was he knew a lot about Root—way too much for Root's liking. Alarm bells were blaring in the back of his mind. Root wasn't going to blow his cover to please Max Shenk.

"Because you're here in Vegas at the same time Ned Bates gets popped," said Max Shenk. "What are the chances?"

"I'm not the only one here in Vegas. Look around. I'm here on a fashion shoot. My models are over at the bar," said Root, gesturing toward them.

Max Shenk heaved a long sigh. "You're not coming clean. We're on the same side. We want what's best for the country. Where's the money meant for Ned Bates?"

"I have no idea."

"It's *our* money."

"The same answer."

"I have powerful allies. It's in your best interest to help Cobalt Green Tide."

"I never met Ned Bates."

"What about Damian Playa?"

"What about him?"

"Don't act stupid. Do you know him?"

"No."

"He's CJNG's bagman."

Root said nothing, his face blank.

Max Shenk stared at Root for several seconds, produced his business card, and handed it to Root. "Contact me when you find out where our money is. It's crucial we get that money."

Max Shenk got up and left.

Root was starting to connect the dots, but he didn't know what he wanted to know most—what Cobalt Green Tide was planning to do with the money from Don Gaetano once they got their dirty little hands on it.

Chapter 82

Hair cropped, forty-two-year-old police chief Roderigo Casilla Zendeja was driving his spotless silver Dodge Durango home from the Guadalajara Police Department. Despite the air conditioning he felt hot, had stripped off his uniform's shirt, and was driving in his olive drab wife beater.

He kept himself in shape, worked out at the police gym four times a week. He ran on the treadmill and lifted weights. He could bench press three hundred pounds. He didn't let himself go to pot like other middle-aged cops he knew with their beer bellies and love handles. He wanted to set an example for his men by taking care of himself.

He glanced to his right at a pink gift-wrapped shoebox lying on the passenger seat at his side. His seven-year-old daughter's birthday was today and he had bought her a new pair of Air Jordan sneakers after he had got off work.

Rounding a curve he slammed on his brakes when he spotted a black Lincoln Explorer parked catercorner across the narrow road blocking traffic.

Damn idiot was an accident waiting to happen, he thought, his head jerking forward from his abrupt braking.

If the SUV had broken down, why was it parked in the middle of the street where it blocked traffic? wondered Zendeja. He had to write the driver up.

Before he had time to get out a citation pad he saw in his rearview mirror a black Chevy Suburban screech to a halt within an inch behind him. His heartbeat accelerated at his hairbreadth escape from yet another accident within seconds. He blew out his cheeks with relief.

Which didn't last long.

Two men with AK-47s sprang out of the Suburban and accosted him. He thought about reaching for his Glock.

"Don't move," said Michael Corleone Casa.

Zendeja decided he would be cut down before he had a chance to reach his holstered Glock. He froze in his seat.

"Get out," said Michael.

The thugs weren't wearing masks, noticed Zendeja. A bad sign. It meant they didn't care about being ID'd. He could draw only one conclusion.

He climbed out of his Durango.

"Toss the gun down," said Michael, training his AK on Zendeja's chest.

Zendeja reached for his Glock.

Michael brandished his AK. "Slow."

Zendeja followed instructions, plucked his nine mil out of its holster, and flicked it to the roadside.

Michael prodded Zendeja with the muzzle of his AK, guiding him to his Suburban.

"Get in," said Michael.

Palms sweaty, Zendeja climbed into the back of the Suburban, where two cartel operatives sat waiting with pistols aimed at him.

Michael signaled to the Lincoln Navigator, which righted itself on the road and drove off.

He climbed into the Suburban's driver's seat.

"They'll know something's wrong when they find my car abandoned here," said Zendeja.

"So what?" said Michael. "By then it'll be too late."

"Who are you?"

"You cut *Toros Rojos* a better deal than you cut us, huh?" said Michael over his shoulder to Zendeja.

"My seven-year-old girl is waiting for me. Today's her birthday."

"Don't worry," he said. "She's gonna see you on the news pretty soon. You'll be famous."

Zendeja said nothing. He ground his teeth. *Toros Rojos*, he thought. It had to be their archrivals the *Cartel Jalisco Nueva Generación* that was kidnaping him.

"You see the error of your ways, chief?" said Michael.

Zendeja said nothing, face grim, sweat beading above his upper lip.

"Are you prepared to admit your guilt?" said Michael.

"Guilt for what?"

"You'll admit it when I get through with you."

They weren't wearing masks. It could mean only one thing. A chill ran down his spine at the thought.

They were going to kill him, decided Zendeja.

Chapter 83

Valentina was shedding her black leather Gestapo trench coat to reveal her mauve thong bikini as Don Gaetano, naked save for a towel around his waist, watched her from his bed in his hacienda bedroom. She was wearing her black Allgemeine SS hat tilted rakishly to the side of her head.

He couldn't wait to fling off his towel and feel the lash of her whip on his buttocks. All he ever wanted was love. Was Valentina the only one who understood him? he wondered.

A flat-panel TV mounted on the wall distracted him as it broadcast the news.

A video of Guadalajara police chief Roderigo Zendeja was playing on the TV screen.

In the grainy black-and-white recording Zendeja admitted he was guilty of taking a bribe from the *Toros Rojos* cartel and giving them a better deal than CJNG, his voice flat, his face pale and blank, as he sat on a chair, his arms bound behind his back, his body motionless.

The heels of Valentina's knee-high gleaming black jackboots clacked on the parquet floor as she approached him, snapping her riding crop on her naked thigh, reddening the flesh.

"Are you ready to beg for mercy?" she said, removing her bra.

"Wait," he said, eyes glued to the TV set.

The black-and-white clip on TV ended. A high-resolution color clip ensued. The scene shifted to a dirt road with a blanket spread over a supine decapitated corpse's torso with its oxford-shod feet exposed on the roadside. Two armed cops with pixelated faces stood in body armor beside the blanket. Three feet away in the dirt lay two lumpy burlap bags.

"Police chief Roderigo Zendeja's corpse was found today on the roadside not far from his home," said the voice-over of a female newscaster. "His head and his hands were found in two separate burlap bags three feet from the decapitated corpse. Police speculate it was an execution committed by the *Cartel Jalisco Nueva Generación,* who were angry with the police chief for giving the *Toros Rojos* cartel preferential treatment in exchange for bribes."

"*Sic semper tyrannis,*" said Don Gaetano.

"It's time to beg for mercy," said Valentina, standing over him, arms akimbo, her flashing blue eyes savage with lust.

Don Gaetano took one look at her, flung off his towel, and rolled over onto his naked belly on his bed.

Valentina began slashing his right buttock with the riding crop.

Grimacing with pleasure, he rolled onto his back.

She flung her riding crop away and sprang onto him, straddling him.

Don Gaetano's eyes roamed over to Zendeja's corpse on the TV screen. When Valentina mounted him, his eyes rolled up into his head and he gasped.

Chapter 84

Brody was sitting at a bar in the Venetian, exhausted.

At times he was his own worst enemy. He felt like he was poisoning himself with self-hatred for being an epileptic, even though he knew rationally it was pure chance he had been born with the disease. Why should he hate himself for having a disease? If he thought about it, feeling self-hatred made no sense.

But that wasn't the only reason for his self-hatred. He found himself starting to feel something for Melody. Her image kept appearing in his mind unbidden, ghostlike, and it gave him a pleasurable sensation.

He knew he couldn't allow himself to have feelings for her. He was certain she would die violently as a result. He kicked himself and told himself to concentrate on his job.

Maybe if he went to a hooker, he could get Melody out of his system. Vegas was chock-full of hookers. All you had to do was know their price. He had no time. He had to do his job.

Damian. Brody had to get Damian out of here in one piece and back to his sister Araceli.

Brody couldn't allow himself to become paralyzed with self-doubt and self-hatred. He knew he could do his job. He had done it many times. It was just another day at the office. No sweat.

The problem was, no matter what case he took, he could never guarantee the results. He couldn't let the idea of failure defeat him.

He wondered where Damian was. Was Damian holed up in Musante's penthouse?

Brody felt like storming the place, gun in hand, and snatching Damian by force from Musante's clutches.

Brody wondered if it could be done. After all, it would be for Damian's own good. Damian would thank him in the end. Damian's days were numbered as long as he remained under Musante's aegis.

Brody didn't know how Damian could stand being with Musante. Surrounded by underage girls, Musante was obviously a pedo. Cons called pedos *short eyes* in the joint and considered them the lowest form of life.

Brody felt the same way. He hated slot badgers. As soon as he realized Musante was one, just being around Musante made Brody's skin crawl. The underage girls in bikinis, the massage table in Musante's living room, the naked pink blow-up doll hanging from his ceiling, Musante had to be a slot badger.

One less slot badger on earth would make the world a better place, as far as Brody was concerned.

Not that he considered himself judge, jury, and executioner. He wasn't going to go to Musante's penthouse for the sole reason of murdering the pedo. But if the perv got in his way, Brody would have no problem pulling the trigger.

He reminded himself he wasn't in Vegas to make the world safe for children.

In many ways Musante reminded Brody of his father. Brody's father the serial killer had never molested him—the guy was too busy ignoring him and murdering women—but the guy was sick in the head like Musante. The two sickos weren't wired right.

Maybe Musante's resemblance to Brody's father was the real reason Brody wanted to clip Musante.

All Brody knew was he wouldn't be shedding tears when Musante bought it.

Brody's cell phone vibrated in his trouser pocket. He took the call.

"He's after me," said Melody's breathless voice.

Brody tensed on his stool. "Where are you?"

"In the Mirage. Hurry. I can't escape." She screamed. "Let go—"

He heard a crash, her cell phone falling to the floor.

Chapter 85

Brody sprang off his stool, bucketed across the casino floor, out the front door and onto the baking sidewalk. He sprinted across Las Vegas Boulevard against the light, dodging vehicles that slammed on their brakes and blasted their horns at him.

Sweating in the suffocating heat, legs thrusting, he belted across the sidewalk into the Mirage's entrance, where the cool air engulfed him. He scoped out the crowded casino gaming floor.

Where was she? he wondered.

He whisked deeper into the belly of the casino, all the while casting around for Melody.

He heard a commotion emanating from the front desk adjacent to a gigantic aquarium that took up an entire wall. He charged across the floor to the front desk, where guests milled about lugging their suitcases. Some of the guests were staring in the direction of a fracas.

Brody followed their gazes to a struggle between a heavyset man and Melody near the fish tank.

"Get away from me," said Melody, trying to pull free from her husband Dan, who was wrestling with her.

He threw her to the floor, snagged her hair, and started dragging her on her back across the marble tiles.

"Bitch," he snarled.

Sliding across the floor Melody screamed, her face twisted in pain, and clutched her hair so he wouldn't tear it out of her scalp.

"Let her go," yelled Brody.

Dan ignored him.

Brody pulled out his SIG Sauer P365 and trained it on Dan. "Do it or I'll shoot."

Dan looked over at him, glowering, maintaining his grip on Melody's hair and hauling her across the floor. Instead of releasing Melody, he whipped out a Smith & Wesson .357 Magnum Highway Patrolman from his rear waistband and leveled it at Brody.

Somebody in the mob behind Brody screamed, "He's got a gun."

Dan fired in the ensuing panic.

Brody was already moving before Dan squeezed the trigger.

Jacked up with the adrenaline of anger, Dan missed his aim.

Brody fired back at him. But at the moment he squeezed the SIG's trigger, a frantic bystander from behind him jostled his arm, throwing off Brody's aim. The errant bullet perforated the immense aquarium's glass side. A narrow stream of water like a burst from a squirt gun arced out of the bullet hole and splashed onto the floor. Under the pressure of the leaking water, the aquarium's glass wall began to give, spiderwebbing with fissures. Audible cracks rent the air as the glass fractured and burst, pouring water, fish, and shards of glass cascading out of the collapsing aquarium onto the lobby floor.

A manta ray sailed out of the aquarium on a churning cataract of water that flooded the lobby.

The impetus of the gushing water sent Brody and Dan sprawling, forcing Dan to release his hold on Melody's hair.

Screams of terror from the hysterical, fleeing throng of guests.

Brody clambered through the surging water toward Melody, who was flailing in its current as jagged fragments of aquarium glass and bewildered fish streamed near her.

Dan had lost his Smith & Wesson .357 Magnum in the onset of the wall of water.

Braving the flooding water Brody fought his way toward Melody, gun in hand.

Wiping water from his sodden face, Dan spotted Brody approaching with his SIG and decided to retreat, seeing he had lost his revolver in the pouring water. The water was so high now that he broke into a swim to flee Brody.

Brody couldn't swim with his piece in his hand. He jammed the SIG into his waistband and commenced swimming toward the dazed Melody, who was intent on dodging glass shards that kept nicking her as the water rushed over her and consumed her.

Brody felt a floating glass fragment slice into his thigh as he swam through the water. Wincing, he kept swimming, feeling the juggernaut of coursing water dislodge the glass from his flesh as quickly as it had thrust it into him. The worst thing about the glass was that you couldn't see it as it glided in its lethal path through the tumultuous water, making it impossible to evade, decided Brody. You didn't know it was near you till you felt it cutting your flesh.

Her head above water, Melody was staggering around trying to keep her balance as water eddied around her threatening to throw her off her feet.

Brody reached her, stood, and steadied her in the thrusting currents.

By now all of the water had emptied from the shattered aquarium, whose entire glass wall had been washed away save for a few jagged remnants sticking out of their metal frame. The water now flooded the lobby and was sweeping out the entrance into the cluster of shuttles, taxis, and limos parked in the driveway.

Drenched, terrified bystanders fled out the doors, abandoning their suitcases in their haste to flee the building.

Slogging through the water Brody shepherded Melody toward the front door.

"Are you OK?" he said, spitting water out of his mouth.

"I guess," she said, traumatized by Dan's attack on her, shivering, her eyes staring out of her head. "Is he gone?"

"He took off. You're safe."

"Until he finds me again."

Dripping wet, they reached the exit and walked onto the sidewalk, where the water was dissipating as it spread out onto the road reserved for tourist transportation to and from the airport.

Brody made sure his SIG was snugged out of sight in his rear waistband under his soggy leather vest when he heard police sirens' keening.

Speeding squad cars shrieked to a halt in front of the Mirage's entrance to investigate the resort disturbance. Armed cops in bulletproof vests stormed out of their cruisers across the wet sidewalk to the plate-glass doors that led to the lobby.

"Do you want to file a complaint against your husband?" said Brody.

"Not now," she said. "I can't handle it now."

Brody and Melody headed away from the Mirage before anyone could ID them to the cops.

Chapter 86

Musante was getting his back massaged by Toni as he lay naked on his belly under a white Turkish towel on a massage table in his penthouse suite. The thin girl had red pigtails and a sprinkle of faint freckles that straddled the bridge of her snub nose onto her pink cheeks. She was wearing a Catholic prep-school uniform of a short green pleated plaid skirt, a matching necktie, and a white button-down.

Damian stood six feet away from Musante, watching him with a fixed expression tinged with disgust. Toni reminded Damian of Pippi Longstocking. It was enough to make him sick.

"It has come to my attention that you can't deliver on the drug deal we cut," said Musante, enjoying his massage like a cat sitting in the sunlight soaking up the sun's rays, eyes narrowed in pleasure.

"Your information is wrong," said Damian, becoming edgy.

Who had Musante been talking to? wondered Damian. Who would know Damian didn't have the clout in the cartel to cut a drug deal? Had Roberto or one of his hit team been in touch with Musante?

"I don't think so," said Musante.

"Who told you this?"

"A reliable source."

"They're wrong."

"Then where are my goods?"

"You'll get them. You need to be patient. The yayo comes all the way from Colombia to us in Mexico. Then my cartel ships the drugs across the border to you."

"How long do I have to wait?"

"It shouldn't be much longer."

"You're shooting me a line."

Damian glanced over at Dominick and another goon standing in dark blazers near the door to the penthouse watching him and Musante like guard dogs.

Damian was thinking it was time to leave Vegas. Musante's protection was evaporating.

"Patience," said Damian. "Rome wasn't built in a day."

"Don't talk to me about Rome. I'm Italian. You're Mexican."

"You'll get your product if you wait a little longer."

Musante rolled over and sat up on the massage table, his towel covering his lap.

"I'm not letting you out of this room till you fucking deliver," he said. "Do my back, dear," he told Toni in a silky voice, which made Damian cringe.

Toni began massaging Musante's back.

"Why not?" said Damian. "What do you think I'm gonna do?"

"You're not gonna do nothing. You're fucking staying here." Musante paused. His face clouded. "And then I'm gonna invite friends of yours over here to play soccer with your head."

"Friends? What friends?" said Damian, apprehension seizing him.

"You'll see when they get here. It's a surprise."

"I'm not into surprises. Who are these so-called friends?"

"You'll find out soon enough."

Damian didn't have any friends in Vegas. He could read between the lines. The threat was clear. He had to hightail it. The problem was, how? That PI. Could that PI Brody help him? Brody claimed he could. Damian didn't see how Brody could help if Musante locked Damian in Musante's penthouse. Still, Damian had Brody's phone number. It was worth a try.

If he had to remain in this suite under lock and key, Damian was dead meat. It meant Musante was getting ready to whack him. Maybe these "friends" Musante was talking about were going to whack Damian's ass after they beat the crap out of him.

"I have to go to the head," said Damian.

"You know where it is."

Damian made a beeline to the bathroom, closed the door behind him, and produced his burner and Brody's business card.

"I need your help," said Damian into his burner in a low voice.

"I told you, you would," said Brody.

"You gotta get me outa here. Musante's holding me prisoner."

"Take it easy. I'll figure out something."

"They're gonna whack me."

"I need the elevator key to get to the penthouse floor."

"You need to get here fast."

A sharp rap on the bathroom door made Damian jump. He fumbled with his burner.

"Time's up," said Dominick through the door.

"I didn't bring my stopwatch."

"Funny. You're gonna be even funnier when your friends get here. You're gonna be a regular laugh riot. Now get out of there or I'll kick the door in."

"Gotta go," Damian whispered into his burner, and put it away.

"What?" said Dominick. "I couldn't hear you."

"I didn't say anything," said Damian, cracking the door.

Dominick shoved the door open, knocking Damian back on his heels.

"I didn't hear the toilet flush," said Dominick.

"Oh, you're right. I forgot."

Damian turned around and flushed the toilet.

"Outa here," said Dominick, his face humorless, eyes dull stones.

"You worried I'm gonna escape by swimming through the john's pipe?"

"Shut up and move. I love you funny guys when you get it in the neck. And you *are* gonna get it, buddy. Your jokes will turn into screams as you beg for mercy."

"I'm not your buddy."

Dominick straight-armed Damian into the living room, where Musante had returned to lying on his stomach and getting a massage from Toni. Damian stumbled forward.

"Nothing better than a massage, except what comes after it," said Musante, tilting his head so he could ogle Toni with knowing eyes.

"You wish you could be so lucky," Dominick told Damian.

Damian felt like he was going to barf. He had whacked a few narcos in his time, but it was part of his job and he took no pleasure in murder. But slot badgers . . . Their crimes were the pits. He had never stooped to their subhuman level and never would. He had once raped a girl, but she was the same age as him and she was asking for it. None of this slot badger shit. Some things were even worse than cutting a guy's strings.

Damian never should have trusted Musante in the first place. How could you trust a slot badger? Not that Damian had much of a choice. A hit team of *sicarios* was after him, captained by the rabid dog Roberto. There was no way Damian could fend off the lot of them by himself. What he needed was an army.

What he might end up with was a lone PI.

Chapter 87

Brody escorted Melody through the Venetian casino to the elevator to his room, which was the safest place for her at the moment. Her bloodthirsty husband Dan had no idea where Brody was staying.

"Do you think Dan knows where your apartment is?" said Brody.

"I don't know what he knows," said Melody. "I don't know how he found me here."

"Do you think you would be safe in your apartment?"

Melody chewed it over. "No."

"You can stay in my room till you figure out what to do."

"Thanks."

They took the elevator up to Brody's floor, walked down the carpeted hall, and reached his door. He used his key card to enter his room.

"You can take a shower and dry off," he said.

She angled over to the window and gazed outside. "Nice view."

"I have to go."

"You haven't even changed out of your wet clothes," she said, turning to face him.

"Duty calls."

"You need to get off your feet and rest for a second. Dan could have killed you."

"No time," he said, preparing to leave. "You're safer off not leaving the room."

"Why do I always get involved with the wrong man?" she said, as if to herself.

"I don't know when I'll be back."

"He seemed like a decent guy when I first met him. He owns his own trucking company that's going gangbusters.

Everything was working out for him. Why does he go bananas and start treating me like his slave?"

"Anyone can go nuts any time."

"I guess nobody's safe."

"If somehow he tracks you here, give me a call."

Closing the door Brody felt his cell phone vibrating in his trouser pocket. He strode down the hall and took the call, uncertain how he was going to help Damian escape Musante and his goons.

"It's me."

"Who?" said Brody, not recognizing the voice.

"Root. Maybe we can offer your client a deal."

"What kind of deal?"

"The agency can give him a new identity and a new life. A way to escape his enemies."

"Why would the agency want to do that?" said Brody, suspicious.

"A trade-off for intel."

"Intel from Damian? What could he possibly know that you'd want?"

"What do you know about him?"

"I know he needs help. A slew of people are out to kill him, including professional hit men."

"Do you know why?"

"My client didn't tell me. She only told me he's in danger."

Brody reached the bank of elevators and pressed the Down button. He realized he was rushing to save Damian without having formed a plan to exfiltrate him from Musante's penthouse. First things first. He had to get to the Paris.

"He's up to his neck in the underworld," said Root.

"I barely know him. Maybe he doesn't want the new identity you're offering him."

"Believe me, he does. The alternative is . . ." Root's voice trailed off.

"I haven't got him with me yet."

"I thought you were en route to the safe house."

"This is all moot if I can't get him out of Vegas."

What if Root and the CIA wanted to turn Damian over to the feds? wondered Brody. Brody knew the CIA wasn't invested with the power to arrest anyone, but the feds were. The problem with the feds was that some of them in the upper echelons were active in the cabal that was trying to remove the president from office. Which of them were on the up and up?

Brody stepped into the elevator as its doors opened. He held the doors open so he wouldn't lose the signal to his cell.

"His problems aren't gonna end after he gets out of Vegas," said Root. "He's no choir boy."

Brody didn't know where this conversation was leading.

"Are the cops after him?" he said.

"Not that I know of."

Brody didn't want to break the law. "I'm not aiding and abetting a criminal?"

He was glad the elevator was empty so nobody could eavesdrop on him. He didn't see anyone approaching in the hallway. He continued holding the doors open.

Root didn't answer right away. "I'm not aware of an arrest warrant out for him."

"I can't speak for Damian. I don't know if he wants to cut a deal with you."

"But you can contact him and ask him."

"Maybe."

"Where is he?"

Brody debated whether he should tell Root Damian's whereabouts. Would Root, a fashion photographer, help rescue Damian from Musante? Somehow Brody doubted it. Brody wasn't convinced Root really was CIA, though Root *did* seem to know a lot about Damian and he knew about Cobalt Green Tide. How would a professional photographer know about Cobalt Green Tide? The guy had to be CIA, and

he had arranged a safe house in Big Bear for Brody and
Damian. The bottom line was Root had to be on the level.

"I'm trying to find him," said Brody.

"You and half the town."

The elevator doors kept trying to close.

"Get Damian to the safe house ASAP," said Root.
"Remember to tell him he has a new life and a new identity
awaiting him, if he agrees to work with the agency. This
deal's almost too good to be true."

"That's what I'm thinking," said Brody, skeptical.

"As my sainted mother used to say, don't look a gift horse
in the mouth. The deal won't be on the table forever."

"I'll pass it on."

"One more thing. Do you know an FBI agent named Max
Shenk?"

Not another fed, decided Brody. Max Shenk?

"Never heard of him," said Brody.

"He's looking for Damian. Max Shenk knows a lot. He
could be a problem."

"Why's he looking for Damian?"

"That four hundred grand that's missing was meant for
him. He isn't happy."

"Cartel money meant for a fed? That makes no sense."

"It does when you understand the big picture."

"Which is?"

"Classified."

Brody had a feeling there was a lot Root wasn't telling
him.

"Did he say anything about me?" said Brody.

"You don't want to meet up with Max Shenk. Trust me."

Root terminated the call.

Brody allowed the elevator's doors to close behind him.
He rode down to the lobby. He stepped out into a knot of
grumbling waiting guests. A thirtyish couple clad in white
tennis outfits shot glares at him.

He didn't have time to think about Max Shenk. If he didn't act quickly, Damian wouldn't be alive much longer for anyone to find, including Max Shenk.

Chapter 88

Brody strode down the baking sidewalk to the Paris. The sun and the heat helped dry his soggy clothing. By the time he reached the Paris his clothes were still damp, but not as noticeably wet. They didn't become uncomfortable till he entered the air-conditioned casino, making them feel clammy.

He cut across the casino gaming room to the front desk. He had concocted a plan to obtain the elevator key to Musante's penthouse floor.

Brody's spirits deflated as he set eyes on the front desk, where a long, winding queue of tourists bogged down with suitcases stood checking in and out. He noticed the concierge's desk had no queue in front of it. Maybe because nobody was manning it. Nonetheless, Brody decided he'd take his chances there and ring the bell on the desktop.

As he approached the desk, a thirtysomething woman wearing a black blazer bobbed up from behind the counter, smiling, her mahogany hair neatly secured behind her head with a tortoiseshell barrette.

"I need the elevator key to the penthouse floor," he told her.

"That's a private floor, sir," she said with a courteous smile.

"I know. That's why I need the key."

"You don't understand—"

"This is an emergency."

"I'm sorry, sir. That floor is off limits to guests," she said, her voice firm.

"A 911 call was placed to paramedics from Mr. Musante, a resident on that floor. He's dying from a heart attack. I need to help him."

"Who are you?" the concierge said, her brow rucked with concern.

"I'm a paramedic."

She ran her eyes up and down him. "You're not in uniform."

"Every second counts," said Brody, face determined. "Do you want his death on your conscience?"

"Where's your uniform?"

"I'm off duty. My station chief knew I was here and called me because I'm at the scene of the emergency."

"I see."

"Well?"

"Well what?"

"Where's the key? This is an emergency."

"I—uh—I—don't know—I—"

"I'm gonna trash you and your hotel on Yelp if you don't give me that key. You caused a man's death by preventing a paramedic from accessing his room."

A look of horror crossed her face. She bent down, retrieved the elevator key, and handed it to him.

"Not Yelp," she muttered. "Please."

Brody snagged the key from her hand and bustled to the bank of elevators, assuming a self-important demeanor, his mission urgent.

When he disappeared from the concierge's view, he slowed down and blended in with the crowd. Now that he had the key, he wanted to become anonymous, someone no one would remember.

He reached the elevators and took the next one. A Chinese tourist and his wife entered with him. The couple exited on the twelfth floor. Alone, Brody inserted the key in the penthouse floor's lock on the control panel and pressed the floor's button.

Fifty seconds later the elevator doors slid open.

Chapter 89

He stole toward Musante's door.

He tapped lightly on it.

"Maid," he said in a high-pitched voice, and pressed his eye so close to the peephole that it obscured the inhabitants' ability to see his face.

Someone behind the door muttered, "Shit."

Brody heard him undo the lock, whipped out his SIG, and waited for the door to open.

When it cracked, he kicked it open and thrust into the room, gun in hand.

Dominick staggered away from the door, thrown off balance, an open bag of Cheetos in his hand spilling its contents on the carpet. Greasy orange Cheeto crumbs stained the corners of his mouth. A hodgepodge of Cheeto curls strewed the floor at his feet like pine shavings.

"I hope you made out your will," he said, hunching his shoulders.

Brody brandished the SIG at him and scoped out the room. He didn't see Damian.

"Where's Damian?" he said.

"What's all the noise?" said Musante, annoyed, strutting into the living room, bare-chested, a lime green towel engirdling his waist.

He spotted Brody and froze. "Who let that scumbag in here?"

"Where's Damian?" said Brody, and trained his SIG on Musante.

"Get the fuck outa here."

Brody squeezed off a round. The bullet took off Musante's left earlobe and perforated the wall.

Screaming, Musante clutched his bleeding ear. "You shithead."

"The next one kills you," said Brody.

"That was a mistake," said Musante, grimacing, pressing his hand against his wounded ear. Blood trickled down his neck.

One of Musante's goons flew out of the bathroom, his fly open, a Glock 17 in his hand. He fired at Brody. Brody fired back, felling him. The goon crumpled on the floor.

Wearing a sheer scarlet leather dress, a five-five fortysomething woman with bobbed blonde hair sprang out of a room with fear in her exophthalmic grey eyes.

She had high cheekbones which descended into a vulpine chin. An overbite detracted from any glamour her face might otherwise have had. Her mouth had a twist of a sneer permanently etched on it as if she knew how depraved human nature could be and was well acquainted with it—and, indeed, reveled in it.

But now she was scared.

"What happened?" she said, horrified at the sight of Musante's bleeding ear.

She saw Brody with a gun in his hand and froze.

"Who's that?" Brody asked Musante.

Musante said nothing, continuing to clutch his bleeding ear.

Brody fired another bullet at him. It flew inches over Musante's scalp. Musante flinched and ducked.

"Want me to shoot off one of your fingers next?" said Brody.

"You fucking bastard."

"Who is she?" said Brody.

"Alice."

"What's she doing here?"

Musante riveted his eyes on the SIG in Brody's hand aimed at him. "She picks up girls for me. She's interviewing a new prospect."

"Your madam, huh?"

"Jealous?"

"You're sick. You're both sick," said Brody, glancing at Alice and Musante.

"Don't knock it till you've tried it," said Musante.

Brody wanted to belt the slot badger in the jaw, but that wasn't why he had come here.

He contented himself with saying, "Give me an excuse for blowing you away."

Musante sniggered at him.

"She's as bad as you, pimping girls for you," said Brody.

"She enjoys them as much as me, if you get my drift."

"What's happening?" said Alice, shifting her eyes back and forth between Brody and Musante with alarm. "I didn't sign on for anything like this." She turned to Brody. "Are you a cop?"

"No," said Brody.

"He pays these girls fifty dollars an hour for a massage. There's nothing illegal about that."

"There's more than a massage involved."

"I wouldn't recruit girls for illegal or immoral purposes."

"Don't listen to her," said Musante. "She likes the girls' massages as much as I do. Even more."

"What's wrong with getting a massage?"

"Don't act all innocent." Musante snickered. "The massages you get make you climax."

"That's a lie. I know what you do with these girls. You stick it in every hole in their bodies. The cops'll put you away for the rest of your life if I start talking."

"Shut up."

"I'm not going to jail for you."

"I made you what you are today. Without me you'd still be working the sidewalks in a two-bit G-string getting your photo snapped with tourists for a couple bucks."

"You asshole. Wait till I tell them how many hundreds of girls you've had in here. I have photos of you getting blowjobs from naked thirteen-year-old girls to prove—"

"Go on," said Musante. "Keep incriminating yourself."

"I don't have time for this," said Brody. "Where's Damian?"

"He's—," said Alice.

"What makes you think he's here?" Musante cut in.

Alice looked bewildered.

"I know he's here," said Brody. "Get him."

Musante started to leave the room.

"Hold it," said Brody.

"You told me to get him."

"Not you. Tell one of your goons to get him."

"Why do you want him?"

"He's leaving with me."

"He wants to stay here. He wants my protection."

"No, he doesn't. I'm tired of talking. Tell 'em to bring him out."

"Bring Damian out here, Biff," Musante called to another room.

A lantern-jawed goon in his late twenties over six feet tall with a gun pointed at Damian's head entered the living room, using Damian as a shield. One of Biff's brown eyes looked out of true, Brody realized.

He figured Biff had a glass eye. The lack of an eye could throw off Biff's depth perception, Brody knew, which in turn, Brody hoped, would throw off his aim.

"Drop the gun or I'll shoot him," Biff told Brody.

"*You* drop the gun," said Brody, and swung his arm toward Biff. "Or *I'll* shoot *you*."

Biff had black hair cut in a flattop and an acne-pocked face. He had a flattened nose, like it had met a fist head-on and had never returned to normal. His muscular build bulged under his tight black T-shirt.

"How do you want to die?" Musante asked Brody with a leer.

"From old age," said Brody.

"Not gonna happen."

"How would you know? You're not gonna be around when I die."

Musante smiled. "You're wrong. I'm gonna have a ringside seat to your death."

"How 'bout I take you out now?"

"Biff will shoot you. Right, Biff?"

"Yeah, boss," said Biff, black eyes showing no emotion, two lumps of charcoal in a snowman's face.

"You know how many guys I whacked?" Musante asked Brody.

"It doesn't matter," said Brody.

"Too many to count. And Biff's taken out even more than me."

"Then you both deserve to die."

"Except you're the one that's gonna do the dying."

"Let him go," Brody told Biff.

Biff pressed his Glock's muzzle against Damian's temple.

"Drop the piece," he told Brody.

Brody didn't want to run out of bullets. He hadn't brought a spare magazine.

Chapter 90

Brody shot Biff in the head.

The impact of the SIG's bullet knocked Biff backwards. Stumbling, Biff squeezed his Glock's trigger. The bullet soared awry, striking and bursting the inflated pink blow-up doll that hung from the ceiling. Hissing, the deflating doll sank to the floor in a heap.

Biff's knees buckled. He went down hard, slamming the back of his head against the floor.

Musante pulled a gun from under the massage table behind him and whipped the barrel toward Brody. Brody shot Musante in the head. Brody usually double-tapped his victims to make sure they were dead, but he had to count his bullets. He had no idea how many more goons were hiding in other rooms getting ready to come out blasting.

"They were gonna whack me when the *sicarios* got here," said Damian.

"*Sicarios*?" said Brody.

"Musante just got off the phone telling them I'm here."

"We gotta move."

"Behind you," said Damian, staring over Brody's shoulder.

Brody slewed around, gun in hand, not knowing what to expect, ready to fire.

Dominick was pulling a pistol out of the holster on his waist and preparing to fire at Brody. Brody shot Dominick in the head. Dominick lost control of his pistol and plunged to the floor.

Damian lunged at Dominick and scoffed up the gun from the floor two feet away from Dominick's motionless hand.

Brody heard movement off to his side. He picked up on Alice darting to a sideboard and jerking a pistol out from its bottom drawer.

"Don't," said Brody.

Ignoring him she whirled around, leveled the pistol at him, and crumpled as Brody shot her in the head. She moaned, briefly.

Her gun went off. The bullet slammed into a stuffed green frog on a shelf full of stuffed animals on the wall. The frog did a little pirouette and tumbled off the shelf. Musante must have put the toys there to appeal to the girls he and his pimp recruited.

"How many more goons?" Brody asked Damian.

"Dunno," said Damian.

"Let's beat it."

"What about the girls?"

"There are girls here?" said Brody, looking around in surprise.

"They're in a bedroom in the back."

None of them had seen him, Brody decided. It was best he got out of here before they ventured out to see what had happened and spotted him.

The cops were going to be all over these stiffs like flies. It was self-defense on his part, but he didn't want the cops dragging him down to the station to grill him, especially if they were in Musante's pocket.

If he beat it, how would the cops know *he* had clipped the mobsters? wondered Brody. He stooped down and gathered his brass from the carpet. He deposited the spent cartridges in his trouser pocket. With luck the cops would think it was just another mob hit with one faction wiping out another in a turf war. Happened all the time in the Mafia.

Brody took one last survey of the room casting around for his brass and for any goons popping out of doors to other rooms.

"Let's go," he said.

He and Damian made for the door to the hall.

"They were a bunch of pervs," said Damian. "They made my skin crawl. Fuck 'em."

Brody knew the feeling.

Damian spat on the floor in disgust.

"You shouldn't have done that," said Brody.

"Why not? You a neat freak? They're garbage."

"DNA. The cops'll know you were here."

"I'm not in their system."

"How can you be so sure?"

"Don't worry. I'm Mexican. From Guadalajara. The *sicarios* are gonna be here any second."

"They followed you all the way from Mexico?"

"Yeah. They take contracts all over the world."

"How do you know so much about them?"

Damian said nothing.

"I'd like to know," said Brody.

"We really need to get outa here," said Damian, his face breaking into a sweat.

He wiped off the sweat under his nose with the back of his wrist.

Damian was right, Brody decided. They could discuss it later.

They headed out the door.

Chapter 91

Don Gaetano's son Juan pelted into their hacienda's living room, gasping for breath.

"What is it, Juan?" said Don Gaetano, who hid the tiny spoon he had been using to snort cocaine.

"Papa, there's a big pile"—Juan gasped for breath—"a big pile"—more gasps.

"Pile of what?"

Juan leaned forward, hands on his knees, trying to catch his breath, his tongue hanging out.

"Dog crap," he managed to say at last.

"Dog crap?"

"In our yard. Come look."

Juan grabbed Don Gaetano's hand and led him out of the living room, past the pool deck, and into the backyard. Don Gaetano enjoyed the fragrance of fresh-mown grass that suffused the warm air.

It took them a while, but at last they reached the perimeter of their property. Juan pointed at the brown clump surrounded by swooping flies.

"Big dog," he said.

Don Gaetano glowered at the mess on his newly mown lawn. He raised his glare to his neighbor's property.

"It's their Great Dane that did that," he said. "Those stinking slobs. We have the worst neighbors."

He stalked back to his hacienda, Juan in tow.

Wearing a scarlet dress with a broad black velvet belt Carmen saw Don Gaetano enter the living room fuming.

"*Qué pasó?*" she said.

"The neighbors."

"What are they complaining about now?"

"Their filthy dog dumped on our lawn."

Rage consumed Carmen. Her eyes popped.

"Those pigs. They're always complaining about us, and now look what they do. Have they no decency?" she said, stamping her heel on the hardwood floor.

"We ought to make them eat it."

"How dare they?"

"Why can't we have decent neighbors, instead of pigs fit for a sty?"

Clad in a bespoke dark suit and a lime silk moiré tie, a patrician smooth-faced man pushing fifty, all of five ten, levered himself up from the sofa and approached Don Gaetano.

"Don Gaetano," he said, nodding with a polite smile.

Don Gaetano gazed at Mayor Valdez with surprise. Don Gaetano quickly composed himself.

"Mr. Mayor," he said.

"I didn't have a chance to tell you the mayor has come to see you, dear," said Carmen.

"To what do we owe this pleasure, Mr. Mayor?"

"Would you like a drink, Mr. Mayor?" asked Carmen.

"*Una Tecate, por favor*," said Valdez. "*Gracias.*"

Valdez's face became grave after Carmen departed.

"We have a problem," said Valdez. "The media are up in arms about the assassination of our esteemed police chief Roderigo Zendeja."

"How tragic," said Don Gaetano.

"They are saying you had something to do with it. Of course, I told them they're wrong, but they're very persistent."

Don Gaetano paced in a semicircle and came to a halt. "With all due respect, Mr. Mayor, Zendeja had it in for me."

"Believe me, Don Gaetano, I hate to ask you this, but did you have anything to do with his murder? The papers are saying you did."

"The papers," Don Gaetano scoffed. "They say anything that sells copy."

"Zendeja's murder is putting you in a bad light."

"He was cheating my organization." Don Gaetano retrieved his cigar box from the coffee table, flipped open the box's lid, and offered the assorted cigars to the mayor. "A cigar?"

"No, thank you. What should I tell the papers you said to their charges?"

Don Gaetano thought about taking a cigar, decided not to, and put down the cigar box.

"I didn't assassinate him, if that's what you're asking," he said.

"That's good, because I thought we had an understanding."

"An understanding?"

"We don't target each other's leaders." Valdez paused. "Otherwise, when you target one of our leaders, we'll have to target one of yours in reprisal. You don't want the police going after your leaders, do you?"

"Are you here to make some kind of deal?"

"No. That's not my intention. I just want to make sure we have an understanding, a tacit agreement not to target the top of the food chain. This benefits both of us. We could easily start lopping off the heads of the cartels. All I have to do is give the word to the police. Your leaders would end up dead or rotting in jail."

"Are you making a veiled threat?"

"Not at all. I'm making sure our understanding is still in place."

"You sound like you're concerned about your own welfare."

Valdez bristled. "I have this city's entire police force at my beck and call. Why should I be concerned?"

"Then why are you here?"

"To find out if you had anything to do with the assassination."

"My organization will not accept being cheated."

"The assassination of my police chief is unacceptable."

"Zendeja was a bad cop on the take. A man like that is a blot on your reputation as mayor. You should have fired him a long time ago, Mr. Mayor."

"I won't be dictated terms," said Valdez, bridling.

Chapter 92

Carmen brought a glass of Tecate beer for Valdez from the kitchen. Smiling, she set the glass down on the coffee table, but sensed something was wrong.

"I'm not dictating terms," said Don Gaetano. "I'm simply saying Zendeja was a corrupt police chief. He sullied your reputation as mayor."

"I cannot accept assassinations of my officials under my regime."

"I cannot accept corrupt government officials that are cheating my organization. Zendeja was swindling us."

"Are you admitting you had him assassinated?"

"That's not what I said, Mr. Mayor. I said he was corrupt. He had to go."

"This assassination makes me look bad to the public. It makes it look like I can't maintain law and order in our fair city."

Don Gaetano noticed a tic on Valdez's left eye. Valdez scratched the tic to disguise it.

"The media blows everything out of proportion," said Don Gaetano. "It's how they make money."

"An assassination during my term of office could end my career."

"Don't let the media goad you into doing something you'll regret."

"That sounds like a threat."

"It's friendly advice, Mr. Mayor. I'm one of your biggest supporters. You know that. Just think of all the donations I've made to you."

Valdez stared at the coffee table, thinking. "I need to do something. I don't want to look like a weakling. This is my city. I'm not letting it descend into chaos."

"I agree. That would destroy both of us. We have a symbiotic relationship. We must keep up appearances."

Valdez looked up at Don Gaetano, confronting him. "I need to have someone arrested for the assassination, or the media will turn on me like the snakes they are."

"A scapegoat. I understand your dilemma. Nothing is lower than the media when it comes to perfidy and baseness. They get fat off dishing dirt."

"And?"

Don Gaetano mulled it over. "Tell them the Sinaloa cartel assassinated Zendeja."

"They're not active in my city," said Valdez, puzzled.

"They are now."

"I will need to arrest somebody. Leveling accusations isn't enough—not for a crime as heinous as this."

"I'll throw in five million dollars to help you find the assassin. You should be able to find the Sinaloa scumbag with that much money at your fingertips."

Valdez became pensive. "How can you be sure it was the Sinaloa cartel behind the murder?"

"I have informants in their cartel."

"My police haven't been able to infiltrate their organization."

"Of course not. They can smell cops a mile away."

"But you can—"

"We fit right in with them. They can't tell the difference."

"Five million, you say?" said Valdez, scratching his chin in thought.

"Ten million. We want to make sure you catch and execute the assassin."

Valdez liked what he was hearing. He nodded in agreement, planning his speech to the media.

"The Sinaloa cartel," he said. "Yes. They're invading our city. They have to be stopped. That'll play. The media will lap it up. It makes it look like we're being invaded by the biggest, most powerful cartel in the world, and I'm the only one that can stop them."

Valdez pumped his fist.

"You're getting the picture, Mr. Mayor," said Don Gaetano, smiling. "This is gonna enhance your reputation, not besmirch it. By the time it's over, the public will be begging you to run for another term. It's time to turn the tables on your detractors working in the lynch-mob media."

"The people in Guadalajara are going to love you, Mr. Mayor," said Carmen. "They'll erect statues to you."

Valdez regained his composure.

"Don't get any funny ideas. This doesn't make you one of us, Don Gaetano," he said, his bearing erect, his chin held high. "I hope you realize that."

Silence.

"One of you?" said Don Gaetano.

"The ruling class. You'll remain an outsider no matter how much money you donate to us. An unwelcome guest that we tolerate."

"*Tolerate*? You *tolerate* me? You *tolerate* my money?"

"The assassinations must stop. Committing assassinations will not make you one of us. You can't shoot your way into high society."

"It was the Sinaloa cartel, not me."

"Even though you have money, we can't acknowledge you. We'll never let you into the inner circle. We can never be seen with you in public. We can never allow a common criminal into our esteemed ranks."

"Esteemed ranks? Politicians on the pad, robber barons, shysters, oil monopolists, rent-gouging landlords, price-gouging big pharma—you call yourselves *esteemed*?"

"You realize there are some things money can't buy," said Valdez, his face smug.

"Like what?"

"Like respect and dignity," said Valdez, standing straighter.

You have all the dignity of a snake slithering in the grass, thought Don Gaetano. *You corrupt hypocrite, Valdez.*

"I believe we see eye to eye," said Valdez. "When can I expect your donation?"

"I'll have it wired to your dignified slush fund as soon as you leave."

Valdez did a double take.

Recovering his regal bearing, smoothing his jacket with his hand, Valdez took leave of them.

Don Gaetano glared after him. "He walks like he's got a poker shoved up his ass." Don Gaetano turned to Carmen. "He's not too proud to take my money."

"He's a pompous ass, but we need to humor him," she said.

"He better pick a police chief we can deal with to replace Valdez, or the new top cop's career will be short-lived."

"Does the mayor understand that?"

"He gets the message. If he doesn't know how to read between the lines, he shouldn't be in politics. It's the dirtiest game in town based on nothing but lies. You don't make it in that racket without being an accomplished liar."

"What about the dog turd?"

Don Gaetano looked at Carmen.

"We should make our stinking neighbors come over here and pick it up," he said, miffed, jabbing his forefinger at the floor.

"I know. Let's have a loud pool party tonight with a live mariachi band and a bunch of noisy guests and bug those creeps," said Carmen with a grin.

Don Gaetano slapped his thighs and laughed.

"I like the way you think," he said, and hugged her.

Chapter 93

Brody and Damian were entering the Venetian when Brody felt his cell phone vibrate in his trouser pocket.

"Hello?" he said, holding the cell to his ear.

"We need to talk."

"Who is this?"

"Special Agent Max Shenk of the FBI."

The name sounded familiar, decided Brody. Didn't Brockton Root mention Max Shenk to him? Brody didn't have time to talk to Max Shenk. On the other hand, since the guy was a fed, Brody decided he better make time for him.

"I'm busy," said Brody, trying to keep the conversation short. "What's this about?"

"I can't talk over the phone. Your phone might be compromised."

"What are you talking about?"

"The NSO Group might've taken control of it."

"NSO Group?"

"An Israeli cyberintelligence outfit that markets its services. Its Pegasus software can hack into an iPhone and access everything inside it, including phone calls. The NSO Group hacked El Chapo with Pegasus."

"What does this group want with me?" said Brody, bewildered.

Who would want to hack his cell phone? he wondered.

"It depends on who hired them," said Max Shenk.

Was Max Shenk trying to intimidate him by making him paranoid? wondered Brody. Or was the guy on the up and up?

Brody should be leaving town by now, but he didn't want to add feds to the hit team of *sicarios* chasing him. He had enough enemies to deal with.

"Where do you want to meet?" said Max Shenk.

"How about Delmonico's Steak House at the Venetian?" he said.

"Give me five minutes."

Max Shenk terminated the call.

"We got a problem," Brody told Damian, pocketing his cell.

"What?" said Damian.

"A fed wants to talk to me."

"Count me out."

"I'll talk to him alone. You disappear into the casino. Play the slots or something. Stay out of sight. I'll get back to you when we're done."

"How long's this gonna take? We gotta move it."

"I don't know what he wants."

Damian thought about it. "I might be better off splitting on my own."

"Look, I came here to help you. I got a cabin at Big Bear all lined up for us. We'll be safe there."

Damian demurred. "All right. But if this takes longer than fifteen minutes, I'm legging it, cabin or no cabin. The *sicarios* want a piece of me. I gotta get outa Vegas. I'm telling you, Roberto is a stone killer."

Damian ground his teeth.

"I'll get rid of this guy ASAP," said Brody.

Damian nodded and wandered down a row of slot machines beeping and chiming as gamblers fed money into their voracious metallic mouths.

Brody made for Delmonico's, a stone's throw away on Restaurant Row.

He stood at the entrance to the upscale restaurant waiting for Max Shenk. Brody had no idea what the guy looked like. All Brody could do was hang around the entrance and wait. Max Shenk must know what he looked like or why arrange a meet?

Eight minutes later a suit about forty with a round face showed up and studied Brody.

"Let's go to the bar," said the guy.

"Max Shenk?" said Brody.

"That's what I'm called."

Brody narrowed his eyes at him.

"Come on," said Max Shenk. He scanned the casino gaming room. "Humans' addiction to throwing away their hard-earned cash on gambling never ceases to amaze me."

Chapter 94

Brody and Max Shenk claimed stools at the bar that
skirted the lounge where a scatter of smokers relaxed on green
leather-upholstered sofas puffing cigarettes.

"How did you get my phone number?" asked Brody.

"A mutual friend of ours gave it to me."

Brody shook his head in puzzlement at the unenlightening
response.

"Brockton Root," said Max Shenk.

He ordered a Jack Daniels. Brody ordered a Perrier.

"I barely know Root," said Brody.

"That's immaterial. I understand you're looking for
Damian Playa."

How did everyone know so much about him? wondered
Brody. The feds and the CIA had no trouble finding him. Of
course, the intelligence agencies with their state-of-the-art
equipment and know-how could keep tabs on anybody. But
why had they singled *him* out of all people?

"Even if it's true, why is it your business?" said Brody.

"I told you. I work for the bureau."

"I don't see the connection."

"I want to talk to Damian."

"A lot of people do."

"Do you know where he is?"

"No," said Brody, well aware that lying to a fed was
committing perjury and could land him in jail.

He kept thinking about what Root had said about a cabal
of FBI and CIA agents in the deep state who were trying to
oust the president. With that in mind, how could Brody trust
any of them, including Root? Anyone from the two
intelligence agencies could be a member of the deep state
cabal. But Brody didn't see the connection between Damian
and the cabal. Was the cabal after Damian? Why would they

be? Brody realized there was a lot about Damian he didn't know.

Max Shenk changed the subject. "What do you know about Cobalt Green Tide?"

"Nothing."

Max Shenk eyed Brody skeptically.

"What do you know about Damian?" said Max Shenk.

"I know he needs my help. He got mixed up with a cartel."

"How is he mixed up with a cartel?"

Brody glanced at his wristwatch. "They're after him, is all I know. Will that be all?"

"I need to talk to Damian."

"I can't help you."

"Where is he?"

"Same answer."

Max Shenk drummed a tattoo on the polished mahogany counter with his fingers—fingers strangers to manual labor, devoid of calluses, Brody noticed.

"If you know and you're not telling an FBI agent, namely me, you are committing a crime," he said.

Brody said nothing.

"I don't want to see you go to jail," said Max Shenk, his face impassive.

"Are you arresting me?"

Max Shenk didn't answer right away, preferring to see Brody sweat.

"Why do you want to risk a jail sentence for this bottom feeder Damian?"

"Is that what I'm do—?"

"Who killed Ned Bates?"

"I don't know any Ned Bates."

Max Shenk leaned back on his stool, sizing Brody up.

"I had hoped you would see how precarious your situation is," he said.

"I can't tell you stuff I don't know."

"Do you have any idea what you're getting mixed up in?"

"I'm doing my job for my client."

"Who is . . . ?"

"Privileged information."

Max Shenk didn't appreciate Brody's stonewalling. "I could charge you with obstructing justice."

"I want to see a lawyer."

Max Shenk decided not to press the issue. "When you find Damian, will you tell him I need to talk to him?"

"I will."

Max Shenk withdrew his wallet from his jacket breast pocket. He flipped open the wallet, extracted a business card with his forefinger and thumb, held the card up, fiddled with its edge a few times with his thumb as if emphasizing its importance, watching Brody, and handed it to him.

"My phone number's on the card," said Max Shenk.

Brody pocketed the card without looking at it.

"If you find him and don't tell me, you could end up in a world of hurt," said Max Shenk.

"Are government agents in the habit of issuing threats?"

Max Shenk said nothing, jaw set.

"You could end up marginalized," said Max Shenk at length.

Marginalized? thought Brody. Strange expression to use. Sort of like the CIA using the term *enhanced interrogation* when they meant *torture*.

Brody was having second thoughts. Maybe he should just hand over Damian to the FBI and be done with it. But Brody didn't work that way. When he took on a job, he remained loyal to his client. He would lose clients if he did otherwise. To hand Damian over to the feds before delivering him to his client violated Brody's code. However, Max Shenk's intel made Brody wonder if Damian was wanted for a crime.

Brody didn't cotton to the idea of helping a criminal escape the law. But Max Shenk hadn't said Damian was a suspect in a crime.

"Why do you want to talk to him?" said Brody.

"That information is eyes only."

Brody stood up to leave. "I'll give him your card if I find him."

"Wait a second. What do you know about Julius Caesar?"

"He was a Roman emperor assassinated by Brutus and a cabal of senators on March 15, 44 B.C."

Max Shenk hiked his eyebrows. He said nothing.

"What's the point of your question?" said Brody, baffled.

Max Shenk downed his Jack Daniels.

Why had Max Shenk broached the subject of Julius Caesar? wondered Brody. The subject had come out of the blue.

Max Shenk studied his drink, remaining tight-lipped.

Brody had to get moving.

Shaking his head in confusion Brody left Max Shenk at Delmonico's, not without peering over his shoulder to check if the fed was following him.

Chapter 95

Brody walked back and forth on the casino floor a few times, threading his way through the scores of slot machines, making certain Max Shenk wasn't tailing him.

Brody consulted his wristwatch again. Over twenty minutes had passed since he had parted ways with Damian. It was past the time allotted by Damian for Brody to return to him. What could Brody have done? He hadn't been able to shake Max Shenk.

Brody cast around for Damian among the swarms of slot machines. Brody didn't see him. Brody had gone to all this trouble to find him and now it was looking like he had lost Damian. Brody cursed under his breath.

He picked up on a guy playing a *Walking Dead* slot machine, entranced by it, not aware of Brody's presence. From behind it could have been Damian. Brody approached him.

Feeling someone's presence behind him, Damian craned around and looked up from the slot machine at Brody.

"Finally," said Damian, standing up. "I was getting ready to leave."

"Do you know anyone by the name of Max Shenk?"

"Max Shenk?" said Damian, reflecting. "No, I don't think so."

"Have you ever heard of Cobalt Green Tide?"

From the expression of recognition and a trace of fear on Damian's face, Brody figured the name rang a bell. Damian's face turned blank in short order.

"Never heard of it," said Damian.

"Are you sure?"

"Positive. How could I forget a name like that? What is it? A detergent?"

Brody didn't believe him. Which meant Brockton Root could have been telling Brody the truth when he had told Brody Damian was a bagman for CJNG who was supposed to deliver money to Cobalt Green Tide. It would explain why Max Shenk and the feds wanted Damian if Cobalt Green Tide LLC was an illegal shell company. A shell company by definition wasn't illegal, Brody knew. But a shell company receiving money from a drug cartel raised all kinds of alarms.

Now what? wondered Brody. Should he turn the suspected criminal Damian over to the feds? But what if Damian wasn't a criminal? What if Root and Max Shenk were wrong about Damian?

Brody tried to clear his head. Araceli had hired him to find her brother. That was Brody's job. It was his duty to carry it out.

"We need to go to my room before we leave," said Brody.

"Why can't we leave now?"

"I need my suitcase."

"Roberto and his *sicarios* could find us any second," said Damian, scanning the casino.

"What did you do with the money?"

"What money? What are you talking about?"

"The money that was meant for Cobalt Green Tide."

"I don't know what you're talking about."

"Isn't that why the *sicarios* want you dead? Because the money's missing?"

"They want me dead because they hate my guts. They're cartel hit men."

"What did you do to them to make them hate you?"

"I don't have to listen to this. I'm splitting by myself. Who needs you?"

"Wait a second. I'm your best chance. I have a safe house lined up for us."

Damian mulled it over. "I don't understand why you're giving me a hard time."

A rowdy bunch of gamblers roared at a blackjack table twenty-odd feet away, a cloud of cigarette smoke hovering over them.

"Ohmigod!" screamed a peroxide blonde, looking at the cards in front of her.

Damian and Brody started.

Brody couldn't tell if she had won or lost. It could have been a scream of ecstasy or agony.

"I'm trying to find out what's going on," he told Damian.

"Why does it matter?" said Damian.

"If you're on the lam with stolen money, my helping you makes me an accessory to a crime."

"Rest easy. I don't have any stolen money. I don't have any money. Wanna see my wallet?" said Damian, reaching for his trouser pocket.

Brody wanted to believe Damian, because he wanted to complete his assignment. But Brody had doubts about Damian. Brockton Root believed Damian was involved in a conspiracy to overthrow the president. Max Shenk wanted to know what Damian knew about Cobalt Green Tide, a shell company Root believed was connected to the conspiracy.

"Do you have any luggage?" said Brody.

"The hell with it. We gotta get outa here. A *sicario* could step into this casino any second. What do I need with luggage if I'm dead?"

"You said they were going to Musante's penthouse."

"When they find out he's dead, they're not gonna waste any time there."

Damian was right, of course, decided Brody. "Let's go to my room."

Chapter 96

When Brody took out his key card to unlock his hotel room door, he heard rustling inside his room. He tensed.

"What's wrong?" said Damian.

"There's someone in my room."

"Maybe it's the maid."

"She already came this morning."

Brody withdrew his SIG, swiped his key card, saw the light in the lock turn green, shoved open the door, and thrust into the room, swinging his pistol in an arc around the interior in search of movement.

Damian followed him in, gun in hand.

Brody saw someone leaving the bathroom and trained his SIG in that direction.

Melody walked out of the bathroom, wearing only a white bath towel wrapped around her naked torso and one around her wet hair. Her green eyes bugged out in terror at the sight of the guns aimed at her.

Brody saw Damian's gun out of the corner of his eye.

"Don't shoot," said Brody, pushing Damian's gun barrel down, and lowering his own SIG.

"Are you here alone?" Brody asked Melody.

"Did you think I would invite guests?" said Melody, her face apprehensive.

Brody felt relieved he had held his fire. "I forgot you were here."

"Thanks a lot. You almost shot me."

"The cocktail waitress," said Damian, recognizing Melody.

"We've got company?" Melody asked Brody. "I'm waiting for my clothes to dry out," she said, gesturing to the bath towel she was wearing.

"I'm checking out," said Brody, gathering his clothes and throwing them in his suitcase that lay on the portable aluminum-framed nylon luggage rack at the foot of his bed.

"Where am I supposed to go to get away from Dan?"

"I have to protect my client."

"I thought *I* was your client."

"You are, too."

Ready to pack the shirt in his hand, Brody paused, analyzing his problem. He knew he shouldn't have taken her on as a client since he was working on another case, but she had been desperate for help and her life was in danger.

"You're just gonna kick me out and let Dan kill me?" she said with a combination of consternation and outrage.

Folding his shirt Brody tried to decide his next move.

"How are we supposed to get to this cabin you were talking about?" Damian asked Brody. "I don't have a car."

"Neither do I. If we rent a car, we'll have to use plastic, and the *sicarios* will be able to trace us. That's out." Brody paused in thought. "We could take a bus."

"A cab would be quicker."

"The cabbie might remember your face and tell the *sicarios* if they go around pumping the cabbies if any of them saw you."

"By then, we would already be safe at the cabin."

"But the *sicarios* would know where to find us after they questioned the hack. We may be holed up in that cabin for a long time—till they stop looking for you."

Damian screwed up his face. "That could take a while. They're not gonna give up right away. I know those guys."

"I have an idea," said Melody, padding toward Brody on her bare feet, the bottom of the towel around her torso riding up her toned thighs.

"You look like you work out," said Damian.

"Pilates."

"What's your idea?" said Brody, glancing at her white thighs.

"You can use my car—if . . . ," she said.

"If what?" said Brody.

"If you take me with you."

"Sounds good to me," said Damian.

"You could be exposing yourself to even more danger than you're in already," Brody told Melody. "There's a hit team after this guy."

"If Dan finds me, he's gonna kill me," she said. "Now that he knows I'm here in Vegas he's gonna scour every nook and cranny of this town until he finds me. I'll feel safer elsewhere."

"All right. Let's do it."

He was either killing two birds with one stone or killing both of his clients literally, decided Brody, hoping it didn't come to the latter.

Chapter 97

Brockton Root was sitting at a booth in Cleopatra's Barge at Caesar's Palace when he saw John Tool approach. Teresa and Yolanda were sitting at the bar with a third woman they had befriended in the nightclub.

John Tool, thirty-seven, well coiffed, had a lived-in face and watery blue eyes that betrayed his fondness for booze. He was wearing a tan blazer, his white button-down shirt open at the collar. John Tool was a fellow CIA agent, but he wasn't under deep cover like Root, though "John Tool" wasn't his real name.

"Hello, Root," said John Tool, sitting opposite him.

"Small world," said Root. "It took you long enough."

"The heat."

"Make this short, Tool. A member of the cartel could show up here any second. I don't want my cover blown."

"I wouldn't be here if it wasn't important," said John Tool with a raspy whisky voice.

"I'm listening," said Root, glancing at the models, making sure they weren't watching him.

"Those girls at the bar are your models?"

"Two of them are."

"You a fag?" said John Tool. "I heard all you fashion photographers are poofters."

"Sorry, no."

A flash of annoyance crossed John Tool's face. "You got those three hot broads over there and you're sitting here alone. How can you stay away from them?"

"Two hot broads. The other girl is a stranger. Teresa and Yolanda have no idea I work for the agency. They think I'm a fashion photographer, and I want to keep it that way."

"Whatever happened to the good old days with swinging James Bond?" said John Tool with disillusionment.

"I didn't say I didn't sleep with them. There's a time and a place for everything."

"Look, don't get me wrong. I don't care if you're a fag. I'm a lapsed Catholic. I went to Holy Cross. I'm not intolerant. The agency these days, they let anybody in. Trannies, ferries, the works. LGB—whatever. Q—what's Q? And then there's gender-fluid—whatever the hell that is. I don't care. Live and let live is what I say."

"You're wasting time."

John Tool kept his eyes laser-locked on the models.

They were too absorbed in their conversation with the third woman they had befriended, a woman who appeared overjoyed in their presence, to notice John Tool's gaze.

The third woman must have recognized Teresa and Yolanda and asked to join them in a drink, decided Root. Maybe she was a model wannabe and was asking them tricks of the trade.

Root cleared his throat.

"A whistleblower has approached me," said John Tool, managing to tear his eyes away from the girls.

"About what?"

"Cobalt Green Tide."

"How reliable is he? He could be spreading disinformation."

"He works for the CIA."

"That doesn't guarantee his reliability. What's his name?"

"He's a whistleblower. His identity is secret."

"If I know his name, maybe I can vouch for his bona fides."

"You don't know everyone in the agency."

"I know some. I'm suspicious that he doesn't give his name."

"He's afraid of retaliation. Whistleblowers' identities are protected by the Whistleblower Protection Act to shield them from retaliation. You know that."

"I want to know his name."

John Tool shrugged it off. "He says he infiltrated Cobalt Green Tide. He claims it's a shell company that's funneling money to the cabal that's trying to oust POTUS from office."

"That gibes with what I'm hearing. The question is, what is the cabal doing with the money?"

"The whistleblower says Cobalt Green Tide was supposed to receive a payment of four hundred thousand bucks from a Mexican cartel."

"For what purpose?"

John Tool lowered his voice. "For a bribe to grease the palm of the secretary of the Department of Homeland Security."

"Sheila Dmytryk?"

John Tool nodded yes.

"Bribe her to do what?"

"The whistleblower isn't sure."

"The pieces are coming together—if this whistleblower is the real deal."

"I find him credible." John Tool hung fire. "I need to pick your mind. What do you know about any of this?"

"I know the said money is missing. CJNG sent a team of hit men to off the guy that botched the transaction."

"So where's the money?"

Root offered a half smile. "That's what everybody wants to know."

"This whole thing's as dirty as my kid's underpants."

The veins on the back of his hands bulging out, John Tool took a pull on Root's glass of beer.

"Why don't you help yourself to my drink?" said Root.

"I'm dying of thirst. The heat," said John Tool, blowing out his jowly face's cheeks.

"At least it's dry heat." Root scanned the nightclub, checking out the newcomers entering, knowing Roberto or one of the hit team could appear any moment. "Make yourself scarce. You blow my cover, I'm dead."

"I'm not finished. If cartel money is being used to bribe Sheila Dmytryk, we need to know why. What do they want from her?"

"I don't know anything about her."

"There's a rumor making the rounds inside the Beltway that she has a cocaine habit. Supposedly, she has a voracious appetite for the stuff. It's no secret she spends money like water and is in debt. Her husband's a professor at UNC at Chapel Hill and doesn't pull down a big-enough paycheck to satisfy her outsized needs."

Root thought he recognized one of the hit team enter the nightclub. Root's heartbeat shifted into overdrive. From this distance he couldn't be sure it was one of them.

"Beat it for now," Root told John Tool under his breath.

"The bribe meant for Dmytryk is in exchange for something. Do you know who would know what that something is? What does she have that somebody wants bad enough to pay four hundred grand for?"

"I'm not a Beltway insider. I spend most of my time out of the country."

John Tool took a last pull on Root's beer, which didn't escape Root's notice, and lumbered to his feet.

"Be seeing you," he said, and lurched toward the entrance, his unbuttoned blazer waving about him like wings.

John Tool was half in the bag, decided Root, watching the guy's reeling gait. Root wondered if Damian knew why the bribe was meant for Dmytryk. Could it be to get the secretary to go along with the conspirators' plot? Where the hell was Damian?

Chapter 98

Don Gaetano answered his satphone in his hacienda's living room as he sat on a leather recliner and puffed contentedly on a cigar, his feet resting on an ottoman, daydreaming about Valentina's voluptuous body naked under her Gestapo leather trench coat.

"*Patrón*, it's me."

"I was getting ready to call you," said Don Gaetano, a bit annoyed Valentina's image had vanished from his mind, but business called.

"I have important news."

Sitting up straight, Don Gaetano kicked the ottoman away and planted his feet on the hardwood floor.

"Shut up and listen," he said. "I've been trying to contact the mob capo Musante. He has agreed to give up Damian. Musante's not answering his phone. You need to meet him in person."

"That's why I'm calling, *patrón*."

"Go on."

"Musante was going to give us Damian," said Roberto. "We went to Musante's penthouse and found him dead."

"What?"

"Somebody blew him away."

Don Gaetano cursed. "It must've been Damian. He found out they were going to give him up and whacked Musante."

"Musante and half his crew. All clipped. It was a massacre."

"I don't understand. How could Damian whack so many of them? Those guys were Mafia. They were pros."

"He must've had help. That gringo PI Brody may be helping him. That guy was snooping all over the strip for

Damian. I warned Brody to knock it off and split. But he's still here."

"He's a dime-store gumshoe. You can handle him."

"No problem."

"What about my money?"

"No sign of it."

"The traitor Damian must have it. Any sign of him?"

"No."

"My offer stands. The guy that whacks him gets a ten grand bonus."

"He must be nearby. Musante's stiff was still warm when we arrived at his penthouse. Funny thing. He was only wearing a towel."

Don Gaetano heard the crack of a gunshot. He craned his neck around and saw a body crumple in his doorway. He threw down his satphone, snagged a Belgian FN Five-seveN semiautomatic duct-taped under his coffee table's tabletop, and took cover behind an alcove wall. Gun in hand, he peeked around the corner of the wall casting around for the shooter.

He didn't see anyone, other than Arturo's figure lying on the floor.

Don Gaetano bolted to Arturo's side.

Who was attacking him in his own home? he wondered. Stinking Zetas? The mayor? Was this his way of exacting revenge for his police chief Zendeja's murder?

Don Gaetano didn't have time to think about it. The sight of his best and most trusted colleague's bullet-pierced body overwhelmed him. Arturo was still alive, he saw.

"Who did this?" said Don Gaetano.

Arturo tried to speak. Don Gaetano couldn't hear him.

Kneeling beside Arturo, Don Gaetano gently lifted Arturo's head.

"Who?" said Don Gaetano, tilting his ear close to Arturo's mouth.

Arturo gasped. He was having trouble breathing, his rough-hewn face contorted with pain. Phlegm or blood rattled in his throat. His lips parted.

"My—," he said.

Don Gaetano felt Arturo's head become heavier in his hand. Arturo's eyes became doll's eyes fixed in a glassy stare.

"Arturo, Arturo. I don't understand. Who did this?"

Don Gaetano shook Arturo's limp body, trying to bring him back to life. Tears welled in Don Gaetano's eyes.

"My friend," he muttered. "My one true friend, my trusted right arm, what have they done to you?"

He bowed his head in sorrow.

He heard steps. He sprang to his feet, gun at the ready.

Carmen was crossing the living room floor toward him. She screamed at the sight of Arturo's bloody body.

"Dear God!"

"Call an ambulance," said Don Gaetano.

He darted out of the living room onto the pool deck trying to find the shooter. He didn't see anyone.

"Not Arturo," moaned Carmen, collapsing, her scarlet dress pooling around her inert body.

Don Gaetano belted back into the living room, retrieved his satphone, and ordered his guards to stop any stranger in the vicinity and hold him for questioning. Next he summoned an ambulance.

Out of the corner of his eye, Don Gaetano caught sight of a figure in the front doorway. Wheeling around and assuming a crouch, he leveled his pistol at the figure.

Michael held up his hands in apprehension. "It's me Michael."

Sighing, Don Gaetano relaxed, lowering his gun.

"Michael," he said. "Oh, Michael, look what they've done to your father."

Grief-stricken, Don Gaetano approached Michael, who was now staring at Arturo's motionless figure at his feet.

"Papa," said Michael and knelt beside his father.

He snatched Arturo's wrist and felt for a pulse.

"An ambulance is on the way," said Don Gaetano.

"No need," said Michael, dropping Arturo's wrist.

"Michael, dear Michael," said Carmen, who had regained consciousness as she sat up watching him with tears in her eyes.

"Bastards," said Don Gaetano. "I'll decapitate everyone involved in his murder. Stinking bastards. They shot him in the back, the cowards."

"Do you know who did it?" said Carmen.

"No. I didn't see the shooter. Arturo tried to tell me. Ah, Arturo. Poor Arturo," said Don Gaetano, gazing morosely at his dead friend.

Chapter 99

From Cleopatra's Barge, sitting alone watching Teresa and Yolanda sitting at the bar, Root used his burner to call Don Gaetano.

"It's me," said Root.

"What do you want?" said Don Gaetano, irritation in his voice.

"I have important intel."

"Shoot."

There was something wrong with Don Gaetano, decided Root. He could tell from the guy's voice something had upset him.

"The CIA knows about Cobalt Green Tide," said Root.

Silence.

"How is that possible?" said Don Gaetano.

"A whistleblower told them."

"Who is the whistleblower?"

"I don't have that intel."

"Find out who the whistleblower is and call me back."

"I'll try."

"Could it be someone in my organization?"

"I'm in the dark."

"I must find out. If we have a mole, I have to destroy him. He'll sabotage my operation from within."

"I think it's someone in the deep state intelligence agencies here."

"Call me when you find out."

"Will do."

"What about Damian? Did you find him?"

"No."

"Why can't anybody find him?" said Don Gaetano in frustration.

"Is something wrong?"

"We've talked enough."

Don Gaetano terminated the call.

Root didn't know what was bugging the guy.

Root eyed Teresa and Yolanda. They smiled at him. They liked him because he knew how to make them look good in front of the camera. One of the perks of being a fashion photographer, he decided, nursing his beer. He smiled back at them.

Chapter 100

Brody, Damian, and Melody piled into Melody's beat-up ten-year-old silver Ford Focus in the casino parking garage.

"I'll drive," said Melody, opening the car with her remote fob.

"Let me," said Brody.

"It's my car."

"It could be dangerous while we're in Vegas. I better drive."

Melody agreed reluctantly. She rode shotgun.

"Do you know how to get to Big Bear?" she said.

"No."

"I'll program my GPS," she said, lifting a portable Garmin GPS device from the passenger's-side foot well and entering the starting and destination addresses into the device.

"It's cramped back here," said Damian, shifting his knees uncomfortably in the backseat.

"Hardly anyone ever sits back there," said Melody.

"Great. The seat must be dirty, too."

Melody rolled her eyes. She suction-cupped the GPS device to the windshield so Brody could read its screen and plugged its cord into the cigarette lighter on the dashboard.

Brody put on a pair of aviators he carried in his trouser pocket and fired the engine. As he pulled out of the parking garage, a woman's voice told him to turn right. He powered the Focus's windows up and flicked on the noisy AC.

Something about Damian kept nagging at the back of Brody's mind. Brody couldn't understand why the *sicarios* wanted Damian dead.

"Why are the *sicarios* after you?" said Brody, craning around to face Damian when they stopped at a traffic light.

"I told you, they hate me."

"Why do they hate you?"

Pause.

"I used to be a cop," said Damian.

"Oh? Where?"

"Guadalajara."

It made sense, decided Brody. *Sicarios* would hate cops on sight. But why go to such lengths to hunt him down in a foreign country and waste him?

"Did you bust one of them while you were a cop?"

"Something like that."

Brody figured there had to be more to it, something Damian wasn't revealing. Sending a hit team after an ex-cop just because he used to be a cop was overdoing it.

Brody faced forward. The light turned green. Brody drove with the rest of the congested traffic on Las Vegas Boulevard.

"Try to keep down and out of sight while we're in Vegas," he told Damian.

Damian scrunched down, exacerbating his discomfort with his awkward posture.

"This is gonna be a long ride," he said. "At least we got AC."

Brody started when he saw Roberto striding down the hot, pedestrian-choked sidewalk. Brody hoped the guy wouldn't be looking for him or Damian in a car. Brody tried to look unconcerned and inconspicuous.

"Get down," Brody told Damian, trying not to move his lips.

"I am down," said Damian.

Brody wished the traffic would speed up so he could get out of here before Roberto spotted him.

Brody picked up on Roberto's eyes flashing as they caught sight of Melody's Focus.

Christ, thought Brody. Had Roberto spotted him?

Chapter 101

Brody saw Roberto shoving pedestrians helter-skelter as he bulled his way through the mob on the sidewalk toward Melody's Focus. Roberto whipped out a piece. His eyes intent on Brody, Roberto plowed through the crowd kicking and elbowing anyone near him.

"Get down," Brody told Melody.

"What? Why?"

"A shooter's after us."

Melody turned her head and picked up on Roberto shoving tourists on the sidewalk, a gun in his hand.

"He looks insane," she said.

Adrenaline coursed through Brody's blood. The traffic was going so slow Roberto would be able to catch up with the Focus at this rate.

Seeing Roberto's gun, Melody leaned forward and bent her head into the foot well out of sight of Roberto.

Damian peeked out of the passenger's-side window from the backseat.

"Roberto," he said, ducking out of sight. "Shit."

Despite the raft of witnesses surrounding him, Roberto let loose a shot at Brody. The shot flew over the car's roof across the street and into the spine of a fiftyish roly-poly man in a yellow aloha shirt and turquoise shorts walking down the sidewalk, huffing and puffing in the heat, his face red, wiping sweat off his forehead with a handkerchief. He stumbled forward and fell on his belly. He sprawled facedown on the sidewalk in extremis.

Brody couldn't fire back at Roberto without hitting a pedestrian.

Wild-eyed, Roberto couldn't care less who got in the way of one of his slugs.

Brody hammered the steering wheel with his fist in frustration, urging the traffic to move faster. He produced his SIG. Maybe if Roberto saw it, he would think twice about charging the Focus.

The sight of Brody's pistol made no difference to Roberto. He fired again at the Focus. The bullet sang through the air and penetrated the front right fender. Pedestrians near Roberto screamed in terror and ran for their lives trying to get as far away from him as possible.

Brody couldn't believe Roberto was stupid enough or brazen enough to start throwing lead in the middle of a swarm of pedestrians.

"He has a gun," a rawboned guy in a porkpie hat screamed as he fled in panic.

"He's gonna shoot us," yelled a short middle-aged woman with a hunchback, who in short order proceeded to claw through the crowd to escape with her peculiar waddling gait.

In the rearview mirror Brody watched Damian in the backseat pull out the semiautomatic he had commandeered from the dead mobster in Musante's penthouse.

"Don't shoot," said Brody. "You'll hit a pedestrian."

"Roberto's a mad dog. The only thing that's gonna stop him is a nine mil."

"Stay down. Don't let him see you. He doesn't know you're here. He's coming for *me*."

"Whack him. You have to whack him."

His face sweaty with apprehension, Brody noticed a break in the traffic. He accelerated as Roberto was bucketing toward the Focus jinking through the milling pedestrians to reach his destination.

Roberto dashed into traffic on Las Vegas Boulevard after the Focus. He fired a shot at the Focus's rear window. The punctured safety glass spiderwebbed.

Brody hunched in the driver's seat as the bullet exited through the windshield.

Hearing the impact of Roberto's bullet with the glass, Damian scrunched lower in the backseat.

"He's catching up," he said, panic-stricken. "Get out of here."

In the rearview mirror Brody glimpsed Roberto's twisted face. Unhinged with fury, Roberto pumped his legs up and down on the tarmac behind the Focus, running alongside passing cars. He prepared to fire another slug at the Focus. Brody switched lanes.

"Fuckers. Fuckers," Roberto yelled.

Drivers in their cars cursed and honked at Roberto as he ran amok among the vehicles getting in their way.

Brody found an opening in traffic and accelerated into the gap. He started pulling away from the enraged Roberto, who had to dodge cars whooshing by him to avoid getting run over.

The driver of a van with neon pink sides advertising lap dancers sent to your room in ten minutes or less leaned on his horn as he narrowly missed running over Roberto. Text This Number for Live Girls, read the sign on the side of the van. Roberto gave the driver the finger as he stumbled to avoid the van.

"Text this," Roberto hollered, his middle finger extended.

Realizing his peril among speeding motor vehicles, Roberto hightailed it off the boulevard, lunging out of the way of a careering yellow low-slung, wedge-shaped Lamborghini at the last second and tumbling onto the sidewalk.

Damian stuck his head up and peered out the Focus's back window to see Roberto get to his feet, fit to be tied. If anything, he was madder than ever.

Roberto recognized him and, beside himself with rage, jumped up and down on the sidewalk, frothing at the mouth, cursing, pounding the air with his fist and his gun.

Damian grinned back at him, seeing Roberto had given up the chase.

Roberto fired a shot at Damian. Damian ducked. The bullet plugged the trunk's lid.

Roberto tried to flag down a cab. Hacks took one look at the gun in his hand and sped past him in fear.

Roberto heard an approaching police siren and fled from the boulevard to take refuge in the nearest casino.

Chapter 102

Two EMTs rolled a gurney with Arturo's corpse on it back to their meat wagon parked in Don Gaetano's hacienda's driveway. The meat wagon's red lights flashed on its roof.

Don Gaetano stood in his living room talking with the paramedic in charge of the medical crew, a mustachioed guy barely in his thirties wearing a navy blue uniform.

"What happened here, *Señor*?" said the paramedic.

"Somebody shot my best friend."

"Have you called the police?"

"No."

"I have to report the shooting to the police."

Don Gaetano moved closer to the paramedic, sizing him up. "What is your name?"

"Rafael Mendez."

Don Gaetano could see Mendez's last name printed in bold face Arial type on a name tag pinned to Mendez's breast pocket.

"You look like a man who enjoys the finer things of life," said Don Gaetano.

"I'm not a workaholic, if that's what you mean."

"Listen to me, Rafael. I don't want the police involved."

"It's the law. I must report all shootings to the authorities."

"This is a personal matter, and it would embarrass me if anyone found out about it."

"I understand, but it's the law."

Don Gaetano leaned closer to Mendez. "I'll give you a hundred thousand dollars to keep quiet about the shooting."

"USD?"

Don Gaetano nodded yes.

Mendez shrugged. "You're asking me to break the law."

"You're not breaking the law. You're just not reporting a shooting to the cops. Does that feel like committing a crime to you?"

"Uh—uh—no. But if I get caught I could go to jail."

"Why would you get caught? You take the corpse directly to the morgue, where my men will pick it up so we can have a proper funeral. All you have to do is keep your lips sealed about the shooting. Easy as pie."

"A hundred thousand, you say?" said Mendez, his expression noncommittal. "My little daughter needs an operation."

"*Qué lástima.* Your hearing is not so good. A hundred and fifty thousand is what I said."

Mendez looked around to make sure none of the EMTs could see him. "It *does* seem like a stupid law."

"If you don't feel like you're doing something wrong, you're not, is what I always say. Would you feel guilty for keeping my friend's death from the cops?"

"I wouldn't feel guilty. I would feel worried about getting caught and going to jail."

"That's not gonna happen. It's between you and me. Nobody else will know."

Mendez chewed it over. He lowered his voice. "OK. Where's the money?"

Don Gaetano retrieved bundles of hundred-dollar bills secured with red rubber bands from a wall safe and delivered them to Mendez. Uncertain what to do with the bundles, he decided to unbutton his shirt and stuff them inside it.

"I'll take care of everything," he said, buttoning up his shirt to conceal the cash.

"*Buen hombre*," said Don Gaetano, patting him on the back and escorting him out the door.

Chapter 103

After Mendez was gone, Don Gaetano turned to Carmen and Michael.

"We have to find out who murdered Arturo," said Don Gaetano.

"We will execute him," said Carmen, her face set. "Nobody can get away with killing our friends."

Don Gaetano's satphone bawled. It was one of his guards.

"None of my guards saw anyone enter the premises at the time of the gunshot other than Michael," said the guard.

"Are you sure? Only Michael entered?"

"Positive, *patrón*. My guards will swear to it."

Don Gaetano terminated the call.

Bemused, he paced around the living room in a circle, stroking his chin, deep in thought.

"What is it, dear?" said Carmen.

Don Gaetano stopped pacing and looked at Michael. "Did you see anyone suspicious when you were approaching the hacienda, Michael?"

"No."

"You didn't see any strangers?"

"I saw no one."

"How could the shooter escape without your seeing him? Were you coming up the path to the door at the time of the shooting?"

"I heard the gunshot when I was approaching. He must've fled in a different direction. Or maybe he was hiding out of my sight."

Don Gaetano stared holes in the floor. "We got a problem."

"What do you mean?" said Carmen.

Don Gaetano looked up at her. "The guards didn't see any strangers enter the premises at the time of the gunshot."

"So?"

"So the shooter wasn't a stranger. He must be one of my own men—somebody nobody would notice because he's one of us." Don Gaetano sneered. "We have a traitor in our cartel."

"Are you sure?"

"What other explanation is there?"

"I think you're right, *patrón*," said Michael. "The shooter must've known his way around the hacienda and he knew how to avoid detection."

"This is the worst scenario imaginable," said Don Gaetano, his eyes black.

"Who will replace Arturo?" said Carmen. "Nobody can replace him," she said, gazing at the pool of his blood coagulating on the floor near the doorway, her voice quivering with emotion.

Don Gaetano pulled himself together and faced Michael. "Are you man enough to fill your father's shoes, Michael?"

"He's so young," said Carmen.

"I can do it," said Michael, his face set, his eyes steely.

"Did Arturo see his killer?" Carmen asked Don Gaetano.

"I asked him when he was dying in my arms," said Don Gaetano. "He tried to tell me. He passed out before he could finish. It sounded like he said, 'My.'"

"My what?"

"I couldn't make it out."

"He didn't know what he was saying," said Michael.

"Could be," said Don Gaetano. "It could've been gibberish. He could've been incoherent. He was in great pain."

"Our best friend gone," said Carmen, her voice fraught. "Life is unfair."

Don Gaetano summoned Michael to a corner of the living room under a trophy of a stuffed grizzly bear's head mounted on the wall.

"We need to talk business," said Don Gaetano.

"*Sí, patrón.*"

"I'm convinced Damian stole my money. We can't let him get away with it."

"Didn't Roberto catch him yet?"

"No."

"I should have gone with Roberto."

"Nobody steals from me without paying the price."

"How can I help?"

"For now I just want you to be aware of what's happening, since you're taking Arturo's place as my right-hand man."

"Let's crucify the bastard that shot my father."

Grim-faced, Don Gaetano nodded yes. "In due time."

"My father may have been weak, but he didn't deserve to die with a bullet in his back."

"Weak?" said Don Gaetano, startled. "Your father weak? No, Michael. I never met anybody tougher than your father."

"He was weak. He told me I was too young to take cartel jobs. You didn't know him like I did."

"I knew him better than anyone. He was tough as rawhide."

Michael held his tongue, his face impassive.

"Worrying about a son's well-being is not a sign of weakness," said Don Gaetano.

Michael remained impassive.

Don Gaetano searched Michael's face. Nothing. Was Arturo right about his son's mental health? Arturo was worried Michael had emotional issues, that Michael was withdrawn and didn't speak to him.

Don Gaetano shrugged his doubts off. Michael's father had just been killed. Who wouldn't be upset about such a tragic event? That was the problem, Don Gaetano decided. Michael wasn't showing enough emotion. He was bottling it up. Not good.

But then again, decided Don Gaetano, closing himself off may have been Michael's way of dealing with trauma. Everybody had their own way of dealing with grief. Yet, it was fresh in Don Gaetano's mind that Arturo had voiced his concerns about Michael's psychological health . . .

Chapter 104

Root was riding in the ivory leather backseat of a white stretch limo with Teresa and Yolanda sitting opposite him in the mood-lit glitzy interior, where they were supplied with everything from champagne to vintage wines.

Using his Nikon D3X digital single-lens reflex camera, Root snapped photos of the models luxuriating in their seat in gleaming loose jade shantung dresses. Relaxing, Teresa and Yolanda listened to thumping, twanging rock music vibrate the limo.

The two held glasses of Cristal champagne in their hands. Their café au lait complexions smooth, their features chiseled, their expressions blank, their crimson bee-stung lips slightly parted, the models raised their glasses of champagne and toasted Root, as he photographed them living the high life.

Root kept snapping pictures till the stretch limo pulled to a halt in front of the water fountains in the immense pool at the Bellagio Hotel and disgorged them on the sidewalk.

Root commenced sweating as the relentless sun pounded him into the sidewalk.

"I can't last very long in this heat," said Teresa, fanning her face with her hand.

Root scoped out the pool and the row of fountains bisecting it that were jetting water into the air as Elvis's "Viva Las Vegas" blasted from loudspeakers mounted around the pool's perimeter.

"My face is getting sweaty," said Yolanda. "I'll look terrible for the shoot."

"You're both professional models. You know how to look good even in wretched conditions."

"It's hard to look good when you're covered with sweat."

"We'll just snap a couple of pictures and go inside and cool off. The magazine wants a shoot of you in front of a

casino. The fountains look great in the background. Both of
you get up on the wall around the pool and strike some poses
while the fountains are jetting."

"We should get hazardous duty pay for working in this
heat," said Teresa.

"Just get on the wall while the fountains are on. They'll
shut down soon."

"If I pass out from the heat, I'm demanding more money.
Nobody said anything about endangering my health on the
job."

Thanks to her dress Teresa climbed with difficulty onto
the cement rampart that skirted an alcove adjacent to the
sidewalk. A twenty-foot-high mesquite growing out of the
sidewalk provided what little shade there was.

Yolanda climbed up after her. "I don't like heights."

"We're not that high up," said Teresa.

"Don't look down," said Root.

"Easy for you to say. You're still on the sidewalk. Why
don't you climb up here with us? Then you'll know how it
feels."

"Take it easy. Relax."

"I feel lightheaded," said Yolanda.

"Look like you're enjoying yourselves basking in the
sun."

"Right."

"That's great," said Root, snapping pictures of their poses
on the rampart, the fountains mushrooming into the dazzling
blue sky behind them.

A black Lincoln Navigator shrieked to a halt behind Root.
Startled, he spun around.

"Get in," Roberto yelled through the open driver's-side
window. "I found Damian."

"Let me finish the shoot."

"Fuck the shoot. This is urgent."

"Wait for the girls to climb down."

"Fuck the girls. If you can't fuck 'em, kill 'em, is what I say."

Roberto whipped out a MAC-10 machine pistol and trained it on Teresa and Yolanda. They screamed. He fired a burst at them, cutting them down with a scythe of bullets. The bullet-riddled bodies of the two women plummeted into the pool, where they floated, their dresses billowing around them, their blood dyeing the water with carmine clouds.

"They're just props," said Roberto. "The shoot's over. Get in."

"You—," said Root, his face livid with rage.

"Get in or you're next," Roberto told Root, brandishing his MAC-10.

Root glowered at Roberto, aching to kill the psycho butcher.

Pedestrians on the sidewalk screamed and skedaddled, fearing a mass murderer was on the loose once again in Vegas. First it had been an insane sniper at Mandalay Bay. Now it was a nut in an SUV at the Bellagio that was slaughtering innocent people.

"It's only a movie," Roberto yelled out his window at the crowd.

Muttering, the crowd simmered down. Some of them giggled at their overreaction. They gazed at the corpses of the models floating in their own blood in the pool and smiled. It was only a movie.

Putting a lid on his anger Root clambered into the back of the Navigator, where the rest of the team of *sicarios* were sitting, stone-faced, armed to the teeth.

Roberto peeled off into traffic, cutting off a fluorescent lime Dodge Challenger with black stripes running from the bottom of its windshield down its hood. Stamping his brakes the teenage blond driver leaned on his horn, stuck his head out the Challenger's window, and screamed obscenities out the window at him. Roberto shoved his MAC-10 through his open window and fired a burst at the teen.

Terrified, the teen ducked back into his car and slowed down.

"You'll have every cop in Vegas down on us," said Root.

"Shut up," said Roberto, and put on speed, the Navigator lurching as it accelerated. "I don't care if you *are* our mole in the CIA." He aimed his MAC-10 over the front seat at Root. "I'll pop you if you get in the way."

Root believed him, his heartbeat jackhammering with fear for his life and with anger at Roberto, the cold-blooded murderer of Teresa and Yolanda.

"That's better," said Roberto, lowered his MAC-10, and concentrated on driving.

Root seethed. "Is that your answer to everything? Shoot everyone?"

"It's effective."

Chapter 105

Brody drove Melody's Ford Focus on the I-15 through the
Mojave Desert toward California. He glanced in the driver's-
side mirror. He didn't see anybody tailing him. The desert
was flat, tan, and empty save for rows of wind turbines
standing like rowels in the distance.

Every once in a while he spotted an odd Joshua tree or
saguaro.

Riding shotgun Melody looked concerned.

"What's wrong?" said Brody.

"I'm worried about Frenchie."

"Frenchie?"

"My French bulldog. I didn't have time to take him with
me. I don't know what Dan's gonna do to him."

"Not much you can do about it now—unless you have a
neighbor who could check on your dog."

"What if Dan decides to take out his anger at me on
Frenchie?"

"Dan's still in Vegas. He can't hurt Frenchie now."

"When he returns home."

"The most important thing is to get you to a safe place.
We can worry about your dog later."

"You obviously don't own a dog."

She was right, decided Brody. He spent too much time
out of town to own a pet. He checked out Damian in the
rearview mirror.

"Where's the money?" Brody asked Damian.

"I don't have it."

"They're not gonna stop chasing you till they get it."

"It's over with."

"What's over with?"

"My life."

"It's not over till you're dead."

"I will be soon at this rate." Damian paused. "I want to start a new life. That's what this was all about in the first place. I want to have my own auto shop."

"You're not alone," said Melody. "I want a new life, too."

"I'm sick of my job . . . all the killing."

"Killing?" said Brody, cocking up his head.

"Uh—uh—I told you, I was a cop."

"Your plan was to jack the cartel's money and start a new life?"

"What's wrong with that?"

"The consequences."

"You don't understand," said Damian, massaging his furrowed brow.

"Give them back their money, and they'll let you be."

"Haven't you been listening? I don't have it."

"Where is it?"

Damian gazed out his window into the blank desert. "It's gone."

"I want a new life without Dan," said Melody. "Without all the drunken violence."

"Violence?" scoffed Damian. "You don't know anything about violence. I'm from the slums of El Tapatio. People get murdered there every day. That's violence. The only way anyone can stand living there is by taking drugs."

"You worked hard and you escaped," said Brody.

"I escaped the slums, but not the violence. The violence follows me around like my shadow."

"If you don't have the cartel's money, you have nothing to worry about."

"You don't know these guys like I do. Especially Roberto. He's not gonna stop coming after me till I'm dead."

"He sounds like Dan," said Melody, half to herself.

"He's worse than Dan. He's worse than anyone I've ever met."

"Who did you give the money to?" said Brody.

Damian ignored him. "Except maybe Don Gaetano. He's gonna rape and murder my mother, sister, and girlfriend, if I don't give him the money. And I *can't* give it to him," said Damian, throwing up his hands.

"Your sister's safe."

"You think she's safe because she's in California? You don't know anything about Don Gaetano and Roberto, if you think that. No border wall's gonna stop them from whacking anyone they want."

"Who did you give the money to?"

Damian heaved a sigh. "I lost it."

"How could you lose all that money?"

"On a bet at the roulette wheel." Damian hung his head. "My whole life's ruined thanks to one spin of the wheel."

"It's not just the cartel that's after you. What about Cobalt Green Tide? The money was meant for them."

"What were you thinking?" said Melody.

"I was gonna double my money, keep half for myself, and deliver the other half to the bagman Ned Bates," said Damian. "Everybody would get their money and be happy, and I'd start a new life in this country."

"Nothing's that easy," said Brody.

"Tell me about it. But I was sure I was gonna win. Just one bet. One spin of the wheel. That would be all it would take to free me from the cartel. Freedom was so close I could taste it." Damian started punching himself in the head. "And I blew it. I. Blew. It. Jeeeeez. Now me and my whole family's gonna die."

"How do you know the roulette wheel wasn't rigged?"

"Rigged? They rig the equipment in Vegas?"

"For that kind of money, I wouldn't bet against it."

This was worse than he had expected, decided Brody. Damian's sister Araceli didn't know half of what her brother was into. It was better for her that she didn't know, or she would be worried sick—not only about her brother's life but about her own.

Brody wasn't sure he should continue helping Damian. Brody didn't take on cases to assist criminals. Damian had admitted he had gambled away the cartel's money. In effect, Damian had stolen it and lost it. Yet the money belonged to a cartel engaged in a criminal enterprise. Why should Brody be concerned if Damian had stolen dirty money? The cartel would never report Damian to the cops.

As Brody saw it, he wasn't helping a criminal escape, he was helping a hapless loser escape a gang of ruthless criminals bent on clipping him.

It was OK, then, Brody decided. He would complete his case and deliver Damian to Araceli.

Chapter 106

Root felt his burner vibrate in his trouser pocket in the backseat of the Navigator, as he sat among the armed *sicarios* who were grooving to monotonous rap music blasting out of the SUV's stereo speakers.

Root figured he better take the call. It could be urgent.

"You can't let the cartel get their hands on that money," said John Tool.

"What happened?" said Root, keeping his voice low. "What's all that racket? I can hardly hear you."

Root repeated his question.

"I found out what Cobalt Green Tide is gonna do with the money," said John Tool.

"You said they were gonna use it to bribe the DHS secretary."

"But now I know why."

"How did you find out?"

"The whistleblower's still singing."

"And they want to bribe her because?"

"Because they want her to vote with others in Ransom's cabinet to declare Ransom unfit for his job in the White House because he's insane and oust him by using the Twenty-fifth Amendment. With her vote there's a majority in the cabinet to force Ransom out and replace him with Dealey. *You can't let that money get into Dmytryk's hands.*"

Root gripped his burner, nonplussed. Foreign money. Dirty money. Cartel money. A bribe. All to accomplish a coup d'état so Vice President Dealey could seize the reins of power.

"Is the whistleblower believable?" said Root at length.

"I believe him."

"This is fantastic."

"Fantastic, but true. A cabal of deep state operatives in the intelligence agencies is trying to take down Ransom. You have to stop them by intercepting the cartel's bribe."

"Who are you talking to?" said Roberto, glaring at Root in the rearview mirror.

Root terminated the call.

"What?" he said, gesturing to his ear to indicate he couldn't hear because of the din of the rap music.

"Who were you talking to on the phone?"

"The magazine editor who commissioned the photo shoot I was doing with the models."

Roberto looked skeptical. "Did you tell him I whacked them?"

Root glared at him, the memory of Teresa's and Yolanda's murders fresh in his mind.

"No. I told him they're sick on account of the heat," he said.

"No more talking on your phone unless I say so."

"I'm not a member of your hit team. I don't take orders from you."

"I'm in charge of this mission, not you. Do as I say or I'll tell Don Gaetano."

Discretion was the better part of valor, Root decided. He chose to cooperate. Roberto was a keg of dynamite waiting to go off. Root saw no percentage in lighting Roberto's fuse. Root pocketed his burner. He would try to sneak in a call later.

He wanted to contact Brody to see if he had found out anything about the four hundred grand. It would have to wait, Root decided. Root didn't want to risk another call at this time lest Roberto confiscate Root's burner.

Coopted into the hit team, Root wouldn't be able to participate in any clandestine tête-à-têtes with Brody. The only way Root could contact Brody now was by phone when Roberto wasn't looking, decided Root, picking up on

Roberto's scowl at him in the rearview mirror from the driver's seat.

Chapter 107

His lime guayabera shirt unbuttoned, Don Gaetano was sitting in black jeans and leather huaraches on a chaise longue on his pool deck, negotiating a deal by satphone to use a Colombian narco-submarine to ship cocaine into the USA.

Normally, the Colombians shipped their coke to Mexico, where Don Gaetano's cartel transported it the rest of the way by land across the American border, but Don Gaetano wanted to expand his business.

He figured he could ship ten thousand pounds at a time via submarine to the California coastline and earn hundreds of millions of dollars at one blow.

Don Gaetano knew the Colombians used their submarines only once and then scuttled them. Why not get more mileage out of them?

"I want to buy one of your submarines," he said on his satphone.

"They're not cheap, *mi amigo*," said Don Diego, the chief of Los Machos, a Colombian paramilitary organization running narcotics, the principal source of the coke Don Gaetano shipped to the US.

Don Gaetano didn't like Colombians and he didn't like paramilitary organizations, but Los Machos produced the lion's share of the yayo on the market and he had to put up with dealing with them. He knew they were screwing him with their prices and they knew he couldn't do anything about it. They could always take their business to another Mexican cartel—like the despicable Zetas, or the equally despicable Sinaloa cartel.

"With all due respect I'm not your *amigo*, Don Diego," said Don Gaetano. "This is business."

"Of course. We are both businessmen. That goes without saying."

"I have a business proposition for you—one you can't refuse."

"Go on."

"I want to buy one of your submarines after it completes a delivery here."

"So you can compete with me shipping blow from Colombia to Mexico?"

"I don't want to compete with you, Don Diego."

"Then why do you want it?"

Don Gaetano didn't think it was any of Don Diego's business what he wanted it for. However, he had to say something to allay Don Diego's fear of competition in the cutthroat narcotics marketplace.

"I want to use it to make shipments from here to the US," said Don Gaetano.

"My submarines are expensive. They cost millions of dollars to construct."

"But you scuttle them after you send them here."

"What's your point?"

"I'll pay you a million bucks for it after it makes its delivery. Your net profit is a million bucks. Do you really want to walk away from a million bucks on the table?"

"Five million. They cost me twenty million to make. Since it'll be used, I'll sell it for five. You're getting a sweet deal."

Don Gaetano found that hard to believe. He knew Don Diego was cheating him—as usual. But Don Diego knew he could drive a hard bargain. He had the whip hand. You couldn't buy a narco-submarine on the open market. Knowing that Don Gaetano wanted the sub as much as Don Diego's blow, Don Diego could charge outrageous prices. But sometimes the sheer gall of Don Diego got to Don Gaetano.

"Two million, max," said Don Gaetano.

Don Diego fetched a sigh of disappointment. "I guess you don't want my sub."

Don Gaetano felt the urge to slam his satphone down in anger, but he reined in his temper.

"Two and half, max," he said, voice calm.

Don Diego paused two beats. "For you, I will agree. But only because it's you."

The price-gouging prick, thought Don Gaetano. "Excellent."

"I will tell my men the next narco-sub that makes a delivery to you is yours."

"*Patrón*," said Paco, a teen member of CJNG who was striding across the pool deck toward him in baggy jeans, jogging shoes, and a Gucci T-shirt. "I must speak with you. Am I interrupting?"

"No, Paco."

Don Gaetano terminated the call. "*Qué pasó?*"

Paco shuffled nervously on his feet. "I—I—I—uh—"

"Spit it out, Paco. I don't have all day."

Wincing, Paco bit his lower lip. "I saw who killed Arturo."

Don Gaetano sat bolt upright. "Who did it, my son? Tell me."

"I don't know how to tell you this."

"What kind of an answer is that?" said Don Gaetano, becoming angry.

"You won't be happy," said Paco, gulping.

"*You* won't be happy if you don't tell me."

"I didn't tell you earlier because I know how you feel—"

"Out with it, damn it."

"I saw Michael Corleone shoot him."

Don Gaetano sat speechless.

"You must be mistaken, Paco. Michael is Arturo's son."

"I know that, *patrón*. But I saw it with my own two eyes. I swear to you," said Paco, shivering, terrified Don Gaetano would punish him.

"Why would Michael kill his own father?"

"Michael told me his father was a coward. Michael hated cowards."

"Arturo was no coward. He was the bravest man I've ever known."

"Michael said it, *patrón*. Not me."

"He called his own father a coward?"

"He did, *patrón*. He called him a quivering jellyfish."

Don Gaetano clutched his brow and shook his head, unable to come to grips with Paco's words. He couldn't believe it.

"You can go now," he told Paco.

Paco hurried off, uncertain he had done the right thing by confiding in Don Gaetano.

It couldn't be, decided Don Gaetano. Yet Paco sounded sincere. Why would Paco tell him such an unbelievable story if it wasn't true? Could it be true? Arturo had suspected his son might have psychological issues, calling him withdrawn. *But to kill his own father?* It beggared belief.

Chapter 108

The tortoise lumbered across the interstate highway in the Mojave Desert under the burning sun that baked the horny keratin plates in his carapace. It was a long walk to the other side of the highway, but he had all the time in the world. Time had no meaning for him.

The sun made him feel uncomfortable. He didn't like the sun. He spent most of his time in his burrow, where it was cool. He had survived over eighty years, and he knew the sun dehydrated him.

He hadn't eaten in many days, but he knew he could go many more days without eating. He had survived many things during his long life.

He had survived the A-bombs the US government had dropped on its own land in Nevada that shook the earth and discharged toxic mushroom clouds gushing into the sky during the fifties through the early sixties when he was young. As a result, auto traffic ramped up as tourists came from miles around to witness the spectacular nuclear blasts from the windows of Las Vegas resorts. And then came the underground detonations that rocked the earth for decades.

The earth didn't shake as much these days, except for earthquakes, and the air was more breathable without the radiation, but the desert continued to hold enemies for him.

The birds, he thought, craning his head up into the sky. He hated the birds. They swooped down and attacked him trying to peck through his shell to eat him. The big birds, like ravens and eagles, were the worst culprits with the biggest, most destructive beaks that could crack open his shell like a church key.

He didn't see any birds at the moment.

But that didn't mean he was safe. He had to hide from certain land animals as well, namely badgers, kit foxes, and roadrunners.

All of these predators were more dangerous when he was young with a softer shell. However, any determined predator could kill him in his old age if it set its mind to it.

And then there was his worst enemy of all. The two-legged killer, man. One of them could pick him up, hurl him against a boulder, crack open his protective carapace, and leave him to die in the desert, where his other predators could finish him off by pecking or chewing through his damaged shell and consuming him.

He didn't worry about it. It was pointless to worry. He had learned that lesson in his eighty years on this planet. Worrying about being attacked wouldn't prevent it from happening. He had met each challenge and overcome it, the same way he had been doing all his life.

He felt tired and needed to rest on the tarmac. Maybe he would rest here for hours.

He didn't see the silver Ford Focus speeding toward him, its outline blurry in the thermals that shimmered around it on the black ribbon of road.

Chapter 109

Brody was falling asleep at the wheel, played out by adrenaline rushes from both his shootout with Musante's family and his flight from the *sicario* Roberto.

Brody didn't see the motionless tortoise in the sun's blinding glare until the last moment. When he picked up on it, he thought it was a boulder. He veered to the right in the nick of time to avoid hitting the tortoise.

The Focus skidded off the road and onto the dirty shoulder, where Brody slowed and righted the vehicle.

"What happened?" said Melody.

"There was a tortoise in the road," said Brody.

"Did you hit him?"

"No. I turned in time. He's still out there."

"Somebody ought to move him off the road before he gets hit."

Brody halted the Focus on the shoulder.

"It's illegal to pick up a tortoise in the desert," he said.

"I'm not gonna report you. He's gonna get hit by another car."

"Tortoises are tough."

"He won't survive a two-ton car running him over."

Brody knew he had just missed the tortoise. The tortoise might not be so lucky the next time a vehicle bore down on him.

Brody got out of the car, stepped into the burning heat of the sun, and darted over to the tortoise while the highway remained deserted. The tortoise had retreated into his shell. Brody lifted the ten-pound tortoise, carried it off the highway, and set it on the sun-parched, -cracked desert ground.

Sweating, he returned to the Focus and closed the door to keep the scorching heat at bay.

"My good deed for the day," said Brody.

"I can't believe your father was a serial killer," said Melody, crossing her legs.

"Just because I helped a tortoise?"

Brody noticed her skirt riding up her crossing legs. No hiss. No nylons. Naked. Which explained the gleaming whiteness of her thighs.

The sins of the father, he thought. Was he going to grow up to be a serial killer because his father was? Was his father an epileptic like him? His father had never said anything about it to him. Brody had no idea if his father had epilepsy. Maybe the epilepsy gene had lain dormant in his father's DNA and had been passed on to Brody without affecting his father. What about his father's serial killer gene? If there was such a gene, would it inevitably become active in him at some later date? Was the gene inside him lying in wait to be triggered? Triggered by what? An epileptic seizure?

Was he afraid of becoming involved with another girl because he was afraid she would be murdered or because he was afraid *he* would murder her? he wondered with a start. He had no desire to murder Melody. It was crazy to think that, he told himself. Why was he torturing himself with such thoughts?

"Are you trying to atone for your father's murders by being a PI?" said Melody.

"I can't help what he did," said Brody.

"Then you shouldn't let it interfere with your life."

"What he did is on him, not on me."

"Do you really feel that way, or are you just saying it?"

"This is what I get for helping you? A cross-examination?"

"I don't think you should blame yourself for what your father did."

"I'm not blaming myself. Why do *you* blame yourself for your husband beating up on you?"

Melody turned inward. "I used to blame myself, it's true. But not anymore. That's why I'm running away from him." She paused. "I'm not running way from all men, though. You're running away from all women because you believe they'll end up murdered like your father's victims if you get involved with any of them."

"I don't buy that. My father has nothing to do with it," said Brody, put out. "Why are you running away from your husband?"

"Because he's gonna kill me."

"It's all about fear. You're running away because you're scared of him."

"Because he's gonna kill me."

"You should talk," said Damian. "I got an entire hit team trying to kill me."

"Where there's love there's no fear." She paused. "Why did that tortoise decide to sleep in the middle of the road?"

For the same reason I was falling asleep at the wheel, thought Brody.

"He's an idiot," said Damian.

"He looks like an old-timer," said Melody, craning around to look at the tortoise. "You don't get to be that old by being an idiot."

"He's probably been around longer than any of us," said Brody.

"Don't tortoises have any natural predators?" said Damian.

"Nobody wants to deal with that shell," said Melody.

"The desert isn't any friendlier than a jungle," said Brody, surveying the arid, desolate landscape.

"If we hang around here any longer, the *sicarios* will catch up to us," said Damian.

Tormented, Brody peeled off onto the highway.

If he couldn't succeed in escaping the demons inside him, maybe he could at least succeed in escaping the *sicarios*.

Chapter 110

Don Gaetano paced in his huaraches around his hacienda's pool under the mackerel sky, watching the aqua water glimmer under the sun like a living thing, his satphone to his ear, listening to Roberto.

"I saw Damian, *patrón*," said Roberto.

"Do you have him and my money?" said Don Gaetano.

"We're chasing him now."

"Don't call me back until you have him and my money."

Don Gaetano terminated the call, nettled, not only by the elusive Damian, who seemed impossible to catch, but by the decision he had to make concerning Michael. Though he felt compelled to question Michael about Arturo's murder, he didn't look forward to it. Don Gaetano had to know if it was true that Michael had slain his own father.

Don Gaetano couldn't believe that any son would raise his hand against his own father, but he had to find out for sure. He had to interrogate Michael.

Don Gaetano sat on a chaise and called Michael on his satphone for a meet.

Fifteen-odd minutes later Michael drove his growling carmine Ferrari Portofino past the guards under the porte-cochere at the entrance of Don Gaetano's driveway. Michael tooled up the driveway, killed the throaty V8 engine, parked, got out, and walked the rest of the way to the pool in the backyard to greet Don Gaetano.

Don Gaetano watched Michael strut along the cement and terrazzo deck toward him in jeans and a button-down silk apricot aloha shirt with green palm-frond prints on it.

"We have to talk, Michael."

"*Qué pasó, patrón?*"

"You don't seem upset by your father's murder."

"I'm not a crybaby. You know that."

"Still, it is a horrible thing to happen at your young age."

"I'm not a baby."

"For that matter, it's a horrible thing to happen at any age."

"Weeping won't solve anything."

"I know you must feel pain inside."

"I feel anger."

Don Gaetano gave him a look. "Before he died, your father told me you were growing up too fast. He was worried about you."

"He was a coward and had great fear. He lived in constant fear."

Don Gaetano shook his head. "Arturo never feared anything in his life. I knew him better than anybody. I don't want to hear another word about his being a coward."

"With all due respect, *patrón*, *I* knew him better than anybody. I was his son."

Don Gaetano stood up and held out his hand. "Let me see your gun."

"My gun?"

"You don't go anywhere without your piece."

"I don't understand."

"Let me see it," said Don Gaetano in a no-nonsense voice.

Michael leaned forward, withdrew his SIG P226 from his ankle holster, straightened, and handed it to Don Gaetano.

Don Gaetano lifted the pistol to his nose and sniffed the action.

"It's been fired recently," he said.

"That's right."

"What were you shooting at?"

"I was using it for target practice. What's the point of this questioning?"

Don Gaetano was beginning to believe Paco was right, that Michael had shot his own father—no matter how inconceivable the idea of patricide. But why? Did Michael hate Arturo that much? What would drive Michael to shoot his father?

Don Gaetano didn't know how to say this. But he had to clear the air. He had to know the truth. He had to know who he was dealing with. Don Gaetano had promoted Michael to his right-hand man. His right-hand man had to be someone Don Gaetano could trust implicitly—a man like Arturo.

"I need to ask you a question," said Don Gaetano.

"Can I have my gun back?"

"In due time."

"What's going on, *patrón*?" said Michael, flummoxed.

"What should we do to your father's killer?"

"Put him down like a dog."

"Is that what I should do?"

"*Sí, patrón.*"

"Hmm," said Don Gaetano, studying Michael's SIG in his hand. "I have an eyewitness who says he saw who shot your father."

"What eyewitness?"

Don Gaetano locked his gaze on Michael's eyes. "He says *you* were the one who shot Arturo."

Michael looked blank.

Not the reaction Don Gaetano had expected from him. Don Gaetano had expected a vociferous denial.

"Well?" said Don Gaetano. "What do you have to say?"

Michael's lack of emotion sent a chill down Don Gaetano's spine. Don Gaetano wished Michael had cursed him out for such an accusation.

Michael's wooden expression remained in place.

"Do you deny it?" said Don Gaetano. "Your gun has been fired recently, and an eyewitness says you shot your father. What do you say?"

Michael's silence was unnerving, decided Don Gaetano.

At last Michael spoke.

"My father was a weak man," he said. "He didn't deserve to be second-in-command, *patrón*. You need a strong man at your side. The *cartel* needs a strong man at your side, a young man. Like our name says, Jalisco New Generation cartel. A new generation must lead."

"Are you confessing?"

"He was too weak. He had to go. The Jalisco cartel would have fallen apart if he had ever taken the helm."

"I accept that as your confession."

"A 'confession' makes it sound like what I did was something evil. What I did had to be done for the survival of the cartel. There is no need for a 'confession.' His elimination was a necessity."

Don Gaetano was at a loss for words.

"Why didn't you admit it to me in the first place?" he said, finding his tongue.

"I didn't think you would approve. Though, the truth is it had to be done. The cartel empire would have crumbled under his leadership."

"He wasn't the one in charge."

"I know, *patrón*. He was number two. But if something happened to you, he would have become the new *jefe*."

"You killed him to prevent that?"

"I did."

"Why didn't you tell me what you were going to do before you took matters into your own hands?"

"You would never have agreed to it."

"And I am the *patrón*."

"*Sí, patrón*."

Don Gaetano stood a long moment marshaling his thoughts, his face unreadable.

"You can go now," he said.

"Can I have my gun back?" said Michael, holding out his hand.

"I'll give it back to you when I'm ready."

Michael turned and stalked off to his Ferrari.
Don Gaetano studied Michael's SIG in his hand.

Chapter 111

Roberto at the wheel, the black Lincoln Navigator catapulted down I-15. Roberto picked up on a tortoise in the middle of the opposite lane. Swerving over the solid double yellow lines, a glint in his eyes, sneering, he ran over the tortoise.

The Navigator bounced over the tortoise's shell, crunching it.

"What was that?" said the startled *sicario* sitting opposite Root.

Roberto veered back into his own lane.

"A stupid tortoise in the road," he said over the blaring rap music shaking the Navigator. "I don't let nobody get in my way."

"Any sign of Damian?" said Root.

"No. He's heading west. I'm sure of it. He was heading west out of Vegas the last time I saw him."

"Maybe he turned off the highway."

"There's nowhere to go in this desert. He's gotta be making for California. We'll catch up to him soon enough," said Roberto, and stepped on the gas.

"You don't want to get a ticket, do you?"

"I don't see any cops," said Roberto, stealing a glance in his rearview mirror.

"They use radar around here."

"Maybe," said Roberto, not convinced. "Whenever I see one of those radar-patrolled signs on a highway I figure it's a lie to scare drivers into slowing down."

"If a cop pulls us over and writes you up for speeding, it'll slow us way down."

Roberto eased up on the gas and drove ten miles over the posted speed limit.

"That's not gonna happen," he said.

"What makes you think they're heading for California?"

"I know Damian. He was always talking about retiring in California. I bet that's where he's going."

"It's a big state to hide in."

"That's another reason he's headed there. We'll catch up to him before he crosses the California border."

"What if he doesn't have the money?"

"He has it. Where else could it be? The son of a bitch jacked it and he's making a run for it."

"We don't know that for sure."

"He's dead either way." Roberto gritted his teeth. "Nobody cheats the cartel and gets away with it."

Root couldn't let Roberto lay his hands on the money. If Roberto ever got hold of it, he would deliver it to Cobalt Green Tide. They would bribe the secretary of DHS Sheila Dmytryk to vote to oust President Ransom from office, and the coup by the cabal burrowed inside the deep state intelligence agencies would be complete. Root had to do everything he could to stop that from happening.

Meanwhile, his eardrums pounded with thumping rap music.

"Do you ever turn that noise off?" he said, grimacing.

"No," said Roberto. "Rap gets me high. It's like snorting yayo."

"It's like putting my head into a buzz saw."

One hand on the wheel, Roberto poured cocaine powder out of a vial he carried in his trouser pocket onto the back of his hand and did a bump.

"Don't get me mad," he said. "Let me tell you about a *sicario*, who I thought was my amigo."

"I can't hear a word you're saying," said Root, shaking his head.

"He tried to cheat on me by macking on my girlfriend. I broke every bone in his body with a ballpeen hammer. It took me four hours. You can't believe how many bones there are in the human body. I turned him into a slug. He was alive after I finished, but his entire body was black and blue. He was bawling like a baby. What did I do next, you may ask? I'll tell you. I took that misshapen sucker, that quivering slug of pulverized bones, and threw him into a river full of piranhas. In his condition he couldn't swim to safety." Roberto guffawed. "The river was bubbling with blood in no time. You should have been there, Root."

The stretch of highway in front of Roberto was devoid of cars.

He powered down his window, pulled out his piece, and shot at a jackrabbit scampering across the desert. The jackrabbit hightailed it.

Feeling the blast of the furnacelike heat Roberto powered up his window.

"I'm having a ball," he said, sniffing, his eyes watery. "It's all about having fun. The most fun of all will be blowing away Damian. If only the gringos had piranhas in this backward country."

The Navigator throbbed with rap music.

Chapter 112

Don Gaetano sat with Carmine on a mahogany leather sofa in their living room. Carmine was wearing a strapless emerald green dress. Disconcerted, Don Gaetano had to make a difficult decision about what to do with Michael—if he should do anything at all.

"I need to talk business with you, Carmine."

"*Qué pasó, querido?*"

"Without Arturo I have no one to confide in."

"You can always confide in me. You know that."

Don Gaetano nodded, his face glum. "It's about Arturo."

"A no-brainer. We need to execute his murderer. We can't let our enemies assassinate your right-hand man without retaliating. To do nothing sends them the signal that you are weak."

"That's the problem."

"I don't understand."

"I learned from a reliable source that Michael murdered Arturo."

"I can't believe Michael would murder his own father," said Carmine, taken aback.

"I confronted him with the accusation—"

"And he denied it."

"No, he didn't. He admitted he killed Arturo."

"What in God's name for?" said Carmine, appalled.

"Michael said Arturo was too weak to lead the cartel. Arturo was second in command. If something happened to me, Arturo would take my place. Michael said the cartel would disintegrate under Arturo."

"Michael is too young to make these kinds of decisions."

"He has grown up fast. Too fast, according to Arturo." Don Gaetano paused in thought. "I wanted to kill him when he told me at the pool that he had done it. But I couldn't bring myself to kill Arturo's son. I loved Arturo like a brother."

"I know, *querido*. I did, too."

"I don't know what to do."

"If you *don't* kill Michael, it would make you look weak," said Carmine, her gaze pensive.

"Only if people found out Michael killed Arturo."

"How many people know?"

"Other than me and you, there's only one other person besides Michael that knows Michael did it. The eyewitness Paco."

"Do you think you can trust Michael enough to let him take Arturo's place at your side?"

Don Gaetano held his brow. "I don't know. If I kill him, it would be like killing my own flesh and blood. The son of my brother. Arturo was *that* close to me."

"He might think you're weak if you let him live, since you know he's the murderer."

"And then what? You think he'd kill me, too?"

"I don't know what's going on in his mind. He's not ready to be boss. He's too young. He makes rash decisions."

"I know that, and you know that. But does he know that?"

"Certainly, the others in the cartel will think you're weak if you don't kill him."

"Only if they find out he killed Arturo."

"What's to stop Paco from telling the others the same thing he told you about Michael? Maybe he's done so already."

"No. I don't think so. He was very nervous about telling me. I doubt he would dare tell anyone else before he told me first."

"Can you be certain of that?"

Don Gaetano stared at her. "You really think I should kill Michael?"

"I didn't say that. I was talking about appearances. The way others see you. You must appear strong at all times. You can never let them see you as indecisive."

"He could have killed me as easily as he did Arturo. I would never have expected it. But he didn't."

"Do you think you can trust him as your second-in-command?"

"I either kill him or promote him to take Arturo's place at my side. There are no other choices that I can see. What do you think I should do?"

Carmen thought about it. "Michael could turn out to be a mortal enemy to us. Anyone willing to kill his own father for power has to be considered a viable threat. His lust for power is unquenchable."

"He saw his father as weak. I don't think he sees me as weak. If he does, he'll make a move on me."

"You must never appear weak to him."

"It'll be like living with a rattlesnake coiled around my throat waiting to strike at a moment's notice," said Don Gaetano, tugging uncomfortably at his collar.

"It will keep you on your toes."

Face grim, Don Gaetano nodded yes. "It'll remind me that not only to do I have to appear strong to my enemies but to my followers as well."

"You'll have to be careful, but you must always appear in control."

"Or should I kill him like a rabid dog and be done with him?"

"I'm not going to tell you what to do, *querido*. You are the *jefe*. I'm only telling you how I think the appearance of your actions will affect others."

"There must be punishment."

"As you say."

Don Gaetano stood up with determination, Michael's gun in his hand. "I will avenge Arturo's murder."

Carmen said nothing, her face impossible to read.

"Was Michael mad at you when you confronted him?" she said.

Don Gaetano shrugged. "He seemed relieved to get it off his chest. Killing means nothing to him. It's a means to an end. Nothing more." He frowned at Michael's gun in his hand.

"What are you going to do, *querido*?"

Chapter 113

It was dark and cool when Brody drove the Ford Focus up Big Bear Mountain to the safe house. His back was aching from the hours of nonstop driving. He wished he had a Tylenol. He hadn't wanted to take a break because he was concerned Roberto and his henchmen would catch up to him.

The female GPS voice told him where to turn so he could reach the safe house. He wouldn't want to drive around here with just a map. The roads were narrow, twisty, and unlit. It would be easy to get lost.

He drove on a tortuous road up a rise populated with oak trees and a variety of pine trees, including Ponderosa and lodgepole pines.

He didn't see anybody behind him in the rearview mirror. With any luck they had lost the *sicarios*, who had no idea where he was headed. The *sicarios* had probably figured he was on I-15 heading west since Roberto had seen him heading in that direction. When Brody had turned off I-15, it was a good bet he had lost their tail.

"Do you know where you're going?" said Damian.

"I thought you were asleep," said Brody, who was having trouble keeping his eyes open thanks to his fatigue.

He leaned close to the rearview mirror and startled himself with the sight of two bloodshot eyes peering back at him. The eyes of Dracula.

"Not anymore," said Damian. "Just tell me we're not lost."

"I'm following the GPS directions. We should be there soon."

They drove up a steep bluff. Brody felt his ears popping. The air became cooler as they ascended the mountain.

He took several hairpin turns that snaked up the bluff and arrived at a long driveway. The GPS voice told him to turn here.

"One minute we're in the desert, the next we're in the woods," said Melody, surveying the gloomy forest that surrounded them. She shivered. "I'm turning down the AC."

"Good idea," said Damian. "I didn't bring my jacket."

Brody drove up a sinuous narrow asphalt driveway and reached a cabin that overlooked a tarn.

"The middle of nowhere," said Melody.

"That's the idea," said Brody, pulling to a halt in front of the cabin.

"Dan will never find me here."

Damian squinted through the rear window into the darkness for any sign of Roberto's Navigator. "Roberto won't find us here either."

Brody killed the engine.

The three of them piled out of the Focus. They stretched and walked around getting their circulations going before heading to the cabin front door.

It was a white clapboard one-story cabin with a pitched roof, a red brick chimney climbing its side, dark windows, the curtains drawn shut, and a wraparound porch. Weathered green Adirondack chairs stood on either side of the front door.

It was no doubt a popular place in the winter when Big Bear had skiing, decided Brody.

The cabin commanded a spectacular view of the glittering lake that spread far below it under the starlit indigo sky where fitful wraiths of mauve clouds scudded with abandon.

"I hope it's not locked," said Melody, climbing the creaky wooden steps that led to the front porch, gripping the banister's handrail in the dark.

Brody climbed after her.

Bringing up the rear Damian tripped on a step, pitched forward, and slammed his head into a tread. He groaned.

Chapter 114

"Jesus. What happened?" said Melody, wheeling around at the racket.

"He tripped and fell," said Brody, scoping out Damian.

Brody bounded down the steps to help Damian to his feet.

"Give me your hand," said Brody, reaching out to Damian.

Damian sprawled facedown motionless on the steps.

"What's wrong with him?" asked Melody.

Brody hunkered down and turned Damian over to get a good look at Damian's face. A deep gash scored Damian's forehead, dripping with blood.

"He's out cold," said Brody.

He lifted Damian in his arms, draped Damian's arm around his neck, and hauled Damian's inert body up the steps onto the front porch. Brody laid him on his back on a thin carpet of fallen desiccated brown pine needles that mantled the oak floorboards.

Melody tried the cabin's doorknob.

"I hope you have a key," she said.

Root had told Brody the owner kept a spare key wedged under the porch light. Brody reached over his head to the light fixture above the door and felt around for a key.

"He looks dead," said Melody, eying Damian with alarm.

She squatted beside him and felt for a pulse in his throat with her fingers.

"How is he?" said Brody.

"I feel a pulse, barely."

"He must have a concussion," said Brody, fingering the light fixture in the dark.

It would help if he had some light, he decided.

He fished his cell phone out of his trouser pocket, tapped on the flashlight, and shone the beam on the light fixture.

"What are we gonna do with him?" said Melody.

"We have to stop the bleeding. Do you have a handkerchief?"

Melody withdrew a handkerchief from her purse.

"Press it against the wound," said Brody, while feeling around for the key in the light fixture.

Melody stanched the bleeding from Damian's gashed forehead with her handkerchief.

Brody shone his cell phone's flashlight on a nub he had felt along the fixture's metal rim. He plucked the nub with his thumb and forefinger and extracted a key.

"Got it," he said.

He proceeded to insert the key into the Schlage dead bolt lock above the doorknob and unlocked it. Then he used the key to open the doorknob's lock. He had to give the door a slight shove because it was stuck in its frame from lack of use. The cabin's musty air greeted him.

Once inside, he phoned Araceli.

"I got Damian," he said. "He's safe with me."

"What a relief," she said. "Where are you?"

He gave her the cabin's address.

"Why didn't you bring him back to your apartment?" she said.

"We're lying doggo. A group of hit men are after him."

"What time is it?" she muttered to herself, as if looking at her watch. "It's too late for me to drive there now. I'll be there tomorrow."

She terminated the call.

"Who was that?" said Melody, entering the dark living room and searching for a light switch.

"My client."

"I thought *I* was your client."

"My second client. I told you earlier I would be handling two cases if I took you on."

Nodding, Melody located the switch and flicked on the overhead light.

"He'll be glad to see her tomorrow," said Brody, peering out the door at Damian lying on the porch.

"If he's conscious."

Brody returned to the porch and carried Damian into the living room, where he laid him supine on the sofa.

"I stopped the bleeding," said Melody, her bloody handkerchief in her hand.

Brody yawned. "I'm beat. We need to get some sleep."

"What do we do with him?"

"Let him rest."

"Don't you want to check this place out?" she said, casting around the sparsely furnished living room.

It contained two bentwood fir chairs and a rectangular cherrywood coffee table with round white marble knobs on its two drawers and several outdated *Ski* magazines lying askew on its surface. A zebra-patterned runner on the hardwood floor led to the front door.

"We can do it tomorrow when it's light," said Brody.

"Mountain-cabin chic. All that's missing is a lion's head trophy over the fireplace and one of Hemingway's six-toed cats."

"As long as we're safe here. That's what counts."

They found two bedrooms, each with one stripped bed and one varnished deal bureau and not much of anything else.

Brody yawned again and made for one of the bedrooms.

Melody took the other.

Brody would have been asleep as soon as his face hit the pillow, except for something niggling at the back of his mind—what Max Shenk had said about Julius Caesar. Brody didn't think it was a fluke Max Shenk had brought up the subject of the assassinated Roman emperor. There was a new member of the Elysian Fields chat group called Julius Caesar. Could that have anything to do with Max Shenk's remark?

But how would Max Shenk know the new member in the Elysian Fields group was called Julius Caesar? Unless Max Shenk and the FBI had hacked the group's website. Which begged the question, was Max Shenk a legit member of the bureau or a member of the deep state cabal?

Or was Brody's paranoia working overtime?

Brody was too exhausted to think anymore. He fell asleep.

Chapter 115

Don Gaetano arranged for Michael and Paco to meet him at his pool the next morning.

The three of them stood on the pool deck bathed in the chill, oyster light of the rising sun. Michael and Paco stood near the pool as Don Gaetano faced them. Paco looked nervous, sneaking fearful glances at Michael, who stood calmly beside him. Paco stroked the silver crucifix that hung from a silver chain about his neck.

"Do you know why I have brought you here this morning?" said Don Gaetano.

"No, *patrón,*" said Michael.

"No, *patrón,*" said Paco.

Juan rode his tricycle around the pool, churning the pedals as he worked up speed, his face intent. He approached Don Gaetano.

"Stop riding and take a rest, Juan," said Don Gaetano.

"I like riding," said Juan, pedaling.

"I don't want you to get hurt."

"I'm not gonna get hurt from riding."

"Do as I say and stop riding for fifteen minutes," said Don Gaetano with patriarchal authority.

Juan pouted and drove his tricycle to the chaise longues, where he parked behind Don Gaetano and watched the grown-ups.

Don Gaetano took out Michael's SIG P226 from behind his jeans' waistband where he had wedged it. He inspected the SIG.

"I found out who killed my best friend Arturo," he told Paco and Michael, "and I have decided what I must do about it."

He looked at Michael.

Michael must have had ice water in his veins, because his face showed nothing, decided Don Gaetano.

"I don't understand," said Paco, sweat pouring out of his face.

"The accused has the right to defend himself from the accuser."

Michael stood stock-still, watching Don Gaetano.

Paco looked more nervous than ever. His left hand began to tremble at his side.

"Paco, tell Michael what you told me," said Don Gaetano.

"About what?" said Paco, fear creeping into his voice.

"About who you saw kill Arturo."

Taken aback, Paco said nothing.

"I'll tell you in private," he said, managing to collect himself after a fashion.

"Tell me here. Now."

"Are you sure?" said Paco, stalling for time.

"Do it, Paco," said Don Gaetano, fingering the SIG.

Paco couldn't stand the tension any longer.

Fetching a sigh of anguish he said, "I saw Michael shoot Arturo."

"What do you say, Michael?" said Don Gaetano. "Do you deny it? If Paco is lying I must kill him to stop him from spreading lies about you."

Michael thought about it. All he had to do was call Paco a liar, and he would escape Don Gaetano's wrath. Paco would become the villain. It was an easy way out.

If Michael was frightened, he would have taken the bait and called Paco a liar. But Michael had no fear.

"I did what had to be done for the sake of the cartel," he said.

"You admit you killed your own father?"

"I do," said Michael, his expression stony.

"Then Paco is telling the truth?"

"He is."

Nodding, Don Gaetano examined the SIG's action and turned toward Paco.

"Paco, stand farther away from Michael and closer to the pool," said Don Gaetano, training the SIG on Michael.

Bewildered, Paco did as he was told. With the gun aimed at someone else, he was beginning to feel less afraid.

Which was a mistake.

Don Gaetano raised the SIG and double-tapped Paco in the heart. Paco fell backward into the pool, windmilling his arms.

"I didn't want blood to get on the deck," said Don Gaetano. "It's hard to clean up."

Paco's heart pumped its last beats spilling blood into the pool's turquoise water. A corolla of blood hung suspended in the water beside Paco's floating body like a discarded rose.

"I hate snitches," said Don Gaetano, and handed Michael his gun back to him.

"*Gracias, patrón*," said Michael, accepting his piece and snugging it in the waistband of his jeans.

"If you had called Paco a liar, I would have shot you instead of him for being a coward afraid to admit what you did. You *do* realize that?" said Don Gaetano, his black eyes locked on Michael's.

"*Si, patrón*. I would have done the same in your shoes."

"You're a man I can trust, Michael. Make me proud of my decision to spare your life."

"I *am* the best man for the job."

Juan rode his tricycle to the edge of the pool and, as if mesmerized, watched Paco float in the water. The bloody water lapped against the cement sides of the pool.

"Go and play now, Juan," said Don Gaetano.

In a flurry of pedaling Juan tore around the pool.

Don Gaetano's father Javier powered his electric wheelchair out of the living room to the pool. Javier stopped at the pool's edge and gazed at Paco's corpse with concern. Excited, he tried to talk.

Javier must have heard the gunshot, decided Don Gaetano.

Javier spoke gibberish.

"Don't worry. We'll have the pool cleaned, Papa," said Don Gaetano.

Javier looked at Michael and, disconcerted, gaped at him.

"What's wrong with him?" said Michael.

"My father has Alzheimer's," said Don Gaetano.

Michael nodded. "I know. But why's he so excited?"

"Things upset him. Have the pool drained and cleaned," said Don Gaetano. "I don't want my father to become too upset. He might have a heart attack."

Anxious at Michael's presence, his eyes bugging out of his head, Javier mumbled and began drooling on himself, his bony black-veined hands grasping at air. The skin on the back of his hands was translucent like a glass frog's skin, and Don Gaetano could discern Javier's bones and the network of dark purple veins underneath it.

"*Sí, patrón*," said Michael.

Javier became increasingly agitated at the sound of Michael's voice.

"If I didn't know better, I would say he's frightened of you," said Don Gaetano.

"That's odd," said Michael.

"Come, Papa," said Don Gaetano. "Michael is our friend. Let's go back inside."

He took control of Javier's wheelchair and wheeled him back to the living room.

Chapter 116

When Brody woke up the next morning, the sun was already in the sky. He felt cold. He wished he had had a blanket. He felt his cell phone vibrating in his trouser pocket. He sat up on the tick and took the call.

"The owner of the safe house is coming to meet you today to make sure you're OK," said Brockton Root in a barely audible voice drowned out by thumping rap music.

"Root?" said Brody. "Is that you? What does this guy look like?"

"He'll be wearing a green New York Jets football cap."

"Damian cracked his skull on the cabin steps."

"What? Is he dead?"

"No."

Root terminated the call.

Maybe the owner would bring some breakfast with him, decided Brody.

Hungry for bacon and scrambled eggs, Brody climbed out of bed and entered the living room to check on Damian.

Damian was out cold.

Brody checked Damian's pulse. It was faint and slow, but steady.

"Is he still out?" said Melody, startling Brody from behind with the sound of her voice.

"Yeah," said Brody, turning to face her.

"Shouldn't we call paramedics?" she said.

"I can't protect him in a hospital. He's better off here."

"What if he's dying?"

Brody didn't want Damian's death on his hands.

"I'll let his sister decide what to do with him," he said.

"Is she coming here?"

"This morning."

Melody yawned. "I'm hungry."

"Me, too. Let's raid the kitchen."

They repaired to the kitchen and rummaged around for food.

Maybe there was an old box of cereal hanging around in the cupboard, decided Brody, but it didn't look like anybody had lived here recently.

Melody opened the refrigerator. It was bare. It wasn't even plugged in.

Brody managed to scrounge an opened, outdated box of Corn Pops from one of the cupboards. He shook the carton.

"Half full I'd say," he said. He inspected the expiration date. "Six months past its expiration date."

"I don't know if I'm *that* hungry."

"We can take our chances with these—or starve," said Brody, opening the cereal box.

"We don't have any milk."

Brody approached the aluminum sink and turned on the cold water cock. The pipes knocked. Water streamed out of the faucet with a hiss.

"We won't die of thirst anyway," he said.

Melody pulled a face. "Corn Pops with water doesn't work for me."

"Eat 'em dry."

He dug a yellow Corn Pop out of the cereal box and flicked it into his mouth. "Delicious."

"Say it like you believe it."

He strolled into the living room, cereal box in hand. "It's either this or drive around and find the nearest store or restaurant."

"Let's go for a restaurant. There must be one around here somewhere."

Brody peeked through the front picture window and pulled away from it.

"What's wrong?" said Melody, following him into the living room.

"Somebody's coming. Stay out of sight."

Hiding behind the window frame, he watched a blue BMW sedan tooling up the driveway.

"Who is it?" said Melody.

"Dunno."

"Could it be the team of hit men chasing Damian?"

"I have no idea how they could have found us here. I never saw a car tailing us."

Nevertheless, Brody felt his pulse rate ratchet up. He withdrew his SIG P365 from his waistband.

Chapter 117

"How many of them are there?" said Melody.

Brody saw the BMW's driver's-side door open. A woman dressed in a white button-down blouse and a short black leather skirt clambered out, looking unsure as she eyed the cabin. Brody relaxed, lowering his pistol.

"It's Araceli," he said. "Damian's sister."

Brody opened the front door and waved to Araceli.

She strode up the driveway in her black patent leather boots to the cabin.

"I wasn't sure this was the right place," she said, ascending the creaky steps to the front porch.

"Watch your step," said Brody.

"What?" said Araceli, puzzled.

"We had an accident last night. Damian fell and hit his head on those steps."

Brody retreated into the living room. Araceli followed him inside.

"Oh no. Where is he?" she said, worried, her hand clenching her purse.

Brody gestured to the sofa where Damian lay unconscious. "Over there."

"Is he OK? He looks dead."

Araceli knelt beside Damian, taking in his pallid face with concern.

"We think he has a concussion," said Melody.

Araceli noticed Melody for the first time and stood up. "Who's this?"

"That's Melody. She was in a bit of a bind, and I'm helping her out."

"Nice to meet you," said Melody.

Araceli offered her a thin smile then turned to Brody.

"Why are you hiding here in this cabin?" said Araceli.

"Your brother has a cartel hit team after him. They think he has their money."

"What money?"

"Four hundred thousand bucks."

"Where is it?"

Brody heard car tires crunching gravel on the driveway. He darted to the window to catch sight of another car pulling in behind Araceli's BMW. It was a late-model black Mercedes sedan.

"We got company," he said. "Stay out of view."

Remembering what Root had told him Brody hoped it was the owner of the cabin, but he pulled out his SIG P365 just in case. Entirely too many visitors were showing up at a sequestered safe house for his liking.

The Mercedes parked behind the BMW. The driver killed the engine and swung open his door.

He was a paunchy middle-aged guy wearing cargo pants, an expensive navy blue down vest, and a green New York Jets hat, a well-to-do guy dressed for a vacation at the lake. Pegging him for the cabin's owner, Brody relaxed and put away his gun.

He opened the door and strode out onto the front porch.

"Hello," he said, waving and smiling at the guy.

Returning the wave and smile the guy walked up the driveway toward him.

Araceli bolted out of the cabin behind Brody, shoving him out of her way, and, gun in hand, fired three shots into the guy's chest. The guy clutched his chest and crumpled to the asphalt.

"What are you doing?" said Brody, thunderstruck.

"That's a hit man," said Araceli, holding a 9 mm Beretta Px4 Storm Compact. "I saw him tailing me here. I guess they thought I knew where my brother was and were following me."

"He's the owner of the cabin," said Brody.

He sprang down the steps and pelted to the guy sprawled on the driveway. Blood was leaking out of the guy's bullet-ripped down vest. Hunkering down, Brody pressed his hands against the guy's chest to stanch the bleeding. He had a feeling it was too late. At least one of Araceli's bullets had torn the guy's heart apart. His fingers bloody, Brody felt for a pulse in the guy's throat. The pulse was faint and guttering out.

Grim-faced, Brody rose from the body. "You killed him."

"He was a hit man that was tailing me," said Araceli, gun in hand.

"You shot him in the heart. Where did you learn to shoot like that?"

"I grew up in Ciudad Juarez. Learning how to handle a gun is part of growing up there. It's like learning to drive."

Brody didn't know what to believe. Root had told him this guy was the owner of the cabin, identified by his green Jets hat. Could Araceli be right about the guy being a hit man? Was the whole thing a setup by Root to entrap and kill Damian?

"You're wrong," said Brody, tentatively. "He's the owner of the cabin."

Brody heard the rumble of a car engine in the distance. He spotted a black SUV climbing the road through the pines to the cabin.

Melody dashed down the steps to see what was going on. She grimaced at the corpse lying on the driveway.

"Who's that?" she said.

Maybe Araceli was right about the guy she had shot, decided Brody. Maybe he was the advance guard of the hit team, who were now approaching the cabin in the SUV. And maybe Root was in on it. Maybe he really was working for the cartel, despite his claims he was working for the CIA and posing as a fashion photographer to infiltrate the cartel. Brody couldn't take any chances.

"There's no time," said Brody. "Let's get back inside."

"What's wrong?" said Melody.

"There's another car coming. Our safe house's been compromised."

"How could that happen?"

Brody shook his head in puzzlement. "We'll figure it out later. Right now we need to get inside and lock the doors."

Chapter 118

Brody, Melody, and Araceli belted back to the cabin, charged up the protesting porch steps, and took shelter inside.

"Now what?" said Melody.

"We need to find those guns," said Brody.

"Guns? What guns?"

"Root told me the owner stashed MP5s in this cabin." *If Root could be believed.*

"I don't know an MP5 from an LP," said Melody, bemused.

Brody's cell vibrated in his trouser pocket. "I need to take this call. Try to find the guns."

Brody put his cell to his ear and answered.

"This is Max Shenk. Where's Damian?"

"I have him," said Brody.

"Where are you?"

Brody didn't trust Max Shenk. "We're OK. What do you want?"

"The money. Where's the money?"

"I'm in the middle of something."

"You don't understand your position. You're a member of an online anarchists' group dedicated to the overthrow of the government. I can have you arrested for treason."

"That's insane. We're not anarchists."

"Do you deny you're a member of the Elysian Fields chat room?"

"What if I am?"

"We have a whistleblower there who says you're unhappy with the way things are, and your group is plotting to overthrow the government."

"What whistleblower? What are you talking about?"

"I'm not naming names. He's a federal employee. His name's protected by the Whistleblower Protection Act."

"Then how can I defend myself against him?"

"Give us the money."

"That's blackmail."

"Call it anything you want. Give us the money, or we're arresting you for treason. You don't have a leg to stand on."

Picking up on Damian opening his eyes, Brody terminated the call. Max Shenk couldn't bust him if he didn't know where Brody was, decided Brody. Elysian Fields wasn't a group of rabble-rousing anarchists. The guy was misinformed.

Brody strode over to Damian on the sofa. "Are you OK?"

"Yeah. What happened?" said Damian, looking around.

"I found two guns," said Melody, entering the living room with two MP5s cradled in her arms.

"You tripped and hit your head on the stairs," Brody told Damian.

Damian grimaced.

"No wonder my head aches," he said, trying to sit up.

"I'm glad you're OK," said Araceli, watching him.

"Who are you?"

Taken aback, Brody didn't get it. "That's your sister Araceli. Don't you recognize her?"

"I never saw her before in my life."

"Maybe he lost his memory because of his concussion," said Melody. "He was out for at least twelve hours."

"Some patients with concussions *do* suffer memory loss," said Brody, contemplating Damian with a studious expression.

"I didn't lose anything," said Damian. "That's not my sister. Don't you think I'd recognize my own sister?"

Araceli trained her Beretta on Damian's face. "Where's the money, Damian?" She saw Brody make a move and swung the Beretta toward him. "Everybody, stay put."

"What's going on?" said Brody.

Damian's eyes widened in fear at the sight of the gun's muzzle staring at his face. "I don't have any money."

"CJNG's four hundred grand."

"How do you know about that?"

"I'm working for Don Gaetano. He hired me to get his money back from you."

"And you hired me to do your job for you," said Brody, feeling like a sucker. "Is that it?"

"I'm a *sicario*, not a private eye. I figured you'd do a better job of finding him than me since the papers say you're such a great PI and you wasted a lot of Don Gaetano's men. And you're an American—you know the lay of the land."

Brody remembered the write-up in the LA papers about a previous case where he had helped Deirdre Fox defend herself from Don Gaetano's cartel hit men.

"You're not American?" he said.

"I'm Mexican. I was born in a slum in Juarez, Chihuahua. There was only one way out of poverty. A life of crime. I didn't want to hook for a living, though men drool at the sight of me and I could've made a good living at it. I chose the life of a *sicario*. They make good money, and they don't have to sell their bodies to a bunch of drooling slobs."

"You know what they say. Live by the sword, die by the sword."

"Only if you're inferior at your job. I'm the best in the business. That's why Don Gaetano hired me. I have over forty kills to my name."

"What about those *sicarios* outside?" he said.

"They work for Don Gaetano, too. He *really* wants his money back. And . . ."

"And what?"

"And there's another reason I hired you. Your name happens to be on my hit list. He wants you dead for killing his men in LA."

"I do your job for you. Then you waste me. It has a certain symmetry. Cute."

"Thank you," she said, pleased with herself. "I wanted to get some mileage out of you before I whacked you."

"What's your real name?"

"Not that it matters. Francesca." She trained her Beretta on Damian's head. "Give me the money. You lie, you die."

"I don't have it."

"Bullshit." Francesca jutted her Beretta at Damian's head, her eyes flashing. "I mean business."

"I gambled it away on roulette. I swear. Every penny's gone," said Damian, holding up his hands as if in surrender.

"Lying won't save your skin."

"It's true. I want out of this business. I came here to start a new life—"

Francesca shot him between the eyes in disgust.

At that moment gunfire erupted outside. A burst of bullets tore through the picture window, hurling glass shards helter-skelter tinkling on the floor.

Chapter 119

Brody took advantage of the distraction outside and double-tapped Francesca in the head. Her head jerked back, fragments of brain-smeared bone hurtling out the back of her skull onto the zebra-patterned runner, where they splatted.

Francesca collapsed to her knees, toppled forward, and slammed the floor facedown.

"There goes my paycheck," said Brody.

"Why are they shooting at us?" said Melody.

"Stay away from the window," said Brody, taking up station next to the window frame and waving at Melody to stand back.

Brody drew the blinds shut.

One of the hit men fired a burst into the window, shattering more glass. Fragments strewed the floor, clinking against the hardwood floorboards. The curtains prevented the glass from flying all over the place, but they didn't prevent the slugs from tearing holes in their cloth.

Melody took refuge in a corner of the room, her back against the wall.

Brody could see the MP5s in her arms were loaded with thirty-round, slightly curved steel magazines of 9 mm Parabellum rounds.

"Slide one of those MP5s over here," he said.

She laid one down and slid it over the hardwood floor toward him. The MP5 didn't make it all the way, skidding to a halt five feet short of him.

"I was never any good at shuffleboard," she said.

Even though he had drawn the curtains shut, he didn't want to risk drawing the fire of the *sicarios* by walking behind the curtains lest the *sicarios* could make out his outline through the sheer fabric.

Brody hunkered down on his knees, crawled under the windowsill, and retrieved the MP5 without drawing fire. He crawled back to his original position and inspected the MP5.

To his satisfaction he found it was set to full auto, which meant it could fire continuous bursts. It helped even the odds in his battle against the *sicarios*, though they outnumbered him by at least six to two. He had seen six of them, but there could easily be additional soldiers occupying the Navigator.

"What about spare magazines?" he said. "Did you see any?"

"The guns were next to a pasteboard box. I didn't open it."

"I need you to check it out for spare magazines."

She retreated into another room.

Brody pulled the curtains back a smidgen and peeked out at the *sicarios*. They were hiding behind the cars, scoping out the cabin, and talking among themselves, plotting their assault strategy. He couldn't hear them from this distance, but their intentions were obvious.

They weren't going to lay siege to the cabin, decided Brody. They were going to launch a full-scale attack.

Brody figured how he would do it if it was up to him. He would surround the cabin with his men and storm it from all sides at once. Not good. Not only were Brody and Melody outnumbered, Melody wasn't an experienced fighter. At least the two of them had submachine guns. The one thing they had in their favor was the protection provided by the cabin.

Melody returned to the living room carrying a pasteboard box. When she reached the corner, she set the box down on the floor and withdrew a magazine.

"Was this what you wanted?" she said.

"Yeah. How many are in there?"

Melody inspected the box. "About a dozen."

Brody peeked around the curtain, saw that the *sicarios* were engrossed with talking to each other, and dashed past the curtain to the pasteboard box beside Melody.

He gathered four magazines from the box and stuck them inside his trouser pockets.

"We need to check out the cabin and make sure the curtains are drawn shut," he said.

They split up, hurried around the cabin shutting all the drapes that were open, and returned to the living room.

"Damian, come out now and surrender," called out Roberto, cupping his mouth with his hand, addressing the cabin's front door.

Brody didn't answer.

He peeked out the shattered front window. He saw Roberto standing behind the Navigator and the *sicarios* splitting up, preparing to surround the cabin.

"Come out now and we'll let you live, Damian," said Roberto.

Brody wondered if he could stave off an attack by talking to Roberto. Brody cracked the front door.

"Damian's dead," he yelled through the opening.

"Where's the money?" said Roberto.

"He gambled it away in Vegas."

"Bullshit. Give us the money, and we'll let you live."

"There isn't any money."

"Get Damian. We know he's in there."

"I told you, he's dead."

"Let us inside so I can see for myself."

Not gonna happen, thought Brody. Roberto was a professional hit man. There was no way Brody could trust him. If Brody dropped his guard, he was convinced Roberto would kill him.

"He's dead," said Brody. "There's no money. It's over. Go home."

"Not till I see him and check out the cabin for the money."

Brody wasn't going to allow a team of armed hit men enter the cabin.

"OK. Come in by yourself," said Brody. "Leave your men outside."

Roberto sniggered. "So you can hold me hostage? The deal is, my men and me enter together."

"You're wasting your time. There's no money."

"Amigo, *you're* wasting my time with all this talk. The time for talk is over. Let us inside or we're coming in, guns blazing. You have no chance against us."

"You alone can enter."

Roberto shook his head no. "The only way you get out of this alive is by letting us in now."

He fired a burst at the cabin's front door with his MAC-10.

Adrenaline coursing through his body, Brody slammed the door shut and stepped aside to avoid the slugs penetrating the wood. When the gunfire ceased, he locked the door.

So be it, he decided.

Chapter 120

Brody watched Roberto's men disperse around the cabin.

"You need to cover the back door," Brody told Melody. "I'll cover the front. They're the only two ways they can enter."

"I don't know anything about shooting guns."

"That MP5 in your hands is set to full auto. Just aim it and squeeze the trigger. You're bound to hit something with the spray of bullets."

She eyed the weapon in her hands uncertainly. "I'll try."

"We don't have any choice. If they get in here, we're dead," said Brody, feeling his heartbeat hammering out of control.

Brody heard the crack of gunfire. Bullets burst through a side window, tearing and fluttering its curtains. He charged the window, peeked through it, aimed his MP5, and returned fired with a short burst at the shooter who was leveling a TEC-9 at the window.

Brody's slugs stitched bloody holes in the *sicario*'s throat. The guy screamed, dropped his TEC-9, and clutched his blood-spurting throat with both hands. It wasn't long before he lay sprawled on the ground, his torn carotid artery jetting pulsating streams of blood that became progressively thinner until they turned into trickles that died out.

Brody heard another window shatter. The sicarios were attacking simultaneously. Brody belted into the adjoining bedroom, reached the window, and searched for the shooter.

A bearded, rawboned guy wearing a Castro fatigue hat was firing from behind an oak trunk.

Brody stuck his MP5 out the broken windowpane and let loose a burst at him. The shooter ducked behind the oak, as Brody's slugs ripped off chunks of bark that sprang off the trunk like grasshoppers.

More shots from the other side of the cabin, as bullets blasted cabin windows.

Which was the diversion and which was the main assault? Brody wondered.

He heard gunfire emanating from the back door in the kitchen. He bolted to the kitchen doorway and picked up on Melody peppering the door with bullets.

Brody thought he heard a thump like a sack of potatoes falling on the back porch.

"I saw the doorknob turning," said Melody. "Somebody was trying to get in."

Brody wasn't taking any chances. He fired into the door and ran out of rounds. He swapped magazines and let the door have another burst.

The doorknob wasn't turning anymore.

Gunfire exploded at the front door. Bullets singing through the wood spat wooden splinters across the floor. Brody wheeled to face an ensuing attack. He figured the main assault would come from either the front or the rear. He doubted the *sicarios* would try to enter through the cabin's cramped side windows, even though they were shooting out the windowpanes. The flank attacks had to be diversions, decided Brody.

Brody picked up on a silhouette gliding past one of the side windows. He squeezed off a burst through the pane at the silhouette. He heard a groan from outside.

Automatic gunfire ripped into the front door. Whoever was firing was trying to blow the door's dead bolt lock apart.

Brody couldn't tell if the shooter was standing on the porch or farther away in the front yard. He heard gunfire. Slugs flew through the disintegrating wooden door. The bullets had an upward trajectory, suggesting the shooter was standing in the yard below the porch.

Brody fired a burst downward through the door, hoping to hit the assailant with a lucky shot. Brody didn't like his chances. It was too hard for him to calculate the angle of the shooter's trajectory doing it on the fly. Brody had to make a guesstimate and take his chances.

The front door lock wouldn't hold much longer. Another burst riddled the door. Splinters spat out from the jamb and the immediate area around the doorknob. The entire door shuddered in its frame.

He had wasted one of the *sicarios*—maybe even three. Two for him and one for Melody, if he was an optimist. But he wasn't. He was sure of only one kill. He and Melody might have only winged the other two *sicarios*.

Somebody blasted the back door with automatic fire and kicked the door in.

Melody screamed.

Brody slewed around from facing the front door, spotted a portly hit man unleashing bullets from his MAC-10 as he barreled through the cracked back door, his red face a mask of hate.

Brody's magazine ran dry.

Melody stood nonplussed.

A bullet grazed Brody's thigh. He dropped his MP5, whipped out his SIG P365 from his waistband, and double-tapped the *sicario* in the forehead. Brain dead, the guy plunged forward and slammed against the kitchen's yellow linoleum tiles, dropping his MAC-10, which clattered on the floor.

Brody rushed the open door and slammed it shut seconds before a barrage of bullets tore into it from outside. Its lock broken, its jamb cracked and riven by the intruder's kick, the door wouldn't hold.

Brody saw his trouser leg turning red as blood soaked it. He had no time to treat it. He took a head count. In the best of all possible worlds, he and Melody had killed or incapacitated four shooters, leaving two alive.

But Brody, a pronounced skeptic bordering on a cynic, had a Voltairean view of this best of all possible worlds.

He heard more gunfire. Bullets pelted the front door.

The *sicarios* were closing in on them, Brody realized.

He didn't like his chances. He wondered if he was close to dying. Was this how it would end for him—gunned down in an isolated cabin at Big Bear?

Chapter 121

Brody put away his SIG, recovered his MP5 from the floor, ejected the spent magazine, and replaced it with a fresh one.

"Let's regroup in the living room," he said.

Brody and Melody dashed into the living room.

He heard a hit man kick open the back door.

Brody heard the guy's footsteps in the kitchen amidst the gunfire raining down on the front door, which rattled loose in its frame and now hung ajar. His back flat against the wall, he trained his MP5 on the doorway that led from the living room to the kitchen, expecting the invading hit man to enter any second. Brody kept glancing at the front door, making sure nobody was charging through it, now that it had been breached.

"Watch the front door," he whispered to Melody.

Standing beside him she nodded yes and directed her MP5 at the front door, her eyes huge with fear.

Brody's pulse was racing out of control, supercharged by adrenaline, as he waited for the hit man to enter from the kitchen. At the same time he heard the creaking of the wooden steps to the front porch.

A burst of bullets peppered the shredded, perforated front door. The door eased open on squealing hinges.

Brody wheeled around and fired at the front door as he glimpsed through the mangled door a man's figure standing out on the front porch. The guy returned fire and kicked the door open as the other hit man in the kitchen appeared at the entrance to the living room. Mistaking Brody's shots for those of the guy in the kitchen doorway and jazzed up with adrenaline, Roberto, rushing in from the front door, blasted his cohort by mistake in the heat of battle.

The guy in the kitchen collapsed to the floor, cut down by Roberto's slugs. Roberto saw Brody.

Too late.

Brody squeezed off a burst at Roberto, felling him.

Brody barreled to the open front door, MP5 in hand, prepared to confront the next assailant. He heard movement behind him. Caught off guard, he slewed around. A burst fired before he could complete his spin. He thought the hit man behind him had him dead to rights. When Brody about-faced he spotted a hit man framed in the kitchen doorway standing near his cohort's crumpled bullet-riddled corpse at his feet and looking in Brody's direction as if in astonishment.

Melody emptied another burst into the guy. He crumpled, realizing he was dead from Melody's previous gunfire.

Brody gave her a brief nod in gratitude.

He wheeled around to face the front door, concerned additional *sicarios* would mount assaults. He approached the door.

He picked up on a bald guy clambering out of the Navigator and stealing toward the cabin. The guy looked unarmed.

Brody scanned the area. He didn't see any other hit men. Descending the porch steps he drew a bead on the guy, but didn't pull the trigger.

It was Brockton Root.

Approaching Brody, Root waved at him.

Tentatively, Brody headed down the driveway to meet him midway.

Brody couldn't get his head around it. Why had Root been in the hit squad's vehicle? he wondered.

"Hold it," said Brody, keeping his MP5 directed at Root.

"What's the problem?" said Root, balking. "You found the safe house."

"Yeah. That's the problem."

"I don't understand. I told you you'd be safe there."

"So how did the *sicarios* find me? You were the only one that knew I was here."

"I didn't tell them. Is that what you think? Why the hell would I do that? I'm the one that arranged the cabin for you."

"Then why were you in their Lincoln?"

Out of the corner of his eye Brody saw Melody approaching them from the cabin, her MP5 aimed at Root.

"Why are you keeping him alive?" she said. "They tried to kill us."

"He works for the CIA," said Brody.

"What's he doing with them?"

"That's what I'm trying to find out."

"They forced me to go with them at gunpoint," said Root, eying Melody's gun warily.

"Why didn't they kill you?" said Brody.

"I told you before, I'm under deep cover. The cartel thinks I'm working for them. They don't know I'm really working for the CIA."

Melody lowered her weapon.

"That's better," said Root, relaxing.

Brody wasn't convinced. He kept his MP5 leveled at Root.

"If you didn't tell the *sicario*s where Damian was hiding, who told them?" said Brody.

"Good question." Root peered at the cabin. "Where's Damian?"

"He's dead."

"I see," said Root, dejected. "Roberto got him?"

"No."

"You did it?" said Root, puzzled.

"His sister who wasn't his sister took him out."

"Run that by me again."

"She was my client. She hired me to find her brother Damian. She said she was his sister Araceli. Her real name was Francesca. She was another *sicario* working on her own for the cartel."

"A freelancer."

"Yeah."

Root nodded. "She used you to find her target for her." He peered at the cabin's open door. "Where is she?"

"She was gonna kill me and Melody. I shot her."

"That's it, then."

"What's it?"

"She must be the one that told the cartel where Damian was holed up. That's how Roberto knew where to find you."

Brody had to admit it was possible. However, he didn't trust Root.

Root might indeed be a CIA agent that had infiltrated the cartel as he claimed, but he still could be working for the cabal of deep state CIA and FBI operatives that were trying to oust President Ransom.

"We need that money," said Root.

"There isn't any," said Brody. "Damian gambled away the whole wad."

Root shrugged. "At least Cobalt Green Tide didn't get it. That's the important thing. That's the money the cabal was going to use to bribe Dmytryk to get her to vote in favor of removing Ransom from office with the Twenty-fifth Amendment. Her vote would have given them the majority of the fifteen members of the cabinet needed to oust Ransom calling him unfit to govern by reason of insanity."

"So what's the cabal gonna do now?"

"They'll try to get more money from the cartel."

"And?"

"And the cartel will give it to them. The cartel wants Ransom replaced because of his support for beefing up security on the border. They're convinced his replacement Vice President Dealey will open up the border, making it easier for them to smuggle their narcotics into the States."

"Is Dealey involved in the conspiracy?"

"We believe he's running it."

"Why doesn't Ransom fire him?"

"The vice president is the only member of the cabinet the president *can't* fire. The House and the Senate are the only ones that can remove VPOTUS, and the Senate has to vote to remove him with a two-thirds majority. In other words, the only way to remove him is by impeachment. Ransom has no say in the matter."

"Ransom picked Dealey to run with him, but he has no say in firing him. How does that figure?"

"Whether it figures or not, it's in the constitution. And besides, Ransom doesn't even know about the conspiracy."

"Why hasn't the CIA told him?"

"I wasn't sure the conspiracy existed, though I've suspected it for some time. I believe we've got enough intel now to expose the plot."

"Is any of this for real?" said Melody, bewildered by Root's words. "I'm just an ex-lifeguard trying to escape my abusive husband. I don't know anything about any international conspiracies."

"It's as real as the bullets they're using," said Brody.

"Are you really a private eye or are you something else? You sound like a spy. Are you pretending to be a private eye? Is this a big lie?"

"It's no lie. I was doing my job and got ensnared in this mess like you."

"Conspiracies don't exist."

"Who told you that?" said Root.

"I read it somewhere or saw it on TV. Conspiracies are invented to explain historical events that people can't understand—like Kennedy's assassination."

"This conspiracy doesn't involve an assassination."

"Same difference. People can't accept the idea that a nut-case lone gunman like Lee Harvey Oswald could kill the president of the United States without any help. They believe there had to be a conspiracy behind it so they invent conspiracies with the Mafia, the CIA, the KBG, Castro, LBJ, and a hundred others. But conspiracies don't exist."

"Tell that to John Wilkes Booth, Lewis Powell, David Herold, George Atzerodt, and Mary Surratt."

"I've heard of Booth, not the others," said Melody, bemused.

"They all took part in the conspiracy to assassinate Lincoln, Vice President Andrew Johnson, and Secretary of State Seward."

"I never heard of them," muttered Melody.

"Booth gets all the attention. Anyway, this has nothing to do with Lincoln or Kennedy," said Root. "It's here. It's now. It's a coup by a cabal of deep state operatives financed by a Mexican cartel who are bent on removing President Ransom from office."

Melody gaped at him.

"How are we supposed to stop the conspiracy?" said Brody.

"The cartel will get their money to the conspirators sooner or later. The cartel has an endless stream of incoming cash. We got lucky this time because the bagman lost the cartel's money, but there are too many ways for the cartel to deliver the laundered money to Cobalt Green Tide for all of them to fail."

"Then how do we stop the conspiracy? We can't go to the FBI or the CIA because they're compromised. We don't know who we can trust there."

Root chewed it over, pacing back and forth on the front yard, plucking at his earlobe. "We have to find some way to expose their plot."

"How?"

"The only thing as powerful as the government is the media. We'll expose it in the news outlets."

"Why do you think the news outlets will publish it?"

"It'll make good copy."

"They only publish stories that support their narrative."

"We'll give them proof. NBC, CBS, ABC, CNN, MSNBC, FOX—one of them is bound to air the story. If not them, there's the *New York Times*—"

"What kind of proof do we have? The bagman Damian took his secret to the grave. He was our only proof."

Silence.

"Or there's another way," said Root, "and this might be the best way. We go directly to President Ransom himself and tell him about the conspiracy. That way the deep state cabal won't be able to block us, and we won't have to rely on the media."

Brody heard the crack of a gunshot. He whirled around and spotted Roberto lying on his stomach in the cabin front doorway training his MAC-10 on them, his hands streaked with blood, a rictus of hate twisting his face. Brody fired a burst from his MP5 in retaliation, tearing apart Roberto's skull, which catapulted fragments of bone, gouts of blood, and dollops of brain into the cabin.

"Everybody OK?" said Brody, facing Melody and Root.

"Except Roberto," said Root. "Most of his head is missing."

Brody fired another burst at Roberto's head, pulverizing what was left of it. "Now all of it is."

"I hope the others are dead in there," said Root, eying the cabin with unease.

"How do we expose the cabal?"

"Tell President—"

Another shot rang out.

Chapter 122

A high-velocity bullet from a sniper's rifle cleaved Root's forehead. He collapsed in a lifeless heap, minus the back of his skull.

"Get behind the car," said Brody, not sure where the bullet had come from, adrenaline shooting through him and triggering hyperacuity in all of his senses.

He and Melody ducked behind the Navigator.

"Who was that?" said Melody.

"I don't know, but he's got a sniper's rifle. He could be a long way from here." Brody cast a dispirited glance at his and Melody's MP5s. "Well out of our range."

"Why did he kill a CIA agent?"

"I have a feeling he's gonna kill all of us."

"Why is everybody trying to kill us?"

"I'm thinking the sniper's a member of the cabal sent to tie up loose ends by taking out everyone at the cabin."

"How did they know we were here?"

"The CIA and FBI are riddled with the cabal's deep state moles. The security agencies have the technical ability to tap anybody's phone. One of the moles must have intercepted Root's conversation with the cabin's owner arranging the safe house for us."

"But why kill *us*? Damian's the one they want, and he's already dead."

"They must suspect we found out about their conspiracy to oust the president."

A gunshot cracked.

The bullet penetrated the Navigator's metal doors and whistled past Brody and Melody.

"Christ," said Brody. "Armor-piercing bullets. He must be using a .50 caliber sniper rifle like an M107." He crouched behind the Navigator. "Stay out of sight so he can't pinpoint our position."

"Where can we go?" said Melody, squatting beside him.

"We're not safe here. He could keep blanketing the four-by-four with gunfire until he gets lucky and clips both of us."

"Maybe he'll run out of ammunition."

"We can't count on that. This guy's a professional. They're not gonna send an amateur sniper after us. He's a marksman. He'll be prepared."

Brody had to think fast. His throat tightened with apprehension. He turned over plans in his mind. They could sprint to Melody's Focus and drive away. He gazed at the Focus. It was too far away. The sniper would cut down at least one of them en route. Maybe even both of them.

He straightened up and peeked into the Navigator at its ignition.

"What are you doing?" said Melody with concern.

A bullet slammed through the windshield and through the Navigator's metal door, missing Brody by inches.

He dropped down to his haunches.

He had glimpsed the muzzle flash of the sniper's rifle in the distance and knew the position of the sniper now. Brody's MP5 wouldn't be of any use.

"No car key," he said.

That left Francesca's BMW and the cabin owner's Mercedes. Brody doubted Francesca had left her keys in the ignition. The same with the cabin owner.

"You *do* have the keys to your car, don't you?" he said.

"Yes," she said, her voice tense.

"Yours is the only car we can count on."

"My car's blocked by all of these other cars in the driveway."

"You'll have to drive onto the lawn to get around them."

"You make it sound like I'm going alone."

"We're both not gonna make it to your car. I'll have to act as a diversion and draw the shooter's fire, while you run to your car and get out of here. You're gonna have to do everything in fast motion to avoid getting shot."

"What are you gonna do?"

"I'll run into the woods firing at him, drawing his fire while you make your getaway in your car."

"My car isn't made for driving on the dirt. My tires don't have deep treads."

"As long as the dirt's not muddy, you'll be OK."

"What about you? He's gonna kill you if you're out there running around without anywhere to hide."

Brody scoped out the terrain. "If I can make it to the trees, I should be OK."

The sniper fired again.

A slug gored the Navigator's door less than an inch away from Melody's neck, hissing past her and thudding into the lawn.

"We have to go now," said Brody, his entire body tense, ready to spring into action.

"Why can't we both run to the car?"

"We won't make it. I have to draw his fire away from you. It's me he wants first. Then he'll come after you."

"Why? I don't know anything about any conspiracy."

"The sniper doesn't know that. And you're a witness to this massacre."

"I don't want to die."

"I doubt he'll shoot at you when I make a run for it, but zigzag to throw off his aim when you run to your car."

Brody's face broke into a sweat. He didn't know what he was going to do once he reached the trees. It wasn't a thick forest. The trees were thin and isolated, but they were the nearest cover—unless he ran into the cabin. But if he chose the cabin as his destination, the sniper would pick off Melody on the way to her car and come for him later, knowing he had

Brody trapped inside. The sniper might even torch the cabin—with Brody inside. In any case, the cabin wasn't any closer than the trees.

Brody's making a dash for the trees would occupy the sniper's attention long enough for Melody to reach her car and drive away in safety. Or so he hoped.

"Hold my hand," she said, extending her hand to him.

He took hold of it. "We'll make it."

They stood like that a full minute, gazing into each other's eyes, warmth passing through their clasped hands, their faces grave.

Brody broke his grip. He popped up and fired over the Navigator's hood in the direction of the sniper.

"Now," he said.

Bryan Cassiday

Chapter 123

Firing another burst at the sniper Brody bolted for the woods, jinking on the way to make himself a more difficult target.

Melody tore along the driveway in the opposite direction toward her car.

The sniper fired at Brody. A cloud of dirt puffed a few feet from Brody's feet as he ran. Heart pounding, Brody took cover behind a narrow pine trunk. He wondered if it was a good idea. The sniper's .50 caliber bullets might be able to rip through the trunk. The trunk was at least six inches in diameter, but it could have a rotten core for all Brody knew, making it a piece of cake for a high-velocity armor-piercing bullet to penetrate.

He saw Melody clamber into her Focus and fire the engine. The car lurched onto the front yard, made a U-turn, and jounced over the lawn to the driveway. Melody cut onto the driveway behind Roberto's Navigator.

Brody peeked from behind the pine toward the direction of the sniper and let loose another burst emptying his magazine. He ducked back behind the pine, ejected the spent magazine, and replaced it with a fresh one from his trouser pocket.

He sprinted toward the nearest pine, firing his MP5 at the sniper. A bullet kicked up pine duff at his feet. Breathing hard he took cover behind another pine.

He saw Melody speed along the rest of the driveway to the tortuous road that wound down the bluff.

Sweating, pressing his body against the trunk to make himself as inconspicuous as possible, he hoped she would make it all right.

A bullet thwacked into the trunk he was pressed against. He had to get out of here. Firing a short burst he juked to another pine. He had to keep the sniper's attention diverted from Melody as long as possible to insure her safe escape.

He watched her drive with abandon down the mountain road. He hoped she didn't go so fast she would lose control, career off the road, and go tumbling down the mountainside.

A bullet thudded into the pine in front of him.

He pelted to a gnarled oak tree, trying to draw sniper fire by firing another burst in the sniper's direction.

He watched Melody's Focus disappear from sight down the road. He hoped she had gotten a good-enough head start that the sniper wouldn't be able to catch up with her. For sure he couldn't target her now without altering his position. Brody was certain she had disappeared from the sniper's coign of vantage.

Brody surveyed the landscape behind him. The edge of the bluff was thirty-odd feet from where he stood. Directly below the bluff stretched the tarn. He wondered how far the drop was to the tarn.

A bullet ripped into the oak bole. Shreds of craggy grey bark exploded into the air.

He had to get out of here.

He emptied his MP5's magazine at the sniper and sprinted toward the bluff's edge, his legs pumping like pistons. He zigzagged to fake out the sniper, straightened his course, charged the bluff's edge full tilt, tossing away his MP5, hearing the crack of the sniper's rifle behind him in the distance as he leapt off the bluff and dropped through the air toward the glassy surface of the tarn, flapping his arms at his sides in an effort to create drag on his speedy descent.

It was a long way down.

He heard the wind screaming past his ears.

He had to live long enough to tell President Ransom about the conspiracy.

Chapter 124

Wearing a shepherd's check blazer the thirtyish blue-eyed woman with a frosted blonde perm read the teleprompter in front of the TV camera.

"In fast-breaking events, President Ransom has fired Department of Homeland Security chief Sheila Dmytryk. The president said Dmytryk was too lax in implementing his border control policies. We're also getting reports of a rift between the president and Vice President Dealey. As you know, a president cannot fire a vice president. The only way to remove a vice president from office is by impeachment.

"In a related story, the Department of Justice is opening an investigation into charges that a Mexican drug cartel is funneling narco money through shell companies to bribe top-ranking United States government officials. Meanwhile, Attorney General Martin Holcroft has named US Attorney Robert Elkins of Connecticut as federal prosecutor to investigate charges that a deep state cabal in the upper echelons of the FBI and CIA is plotting a coup against the president.

"On the local front, ten bullet-riddled corpses were found at a remote cabin in Big Bear. Authorities are calling it a domestic dispute that ended in tragedy."

ABOUT THE AUTHOR

Bryan Cassiday writes thrillers and horror fiction. His first Scott Brody crime thriller was *Bolt*. He wrote *Zombie Apocalypse: The Chad Halverson Series*. His short stories have appeared in anthologies, such as *Shadows and Teeth Volume Two*, which won the International Book Award for best adult horror fiction anthology series 2017. He lives in Southern California.